Virginia Macgregor was brought up in Germany, France and England by a mother who never stopped telling stories. From the moment she was old enough to hold a pen, Virginia set about writing her own, often late into the night – or behind her maths textbook at school. Virginia was named after two great women, Virginia Wade and Virginia Woolf, in the hope she would be a writer and a tennis star. Her early years were those of a scribbling, rain-loving child who prayed for lightning to strike her tennis coach. After studying at Oxford, Virginia started writing regularly while working as an English teacher and housemistress. Virginia lives in Berkshire with her husband, Hugh, and their baby daughter.

Virginia Macgregor

SPHERE

First published in Great Britain in 2014 by Sphere

A CIP catalogue record for this book
is available from the British Library.

Hardback ISBN 978-0-7515-5424-3
Trade Paperback ISBN 978-0-7515-5425-0

Typeset in Granjon by M Rules
Printed and bound in Great Britain by
Clays Ltd, St Ives plc

Papers used by Sphere are from well-managed forests
and other responsible sources.

MIX
Paper from
responsible sources
FSC
www.fsc.org FSC® C104740

Sphere
An imprint of
Little, Brown Book Group
100 Victoria Embankment
London EC4Y 0DY

An Hachette UK Company
www.hachette.co.uk

www.littlebrown.co.uk

For the two people who have loved me into being a writer: Mama and my darling husband, Hugh.

ACKNOWLEDGEMENTS

At 00:17 on the 2nd of October 2012 an exceptionally talented young woman changed my life: my wonderful agent, Bryony Woods. Bryony understands the heart of my writing better than anyone, has an exceptional eye for detail, a fantastic business brain and is more efficient than Mary Poppins – thank you for everything, Bryony.

'Team Milo' at Little, Brown have worked their magic to bring a special little boy to the world: thank you to Manpreet Grewal, my exceptional editor; Sophie Burdess who designed the striking cover; Thalia Proctor whose eagle eye helped me make Milo sparkle; Kirsteen Astor and Emma Williams, the stunning publicity and marketing duo who got out their megaphones and made Milo's voice heard above the din, and the rights team who packed Milo on a plane, took him on a round the world trip and taught him some exciting new languages.

On a personal note, thank you to the lovely young men and women in my creative writing group at Wellington College: your encouragement means so much. Keep scribbling! Thank you to Helen Dahlke, Liz Martinez, Joanna Seldon and Jane Cooper: my writing buddies. To Mama, who believed in me as a writer from the moment I held a pen. To Anne Holtz and Tata Suzanne for loving me and for being my family. To Windmill for keeping me going. To Viola and Sebastian, my white, feline friends who have kept me warm, loved and entertained during long days spent at my desk. And finally, thank you to my beloved husband, soul mate and first reader, Hugh: one day the world will see how brilliant you are.

1

Milo

Milo sat at the computer on the landing listening to the shush-shushing of the firemen's hose on the drive. The firemen had only just let them back into the house.

'I want a list of nursing homes,' said Mum.

'Can't Gran stay till Christmas?'

Gran was Dad's gran and Milo's great-gran but everyone just called her Gran.

Milo turned his head to look at the fairy lights he'd wound round the banisters leading up to Gran's room. He'd had the idea when he saw her struggling to find the light switch.

Mum guided Milo's head back to look at her and said 'No.'

'But ...'

'Don't insist,' said Mum and then pinched shut her mouth. *Don't insist* was Mum's favourite phrase of all time.

'But Mum – the fire was my fault, I should have gone down to check.'

And it was true. Every morning when Gran padded down

the stairs from her room under the roof all the way to the kitchen and made her cup of sweet, milky tea, it was Milo's job to make sure she was okay. He'd lie in bed and listen for the clues:

1. The clink of Gran's tartan mug as she pulled it off the mug tree.
2. The suck and pop of the jar with the tea bags.
3. The rattle of the cutlery drawer as she took out her favourite teaspoon, the one made of real silver with a kink in its handle.
4. The kettle filling up (though usually Milo tried to remember to fill it up the night before because Gran's wrists were weak and she struggled to hold the weight of so much water).
5. The click of the switch on the kettle.
6. A pause.
7. And then the water heating, steam pushing at the lid, bubbles rolling over each other like a hot sea, and then another click when it was done.
8. Sometimes, after step 3, Gran forgot they had a kettle and she'd open the saucepan drawer and fill a pan up and light the stove. That was the cue for Milo to swing his legs out of bed and come downstairs. They had a gas hob and Gran wasn't allowed to use it.

Milo didn't know why he missed the sound of the saucepan drawer that day. He must have been sleepy or maybe Gran was extra quiet, but by the time he felt the flutter in his chest which told him that Gran needed him, and by the time

Hamlet was squealing his head off in the garage because he'd swallowed too much smoke, it was too late, the kitchen was on fire.

'It's not your responsibility to check on your gran,' said Mum.

She leant in and kissed Milo's hair. She was always doing that: telling him off and then kissing him. She smelt of burnt things and sticky perfume and sleep.

'When all this is over, I'll let Hamlet stay in the house,' she said.

Milo leant under the desk and gave Hamlet a rub between his ears. The only reason he was allowed up here now was because the fire had scared him. Milo hated the fact that Hamlet had to live in the garage all by himself: the garage was cold and damp and didn't have any windows. No one should live like that. But if Milo had to choose between Hamlet coming out of the garage or Gran getting to stay with them, he'd have to pick Gran. Hamlet would understand.

Mum looked over Milo's shoulder at the computer screen. 'We don't want anywhere fancy, Milo, Gran wouldn't like that.'

So Milo tried typing *not fancy nursing homes* into Google but Google didn't get it and wrote back: *did you mean fancy nursing homes?*

Once Milo had stationed Gran safely on the drive and once he'd yanked open the main door to the garage and got Hamlet out of his cage and given him to Gran to look after, he'd come back inside and screamed: *Fire! Fire! Mum! There's a fire!*

Mum had come tearing down the stairs and out of the

house, her non-make-up face all pale and puffy. When she saw Gran she didn't ask how she was and she didn't say she was relieved that Hamlet was safely out of the garage and she didn't tell Milo well done for having saved everyone. She just yelled the same words over and over:

This is the last straw. This is the last bloody straw.

Milo and Gran both knew what the last bloody straw meant: it meant that Gran was going to a nursing home.

Mum jabbed a chipped pink nail at the computer screen. 'Those rooms are far too big,' she said. 'Gran will feel lost.'

So Milo did a search for nursing homes with small rooms. But then he thought about all the stuff Gran had upstairs, like Great-Gramps's bagpipes and his uniform and the boxes of letters he'd written her and her map of Inverary and the picture of her fishing boat and her small radio and how she'd want to take it all with her.

'It's not coming up with anything.' If Milo made Mum feel it was a hassle, maybe she'd back down.

'Oh, for goodness sake, Milo.' Mum looked up the stairs to Gran's room and scratched a red bit on her throat. Then she leant in and whispered, 'Just find somewhere cheap.'

Mum wrote the word CHEAP on the back of an envelope and placed it right in front of Milo so it wasn't lost in the fuzzy bit of his vision. He ran his fingers over the word; she'd pressed so hard on the pencil that the letters felt bumpy.

'I've got to make the firemen some tea.'

Still in her nightie (the frilly one that looked like the kitchen curtains, or how they looked before they caught fire and turned into black moths on the linoleum floor), Mum rushed back downstairs. Milo heard the cupboard door open and the rustle of the Hobnobs packet. The plastic kettle had

4

melted, so Milo didn't know how Mum was going to boil water for the tea.

Milo wasn't going to let Mum stick Gran in a nursing home. He'd pretend to go along with it and then Mum would calm down and realise that Gran belonged right here in the small room Dad had converted for her under the roof, and that Milo was the best person to look after her. Then they'd have a proper Christmas, the four of them: Milo, Gran, Hamlet and Mum.

Milo scanned down the list of homes on the screen. They all had garden centre names like Acorn Cottage and Birdgrove and Beechcroft Hill and Bird Poo View. He made up the last one.

Milo typed: *not cheap nursing homes* into Google and waited for a new page to load.

'Found anything yet?' Mum called up the stairs.

The burnt smell had crept into the carpet and curtains and walls and was making the back of Milo's throat tickle.

He coughed and called back: 'Nearly!'

'Well, when you have, give me the phone numbers and I'll organise some visits.'

Milo didn't answer.

Above him, the floorboards creaked and then water juddered through the pipes. He hoped Gran would remember to turn off the tap. As soon as he'd finished making this stupid list, he'd go up and tell Gran that there was no way he was going to let Mum kick her out. He'd work out a plan that guaranteed she could stay, and not just for Christmas.

2

Lou

Lou closed her eyes. She felt Milo hold his breath, heard the buzz of his thoughts, saw him narrow his eyes at the screen. Ever since he'd been diagnosed she'd trained herself to see the world as he did: through a pinhole. Funny how, when so much was slipping in her own mind, what Milo saw drew closer and sharper.

Then the tap, tap, tapping of his small fingers on the keyboard. So that's all it took, a few taps to find her a new home.

She felt the rhythm of his heart, heavy this morning. She should have prepared him better, should have helped him see that it was time for her to go.

Lou opened her eyes, stood up and went to look through her bedroom window. She watched Sandy standing on the drive, her knickers cutting into the thick rolls of her backside and pushing up against her nightie. Men in heavy boots and yellow hats thudded and pulled and kept looking over at Sandy's blue dimpled thighs.

Mr Overend from across the road twitched his bedroom curtains. Always sleeping, that man, sleeping or spying or whistling. Lou had listened to him for five years and still she couldn't work out the tune.

And then Sandy's mules on the kitchen tiles, clippety-clop, like she was tap dancing. Always showing off, that girl, and now hollering up the stairs to Milo, getting the little boy to do the things that Andrew should have been here to do.

Lou breathed in. It was surprising how far it had crept up, the smell of damp smoke, of burnt chipboard, of melting plastic. She looked down at her hands and turned them over: streaks of ash traced her lifeline.

She rubbed her hands together and imagined Milo teasing her: *You wouldn't make a very good criminal, Gran. You leave too much evidence.*

She hoped that, for once, Milo hadn't noticed what she'd done.

But it had been the right thing to do, hadn't it? A definitive act, something big, to persuade Sandy that she had to go. And it was right for Milo, too – he spent too much time looking after her already.

It had taken a while to find the matches. And it hadn't been easy to get the angle of the strike just right. Her silly, clumsy fingers. But then the flame had leapt out of her hands like a bird. It had caught the loose edge of the kitchen roll, a white bird, then a black bird with paper wings, then grey feathers of ash falling around her.

And then Milo's hand in hers, soft as dough, guiding her out of the house.

It's okay, Gran, everything's okay.

Lou walked over to the bathroom and stood at the sink.

She turned the tap and watched as the water fell through her fingers, ash washing down the drain.

Her eyes stung. A tear fell onto the back of her hand.

Dear, dear Milo.

Don't cry, Gran, she heard him say.

Lou looked at her reflection in the mirror. She saw flames dancing around her head. How had it happened again?

An accident. Yes, it had been an accident, that's what she'd told the firemen.

The gas hob. That's right.

I forgot we had a kettle, she'd written on her pad, her voice still lost. *Silly, silly me.* And then the knob turned to the picture of the big flame, a sudden whoosh, a piece of kitchen paper left too close.

An accident, yes.

I'll tell Mum it was me, said Milo, knowing how Sandy would respond. And then he'd placed the small white pill in the palm of her hand. He never forgot, even on a morning like this.

Hours of waiting on the cold drive.

The wail of the fire engine. The thud of heavy boots, an army drowning the house. And then let in again, thirty-two stairs to the top, up past Milo's room, past the fairy lights he'd put up for her and then up, up up to her room under the roof, like Rapunzel.

3

Milo

A week later, Milo buckled Gran into the back seat of the car and climbed in beside her.

He placed her pad and her pencil on her lap in case she wanted to write anything while they were visiting the homes. Milo had never heard Gran talk out loud, but he still knew what her voice sounded like. Even when she wasn't writing on her pad or sitting beside him, her words came into his head, soft and clear.

'Not in the back, Milo,' said Mum. 'I need you up front to operate the machine.' She waved her hand at the satnav clamped to the windscreen. Milo tried to exchange a look with Gran, but Gran wasn't paying attention. She sat with her hands folded in her lap, staring out of the window.

She'd had that same empty look when Milo went up to her room earlier to help her get dressed. *You'll be back for Christmas*, he'd promised as he pulled her pop socks over her calves. But she'd just gazed down at the lines in her palms.

When he went back downstairs he didn't tell Mum that there was a wet patch on the carpet because Gran had left the tap running.

Milo didn't tell Mum half the things he knew about Gran.

Like that she'd get up in the middle of the night and come into his room and say that she was going on her honeymoon to Greece and that Great-Gramps was waiting for her.

Or that sometimes she got the shakes so bad he was worried she'd keel over and bang her head on the corner of the dresser and knock herself out.

Gran had a sticky streak of jam on her chin. He should have wiped it off with her flannel before they left.

'Let's go to the best one first,' said Mum, winking at Milo.

Milo typed in the postcode of the first nursing home on his list. Then he snuck his arm past the gear stick and the handbrake and put his hand on Gran's.

Her wrinkly fingers tremored under his.

Mum narrowly missed crashing into the old Volvo parked outside Mr Overend's house. 'That stupid car, taking up all that space and never getting used. Someone should take it to the scrap yard.'

As Milo looked up he saw a fuzzy shadow leaning into Mr Overend's bedroom window. He wondered how long it had been since Mr Overend got behind the wheel of his car – in fact, he wondered how long it had been since Mr Overend had last left his house.

As Milo shifted his head and focused in on the images through the small 'O' of his vision, he felt kind of lucky that he didn't have to see it all. At least he only got a bit of the grey sky and the grey pavements and the grey leafless trees. People who saw everything at once must feel drowned by the world. All Milo had to do was to move his head and focus on something else and pretend the bad bits weren't there.

He remembered that day in January when he'd sat in Dr Nolan's examination room. He'd liked the feel of the big chair with the tall headrest and all those machines that made his eyes go funny. The room was underground so it didn't have any windows. There were posters all over the walls of what eyes looked like from the inside: as Dr Nolan explained what was wrong with Milo's eyes, he'd pointed to the nerves and veins and muscles, like a map of the London Underground only messier. And then he'd shown Milo the picture of an orange moon and said that was what his retinas looked like, that the lighter bits of orange were the reason why he could only see part of the world, the bit through the pinhole. That's when Mum had started crying, which meant Dr Nolan had to get some tissues from the loo, but Milo hadn't been able to stop staring at that orange moon. It was beautiful.

Milo sat back and looked up into the trees. He couldn't wait for summer. He would take Hamlet out for walks in the park, which along with Gran's room under the roof was his favourite place in the whole world. He'd sent off for Hamlet's licence to prove that he didn't have any diseases like foot in mouth that would kill all the sheep and cows in nearby farms. Not that there were any sheep or cows or farms near Slipton.

As they drove past the big black gates to the park, Milo pressed his nose to the window. Behind the NO FOULING sign with the black dog in a red circle squatting over a pile of steaming poo, a man with ruffled hair and brown skin knelt on a sleeping bag.

He held his hands to his ears, and then bent forward and touched his forehead to the ground. He was doing the Downward Facing Dog from Mum's yoga DVD. Because of his eyes, Milo didn't get to do normal sports, so sometimes Mum made him do yoga with her. *You don't want to get love handles like your father*, Mum said, pinching the soft bits at the side of Milo's waist. Except they hadn't done yoga in months, not since Dad left, and now Mum's love handles were ten times bigger than Dad's.

Milo turned round, gave Gran's hand a squeeze and whispered *Look*, nudging his head towards the park.

When Gran spotted the man doing his exercises, her mouth tilted up at the sides.

'Turn round and focus on the machine,' snapped Mum. 'I need to know when to turn off.'

Mum didn't like the satnav woman's voice. Dad used to call it sexy and said that it turned him on – like the power switch on the computer, thought Milo. So now Milo kept the satnav on mute and called out the directions himself.

'Right turn ahead in 0.4 miles.' He used the low announcement voice you heard in train stations, except no one heard how good it was because a plane flew overhead and drowned out his words. That was what living in Slipton was like: every few minutes you'd miss part of what was going on because a Boeing 747 tore through the sky. At peak times, it got worse.

'What did you say?' Mum yelled as she drove past the turning.

4

Milo

At lunchtime, they sat in the car outside Poundland, munching meal deal sandwiches, Gran dozing in the back. So far, Mum hadn't liked any of the places on Milo's list.

'What about this place?' Mum asked, jabbing her chipped red nail at the last home on Milo's list: *Forget Me Not Homes.*

Hoping that Mum might not notice it, Milo had written the name of the last home right at the end of the list using his smallest, tightest letters. It was the only old people's home that he liked, so he thought he should add it: if Gran had to leave them, she should get to live somewhere nice. Though he was torn. If Mum liked it too, he'd never be able to persuade her to let Gran stay with them.

In the photo-gallery of Forget Me Not Homes, the old people smiled and they didn't look too wrinkly and they didn't all walk around with Zimmer frames. Everything looked clean and tidy and fresh and there were lots of pictures of this beautiful garden. Gran loved gardens. And when he'd phoned to make an appointment, this really nice nurse had answered and said that of course they could come and visit, that she'd show them round herself.

'Mum, it's too expensive—' And then Milo looked back at Gran and remembered that she heard things, even when she was asleep.

'I don't think you'll like it, Mum.'

But Mum had already started the engine. 'Let's go and see.'

And she did like it.

She liked the nurse in the white uniform with the glowing white teeth and the scraped-back grey hair who ignored Milo and greeted Mum like she knew her already. And she liked the fact that, within five minutes of them walking through the door, Nurse Thornhill had told Mum about the Forget Me Not Payment Plan. None of the other nursing homes had payment plans.

'You'll be charged a small amount of interest, but it means you don't have to pay everything up front. It eases the burden.'

Mum's eyes lit up.

Gran and Milo walked a few paces behind.

The white nurse looked like a skeleton: tall and sharp and bony. He expected her to rattle as she moved. She didn't look at all like she'd sounded on the phone.

Even though they were in a public place, Milo didn't let go of Gran's hand.

'As Director of Forget Me Not, I live on the premises, so I'm available night and day.'

Everything looked squeaky white, like the nurse: the walls and the doors and the floor.

'We're a very friendly little community here.'

Mum kept looking back and saying, 'Isn't this nice?' her eyes screwed up into twinkly slits, and 'It's so close, you can come and visit Gran whenever you want.'

Milo didn't answer and Gran wasn't listening.

Then a woman appeared at the end of the corridor carrying an old tape player under her arm with music blaring out of the speakers that sounded like the Bob Marley album Dad used to play in the car. The old woman tapped her cane to the reggae beat.

Gran's head shot up.

'Who's that?' asked Milo. She was the most interesting thing he'd seen so far.

'Please excuse me.' Nurse Thornhill charged down the corridor.

Because of his eyes, Milo's hearing was extra sharp. As Nurse Thornhill squeaked away in her white plastic clogs, he heard her mutter, 'Silly woman, she knows she's not allowed out here.'

Milo looked through the pinhole: as Nurse Thornhill approached, the old woman turned round and started walking away. She had a lovely smiley face with chubby cheeks and skin as dark and shiny as a conker. But then, as he shifted his head, he noticed a wet patch on the back of the woman's dress. Nurse Thornhill grabbed the woman's elbow and steered her round the bend in the corridor.

'Must require such commitment,' said Mum, 'looking after all these patients.'

Within a few minutes, Nurse Thornhill was back at Mum's side.

'Mrs Moseley – she likes to wander.' She sighed. 'Such a dear,' she said through tight lips.

When they went past the kitchens, Gran let go of Milo's hand and walked to the swing doors.

'What is it, Gran?' he called after her.

She reached onto her tiptoes and peered through the round window.

'Gran?' Milo went and stood beside her. He wondered whether, when people looked through these windows, they saw the world like he did.

A man with tanned skin and curly dark hair and dark eyes stood over a pan of bubbling water. He sang a song that came out fast and bumpy and made Milo think of how voices sound when you record them and play them back in fast-forward. But the words he sang weren't English or any other language Milo had ever heard before.

Gran's face went soft and it was the first time since the fire that she stopped doing her spaced-out staring thing. She came back down off her tiptoes, closed her eyes and stood there swaying, listening to the man's singing.

'Milo, what are you doing? Bring your gran over here!' Mum called from the end of the corridor.

Milo didn't think you were meant to raise your voice in places like this. He looked at the white nurse to see whether she was cross at Mum, but the nurse smiled, revealing a set of big white teeth. The smile reminded Milo of those stickers you get as a kid where you can mix up lips and eyebrows and moustaches to make freaky lopsided faces.

When Gran and Milo caught up with them, Mum said: 'It's all settled – Gran's moving in on Monday.'

Monday? As in the day after tomorrow? Milo thought he'd have ages to come up with a plan to change Mum's mind.

'Aren't there waiting lists?' Milo asked the nurse. There'd

been waiting lists on most of the nice places he'd found on the internet. 'Or forms to fill out?'

The nurse shook her head. 'At Forget Me Not Homes, we're always open to new clients.'

'Client' was what the bank manager called Mum when she went in to ask for money, which she needed for the beauty salon she ran from the shed and to pay for the mortgage. Mum needed money because of Dad. *Your dad's buggered off to Abu Dhabi with His Tart*, she told Milo when he came home from school one afternoon last June. And The Tart was pregnant, which made it worse, and Dad had emptied their joint bank account saying that the money belonged to him and that Sandy should get a job that earned money for a change. That made it worse than worse.

Come to think of it, The Tart had a voice a bit like the satnav. Maybe that's why Dad preferred her to Mum.

'What about Dad?' asked Milo. 'Shouldn't we see what he thinks?'

Another plane rumbled overhead. The soundproofing in Forget Me Not was worse than at home.

Mum used the noise from the plane as an excuse not to hear.

Milo spoke louder. 'We have to tell Dad, it's his decision too.'

He knew he was Insisting and that Mum wouldn't like it, but Gran was Dad's Gran. She was the one who'd looked after him when he was little and his parents were busy with their jobs in Edinburgh, and he was the one who took her in when they said they were too old themselves to look after an old lady. Dad loved her and he understood how much she meant to Milo.

17

Milo knew it wasn't right to feel this but sometimes he wished it was Mum who'd gone to Abu Dhabi and Dad who had stayed here in Slipton.

'Your dad's busy,' snapped Mum.

Mum held out her hand to Nurse Thornhill and kept saying thank you, which Milo thought was pretty stupid as they were the ones paying for Gran to come here.

'Do you allow pets?' he asked.

The nurse looked down at Milo and her sticker smile fell off and dropped to the floor.

Mum yanked Milo's arm.

'I'm afraid not,' said Nurse Thornhill.

If Gran had to stay here until Milo found a way to get her out, he wanted her to have Hamlet.

Mum didn't know, but Hamlet spent loads of time with Gran in her room under the roof. When Gran got cold, Hamlet felt it and snuggled in close and when she did weird things like putting shower gel on her toothbrush (which made her mouth foam for ages) or like taking the radio into the bath (which could have got her electrocuted), Hamlet would grunt and squeak until either she snapped out of it and realised what she was doing or until Milo heard and came upstairs to sort things out.

Hamlet was the one who picked up on the fire. His nose was more sensitive than a sniffer dog's, so when he smelt the smoke he squealed his head off until Milo woke up and came downstairs and found Gran standing over the hob.

Plus, with Hamlet, Gran wouldn't feel so alone living between these white walls with all these white people with their white teeth and their white uniforms and their squeaky white shoes.

'I think we've found the perfect place for Gran, don't you, Milo?' Mum asked as they drove back home. 'Did you know that they have Forget Me Not Homes all over the country?'

Milo shrugged. It sounded a bit suspicious, like it was a Pizza Hut rather than a place to live. He took Gran's hand and squeezed it harder than he'd ever squeezed it before.

5

Tripi

Stupid English food! thought Tripi as he lifted the pan of boiled potatoes off the stove.

He took the potatoes over to the sink and tipped them into the colander. Steam rushed at his face and scalded his eyes. He leapt back, sloshing water from the pan onto the floor.

'For goodness sake, be careful!' Nurse Thornhill made English words land like bricks. 'I thought you were meant to be a trained chef?'

Tripi *was* a trained chef, he just wasn't trained to peel and chop and boil potatoes twenty-four hours a day. Potatoes and meat that looked like old leather left out in the sun. Potatoes and runny, reheated stew from those tins she ordered. Potatoes and pre-cooked vegetables the colour of the uniforms worn by the rebels in Syria: a pale mossy green. He tried his best to make something of the ingredients, but there was a limit to his skills.

He thought back to Four Seasons in Damascus – the chandeliers, the restaurant buzzing with tourists, the head chef who taught Tripi how to make the perfect meringue. He'd written a letter of recommendation for Tripi to help him get a job when he reached England. *One day I'll come and eat in your restaurant*, he'd said. They'd thought there'd be plenty of time to say a proper goodbye, but it turned out those were the chef's last words to Tripi.

'We can't afford to be making a mess, Tahir,' said Nurse Thornhill.

Tahir was his proper on-paper name, but everyone back in Syria called him Tripi. It was the name his little sister gave him when she learnt English and found out that the verb 'to trip' meant to fall over things. *It's what clumsy people do*, she said. *People who fall over their big feet.* She looked up from her dictionary, her brown eyes sparkling. *From now on, I'm calling you Tripi!*

'I'm sorry, Nurse Thornhill.' Tripi took some kitchen paper and mopped up the spilled water.

'I need your address.' She placed a blue form by the side of the sink and pointed to a column of empty boxes.

Steam from the colander curled the edges of the paper. Tripi stared at the words with the blanks next to them: *street, city, county, country, telephone number.* There were other boxes, too, like *National Insurance Number*, but Nurse Thornhill said not to worry about those.

His address? The wet grass that made his knees creak as he bowed down to do his prayers. The thick grey sky that swallowed the sun and thundered with planes. He closed his eyes and thought of Damascus. The reds and purples of the souk, the smell of raw coffee steaming in glass tumblers, his little sister sitting on a high stool in the kitchen telling him what she had learnt at school that day.

'Tripi, did you hear what I said?'

Tripi opened his eyes and nodded quickly. 'Yes, yes, my address. I will get it to you.'

He watched the thin white nurse walk to the big swing doors. The first time he saw her he'd been impressed – so neat and tidy and clean, devoting her life to these old people. He'd felt sorry for her too, living here in the nursing home in her small flat, no husband, no family.

Before she left, Nurse Thornhill turned and looked at him with her pale, washed-out eyes.

'And no more of that foreign singing. Our visitors don't like it.'

As Nurse Thornhill pushed out through the kitchen doors, Tripi thought of that small round wrinkly face staring through the window, and then the little boy's face beside hers. They had smiled at his singing.

6

Milo

A thump.

Milo's eyes flew open.

A crash.

Hamlet squirmed his way up the bed covers and stood on Milo's chest, his ears pinned back.

The floorboards shuddered overhead. A bit of plaster dust came loose from the ceiling and landed on Hamlet's black ear. Milo blew it away and gave Hamlet's ear a kiss.

And then Hamlet and Milo waited to hear what came next.

It was a game they played with Gran, listening really hard and trying to make out as many sounds as possible. Gran had invented it when Milo came back from the first appointment for his eyes with Dr Nolan.

We need to sharpen your other senses, Gran had scribbled on her pad.

Gran's theory was that if Milo could hear, smell, taste and feel things better than everyone else, and listen to that voice in his gut too, it would make up for the things he missed in his periphery vision.

Milo screwed shut his eyes and listened harder.

A thud like someone had dropped a really heavy book.

The creak of footsteps walking from one end of the attic to the other.

Something being zipped open and zipped shut again.

And then a smash.

And after that a sigh – not so you could hear, Gran didn't do things out loud, but a big, fat sigh inside her head and her heart, so big that Hamlet and Milo felt it too.

Milo rubbed his eyes and turned his head towards the window. It was still dark outside. The orange street lamps buzzed.

'Come on.' Milo scooped Hamlet up into his arms. 'Gran needs us.'

Milo crept past his mum's bedroom and stopped for a second to check that she was asleep. When Dad first left, Milo would hear her creaking down the stairs, moving around in the kitchen, the suck as she opened the freezer and the clunk as she closed it again and then the low buzz of the telly from the lounge. The next day he'd find her asleep on the sofa, a soup spoon and a soggy tub of Cherry Garcia ice cream lying in a sticky mess on the coffee table. She hadn't done it for a while, but she still had bad days.

When he thought he could hear Mum's sleep-breathing, Milo moved on to the stairs in the attic. As the fairy lights blurred in and out of focus through his tired eyes he felt a fluttering in his chest, which meant that Gran must have the flutter too, which would explain why she couldn't sleep and why she was clomping around and sighing so much.

Milo hated the thought that this might be the last night he'd come up these stairs to find her, that soon the nurse in her white uniform with her white teeth and her plastic smile would be looking after her.

He knocked lightly on her door, waited a second and then walked in.

Moving his head an inch at a time, he scanned the room.

It was like a bomb had exploded. The floor was scattered with Gran's things: her bagpipes and her map of Scotland and her painting of the bay where she grew up in Inverary and the picture of Gramps in his military uniform and all her clothes and shoes and books. Bits of Gran's favourite yellow vase poked up out of the carpet like bits of shrapnel. And in the middle of it all, like one of those suicide bombers they went on about on the news, who'd managed to stay alive despite the blast, stood Gran, her grey hair sticking up in tufts, her eyes wide and glassy.

'It's okay, Gran.' Milo walked over to her, took her hand and guided her back to her bed. She was shivering. 'Here.' He placed Hamlet on her knees. 'He's better than a hot-water bottle.'

Milo placed Gran's fingers over Hamlet's small, warm body and then stroked the top of her hands. Her skin was as thin as tracing paper, barely covering the spiderweb of purple veins.

She looked up and her face relaxed a bit.

'Just wait here a minute,' said Milo. He kissed the top of her head and went to the bathroom.

He clicked open the bathroom cabinet and fixed his eyes on one bottle at a time. There was the bottle with the small pink pills that Gran took because she had too much sugar in her blood. She was skinny as the boys on the football team at school but she lived off shortbread and sugary tea and liked to suck on sugar cubes, so the doctor said she was *at risk*. Then there was the bottle of green and white pills that were meant to help Gran sleep. The doctor said the pills were good for calming her down too when she got into one of her muddles. Except on very special occasions, Milo avoided giving Gran those pills because they made her drowsy and out of it and not like Gran at all.

He shifted his focus to the next bottle. The magic untangling pills for the times when Gran's brain shot off in a million different directions and made her forget where she was and what she was meant to be doing and even sometimes who Milo was. He reached out for the last bottle, pushed and screwed open the lid and tipped a pill into his palm.

When he came back, he put the small white pill into Gran's hand, gave her a glass of water and then went to get her pad, which she kept on the windowsill.

The sky was getting a little lighter now, an inky grey, and through the sky came a chirruping, like a bird, only sharper and more human.

Hamlet squirmed off Gran's lap and onto the bed and he plodded across the mattress to the window. Milo picked him up and they both looked out.

Under a crescent of moon, thin as an onion ring, Mr Overend stood at his window. Sometimes Milo wondered whether Mr Overend was a ghost and whether only he and Gran ever saw him. Mr Overend pressed his lips together and whistled again. He liked to imitate the birds at dawn.

'He's at it again,' said Milo.

Gran didn't seem to hear.

He placed the pad in Gran's lap and then looked around her room. It was all such a mess, he didn't know where to start.

'So you've been packing, Gran?'

She nodded.

'You don't need to bring everything, you know.'

Gran's face didn't change and she didn't write anything on her pad.

Milo came over and crouched beside her. 'You're only going for a while, until I can work out how to get you back. Just bring a few essentials – like ... Like you're going on holiday, Gran. You need to pack light, fit everything in one bag.'

Gran's face still looked confused. Sometimes it took a while for the untangling pills to kick in.

'I'm going to make three piles, Gran.'

Milo took Gran's pad, wrote *Go* on one piece of paper, *Stay* on the next one and *Not Sure* on a third, ripped them off and handed them to her.

'I'll point to your things one at a time, Gran, and you can hold up the piece of paper to direct me with the packing.' Milo grinned. 'It'll be like one of our games.'

Milo had thought Gran would like it being a game but she frowned and her cheeks flushed pink and her eyes misted over. She'd probably worn herself out trying to pack all by herself. Milo had helped her to start packing days ago but she kept changing her mind about what she wanted to take and what she wanted to leave – and now she'd left it to the last minute and was trying to do it all by herself and she was wearing herself out. She'd be better off having a rest, but they had to do this now: Gran was leaving for the nursing home first thing in the morning and if Mum found out that the packing wasn't done she'd flip and do it herself and Gran wouldn't get a say in what she got to take with her.

Milo spotted Hamlet's back legs and curly tail poking out from under the bed and pulled him out and put him back on Gran's lap, which made Gran smile and look better.

'So, let's start with the essentials.' Milo pointed to Gran's underwear. The big, baggy knickers and the bras with lots of straps and hooks and the thick caramel-coloured tights.

Gran held up the *Go* sign.

'You see, Gran, this is going to be fun.'

Milo pulled out Gran's old suitcase that had stiff cardboard-like covers and sharp reinforced corners, snapped it open and carefully started folding Gran's knickers.

Hamlet came over and sat on the soft bit of Gran's bagpipes and Gran got into holding the bits of paper up and Milo got into a really good rhythm of folding and putting away.

'You'll be back by Christmas, Gran,' he said. 'You'll see.'

He stuffed Gran's shoes with her caramel tights.

'And while you're away, you should have fun. There'll be people your age and stuff.'

He took a breath and looked around. Gran's room was starting to look tidier.

'And I'll come and visit you every day. It won't be that different from how things are now, will it, Hamlet?' Milo felt his voice go wobbly and he kissed the top of Hamlet's head to make the lump at the back of his throat go away. 'And I'll sneak Hamlet in too, even if that silly nurse said pets aren't allowed.' Milo scanned the carpet through his pinhole, picked up the bits of the vase one at a time and carried them to Gran's bin.

The door flew open.

Hamlet squealed and started to run around in circles.

Milo felt Gran's shoulders drop.

'What on earth?'

From where he was crouching, all Milo could see was the outline of the door and the edge of Mum's frilly nightie and her bulging pale thighs and her pink slippers and her chipped pink toenails.

'I was only helping Gran . . .'

Mum ignored Milo and turned to Gran.

'Lou, it's five thirty in the morning, Milo should be in bed. He's got school in a few hours.'

Gran shrugged.

'It's not her fault,' Milo said, feeling the heat from all the packing rising up into his cheeks. 'If you weren't making her go, she wouldn't have to pack.'

A silence dropped between them. Even Hamlet stopped running around. The only sound came from Mr Overend's low whistling, not a bird this time, more like a warning siren.

'Go to your room, Milo.'

Milo picked up Hamlet. 'We're staying with Gran.'

Gran scribbled something on her pad. Milo noticed a tremor in her fingers and when he looked at the letters, he saw that they were all wobbly. He went over and read them out loud:

Please . . . don't . . . fight.

'We're not fighting,' Sandy snapped. 'I'm just giving Milo

an instruction and he'd better do what I say or ...' She chewed the nail of her small finger. 'Or I won't let him visit after school.'

Milo felt the heat rise from his cheeks into his eyeballs. The pinhole narrowed. All he saw was Mum's stupid lips, puckered and mean. It was bad enough that she was making him go to school, which meant that he couldn't be with Gran when she moved into her new room at the nursing home, but now she was threatening not to let him visit? If she did that, he'd pack his own suitcase and move out and live with Gran in Forget Me Not. That would teach her.

Gran held up the piece of paper that said *Go* and stared at Milo.

He blinked.

'You want me to go, Gran?' his voice wobbled.

She nodded slowly.

'Good, we're agreed for once,' Mum said. 'And make sure you put that pig back in the garage.'

Milo hugged Hamlet tighter and walked out to the top of the stairs. He was about to slam the door when he changed his mind. Instead he clomped down the stairs to make it sound like he was going back to his room and then crept back up really slowly, kneeled on the carpet and looked through the small crack he'd left in the door.

'He's got to get used to you not being around,' Mum said, pushing the suitcase out of the way. 'It's got out of hand, Lou, his helping you like this.'

Milo saw Gran's eyes go watery and then she scribbled something on the pad but it was too far for him to read.

He clenched his fists. Gran didn't ask Milo to help, he did it because he wanted to. And maybe if Mum stopped feeling

30

sorry for herself and thinking about Dad and his Tart for a second and helped look after Gran too, then he wouldn't have to worry about Gran so much.

'Come on, Lou, it's time for you to rest.' Mum's voice was softer than Milo expected. And then she stroked the top of Gran's head, which she never did when Milo was looking. She eased the pad out of her fingers, put it on the windowsill and then lifted Gran's limbs so that they were straight on the bed. Then she pulled up the sheets and the blankets and tucked Gran in, like she used to tuck Milo in, all the way round until he could see the shape of his body. She hadn't done that in ages.

Milo rubbed his eyes. Packing up Gran's things had used up all his vision energy, but he didn't want to leave, not yet.

He looked again through the crack in the door.

Mum sat next to Gran on the bed and held her hand, just like he'd done earlier.

'Forget Me Not's a nice place, Lou. They'll look after you properly there.'

Milo felt a flutter in Mum's chest like the one he'd felt walking up the stairs looking at the fairy lights.

Mum let out a sigh. 'It's for the best, it's all for the best.'

Through the pinhole, Milo saw Gran close her eyes and bob her head up and down.

Mum stayed there for what felt like ages, stroking Gran's hand, waiting for her to fall asleep. She stayed for so long that Milo got sleepy too and worried that Mum would find him asleep outside the door with Hamlet nuzzled into his arm, so he got up really slowly and tried not to make a sound as he crept back to his room.

As he lay in bed, Hamlet nuzzled in beside him, he heard Mum walking around upstairs, finishing Gran's packing.

Mum's words floated behind Milo's eyes, all wobbly and jumbled up like Gran's writing:

Best ... Its ... All ... Best ... For ... Best ....

Maybe if he looked at the words for long enough, he'd start to believe them.

7

Milo

'Milo . . .'

Mrs Harris's voice faded in and out.

Behind his eyelids, Milo saw Gran sitting in her armchair, the white walls of the nursing home pressing in on her. He wished Mum had let him have the day off school to settle Gran in.

'Milo Moon, are you with us?' Mrs Harris's voice was sharper now.

A finger jabbed into his ribs. 'Wake up,' Nadja hissed through her braces.

'He's off on one again,' announced Stan from behind Milo.

Titters of laughter from around the classroom, all except Nadja, but that was only because she didn't want to get in trouble.

'That's enough, Stan,' said Mrs Harris.

Milo felt a kick against his chair from behind. He could smell Stan's BO festering under his dirty clothes. It hung in the air and mingled with Nadja's sweet perfume and the smelly plants Mrs Harris kept on the windowsills and the thick dust pumped into the air by the fan heaters that lined the hut.

He thought he was going to be sick.

'Milo?'

'Sorry, miss.' He sat up, took a breath and rubbed his eyes.

Mrs Harris came into focus, her elbows akimbo, her head tilted to one side.

'As I was saying, Milo, I've printed your test results and put them in envelopes for you to take home to your parents.'

Milo's heart dropped. The last thing he needed was to have Mum nagging him about school.

'Would you like me to hand them out, Miss Harris?' Nadja asked, her back straight as a ruler, her small, sharp nose in the air.

Before Mrs Harris had the chance to answer, Nadja had scraped back her chair and was standing to attention. Milo and Nadja shared the double desk right at the front of the classroom; Nadja because she'd asked to and Milo because Mrs Harris thought it meant that Milo could see the board better. Mum and Dad were meant to have filled Mrs Harris in on the whole Retinitis Pigmentosa thing, but she didn't seem to get it – that if you were further away from something, you could actually see more through the pinhole. And that if you had the whole class behind you, you were a sitting target.

Milo stuffed the letter into his school bag.

'Pack up your things, push your chairs into your desk and line up neatly by the door.'

Milo narrowed his eyes and looked up at the clock. It was

an hour before hometime and already the sky was getting dark. Gran had been at Forget Me Not for hours and hours.

'You'd better be on your best behaviour, Year Five – we want to make a good impression on PC Stubbs.'

Since September they'd had firemen, dustbin men and paramedics in. It was part of them learning to be good citizens – *and it's never too early to be thinking about career choices*, Mrs Harris told them. The problem was, Milo knew he'd be rubbish at any of those jobs. A fireman who missed the flames shooting out of the side of a house or a dustbin man who only picked up half the rubbish or a paramedic who didn't spot that there was a second person lying in the road with a leg dangling off. You had to be able to see properly or you'd miss things and let people down and get sacked.

The lecture theatre was a hut without proper brick walls or a tiled roof. There were chairs all in a row and an old telly on a chipboard shelf. PC Stubbs stood in front of the class dressed in his black uniform and his navy cap with its blue and white chequerboard band and his navy stab vest and his navy tie and navy epaulettes and his white shirt and over it his fluorescent yellow jacket with his walkie-talkie pinned to his chest and all the bits dangling off his belt like his baton and handcuffs and a proper gun and other bits for stopping criminals.

As they walked in, he gave the pupils sticky labels to write their names on.

'Good afternoon.' The policeman's voice was so low and clear that immediately, the class fell silent. Even Stan shut up for a second. Milo wished he had a voice that could do that. 'My name is PC Stubbs and today I'm going to explain how you can all play a part in helping the police to make Slipton a happier, safer place. To start with, I'm going to show you a brief video.'

A cheer rose up in the class. Mrs Harris hardly ever let them watch films.

PC Stubbs raised his hands for silence and cleared his throat. 'What you're about to see is the re-enactment of a crime scene. I want you to watch as closely and intently as you can. Afterwards, I'll be asking you some questions.'

The TV flickered to life.

Milo focused his eyes and stared through the pinhole. He liked tellies with their clear, set frame: they were way easier to watch than real life.

At the end of the film PC Stubbs froze the screen on the face of an old lady with a hair net standing on the pavement outside the RSPCA shop.

'So, let's see whether there are any budding detectives in here,' PC Stubbs said. 'What did you notice?'

'That bloke put his hand in the old woman's purse,' Stan blurted out.

'Hands up, please,' Mrs Harris said.

PC Stubbs squinted at Stan's name tag. 'Okay, thank you, Stan. You're right, that was what happened. I was looking for a bit more detail, though.'

Milo felt pleased that the policeman had put Stan in his place. Everyone saw what the crime was – you didn't have to be a detective for that.

Everyone started chipping in.

'He had a 'tash . . . '

'He was tall . . . '

'No he wasn't . . . '

'Hands up please, class.'

'He was wearing a grey T-shirt.'

'It wasn't grey, it was white.'

'Blue eyes . . .'

'No, green . . .'

'Adidas trainers . . .'

'The old woman had a wig on . . .'

'No, she didn't . . .'

'Yes, she did . . .'

'No, she didn't . . .'

'Class, one at a time, please.'

'There was a second guy standing on the street corner, out-side Bill the Butchers. Six foot two, mousy brown hair, early twenties, a mole on his cheek, brown leather shoes, faded black jeans, a red hoodie. He was the look-out.'

The classroom fell silent.

Everyone stared at Milo.

Mrs Harris's eyebrows shot up so high Milo thought they might disappear into her hairline.

A smile crept into PC Stubbs's mouth.

'And who's this young man?' he asked Mrs Harris.

'Oh, that's Milo. Milo Moon.'

'Well, it looks like you've got a good eye, Milo.'

Stan let out a farty noise through his mouth but this time no one laughed.

Milo wasn't sure what the big deal was. It was easy: you just looked for the thing that you thought no one else would notice. He played the spotting game with Gran all the time: they'd stare out of her window in the attic and look out onto the street and try to notice things that the other person hadn't. It was part of the training Gran did with him to help with his eyes, like the listening game. They did smells, too, and sometimes even tastes where they tried to work out all the ingredients in one of Mum's microwave meals.

On the way out of the lecture theatre, PC Stubbs handed each of them his personal business card and said that if they ever had any questions about what it took to be a policeman – or if they noticed anything strange happening on the streets of Slipton – they should give him a call.

When Milo got to him PC Stubbs stopped him and said, 'You've got a real talent there, Milo. We need boys like you in the force.'

Stan barged into the back of Milo. 'He wouldn't pass the physical.'

'Excuse me?' PC Stubbs asked. You could tell he didn't like Stan.

'He's blind as a wombat,' said Stan. The pupils at Slipton Junior could tell Milo had a problem with his eyes, even if he tried to hide it.

PC Stubbs's cheeks went a deep, purplish red.

Milo felt his eyes burn. He took PC Stubbs's card, stuffed it into the bottom of his school bag, charged down the corridor and headed out of the school gates into the dark December afternoon.

8

Milo

'Gran, Gran!' Milo burst into Gran's room at Forget Me Not, dumped his bag by her bed and went to kneel beside her chair. Although the view wasn't as good, he was glad she had a chair by the window. She liked to look out.

'Gran.' He took her hand. It felt heavier than usual and it didn't squeeze back. 'We had this policeman come to talk to us at school and he said I was really good at spotting things and he gave me his card and everything.' Milo fished the card out of his pocket and held it up for Gran to see.

But Gran didn't open her eyes. She didn't even stir.

'Gran?'

He shook her arm gently and stroked the inside of her wrist, the bit where you could see Gran's blue veins running under her white skin. Gran wasn't a deep sleeper. Usually, when Milo came up to see her in her attic room, she'd have heard his footsteps on the stairs and would be waiting for him, wide-eyed, ready to listen to him and to write things back on her pad. She didn't even sleep that deeply at night.

Milo looked closer. Gran's head hung down and her chin rested on her chest. Her eyelids were clamped shut and her breathing was deep and heavy.

'Gran?' He tried shaking her arm again. She stirred a little, rolled her head up, flickered her eyes open for a second and then fell asleep again.

Maybe the move had taken it out of her, thought Milo.

'I was going to show you this letter too, Gran,' he said, looking over at his school bag. 'I didn't do very well in my tests.'

But it wasn't any good. Gran stayed silent. He'd have to come back another time.

9

Sandy

Sandy swallowed one of her blue and white diet pills, took a gulp of water and picked up the memo pad by the phone. On it was Milo's handwriting, the letters more perfectly formed than any she'd ever seen. Dr Nolan said they'd notice things like this, how sharp and precise he could be about some things; how he'd miss other things altogether.

Samantha cancelled her waxing.

The third cancellation that week. And this was Christmas, a time when people should be queuing round the block to get plucked.

She heard Milo open and close Hamlet's cage in the garage. He'd been giving her the silent treatment ever since she'd signed Lou up at Forget Me Not. She switched on the TV that sat on the counter; the buttons had melted and a film of soot lay across the screen.

'Are you ready for the adventure of a lifetime? Then take a camel trek across the hottest desert in the world . . .'

Sandy stared at the golden sands of the Sahara. Hot, that would make a nice change from Slipton.

Twenty-seven and she'd never got on a plane, never even left England. When she was pregnant with Milo Sandy had watched documentaries about teenage mums and could never quite bring herself to identify with those girls carting prams around housing estates. But that's what had happened: she'd got pregnant too early and then she'd missed out. She told Andy that flying scared her, how the tiniest thing could go wrong and planes would drop out of the sky. But now, with everything that had happened, getting on a plane didn't seem so frightening after all. In fact, Sandy thought she might quite like it, packing up her life in a small suitcase and disappearing into the clouds.

Milo came back in from the garage carrying Hamlet. She shoved the bottle of pills into the cutlery drawer.

Hamlet had only been with them a few months, and already he'd doubled in size. When Andy showed up with him in June, a few days before he left for Abu Dhabi, Sandy said, *no way, we're sending it back*. But Milo insisted that Hamlet would stay small. *Really small, like these*, he said, showing Sandy pictures on the internet. A wet snout, tiny pink trotters, a corkscrew tail. *He won't be any trouble and I'll take care of him, I promise.*

Milo, always taking care of things.

'I'll make you some toast,' said Sandy.

Milo didn't answer. He buried his nose in Hamlet's fur, walked through the kitchen without saying a word and carried him upstairs.

Right from the word go, Andy had been better with Milo than she had. He hadn't taken responsibility for any of the

42

routine stuff like buying shoes and attending parents' meetings and taking him to dentists and, in the last year, to the optometry appointments with Dr Nolan, but he understood what made Milo happy. And then he'd gone and left him.

And now she'd taken Lou away from him as well. He thought it was all her fault, she could see it in those sharp, focused eyes of his.

They're creatures of habit, that's what Gina said last week as Sandy rubbed cellulite cream into her thighs. *He'll get used to it being just the two of you*. Gina had put her mother in Forget Me Not last Christmas.

Sandy toasted two pieces of bread, smeared them with butter while they were still hot, licked the fat off her fingers and spread Marshmallow Fluff on top. She'd bought Fluff as a treat, or maybe a compensation. But for what? For losing the people he loved? For having to live with her?

She layered the pieces of toast on Milo's favourite plate, the one with pigs flying around the rim, and carried it upstairs.

10

Milo

Milo heard shuffling outside. A dull thud as something was placed on the carpet and then Mum's footsteps plodding back down the stairs. He waited to hear her mules clip-clopping on the kitchen tiles before going over to open the door.

Two pieces of toast sat on his favourite plate, the one Gran had bought him as part of a set from the RSPCA shop on Slipton High Street. He smelt the sweet Marshmallow Fluff melting into the hot butter and all the muscles in his tummy stretched towards the plate.

Hamlet trotted up behind him and nudged Milo's ankles with his wet snout. Milo looked at the toast, swallowed hard and closed the door.

He looked around the room. It was the same as always, only Gran was missing.

Milo looked at the bagpipes and at Great-Gramps's Royal Argyll Sutherland Highlanders uniform hanging on the wardrobe. Sometimes Gran put it on for fun and apart from the fact that it was too big, she actually looked like a proper soldier.

Milo had tried the uniform on too once and it had floated around his wrists and his waist and his ankles. *You'll grow into it, Milo*, Gran had written on her pad. But Great-Gramps was a big man, perhaps bigger than Milo would ever be.

As Milo looked around the room he was glad he'd persuaded Gran only to take a few things with her. She'd be back here soon and it would be pointless carting it all back and forth.

He pulled the letter from school out of his back pocket. He wished Gran hadn't been asleep when he went to Forget Me Not, he'd wanted so badly to read it to her. Gran could be relied on to react properly, she wouldn't make her eyebrows shoot up and she wouldn't shake her head and start biting the nail on her little finger or sigh like the end of the world was coming. She'd just listen and write: *there's more to life than exams* and make notes about Great-Gramps and how he'd been this amazing soldier and that he was really clever and liked reading things like Shakespeare, even though he left school early and didn't have any qualifications. When her hands weren't shaking, Gran could write faster than most people talked.

Milo hugged Hamlet in close, took the letter out of the envelope and whispered his exam results into Hamlet's soft ears: the maths results went into his black ear and the English results into his white ear.

When he'd finished, he buried his nose in Hamlet's fur and closed his eyes.

*

By the time Milo woke up it was dark outside. Hamlet lay nestled in the crook of his elbow. Trying not to disturb him, Milo cradled Hamlet in his arms and stood up. Maybe it was the dead weight of Hamlet's sleeping body, but he felt heavier than Milo expected. Mum kept going on about how fat Hamlet was getting, even though Milo explained that he was following the internet feeding instructions. Anyway, she was one to talk, munching her way through all those packets of Hobnobs.

Milo walked over to the window that jutted out of the front of the house. One of the pieces of paper from Gran's pad lay on the side, a message scrawled across the front in her big capital letters: *BE QUIET*. She'd hold it up to the window for Mr Overend who lived across the street. Mr Overend never did anything but mooch around in his PJs, whistling. Sometimes he whistled so loud that he drowned out the planes.

Gran liked looking at the planes and she liked looking across town. From up here, you could see the high street and the church tower and the canal and the Tesco warehouse and the turning to the motorway. And you could see the park, the tops of the trees, the white paths in the moonlight.

Milo noticed the flickering of the park keeper's torch as he walked around, locking the gates. What would it be like to get caught in there overnight? To sleep under the sky with all those trees swaying above you?

He walked back to the middle of the room, put Hamlet down and lay beside him on the carpet under the skylight. Hamlet snuffled back into Milo's elbow and Great-Gramps's special bagpipe song played in Milo's head, the one Great-Gramps had taught Gran before he got sent to Korea. Since she'd turned up five years ago, Gran had been teaching Milo to play, though her breathing had got bad recently so they'd given the lessons a rest. Dad could play too, but he wasn't here now.

As he looked up, Milo felt the moon shining somewhere beyond the pinhole of his vision. He stared hard into the black sky and saw a single star winking at him.

He hoped that maybe Gran was looking at it too.

11

Tripi

In Syria, old people are not put into homes. They live in houses with their families, they sit and tell stories and eat baklava and drink strong black coffee from glass tumblers.

Tripi had wanted to tell the old woman that he would not eat them either, those potatoes, pale as the Syrian sand, nor that stringy beef sitting in its brown puddle of gravy. He wanted to tell her that one day he would cook a feast for her like they made for rich people at The Four Seasons in Damascus.

This was the end of Tripi's third day and Nurse Thornhill had been too busy to ask about the empty boxes on the blue piece of paper, which meant a little more time to find a home.

Back in the park, Tripi hid behind the laurel bush, waiting for the keeper to lock up the gates. Then he unfurled his sleeping bag and said his prayers, too late for the sun. As he breathed in, his lungs ached; already the cold had set in.

At night, as he slept, he felt icicles creeping in between his ribs.

Back home in Damascus it was unusual for the temperature to dip much below ten degrees. And when it did get cold, there was snow. And in spring when it rained raindrops fell fat and clear, swelling the rivers and spinning the wooden norias, the waterwheels, so that fresh clean water flowed through Damascus. Here the rain was small, dirty and cold. The only heat came from Tripi's nightmares, always the same: Ayishah's face on that hot day in July.

He took out the photograph of his twelve-year-old sister and placed it in front of him. Half his age and yet at times it had felt like she was the older one. He prayed that she was safe, that one day they'd be here together on this island where the only sound of gunshots came from the televisions in people's front rooms.

On their last day in Damascus, Ayishah had given him a postcard of The Queen that she'd bought at one of the stalls in the souk.

Look! she said, tracing The Queen's hair with her finger. *If she's in charge, it must be a good place.*

Tripi took the postcard out of his sleeping bag and looked at it again: the pearls in her ears and around her neck and her soft listening eyes and a smile that didn't give too much away. He wanted to believe it, too, that this was a good place. But he wasn't so sure. Being old, should The Queen not make sure that there were nice places for people her age to live?

'He's here!' The light of a torch flickered across Tripi's face. The park keeper was back, another man with him.

Tripi shoved the photograph into his pocket, climbed off his sleeping bag and dashed towards the gates.

'Stop!'

Two full beams blinded him.

When Tripi got used to the brightness, he saw the park keeper and with him, a policeman, their eyes narrow and mean.

'Knew we had a tramp,' said the park keeper.

'Time to move on.' The policeman stepped forward. 'Here's the number of a homeless shelter.' He pressed a card into Tripi's hand.

A London address. Tripi didn't want to go back there.

'The park belongs to the council,' added the park keeper. 'You shouldn't be here.'

How could grass belong to anyone? thought Tripi. Grass and trees and sky.

He went back to the bush and gathered up his sleeping bag and Ayishah's backpack that he'd carried since they were separated, through the two months he spent walking along the Syrian border, looking for her, through those weeks in London, searching for work. And now here.

The policeman pushed Tripi out through the gates and the three men stood under the glare of the orange street lamp.

The park keeper leant in to Tripi's face, beer on his breath. 'Not from around here, are you?'

Tripi had noticed the looks on people's faces as he walked around Slipton. His worn clothes, his skin too tanned under the English clouds.

'You should ask to see his papers, Stubbs,' said the park keeper. 'Bet he's an illegal.'

Tripi's heart jolted.

The policeman rubbed his eyes; he looked tired.

'Just go to that hostel,' said the policeman. Then he turned to the park keeper. 'They'll check him out there.'

Tripi gave a small bow and walked away, counting his heartbeats and his footsteps and watching the white swirls coming out of his mouth.

'And stay out of my park,' the park keeper called after him aggressively.

12

Lou

Lou's head felt thick with sleep. Like a deep fog.

Gran . . . Gran . . . Can you hear me? Milo's little voice flitting in and out of her dreams. *A policeman came to school. He said I was good at spotting things.* She'd tried to wake up, to speak back, but the fog was too thick.

He moved around her, folding her clothes and putting them in her wardrobe, setting the things in her wash-bag out on the shelf under the mirror.

And then his kiss, just by her ear.

I'll let you sleep then, Gran. But I'll come back tomorrow. I'll visit every day.

He pressed a blanket over her knees, tucking her in like a child.

You'll be back home soon. The fire was an accident, Gran, it could have happened to anyone.

When at last she opened her eyes, there was no one there.

*

And now here, sitting in the lounge with all those old ladies.

Soft chairs, better than handcuffs, the hot whisper of Mrs Moseley, the Jamaican woman who sat beside Lou all afternoon listening to her tape recorder. Island music, a place where coconuts grew on trees, where the water was so clear that you could see your toes.

Lou blinked.

A stain on the back of the woman's dress when she stood up.

And the other women.

Mrs Foxton, who spoke to an invisible policeman about a broken pane of glass in her conservatory. *Thugs*, she kept saying.

Mrs Wong, who called out for rice. *I trained the Olympic gymnastics team*, she said, getting stuck as she lowered her old body into a squat.

Mrs Turner, who hid her potatoes and her mushy peas in the pockets of her smock.

Mrs Swift, who wore make-up that looked like it had been applied with a child's crayon. *I could do yours*, she'd offered Lou. No, Lou had never worn make-up. The sun and the sea and the air, that's all her skin needed.

Mrs Sharp, who played a game called Angry Birds on the iPad her grandson had given her. *Got 'em, the little buggers!* she yelled.

And Mrs Zimmer, who sat in front of the television and slept all day.

Sleeping was a good option in a place like this, thought Lou. And she was tired, so, so tired, more tired than she'd ever been.

From their names, Lou supposed that they were all

married, or had been. And so, besides Nurse Thornhill and that young trainee Nurse Heidi, Lou was the only unmarried woman in the building.

Counting herself, that added up to eight old ladies. But hadn't Nurse Thornhill mentioned that they were nine? *Nine clients*, she'd said to Sandy, *one big happy family.*

Names and numbers, Lou had thought they'd be the first to go.

Sunk in her armchair, she no longer felt her limbs. She craned her neck to see a strip of dark sky above the trees, the window too low for stargazing.

At least she could still hear the planes.

Make an effort with your food, Nurse Thornhill said. *We can't have you wasting away.*

And then that nice boy with the brown eyes and the delicate hands who smelt of earth and flowers and sky. *Shh!* He put a finger to his lips, which made Lou think of prayer. *I won't tell Nurse Thornhill*, he whispered.

He tripped over his feet as he carried away her plate.

Having decided that there was no life left in the room, the sensors had switched off the lights. The buzzing continued though, like a fly beating itself against a hot bulb.

You sure we can't take you back to your room? Nurse Heidi had asked.

No. Lou liked the dark, the stillness of standing on the beach looking at the waves.

Well, just pull on the red cord if you need anything.

Cords dangling everywhere like puppet strings.

Lou's eyes felt heavy. Her mind slipped like water over rocks.

*

When Lou woke, the room was cold and still. The shadow of a man stood over her. She strained her eyes in the grainy darkness. A male nurse? No, he didn't have a uniform and this man was old, like her. As he leant over, she noticed a bald patch the size of a Jewish skullcap. His neck smelt of lemons.

'If you want me to help you up you'll need to give me some oomph,' he said, pulling at her fingers.

Oomph? She liked that word.

She nodded. Yes, she wanted to get back to her room now, her small room under the roof, to gaze out at Slipton, Milo asleep below.

'Good,' he said. 'On the count of three, then ... ' A Mediterranean roll in his consonants.

'One ... '

He pulled at her dead weight, her limbs asleep.

'Two ... '

She took a breath and straightened her spine.

'Three ... '

He pulled.

She pushed her weight into her legs, felt the forward swing of her torso and fell into his arms. His soft belly pressed into hers. To feel a man's body. She blushed in the dark.

'Back to your room, Petros.' It was Nurse Heidi. 'Nurse Thornhill has told you often enough, this isn't your job.'

'Yes, yes,' he said to Nurse Heidi. But then he leant in and whispered into Lou's ear. 'Except it is.' He guided her by the arm to the door. 'This is my job.'

13

Milo

After school on Tuesday Milo went to see Gran again. *You can't go and see her every day*, Mum had said. *You need to spend some time with your friends.* But Mum didn't get it – Gran was Milo's friend and he didn't want to spend time with anyone else. Anyway, yesterday she'd been asleep so that didn't count.

He popped the fourth of December chocolate into his mouth. Behind the chocolate there was a picture of three men on camels heading through the desert.

Christmas in twenty-one days – he had just under a month to get Gran home.

On the way, Milo stopped to sit on a bench by the canal to do some thinking. He loved looking into water in the same way that he loved looking at the sky, because it meant he didn't need to shift his head – the picture changed on its own. A new colour, a twig, a red packet of Hula Hoops, a duck floating by, the reflection of a plane nosing through the clouds. Dad and The Tart and the baby in The Tart's tummy had left in one of those planes. He'd looked up the departure times on the computer and worked out the flight path and stared up at the sky wondering whether Dad could see him standing there like a dot in front of the house.

Milo had never been to the seaside but he knew he'd love it, staring at the waves for hours and hours. Before she moved in with them, Gran had lived by the sea in Scotland. On her pad, she wrote that she and Great-Gramps had run into the waves, even in the middle of winter. That's why she loved taking baths. *It's the closest I'll get to swimming around here*, she'd written. And she was right, Slipton was as far away from the sea as you could get.

Maybe he could find someone to stay with Gran while he was at school and Mum was busy with her clients in the shed, like a babysitter but for old people. That way she wouldn't try to do things by herself and end up setting fire to the kitchen or flooding the bathroom. He'd have to find the money, though. He could put a card in the window of Poundland advertising his IT Services. People were always asking him to help them with their computers, like Mum when she asked him to do a search on The Tart and then told him to wipe the search history before Dad used the computer, or Mrs Harris at school who never used computers because she said they damaged your brain but wanted to find out what the mums were saying about her on mumsinaction.com which is where mums rant about crap teachers and plot ways to get them sacked.

As Milo swung his feet under the bench, the sole of his shoe thumped into something soft. He got down on all fours and crawled under the wooden slats. A sleeping bag, rolled up, and two backpacks. Someone must have sat here and put them down and forgotten all about them.

One backpack was big and blue and the other one small and red with a yellow ribbon tied to the one of the straps.

He'd drop the things off at the Slipton Lost Property Office on his way back from Forget Me Not. Milo left shoes and socks and lunchboxes and books behind all the time (anything that sat outside the pinhole); Keith at the Lost Property Office knew to keep aside anything with Milo's name on it. *Milo Moon*, written in big black Sharpie letters on everything he owned. Sometimes he thought he should write it on his forehead in case the whole of him got lost.

'Milo Moon?' A lime green Skoda pulled up along the pavement.

Milo twisted his head round.

'Milo – over here,' said the voice.

He looked to his right. Mrs Harris's head poked out of the car window.

'You okay?' his form teacher asked. 'You're carrying a lot of things.' She nodded at his schoolbag and the two back-packs and the sleeping bag.

'Going to see my gran,' he said and started off again.

'She's not living with you any more?'

Milo shook his head. He felt his teacher go quiet.

'I'm sorry to hear that.' She coughed. 'I need to speak to your mum about your results.'

At breaktimes Mrs Harris sat in her car and smoked. She was wrinklier than Gran, and Milo reckoned she should have retired ages ago. He asked her once about when she was planning to leave Slipton Primary, and she told him to mind his own business. Gran reckoned Mrs Harris kept teaching because she needed the money to pay for all those cigarettes.

'Mum knows,' said Milo, for the first time feeling the weight of all the bags he was carrying. 'She'll get in touch.'

Mrs Harris crept her car alongside Milo. He smelt stale smoke and caught a flash of green at the edge of his vision. Yellowy-green cars always made him think of snot. Bogeys on wheels.

'It's important,' she said, her voice louder now, and croakier.

'Mum's busy with the Christmas rush. She'll call soon.'

'Maybe I could pop by the house?'

Milo walked over to the car and looked his teacher in the eye. 'Mum doesn't like to be interrupted with her clients, it upsets the energy.'

'The energy?'

'Of their relaxation.'

Then he walked on.

'We need to discuss some options . . .'

Milo switched on Great-Gramps's bagpipe song in his head and Mrs Harris's voice faded away.

He came in to find Gran sitting by the window in her room, staring at the grey sky. She didn't look like the Gran from home; she looked like one of those cardboard cut-outs they have of actors in HMV.

Milo put down the backpacks and the sleeping bag, placed his hand on her shoulder and kissed her by the ear. He liked the feel of the cold pearl against his lips. Her skin was cold too though, much colder than at home.

She turned round to face him, a crease as deep as a ditch between her eyebrows.

'Gran? What is it?'

Her eyes reflected the pale light outside the window. It was like she'd floated away inside her body.

Gran pushed herself up but couldn't quite make it so he helped her with the last bit, placing his palm under her bony elbow.

She went over to the table and scribbled on her pad. It was the first time he'd noticed her right hand trembling: usually it was only her left. Her writing was all jaggedy: *I've got to . . .*

'Gran?'

She wrote some more. *The boat.* She drew a picture of a big boat. *David . . .* Gran hadn't spoken since Great-Gramps died, which was donkeys years ago, but Milo didn't mind. He found it fun writing notes, especially when Mum was in the room and didn't know what they were saying, like *Have you seen Hamlet?* (Milo) *He's in the garage, isn't he?* (Gran) and then Gran would draw a smiley face with a wink and they'd try really hard not to give it away by looking at the lump under Gran's duvet.

Gran walked over to her door, clutching onto bits of furniture on the way: the back of a chair, a chest of drawers. She reached up onto her tiptoes and pulled her woolly scarf off the hook, the one she'd knitted when her hands still worked. She made one for Milo too, in bright orange, which was his favourite colour. Gran wound it round her neck so tight Milo worried she'd strangle herself.

He walked up to her and put his hand on hers; they were cold too.

'Gran, why don't you sit down?'

She stared at him for a second as though she'd never seen

him before. He felt a hollow thud in his chest. Maybe Nurse Thornhill had forgotten to give her the untangling pill.

'Gran, it's Milo.'

Her eyes were still pale and far away and she twisted her engagement ring round and round on her finger.

She shook off his hand, reached for her coat, struggled with the sleeves and then gave up and opened the door, the coat half hanging off her body.

Milo felt a throb in his forehead. She hadn't been like this in months.

He reached for her arm but she yanked him off again, harder this time.

Gran was tiny and stooped with no bit of fat on her and her bones weighed less than Hamlet's when he first arrived; Milo didn't understand where she got her strength.

At home, he'd know what to do: he'd put her small radio on to distract her and lock the door so she couldn't get out and fall down the stairs or walk out into the traffic. And he'd give her Great-Gramps's bagpipes and ask her to give him a lesson and Hamlet would squeak along, because he loved music, and that would make Gran laugh and then she'd be fine again.

Milo was the only one who knew about how Gran disappeared into herself. He'd kept it from Mum, who wouldn't understand. Mum already called Gran *a handful*, and he bet she said even worse things when she was talking to Gina in the shed.

Gran kept shuffling along. He had to find someone to help him steer her back to her room.

It would take her a while to get to the front door, so Milo risked leaving her for a few minutes.

He speed-walked through the white corridors looking for someone official who could help, but everyone had disappeared. He heard the sound of television programmes weaving into each other from room to room: the *Emmerdale* theme tune and someone selling a gold necklace on the Shopping Channel and the voice of that presenter from the holiday programme Mum watched all the time, *Honeymoon Hideaways*. In another room someone was yelling like a toddler that she wanted rice and in another one a loud football-match voice called out *Got 'em, the little buggers!* and from a third room a small, tired voice pleading: *You can't ... can't ... can't make me have a bath.*

Milo had hoped that when you got old, people would stop making you do things.

Mrs Moseley, the lady who pottered around with her tape player listening to reggae music, walked past.

'Do you need some help?' she called over her tape player.

Black hairs sprouted above her lip and on her chin, like the ones Gran sometimes got, which Milo yanked out with Mum's tweezers. *Typical,* Gran would write, *years of trying to grow a beard to impress those fishermen at Inverary, and now that I'm land-locked, the stubble sets in.*

'I'm fine, thank you,' said Milo.

It was kind of Mrs Moseley to offer to help but he was worried she'd confuse Gran even more. He smelt wee wafting from her nightdress and considered suggesting she get some of those granny nappies he'd seen in Boots, but maybe Mrs Moseley didn't realise that she smelt of wee and then she'd get offended.

He went and knocked on the door that Nurse Thornhill had pointed out on their first visit when she said, *I'm available night and day.*

No one answered.

He banged harder, and then he noticed that it was on a latch. He pushed the door and looked in.

The first thing he felt was a blast of heat. It was warmer in here than in the whole of Forget Me Not put together. And then he noticed the deep plum wallpaper with swirly bits that felt velvety against his fingertips.

On the wall hung a picture of Harrods in London. In June Dad had taken Milo to the pet department to find a collar for Hamlet. The Tart came along and it turned out she was really good at picking out collars and she chose a black velvet one, which she said was appropriate for Hamlet and that it went with the black bits of his fur and made him look elegant. Milo knew he was meant to hate The Tart, but most of the time she was quite nice, especially when she talked to him about Hamlet, which Mum only did when she had something to complain about. Dad said not to mention that The Tart came along on their trips and that it was probably a good idea to keep acting like he hated her, because liking The Tart would make Mum more upset.

Next to the picture of Harrods hung a newspaper article with a picture of a young man, with dates underneath, which meant he must have died, and next to him a picture of – could it be, Nurse Thornhill? Much younger, but she had the same square forehead and she wore a nurse's uniform, though it looked all dirty, not like the starched white one she wore at Forget Me Not.

Her smile looked different too, less stuck on.

Milo looked closer. Saturday 17th December 1983. *IRA Bombs Harrods.*

Then Milo's attention was drawn up to a massive chandelier like the ones you saw in films hanging from the ceiling, splitting the light into a million diamonds. At the end of the hallway, he spotted a bottle of champagne lying on its side.

'Nurse Thornhill!' he called out.

No one answered.

Milo wondered whether there'd ever been a Mr Thornhill or baby Thornhills, though when he tried to create a picture of Nurse Thornhill with a family in his head, it didn't work.

He strained his ears but didn't detect any movement in the flat, so he closed the door and walked on.

An old man with a yellow corduroy cap sat on the carpet fixing the hinge of the door to the main lounge. Milo hesitated but the man didn't look like the sort of person who'd know what to do, so he kept going.

Then he remembered their first visit, what Gran had seen through those doors.

He darted to the kitchen.

The guy was singing again in that hiccupy language Milo didn't understand and peeling potatoes to the rhythm of his song.

Milo pushed through the door and walked over to him.

'Excuse me?' He tapped the cook on the back.

The cook turned round.

'My gran...' said Milo, out of breath. 'She's... she's not well.'

The cook put down the peeler and wiped his hands on his apron.

'Show me,' he said.

Milo guided him out through the swing doors and back down all those winding corridors towards Gran's room. The cook smelt weird, thought Milo, not dirty like BO dirty, more like the garden after it rained.

They found Gran standing outside the lounge, staring at a painting of a tiny fishing boat being tossed about on massive foamy waves. It made Milo think of Gran's picture back home of the fishing boat she used to take out to make a living. The old man with the screwdriver and the yellow cap was there too, looking at the picture with her.

'Gran?' asked Milo. 'Are you okay, Gran?'

The man stepped in front of the pinhole like he knew about Milo's eyes. He smelt of fake lemons, like the juice that came out of those plastic squeezy lemons Mum bought because they were cheaper than the fresh ones. And the cuffs of his shirt were frayed.

'I was just telling this lady about the picture.' He sounded foreign, like the cook, but his words were curlier.

He must have helped Gran out with her coat because it wasn't hanging off her any more.

Gran turned round and faced Milo; the blue light had come back into her eyes. She looked back at the painting.

'When I moved in, I brought my paintings with me,' said the man. 'I asked if I could put this one up and they never gave me an answer, so I hung it myself.' He adjusted the tilt of the frame. 'It was my wife's favourite.' He traced the movement of the waves with his oil-smudged finger.

Gran looked at the man like he'd said something really interesting.

The man turned round and held out a large, tanned hand to Milo. 'I'm Petros.'

'I'm Milo,' Milo said, and for a moment it felt like they were at a party, introducing themselves and getting to know each other, rather than in this cold, white nursing home.

But Milo didn't want to seem too keen to get to know Petros. Although he was grateful for the help, he wanted to make clear that it wasn't Petros's job to look after Gran, so Milo steered her away from the painting. Petros must have got the hint because he went back to fixing his door.

As Tripi held Gran's arm on the other side he hummed and that made Gran's face go soft. Milo didn't mind Tripi helping.

They settled her back into her chair by the window and then Milo went to look in Gran's washbag for her pills. He tipped them out into his palms and counted them. He was right, she hadn't had one since she left home. He poured some water into her toothbrush goblet and brought her the pill.

'You need to remember to take these, Gran,' he said as he watched her take little birdlike sips from the goblet. 'One every day.'

Gran nodded but Milo knew that he had to find a better way to make sure she took them. Mum used to take little round pills and she had them labelled M, Tu, W, Th, F, Sa, Su so that she never forgot to take one. Maybe he could make Gran a box with a little hole for each day of the week.

The cook walked towards the door.

'Thank you for your help,' said Milo and he wondered whether he should bow, like you do with Chinese people, though Tripi looked a different kind of foreign from Chinese.

Tripi smiled and then his eyes narrowed and he focused

on something past Milo's shoulder. He looked at the sleeping bag and the two backpacks, the blue one and the red one and his brown skin went dark brown to beige, like those caramel lattes Mum liked.

'I found them . . . ' Milo started. 'By the canal.'

Tripi went straight to the red bag. He zipped it open, peered inside and then sighed with relief and closed it again.

'What's going on in here?' Nurse Thornhill strode into the room. 'Tahir, why aren't you in the kitchen?'

'I looked for you in your flat, but I couldn't find you.' Milo said. She definitely looked nicer in her younger version in the Harrods photo.

Nurse Thornhill stared at Milo. 'You did what?'

'The door was open.'

'You never go into my private residence.' Her voice rumbled. 'Do you understand?'

Nurse Thornhill's face went purple like her furry wallpaper.

'But you said you were available—'

Nurse Thornhill wasn't listening. She'd turned away from Milo and was shouting at Tripi.

'You're not to interfere with the clients. Go back to work.' She pointed at the door.

Tripi glanced at the sleeping bag and the backpack and at Milo and then lowered his head and left. Milo shifted his gaze and watched Tripi walk down the corridor with his heavy, clumsy steps.

'He was helping,' said Milo.

Nurse Thornhill ignored Milo. She wedged her fists into her skinny waist, looked down at Gran and said: 'If you need help, use the button.' She pointed at a red switch on the wall by Gran's chair. 'I've shown you before.' She grabbed Gran's hand, pulled out her forefinger, walked her over to the switch and made her press on the button until it lit up. 'There,' she said. 'I don't want to have to tell you again.'

Her grumbling voice reminded Milo of Mrs Harris when she caught the class island-hopping between their desks at breaktime.

Milo knew that sometimes you had to show Gran things several times until she remembered how they worked, but he didn't like how Nurse Thornhill grasped Gran's finger, or the white grip mark she left behind.

Milo stayed with Gran until she fell asleep, which didn't take long. When Gran disappeared into herself like that, all the energy got zapped out of her.

The heating didn't seem to be working in the room, so Milo put a blanket on Gran's knees, kissed her cheek and then picked up his school bag and the sleeping bag and the two backpacks.

'Bye, Gran,' he whispered. 'Next time, I'll bring Hamlet. He'll keep you warm.'

14

Tripi

As he heated up the cubes of lamb in the big, stainless steel pot, Tripi threw in some cloves of garlic that he'd bought at the little market shop in the high street. Garlic was good for old people, it strengthened their immune system. And it would make this pale, tinned lamb taste of something other than the grey English clouds. Tripi listened out for Nurse Thornhill's footsteps going back to the office. Then he put down his wooden spoon and went to stand by the front door to wait for Mrs Moon's grandson.

As the small boy walked towards him, Tripi saw that he had the same build as Mrs Moon: tiny bones, like the sparrows that pecked at the crumbs outside the hotel in Damascus.

Although the boy stared straight ahead of him, his blue eyes stretched open, he didn't seem to notice that Tripi was there.

Tripi waved. 'Milo?'

Milo shifted his head and blinked.

'Are these your things?' asked Milo, holding out Ayishah's backpack.

Tripi nodded.

'I wasn't going to steal them, I just thought someone had left them behind. I found them under the bench by the canal.'

Tripi nodded again. 'My home.'

He'd never told anyone that he lived outside, that he slept on park benches, by canals, in buses. But he trusted this little boy – he liked how he held Mrs Moon's hand as she sat in her chair.

Milo's eyes went wide. 'You live by the canal?'

Tripi pressed his finger to his lips. 'It's a secret.' He nudged his head towards the nurses' station.

Milo nodded hard, then he whispered back, 'Don't you get cold?'

Tripi shrugged. 'A bit.' He coughed into his hand and then pointed to his throat. 'The wind tickles here,' he said, wiggling his fingers by his Adam's apple. 'And here,' he pointed to his ears. With every movement, the boy adjusted his head.

'Why don't you live in a proper home?'

'What do they say in England? It is a long story.' Tripi looked at the kitchen doors. 'I'd better get back to work. More potatoes, always potatoes!'

Milo nodded and placed the sleeping bag and the backpacks in a heap on the floor.

'Could you put them back for me?' asked Tripi. 'I can't have them here.'

'Under the bench?'

He nodded.

'Okay.' Milo picked the things up again. And then he looked up at Tripi and frowned. 'Are you from the Middle East? That's what Mrs Harris told us it's called if you come from bits of the world that are hot and sandy and where people walk around wearing sheets.'

Tripi smiled. It was the kindest way he had been referred to since he had arrived in England. 'Yes – I am from Syria.'

'I don't want to interfere but I wouldn't carry around too many backpacks if I were you.'

Tripi had heard about this: Arabs + Backpacks = Terrorists.

'They could lock you up.'

'Thank you, Milo. I will bear that in mind.'

The squeak of clogs sounded behind them. Tripi looked over Milo's shoulder at Nurse Thornhill heading down the corridor.

If I find you out of the kitchen once more, you'll be on a warning. That's what she'd said when she came to see him after she found him with Mrs Moon and Little Milo. She hadn't explained what *A Warning* was but it didn't sound good. Tripi had to keep this job, it was his only chance of getting a home and applying for asylum and finding Ayishah.

'You'd better go,' whispered Milo. 'Before you get in trouble.'

Tripi nodded and stumbled away down the corridor.

'Thank you,' Milo called after him. 'Thank you for helping my gran.'

15

Sandy

Sandy stared at the bill. £100 deposit, £150 if it wasn't paid by the end of the week. That nurse had forgotten to mention a fine for late payments.

She bit into a milk chocolate Hobnob and brushed the crumbs off the letter.

Forget Me Not Homes: We're Here to Serve You.

Only because we pay you to, thought Sandy. A red rash crept up her throat. She switched on the TV.

St Lucia is a beautiful island paradise . . .

She sat down on a stool and watched the dusty screen. Maybe Milo would come with her. Maybe if they were somewhere hot and beautiful, things would be better between them.

Here, under the swaying palm trees, your troubles will melt away . . .

Closing her eyes, Sandy felt the smooth, sweet chocolate coat the roof of her mouth.

Then the phone rang.

She opened her eyes and reached for the receiver.

'Hello?'

'Hi.'

She put on her beauty salon voice. 'Who am I speaking to, please?'

'Al McCloud.' A deep Scottish accent.

The name that had been scrawled on the message pad for months. One of Andy's relatives who had moved down south and was looking for a place to stay. He'd called out of the blue, a month after Andy left. He'd pay rent, he said. She hadn't told him that Andy no longer lived here, she couldn't bear thinking of the gossip from his family back home in Scotland. *Knew she was bad news, a girl from the south*, that's what they'd say. But she'd kept his name and his number. Maybe she'd already known back then that Gran would have to move out.

'You left a message on my phone. Said you had a room to rent.'

That Scottish accent. As they lay in each other's arms, drifting off to sleep, Sandy would ask Andy to 'speak Scottish' to her: *Guid night an sweit dreams*, he'd whisper. Hearing him speak in that voice made him feel closer, like she was the only one who knew both who he was now and where he'd come from. Maybe if they'd gone back to Scotland to live in the small town by the sea where he grew up, they could have made it work. Maybe Andy's family would have forgiven him for leaving. Maybe Milo would have been happier there.

You can go scuba diving in the crystal clear waters . . . The presenter stood on the beach in a skimpy red bikini. *Or just lie in the sun . . .*

'I need somewhere for the end of the week,' Al said.

She looked back at the TV, pointy green mountains and long stretches of white coastline. It was a joke, considering her name, that she'd never felt the warm sand between her toes. She imagined Andy and Angela walking hand in hand along the beach in Abu Dhabi.

'Are you still on the line, Mrs Moon?'

'Sandy; please call me Sandy,' she said.

She looked round the kitchen. She hoped he wouldn't mind the soot, the mess. Or the planes that flew overhead. Or that pig snuffling around in the garage. Or Milo walking around, so angry at her.

She felt her chest go tight. She wasn't ready to have a stranger living here, peering into her life.

'I'll pay you two months' rent in advance,' he said.

'Well . . .'

'In cash.'

Sandy looked at the letter from Forget Me Not sitting on the kitchen counter.

She took a breath. 'Well, perhaps we can come to some sort of arrangement.'

16

Milo

Milo brought his watch up to his eyes and stared at the big black hands, hoping Mrs Harris would get the hint.

'Milo, are you listening?' She leaned over him to find his gaze but he now looked at the floor. It was one of the good things about having Retinitis Pigmentosa: you could block people out when they annoyed you.

It was Friday and Mrs Harris had kept him back after school *to have a chat about what went wrong in the exams*.

If she did any more chatting, he'd miss visiting time at Forget Me Not.

'Like I said the other day, if I don't hear from your mum by the end of this week I'll have to drop by the house.'

Milo imagined Mrs Harris in her grey suit with her bobbed hair coming into their stinky black kitchen with Mum in her tracksuit bottoms eating Hobnobs and watching *Honeymoon Hideaways*. At least Mrs Harris smelt of smoke – not smoking was one thing Mum would have over her.

His form teacher stood up and fiddled with a bit of her fringe that had gone wonky on her forehead.

'You'll be doing a speaking and listening task soon and if you work hard, you can balance out your written English mark.' Her voice sounded like Gran's bagpipes when they were cold and hadn't been played for ages. Squeaky. Annoying. 'I think you'll like the topic.'

Milo hated talking in front of people.

'You'll be giving a talk on your favourite pet.'

With the phone Dad had given him, Milo had taken pictures of Hamlet, printed them out on the colour printer at school and stuck them all over his files and books. The girls in the class went mental.

'Such an original animal,' said Mrs Harris.

Milo zoomed in on one of her crooked yellow teeth. Whenever she spoke it looked like it was going to twist out. That's something else Mum had over Mrs Harris: nice teeth. She did bleachings for people in her shed so she got to do them on herself for free.

'I'm sure you'll have lots to say. You'll have to *inform*, *explain* and *describe* to your audience how you look after your pig and how to ensure that it's kept in the best possible conditions for its wellbeing. You'll find that easier than writing.'

In a recent test, Milo had drawn a lunar eclipse rather than writing about one because he thought it was a better way of addressing the topic: *Describe An Amazing Experience*. Not that he'd had a real, live experience of a lunar eclipse, but he'd seen them on YouTube and Dad promised that one day they'd go to Australia together to see one because they happened more often over there.

It was speaking in front of people that made Milo's tongue

go swollen like there wasn't enough room for it in his mouth and his palms go sweaty and his legs go wobbly. When he spoke he heard kids sniggering at him from the fuzzy bit beyond the pinhole because they knew they could get away with it, like the class did to Mrs Harris when she turned her back to write on the board. And anyway, compared to Gran, he did plenty of talking already. If she didn't have to speak at all, Milo didn't see why he should have to give a talk in front of the whole class.

Milo couldn't think of an excuse for maths, except that his eyes hurt when he stared at the numbers for too long.

'Can't I do the written exam again?' asked Milo.

'You have to do both, Milo. Your marks in English and maths have raised quite some concern. We're going to have to consider . . . ' And then she went quiet. 'I really must speak to your mum.'

As he turned into Crescent Way, he heard Mr Overend's whistling, louder than usual. Although he stood for hours at his open window in nothing more than his PJs, Mr Overend never seemed to get cold. Today he leant out of the window looking at a motorbike parked outside Milo's house. When he saw Milo, Mr Overend shook his head and kept whistling. What a loon. If anyone should be in a home, it was him.

Milo looked at the motorbike and hoped it meant a new client for mum. Men sometimes came to have their chests or their bums waxed. Mrs Hairy's flat red Mercedes was there too. Her real name was Gina but Mum called her Mrs Hairy because hair sprouted all over her body, even above her top lip. Milo asked why she didn't just shave, like Dad, but Mum said that it would make the hairs come back thicker and blacker and that there'd be more of them than before. Maybe Mum had two clients, that would make her happy.

Milo dumped his school bag in the kitchen and looked around for Hamlet. Hamlet being in the house was part of his deal with Mum. As long as Gran was in Forget Me Not, Hamlet got to stay in the kitchen.

But Hamlet wasn't in the kitchen. Or in the hallway or under the stairs or in the downstairs loo. Hamlet couldn't do stairs yet, so there was no way he could have got to Milo's room.

She promised, Milo said under his breath.

He looked out into the garden and saw a candle flickering in the shed window.

One of these days I'm going to tell the lady in the RSPCA shop about Mum, Milo muttered as he walked into the garage.

And sure enough, Hamlet was there, crouched in a corner of his cage waiting for Milo to come and rescue him. Then Milo saw something else. Stacked up in a corner stood a pile of cardboard boxes with Gran's bagpipes poking out of the top.

Milo's eyes burned.

He grabbed Hamlet out of his cage and climbed up on the chest freezer and reached for the bagpipes. Then he stormed out of the garage, into the kitchen, out through the back door and across the wet grass to the shed.

He pushed open the door.

'Milo!' Mum glared at him, her hand clamped across a wax strip on Mrs Hairy's brown thigh. Mrs Hairy was Jamaican and had skin like the milk chocolate bits of Mum's Hobnobs. 'When I'm with someone, you knock.' Her face

78

kept switching from screwed up and cross at Milo and trying to smile at Mrs Hairy.

'You packed up Gran's things,' Milo shouted, holding up the bagpipes. 'And you shut Hamlet away in the garage.'

Hamlet squeaked like a *hear, hear* to what Milo had just said.

Mrs Hairy drew a blanket up over her thighs and Mum stood up from her swivelly stool.

'Milo,' she said, her voice low and calm. 'I want you apologise to Mrs Downe and then turn round and go to your room. We'll discuss this later.'

'I'm sorry—' Milo wanted to say *Mrs Hairy*, but Mum couldn't afford to lose another customer. 'I'm sorry, Mrs Downe.' And then he looked up at Mum, waited for his eyes to focus on hers so that she knew he was really looking at her. 'But I'm not saying sorry to *you*.'

Hamlet squirmed under his arm. Milo turned round and slammed the shed door, even though it was only a thin plank of wood and didn't slam properly.

He went straight up the stairs to Gran's room. He was going to put all Gran's things back where they belonged.

When he got the landing Milo saw that Mum had taken the fairy lights off the banister.

Hamlet sneezed. There was a funny smell, like deodorant mingled with dirty socks and mouldy cardboard. Milo missed Gran's apricot smell, the perfume she ordered from Paris because it was the one Great-Gramps bought her for her seventeenth birthday.

Milo closed his eyes to focus on the sounds: music and voices, louder than the planes.

He dashed up the last few stairs, pushed open the door

and stood there, shifting his head in small jolts to take everything in.

A massive plasma screen stood in the corner. The news blared out of the telly, someone droning on about a war, loads of poor people crowded behind him with tents and rucksacks and plastic bags and donkeys.

The music came from a stereo that sat on the windowsill – clashy, shouty music that didn't sound nearly as nice as Gran's bagpipes.

Milo shifted his head again and saw a guy lying on Gran's bed with his boots on and a black leather jacket zipped up to his chin. He had a stubbly face and spiky black hair.

Milo stood frozen to the spot.

Hamlet snuffled under his arm.

The bagpipes gave out a low whine.

'I was going to explain ... ' Mum came up behind him, breathless. 'But you were late home from school.'

The guy sat up on the edge of the bare mattress and looked sleepily from Milo to Hamlet to the bagpipes to Mum, who was still clutching the furry wax strip she'd just ripped off Mrs Hairy's thigh.

'We need the money, my love,' she said, reaching out to stroke Milo's hair.

Milo shook off Mum's hand and pounded back down the stairs.

'Milo, where are you going?' Mum ran after him.

When he got to the front door, Milo turned round and said, 'You got rid of Dad and you got rid of Gran. I'll save you the bother of getting rid of me.' He slammed the door behind him. A proper slam this time.

17

Milo

Milo put down the bagpipes and banged on the front door of Forget Me Not until his wrist hurt. Hamlet let out a small squeal.

'Shhh!' Milo whispered. 'You're going to have to be really quiet or we won't be let in.' He squeezed Hamlet down further under his jacket.

At last he heard Nurse Thornhill's squeaky steps coming to the door.

She opened the door and looked down at Milo.

'If no one answers, it means we're closed,' she said.

Closed? She made it sound like she was running a shop, not a nursing home.

Milo straightened up. 'I've come to see my gran.'

'I'm afraid that's not possible. You'd better come back tomorrow.' Nurse Thornhill began to close the door.

Milo put his foot in the way. 'She'll want to see me.'

Hamlet squealed.

Nurse Thornhill opened the door again.

'What was that noise?'

Milo coughed. 'I've got a wheeze,' he said, pointing to his chest. 'Asthma.' He took a breath. 'Please can I come in and see my gran?'

Nurse Thornhill pasted one of those stretched smiles on her face that she'd used on the day they first visited Forget Me Not. 'I'm sure you'll understand that there are times when our clients need some rest.' She paused. 'Even from their loved ones.'

Milo focused his eyes. Down the pinhole all he could see was a long, dark corridor. It was only just gone four and already the place seemed to be shut down for the night.

'Like I said, you're welcome to come back in the morning.'

Milo could see she wasn't going to let him through, so he gave her back a fake smile and walked back down the steps.

Who cared what Nurse Thornhill said. She didn't have the right to keep him away from Gran, not when Gran was the last person he had left. Not when Gran needed him.

He waited until she'd closed the door behind her and then picked up Gramps's bagpipes and walked around the back of Forget Me Not. There had to be another way in, a door that had been left open, a fire exit or even a window.

By the time Milo got to the back door to the kitchen, his hair was dripping and his clothes were drenched. His feet squelched in his school shoes.

He heard Tripi singing, the same song he sang on that first day when they came to look around Forget Me Not. Milo

82

pushed at the door and felt his chest relax. Tripi had his back to him and was scraping soggy dumplings and stringy bits of beef and lumpy mashed potato into one of the bins. Milo darted through the kitchen. If Tripi didn't see him, he wouldn't get in trouble for letting Milo in against Nurse Thornhill's orders.

The fancy visitors' room was locked up as usual but the corridors were dark too and so was the lounge where the old people ate and watched TV.

'Milo?'

Milo jumped. Nurse Heidi floated towards him in her white uniform like a fairy. He liked her better than he liked Nurse Thornhill.

'Why's everything closed down?'

Heidi looked around her nervously. 'We're having an early night.'

'But it's not night time.'

Nurse Heidi lowered her voice. 'Nurse Thornhill is upset.'

'About what?'

Nurse Heidi shook her head. 'I shouldn't be telling you this.' And then she did a double take. 'How did you get in?' She peered closer. 'And what do you have under your coat?'

'It doesn't matter. Tell me why Nurse Thornhill's upset and why everything's dark and where everyone's gone?'

'They're in their rooms, sleeping.'

The home was eerily quiet.

'It's not bedtime,' Milo said.

'They didn't like the food.'

Milo thought about the slimy dumplings he'd just seen Tripi plopping into the bin. He wouldn't eat those either.

'Mrs Moseley started a protest.'

'Are you sure? Mrs Moseley wouldn't know how to start a protest.'

Nurse Heidi shrugged. 'It's what Nurse Thornhill said. That Mrs Mosely was the instigator.'

None of this made any sense.

He started down the corridor towards Gran's room.

'You're not meant to be here – I'll get in trouble.' Nurse Heidi whispered after him. 'Come back!' She was trying to whisper but her voice came out as a loud, raw hiss.

Milo blocked out her voice and kept going. He had to see Gran and he had to find out what was going on.

Gran sat in her armchair by the window, her head dropped down to her chin.

Milo knelt down on the floor beside her and took her hand. She winced. He looked closer and saw that there were some bruises along her wrists. A sick feeling settled in the pit of his stomach.

'How did this happen, Gran?'

She tried to open her eyes but her head just bobbed back down to her chest. He'd never seen her this sleepy at four in the afternoon.

Milo put Hamlet down on Gran's bed and went to get Gran's pad and pencil and placed it on her lap.

'Here, Gran, write down what happened.' He nudged her gently to see if he could wake her.

Gran opened her eyes for a second, tried to hold the pencil with her fingers but she couldn't grip. She let it drop to the floor.

'It's okay, Gran,' he said, putting his arms around her

shoulders and pulling her in close. Gran had always been skinny but now her bones poked out of her skin, he could feel them through his jumper. 'It's okay,' he said again, breathing in the smell of apricots on her neck. 'I've brought Hamlet for you, and Gramps's bagpipes.'

He waited for her to respond but she didn't say anything.

'Let me make you a cup of tea, Gran. And you can have some shortbread, that will wake you up.'

Milo had found a second-hand travel kettle in the RSPCA shop and when he said he couldn't afford it, the woman behind the counter agreed to swap it for the torch Dad had given him last Christmas. Then he'd packed up Gran's tartan mug and some tea bags and some milk and bought a packet of shortbread from Poundland, which didn't look very nice but it was better than nothing and he'd brought it all to Gran's room and set up a little tea station for her. There was something else he'd added to the tea station: a day-by-day pill box that he'd found at Boots. As he looked down at the tray, he noticed something strange.

Someone had added two pills to every day, those green and white pills the doctor prescribed for when Gran had trouble sleeping, for when she needed to be calmed down. Gran hated how those pills made her feel so she wouldn't have put them there. She'd taken all the pills for today so if whoever it was had added the sleeping pills to today's pile, she would have taken those too, probably without realising. No wonder she was so out of it.

Milo's mind raced ahead. That explained why the whole home was quiet so early. Nurse Thornhill must have given those pills to all the old people.

He poked the green and white pills out of the rest of the week and went to flush them down the loo and then came back and kissed Gran on the forehead.

'Don't worry, Gran,' he whispered into her hair. 'I'll figure out a way to get you out of here.' He placed a blanket over her knees, picked up Hamlet and the bagpipes and slipped out of her room.

18

Sandy

'It's past visiting hour,' said Nurse Thornhill standing on the doorstep of Forget Me Not.

Sandy felt like she was back at school, hauled up in front of Mrs Horn, her headmistress. *If you don't pull your finger out, Sandy, you'll end up on the dole.* She hadn't been so wrong.

'I know.' Sandy bit at the nail on her little finger. 'I know. I just thought that maybe Milo had come to see his gran. Could I . . . ' Sandy craned her neck and looked over Nurse Thornhill's shoulder.

Nurse Thornhill shifted her body to block Sandy's view. Amazing how much space such a skinny woman could take up.

'Your son isn't here.'

'But you don't understand. Milo, he's . . . '

What could she say? That her nine-year-old son was so upset with her that he'd run out into the dark streets on his own? That he'd rather Sandy had left and that his dad had stayed? And that the only person besides his dad who made him happy was his gran, so this was where he'd come?

'I understand that it can be distressing,' said Nurse Thornhill, smiling through her white teeth. 'Getting used to a loved one no longer being at home is a phase experienced by all our clients.' She cocked her head to one side. 'Which is why it's important to establish boundaries.' She paused. 'Why don't you come back in the morning?' Then she leant forward and lowered her voice. 'And perhaps you can bring along the fees you owe.'

Nurse Thornhill shut the door before Sandy had the time to reply.

Sandy went and stood on the pavement and looked up at the windows. She thought she saw Lou's face leaning in towards the glass. This was for the best, that's what she'd told herself. Lou needed proper help. But now, with Milo so upset, Sandy wasn't so sure any more.

She leant against the railings outside Forget Me Not. The metal bars pushed through her beautician's coat into the soft flesh of her shoulders. She'd put the coat on for Gina, her last client. The rest of the time she preferred the comfort of her tracksuit bottoms and sweatshirt. She'd been proud of her uniform once, how professional it made her look; *You look like a doctor*, Andy said, kissing her and lifting her off the ground. Underneath, she wore nothing more than her bra and her suck-in pants, anything else added bulk. Women who visited the salon wanted to be treated by someone with a good figure, who looked after herself. Someone who kept her husband.

Sandy took a packet of cigarettes out of her pocket. She only allowed herself to smoke outside the house.

Her head ached at the mess.

Milo, so angry with her.

Gina, abandoned in the shed, half-plucked.

And goodness knows what the new lodger thought, Milo bursting in on him like that. She needed Al to stay. A month's rent and she might be able to persuade the bank that she could keep up with the mortgage payments. And she had to pay the fees for Forget Me Not before Nurse Thornhill piled on the interest.

Sandy blew smoke up at the clouds and cursed at the moon. Bloody Andy, leaving her to deal with all this by herself. She hoped the baby he had with his Tart turned into a demon from hell.

'Good evening.' A man nodded at Sandy and skipped down the steps of Forget Me Not, stumbling on the last one.

He straightened up and looked at the moon. 'Isn't she beautiful?' he asked.

Sandy shrugged and stubbed out her cigarette. The man towered over her. She looked down at her trainers; when had she given up wearing heels?

A cloud swept across the moon. The sky ripped open and drops of rain fell on Sandy's bare forearms. Small, icy darts. Milo struggled to see in the rain, *like the telly when it's fuzzy*, he explained to her. The static swallowed up the sounds he relied on to get his bearings.

The man stood in front of Sandy and bowed his head towards her. 'Your lips, they are blue.'

'Sorry?'

'You are cold.' He took off a green waterproof, the kind you can scrunch up and fold into a neat pocket. Sandy had seen them in Poundland, stacked up in neon colours. 'Have this.' He held out it out to her.

89

'No, really . . .'

'I insist.'

Sandy felt the rain on her forehead. There'd been a time when she wouldn't have left the house without an umbrella, horrified at the thought of her carefully straightened hair turning to frizz. But since the summer she'd cancelled three appointments at Slipton Highlights. She couldn't face the women there, shooting glances at each other in the mirrors when they thought she wasn't looking.

'A lady must keep dry,' he said.

He had huge brown eyes that took over his face and the kind of eyelashes Sandy's clients would die for.

Sandy took the green nylon waterproof, squeezed it over her beautician's coat and lifted the hood over her hair. A man giving her his coat – when had Andy last done that?

The man was already heading down the road when Sandy called after him: 'How will I get it back to you?'

'No need,' he called over his shoulder. 'It is a gift.'

The rain hammered down as Sandy turned to go. She didn't know where else to look but she couldn't go home until she'd found Milo.

As she turned the corner onto the high street, Gina's red Mercedes drove past, white headlights on full beam. The car crashed through a puddle, leaving Sandy behind, drenched.

19

Tripi

Tripi sat on the bench shivering, looking into the canal. Maybe he shouldn't have given away his waterproof, but the woman looked so sad he hadn't been able to help himself.

For a moment, he saw Ayishah's face in the ripples of the watery moon, like the school photograph he had of her, except in the ripples her face was alive. She smiled at him like she had on that last day when they thought they'd made it. An hour from the Turkish border, an hour from freedom. *Everything will be right as rain*, she'd said.

Tripi bit into the salmon sandwich he'd taken from the nursing home. They put nice food out on visitors' days. Nurse Thornhill had instructed Tripi to pack away the cakes and sandwiches the moment the guests left. *They're a sneaky lot*, she told him, nodding at the old people in the lounge. *Leave the things out for a second, and they'll be at them like vultures.*

As Tripi ate his sandwich, he took out the pocket dictionary from Ayishah's backpack and scanned down the
definitions for *vulture*. The first two entries described the big
bird of prey he knew from back home: huge shoulders under
a black cloak of feathers, a sharp, curved beak. But it was
the third definition that made him think of Nurse Thornhill:
a person or thing that preys, especially greedily or unscrupulously,
and then he looked up the strange word with all the vowels:
unscrupulously: unrestrained by conscience. He thought that
Nurse Thornhill must have got her vocabulary wrong.

When she wasn't looking, he'd wrapped a few of the sandwiches in paper napkins and brought them to Mrs Moon. He
hadn't seen her eat anything since she'd arrived.

Tripi closed the dictionary and stroked the front cover. It
was Ayishah's. She loved to learn new words and phrases;
she wrote them in the front cover and in the blank spaces at
the top of the pages. They had a competition for who could
find the most interesting English sayings.

'My teacher told me my work was *tickety-boo*,' she said.
She loved that phrase: it meant that everything was fine.
'When we're in England, everything will be *tickety-boo*.'
Tripi remembered her brown eyes shining and how he wor-
ried that he would not be able to protect her from all the men
who would fall in love with her.

He looked back into the water, searching for Ayishah, but
this time he saw the face of the little boy with the focused
eyes, his skin as pale as the moon.

Tripi turned round and looked at the boy holding – could
it be? – a pig under his arm. And bagpipes, that funny
instrument from Scotland.

Perhaps the cold had frozen Tripi's brain. He blinked and

looked again but the boy was still there with his pig and his bagpipes.

And then Tripi realised that Little Milo was crying: those thick drops that stream down children's cheeks. Ayishah had only ever cried once. Not when their parents left when she was ten and Tripi twenty-two. Not when she came home from school one day and told him how her best friend had not turned up for registration and that the teacher said she was never coming back. She had cried when she did not come first in an English test at school; she had been sure The Queen would find out and be disappointed in her.

Milo sniffed. 'Can I sit on your bench?'

Tripi laughed. 'It's everyone's bench.'

Milo sat down, put the bagpipes in a heap at his feet and rubbed one of the pig's ears.

'Shouldn't you be at home?' asked Tripi.

Milo shook his head.

'But your parents will be worried.'

'No, they won't.'

'But they must be.' Tripi thought of Ayishah and how he did not like her being out in the streets at night, especially in those last few months before they left. Although there was no war in Slipton, this little Milo was younger than Ayishah.

Milo rubbed his cheeks with the back of his hand. 'Dad's gone and Mum's only worried about money and her stupid salon and there's something wrong with Gran and I don't trust Nurse Thornhill, I don't think she's looking after the old people properly.'

Like Ayishah, Tripi thought, *this little boy sees too much.*

'Your gran would not want you to be out here in the dark,' he said.

Milo shifted his head and searched Tripi's face. 'But you're out here, and you're okay.'

Tripi shook his head. 'I need to find a house, otherwise I cannot keep my job. And it is not okay here, it is cold.' He coughed and pointed at his chest.

Milo sniffed again. Tripi gave him his handkerchief and Milo blew hard.

'I thought only old people had hankies like these,' said Milo, handing it back soggy and scrunched up.

'My father thought that having a linen handkerchief was the sign of being a gentleman.' *Who knows when you might need to wipe away a girl's tears*, he'd said.

From Milo's crinkled nose, Tripi guessed that the boy did not yet see girls as people to whom he might lend his handkerchief.

'I know a house where you could live, it's pink.'

'A house?'

'Yes, a house on the corner of the high street.'

'It must be expensive to live on the high street.'

Milo shook his head. 'It'd be free.'

Tripi's wrinkled his brow as he translated the word to make sure he had understood it properly.

'Free? I do not understand . . .'

'I heard it on Gran's radio. If no one lives in a house for ages and ages, you can claim squatter's rights. I walk past the house every day on the way to school and Big Mike, the guy who used to live there, hasn't been back for over a year.'

'What is a "squatter"?'

Milo laughed.

'Why is this so funny?'

'You say it like it's a rude word. Squatters are people like you, who can't afford to pay rent or buy a home. They find empty houses and live there and if they don't get caught, they can stay there for years and years.'

Tripi felt the damp creeping into his lungs again. 'Get caught?' He shook his head. 'I cannot have trouble with the police.'

'You won't get caught, not here. The police in this town are rubbish. Last year, someone broke into Mum's shed and smashed the lights in her sunbed and the police still haven't found out who it was. Anyway, I'll be your lookout.'

But the policeman had found Tripi in the park and thrown him out.

'I don't know,' he kept saying. 'I don't know. What if this man, Big Mike, comes back?'

'Mum says Big Mike went to Thailand to meet his mail-order bride, Lalana, and that he must have decided to stay out there because its nicer living in Thailand than in Slipton.'

A MailOrderBride? Was this an English convention, to order brides through the post? Perhaps Tripi would find a wife more easily than he thought.

'An empty house . . . ' Tripi shook his head again, but this time it was not worried shaking but amazed shaking. Could it be that he might have a roof over his head at last? *An Englishman's home is his castle.* Wasn't that the saying?

Milo got up. 'If you look after Hamlet and keep Gran's bagpipes safe, I'll show you where it is.' The boy's tears had dried on his cheeks and his eyes shone.

'Now?'

Milo nodded.

'Okay,' said Tripi.

He looked at the pig with its white ear and its black ear and its shiny wet snout and thought about that line in the Koran about swine being unclean. Muslims were not allowed to eat pork, but there was nothing that said that you could not live with a pig, was there? *If you do not like it, you will have to forgive me, Allah.*

The pink house rose from the corner at the end of the high street. In Syria the houses sat large and low and flat, here they were skinny and reached up to the sky.

'We're going to have to break in,' said Milo, shoving the front door with his small shoulder.

Tripi looked around the street, nervous that the policeman from the other night might be watching.

'We should try the back,' said Milo. 'Back doors are always easier.'

Tripi followed Milo through a hole in the fence into the back garden. Weeds and long, yellow grass frozen into spikes, a shed with a broken window, cigarette butts on the patio.

Milo picked up a stone. 'You're going to have to smash open the back door,' he said, handing Tripi the stone.

'Why me?'

'Because it's your house now.'

Tripi had never once broken into a house. Before buying false papers to get out of Syria, he had never broken the law.

The papers stated that he and Ayishah had an English uncle waiting for them in London.

Yes, he is our mother's brother, they said to everyone they met.

Yes, we are half-English.

Their father's genes were stronger, of course, that accounted for the darkness of their skin. But *yes*, they assured everyone who cared to ask, *we have English blood running through our veins.*

What choice did they have? They were being bombed out of their home, and anyway, Tripi did not believe in borders, in marking out where people were allowed to live and walk, where others should be kept out. For Tripi, the world belonged to everyone; it was when people built walls and erected fences and locked doors that the problems began.

Maybe the same was true of houses, thought Tripi. Perhaps, as long as some people had nowhere to sleep at night, houses should be considered shared property.

He lifted the stone and threw it hard.

The house was as cold inside as out. A few bits of broken furniture sat in corners, a damp carpet that smelt of mould, cracked walls, a draught blowing through the single-paned windows.

'You see,' said Milo. 'No one's been here for ages.'

Tripi put down his and Ayishah's backpacks and spread out his sleeping bag in the hope that it might dry out a bit. And then he walked over to the mantelpiece and his eyes lit up. That was all a house needed: a fireplace. Now he could keep warm.

Hamlet scuttled around the living room, sniffing at the corners of the walls. Milo propped the bagpipes against an old chair; as they settled, they let out a wheeze, like an old man sitting on a stool in the souk.

'Do you have a spare sleeping bag?' Milo asked Tripi. 'I have one at home but I don't really want to go back there ...'

'You want to stay here?' Tripi looked at the little boy.

'Yes. I'm living here with you until that stupid lodger moves out.'

'Stupid lodger?'

'Mum's put someone in Gran's room to make money and he's messed everything up.'

Tripi shook his head. 'You need to go back to your mother, Milo. She will be worried.'

Milo kicked at a ruck in the carpet. 'I'm the one who found this place. I should get to stay.'

Tripi edged closer to the boy. 'I have a plan.'

Milo shifted his head and fixed his blue eyes on Tripi.

Tripi continued. 'Go home for tonight and try to explain to your mother about the lodger and how it makes you upset. I will stay here with the bagpipes and the pig.'

'Hamlet – he responds to his name.'

'With Hamlet. If things aren't better by tomorrow evening, you can come back and I will let you stay.'

This was the tactic Tripi used with Ayishah when she was in one of her stubborn moods.

'I'm not sure.'

Tripi picked up the small pig and held him up. 'What do you think, Hamlet?' He held the pig to his ear and nodded his head. Hamlet touched his wet snout to Tripi's nose. 'Yes ... yes ... I quite agree.' Tripi turned back to Milo. 'Hamlet is of my opinion, he thinks you should go home and come back tomorrow.'

'I'm not a kid, you know,' said Milo, standing up.

'Of course not. That's why you're going to do the adult thing and go home – you are going to go the extra mile.'

'The extra mile?'

'Make an effort.'

Milo nodded but stared at the floor.

'And if I'm still not happy tomorrow, I can come back?'

'It is a promise.'

Tripi watched the boy walk out through the back door and across the garden. Then he placed Hamlet on the carpet, wiped his hands on his trousers and looked around the house. This was not the home he and Ayishah had imagined when they dreamt of England, certainly not a castle, but it was a start.

He took out the blue piece of paper that Nurse Thornhill had given him and filled in the address. He hoped that she did not know that this house belonged to MailOrderBride-Man in Thailand and the wife he had ordered through the post.

20

Lou

That fog again. Milo coming in and out, fiddling with things, shaking her. Telling her not to take the pills.

Why was she so tired these days? And why did everything feel so far away?

And could it be Alasdair, her great-nephew from Inverary, sitting there in front of her smelling of leather and engine oil, a thick shadow of stubble on his chin, the roughness as he kissed her cheek? Could he be the little boy who'd swum with her in the sea at Inverary? Or was her mind slipping again, shifting discs of time like those big plates moving under the earth?

And then she'd opened her eyes briefly and looked out of the window and seen Sandy. She'd wanted to tell Milo that his mother was there, standing on the pavement in the rain, squeezing herself into that green waterproof. Getting bigger every day, like Hamlet. Poor Sandy, she couldn't help it. Eating to fill up that gaping hole that Andy had left. Eating to numb the coldness she felt from her little boy.

She loves you, you know, she'd written on her pad, but he'd screwed shut his eyes and shaken his head.

If she loved me, you'd still be at home, Gran.

She must tell him to be kinder, to try to see things from her point of view.

And then Milo had left. And Sandy had walked away in the rain. Maybe they would meet on the way home, Lou thought.

The smell of boiled potatoes hung in the air. White cubes bobbed up and down in the toilet bowl. It was a last resort. She'd tried the bin, layering it with newspaper, damp seeping through yesterday's headlines, but Nurse Thornhill had found out and grabbed her wrists and made her clear them out.

Everything smelt here. The walls and the carpets. The old people. Their skin, their hair, their involuntary farts. The stale smell of sleep that came from Mrs Zimmer as she sat, her mouth hanging open, in the lounge.

She walked to the bathroom, her limbs slow, and sprayed some perfume on her neck. A present from Milo last Christmas, a big, thick glass bottle from the market.

Does it smell like the one Gramps gave you? He'd asked. *Like apricots?*

She'd nodded and sprayed it on her old neck and tried not to breathe in. Dear boy.

Footsteps in the corridor, light on his feet for a man of eighty. He'd told her how he danced with his wife every Saturday night in Patitiri, the harbour town of Alonissos.

He's a bit young, Gran, Milo had said. He'd found Petros in her room last time he came to visit.

A bit young for what? she'd written on her pad.

Milo had blushed.

I mean, if he's bothering you, Gran . . .

Always looking out for her, dear Milo.

'Louisa?' A whisper at the door.

Petros crept in, a screwdriver and some masking tape in his creased hands. At first, as she'd watched him hammering at the table leg in the lounge, she'd thought he was the handyman. Always fixing things, like Milo.

'We mustn't let the rain in,' he said.

He went over to the window, his bald patch shining under the moon.

21

Milo

When Milo got home that evening he shook the rain out of his hair. Mum's trainers were missing from the hallway. Good, it would be easier without her in the house.

This was Milo's plan: he was going to tell the guy living in Gran's room that he had to move out, that with his dad gone, Milo got to make the decisions in the house, and that this was one of them. Mum had made a mistake. She'd forgotten that the room was already taken, or would be soon. He'd saved up enough of the pocket money Gran gave him to refund any rent that had been paid. Whatever happened, the guy had to leave. Preferably tonight.

Milo felt his way along the dark bit from the landing to Gran's room and then stood by the door and listened. Loud voices and explosions boomed out from the telly. The door stood ajar so he gave it a small push and looked through the crack. He couldn't see much, except that the guy wasn't lying on the bed like he had been when Milo walked in a few hours earlier.

He pushed the door a little further.

'Hello . . .'

No answer.

Milo swung open the door and moved his body round 360 degrees so he could scan every bit of Gran's room. Newspapers lay spread out on the floor and the telly was still set on that 24-hour news channel. A reporter in a bulletproof vest stood at the front of the screen, white flashes shooting through the sky behind the guy as he ducked his head and said: *There's been no let-up in the fighting on the streets of Damascus . . .*

Files and books lined Gran's shelves and on the windowsills stood one of Mum's saucers, full of stubbed-out cigarettes. Milo made a mental note of that. Mum hated smoking, she gave her clients lectures about how it dehydrated their skin and gave them wrinkles and made their teeth yellow like Mrs Harris's. She also told Milo that it would kill them, like it would kill him if he ever dared try one. At Slipton Primary some of the boys smoked in the woods, but they'd never invited Milo to join them, so maybe he would live for a bit longer.

Milo looked round for more evidence.

He was surprised to find Gran's bathroom empty. No toothbrush or razor or shower gel. When he went back into the room and opened Gran's wardrobe all he found was a pair of faded black jeans and a grey hoodie. No pants or socks. And the bed didn't have a duvet on it or sheets or blankets, just the bare mattress.

The room looked more like an office than a bedroom.

Milo picked up a book lying on the guy's sleeping bag. The cover had a picture of a biker wearing a leather jacket with *Hell's Angels, North Cal* written on the back. The writer's name was in orange: Hunter S. Thompson. Mum said that people who rode motorbikes were thugs, so why was she letting this guy stay under their roof? Milo flipped through the pages of the book: notes in the margin, and then a thick bit wedged between two pages. A small pile of photographs.

Milo looked through them, squinting to make sure that what he saw was really there and not his imagination filling in the blanks like it sometimes did when his eyes got tired. He brought the photos up closer to his eyes and felt his cheeks heating up.

He definitely wasn't imagining things.

Yes! Milo hissed under his breath. If Mum saw these, she wouldn't let the guy stay here, not in a million years.

Milo stuffed the photos under his school jumper.

The front door slammed.

He heard Mum kicking off her trainers, slipping into her clogs and clippety-clopping across the kitchen tiles. Milo took a deep breath and went downstairs.

Mum stood in the kitchen making a puddle on the linoleum floor that still looked grey and dirty from the fire.

'Oh Milo, thank God!' She ran up to him, threw her soggy arms around him and squeezed him so tight he thought she might push all the air out of him. The photos pressed against his tummy.

And she smelt of smoke. Mum never smelt of smoke.

When she stood back her face was blotchy and her eyes

looked wobbly and there was wet on her cheeks, which could have been the rain, but Milo suspected it was something else. Her face had looked like that for weeks after Dad left.

He stepped back. 'What are you wearing?'

Mum looked down at the lime green waterproof, the same colour as Mrs Harris's bogey car. For some reason the waterproof looked familiar but Milo couldn't quite place it.

'Oh, this? It's nothing.' She peeled it off and hung it over a kitchen chair.

There were wet patches on Mum's boobs where the rain had soaked through to her work uniform.

'And why do you smell of smoke?'

The rash on Mum's throat went a deeper shade of pink.

'Oh, I do?' She sniffed at her sleeve. 'Probably one of the clients.'

Except Mum had a big red no-smoking sign up in the shed.

Milo took the photographs out from under his jumper. Now was a good time to tell her, while she was still feeling guilty.

Mum sat down at the table and rubbed her neck and then she saw a piece of paper and her eyes went even wobblier than before.

'No. Please, no.'

Milo came and stood behind her and read the note from Mrs Hairy, her writing big and loopy:

I waited for you to come back. A whole hour, Sandy. I'm afraid I'll be taking my custom elsewhere. Gina.

106

Mrs Hairy was the only client Mum had left.

'Let someone else wax her hairy bum,' said Mum and then she smacked her hand over her mouth. 'I'm sorry, Milo.'

Tears plopped out of Mum's eyes, definitely not rain this time. And then she dropped her head into her hands and sank her fingers into her hair that had gone fuzzy from the rain.

'I don't know how I'm going to pay the bills, Milo,' she said, wiping her cheeks.

'She'll come back, Mum, no one else will want to pluck out all those hairs.'

Milo remembered a time when he'd walked into the shed and Mrs Hairy was lying with her big thighs all exposed on Mum's massage bed. Later, Mum explained it was because Mrs Hairy was going on holiday to Jamaica, which is where her mum and dad came from, and she'd have to wear a bikini and couldn't have tufts of black hair sticking out. Remembering that made Milo think about the photos he'd found in Gran's room. He shoved them back under his jumper; he'd tell Mum about them when her face wasn't wet and blotchy.

A motorbike roared down the road, stopped outside their door and a few seconds later the doorbell rang.

Milo didn't admit it to Mum or Gran or anyone else, but whenever the doorbell rang, he hoped it might be Dad coming home because he was sick of his Tart. Or, since a week ago, Gran. Not that she'd be able to walk back by herself.

'Don't have any keys yet.' The lodger guy stood on the doorstep, his helmet under his arm. He had a Scottish accent, like Gran's voice sounded in Milo's head.

Mum sniffed, slipped off the kitchen stool and came to the front door.

'I'm so sorry, I'll have some cut tomorrow. Milo, go and get your keys, Mr McCloud can have those in the meantime.'

'I need my keys,' said Milo.

Mum stared at Milo. He felt the photographs under his jumper again.

'I've got the rent. This month, and next month too, a thank you for taking me in at such short notice,' said the man. 'In cash.' He winked.

Mum took the envelope and a big sigh came out of her like she'd been holding her breath for ages.

'He smokes,' said Milo.

'What?' asked Mum.

'Mr McCloud smokes.'

'Al, please call me Al. We're family after all.'

Milo blinked. Family? What was he going on about? He kept talking.

'He smokes and he leaves dirty cigarette stubs in your best saucers.'

'I'm sorry about that, it's all I could find.'

As the guy smiled, Mum blushed a bit.

'If you'd rather I smoked outside.'

'It's fine,' said Mum.

Which was just about the most unfair thing Milo had ever heard. What about smoking giving you wrinkles and yellow teeth and killing you in the end?

'Thank you for the payment, it's much appreciated,' she said, smiling back at him.

'And he left the telly on,' said Milo.

'Sorry, bad habits.' The guy shrugged. 'I'd better leave you

108

to it, early night for me.' And he walked up the stairs. He hadn't taken his boots off either and he left dirty soggy patches on the carpet, but Mum didn't seem to notice.

'Milo, go and get your keys and bring them upstairs to Mr McCloud – to Al.'

As Milo clumped up the stairs to his room, he thought of his new friend, Tripi, and the pink house and how he'd much rather be living with him.

22

Lou

Petros pulled a brown paper bag out of his pocket and handed it to Lou. He'd sketched a face in pencil across the front. Lou's eyes and mind, her whole body, felt clear for the first time in days, her heart lighter.

'It is you,' he said, pointing at the picture. 'Back in Greece, I painted portraits of tourists to earn money,' he said. 'That is how I met my wife. She was British, like you.'

Lou wondered whether Petros charmed all the old women at Forget Me Not. When she wasn't swearing at those Angry Birds, Mrs Sharp was beautiful in her way, high cheekbones, and behind her make-up Mrs Swift had a sweet face.

Lou dipped her hand into the paper bag and pulled out a golden square of fudge.

'Maybe little Milo will like them too?'

Lou smiled. Dear Milo, her little man. She had noticed how his eyes would cloud over when he found Petros sitting in her room.

She closed her eyes and let the buttery cube melt on her tongue, the grain of the sugar, the pull at her teeth.

Petros knelt in front of her, his knees clicking. 'You need to eat, Louisa – all bones.' He lifted her wrist. The touch of a man's fingers against her skin, close to her veins.

And then, her body reacting to an impulse she thought had left her long ago: she leant forward and kissed him on the cheek.

He touched the place of the kiss.

She looked at him sitting in front of her in his frayed yellow cap. Did he have any family left? Anyone to visit an old man, to bring him grapes and flowers and kisses?

The door flew open, a white shadow swept in.

Petros leapt to his feet.

When Nurse Thornhill saw him, her mouth stretched into a smile. 'Oh, Mr Spiteri, I didn't see you there.'

Why was it that Nurse Thornhill was nicer to Petros than to the rest of them? Was it because he was a man? Lou had seen them exchange glances. Heard them whispering in the corridor outside her room. And why, if she was so nice to him, did he look scared, in the same way that a little boy might get scared of a fierce teacher at school?

She came and placed a hand on Petros's arm and steered him towards the door. 'Time to go back to your room, Mr Spiteri, you need your rest.'

When Petros left, Nurse Thornhill's smile fell. She ripped the masking tape off the grouting at the window.

'We don't allow bedroom visits between members of the opposite sex.'

One man, eight women and she'd thought up a rule to keep them apart.

Nurse Thornhill walked over to the table and peered down into the box of pills that Milo had brought in for her.

'Where are your pills for the rest of the week?'

Lou looked down. Each day held her small white pill and her pink pill. She didn't understand what Nurse Thornhill was asking.

'Have you been interfering with your medication, Mrs Moon?'

Gran shook her head.

She shook her head. 'Lying is not a wise strategy, Mrs Moon. You need to let us do our jobs.' Her eyes scanned the coffee table again. She wrinkled her nose, picked up the paper bag, peered inside, scrunched it closed and shoved it into her white pocket. She'd already taken away the tea and the shortbread.

'You know one of the greatest causes of disruption, Mrs Moon?'

Lou didn't answer.

'I've told you before, Mrs Moon: one of the greatest causes of disruption is patients eating inappropriate food.'

Nurse Thornhill switched off the light and shut the door behind her.

23

Tripi

At dawn on Monday morning, Tripi washed his hands and his feet and took his sleeping bag into the back garden.

Hamlet trotted behind him, sunk his round body into the frosty grass and snuffled at the earth.

Bending forward, Tripi pressed his palms to the ground and took a breath.

'You're not doing it right.' Milo squeezed through the gap in the fence, walked across the grass and stood above Tripi. He carried a pink bundle under his arm.

Tripi closed his eyes and whispered: *I am sorry, Allah, you must forgive me.* He knew that Allah must like this little boy, though, so earnest and faithful.

Tripi had decided to give Allah some proper time, to thank Him for the house and the job and let Him know that he could now focus all his divine energies on finding Ayishah.

'Milo, my friend.' Tripi stood up, two damp patches on his knees.

Milo put down his schoolbag. 'I'll show you.' He kicked off his school shoes and unfurled the pink roll. 'I brought this for your exercises.' He stepped onto the mat, folded his hands into prayer position, raised his arms above his head and bent over into a Downward Dog.

Hamlet got up onto his stubby legs, ran under Milo's legs and squealed.

Tripi laughed.

'What's funny?' Milo stood up, his face red.

'I'm not doing exercises.'

'Well, what are you doing, then?'

'I'm praying.'

'On an sleeping bag?'

'It should be a prayer mat, but it is all I have.'

'Are you praying to Jesus?' Milo picked up his bag. 'Everyone's praying to Baby Jesus at the moment.' He rolled his eyes. 'They think it'll get them more presents.'

Tripi smiled. 'I pray to Allah.'

'Allah? Isn't he a Muslim?'

Tripi laughed. 'I hope so.'

'You're a Muslim too, then?'

'Yes, if Allah still wants me – I haven't been keeping up my practices very well.'

Milo picked up Hamlet. 'I've got school in an hour but I wanted to come and see how Hamlet was doing.'

Tripi rolled up the exercise mat and handed it to Milo.

'You can have it – Mum's stopped doing her yoga.'

'It belongs to your mother?'

'She won't miss it.'

Milo, Tripi and Hamlet walked across the wet grass to the back door of the pink house.

'You've made it nice,' said Milo, putting Hamlet down and looking around the lounge.

'One day, I will have a house and a wife,' said Tripi. 'Like MailOrderBrideMan.' He looked at a photo of the large man standing with the beautiful woman on the beach.

'Do you have a girlfriend?'

Tripi shook his head. 'Not yet.' He thought about the woman he'd met outside Forget Me Not, how sad she'd looked and how he'd wanted to take her in out of the rain.

'I could help you,' said Milo.

'You could?'

'There are loads of dating sites on the internet. I could build you a profile.'

'I do not think that I will find a Muslim woman on the internet, Milo. But thank you.' Tripi chuckled. Before the power lines went down, it was the same in Syria, the internet was God: you typed a wish into the Google tab and it came up with an answer.

'You can do searches,' said Milo. 'Like eye colour and hair colour and age. I'm sure there's a box for types of religions.'

'I'm a bit old-fashioned, Milo – I believe I'll find my wife walking down the street.'

'Really?'

'Like, what do you call it? A coincidence. And my sister would have to like her.'

'You have a sister?'

Tripi nodded. 'She is a few years older than you, I think.'

'I'm nine. I'll be ten on Christmas day.'

'Ayishah's twelve.'

She'd had her birthday in October, on her own. Tripi

115

swallowed hard. 'She's coming soon, so you'll get to meet her.'

'Where is she?'

'Somewhere in Syria. Or near Syria.'

Milo's eyes widened. 'You don't know?'

Tripi shook his head. He had looked for her for over two months before ducking under the barbed wire separating Syria and Turkey and heading for England. From England it would be easier to find her, he thought, to ask the authorities for help. In Syria, no one listened. The explosions and the gunfire had made people deaf. And maybe she had found a way out, maybe she was in England already. *Miracles happen every day*, Ayishah used to say. *But only if you believe in them.* So as he travelled through Turkey, then Greece, then Italy and France, all the way to Buckingham Palace, he had tried to believe, for her.

'Why isn't she here, with you?' asked Milo.

'Well . . . ' Tripi regretted having mentioned Ayishah. He trusted this little boy but children sometimes say things without thinking.

'We got separated when we were coming to England.'

'Did she miss the plane?'

'In a way, yes.'

'So do your parents live here, then?'

Tripi shook his head. 'We don't have parents any more.'

'What happened?'

'They had to leave us.'

Two years before Tripi and Ayishah headed for the Turkish border, when the fighting started, their parents fled, promising to find a safe place for the family. They never came back.

'Are they Muslims too?'

'My mother was a Sunni Muslim and my father an Alawi Muslim,' said Tripi. And that was what made them flee. The state saw their marriage as a betrayal of their faith, as did the insurgents.

'So what kind of Muslim are you?'

'A bit of both, like Ayishah, which is why we had to leave. In Syria, the Sunnis and the Alawis are at war against each other and we were on the wrong side twice over.'

'At school, Mrs Harris taught us that that Muslims hated the Americans and that Americans hated the Muslims. But she didn't say anything about Muslims hating Muslims.'

'Muslims hate Muslims more than they do Americans. There are big problems in my country now, a civil war. It has been worse this past year, eleven thousand people have been killed. That is why Ayishah and I fled from our homeland.'

'Eleven thousand people. That's the same as if everyone in Slipton died, and then some. The whole town, dead, like a zombie attack.'

Tripi watched Milo's eyes darken like a cloud over the sea, as the thought sunk into the little boy's imagination. Perhaps he should not have told him about this.

'A bit like that, yes.'

'So why did you come to England?'

'Well, my sister, she wanted to meet The Queen.'

Milo laughed. 'The Queen? You can't just meet the Queen.'

'Well, Ayishah was sure that The Queen would see her. And I wanted to live on an island.'

Tripi was tired of having borders on all sides. Jordan, Iraq, Lebanon, Israel. Even the Mediterranean Sea felt like it belonged to someone else. *Squashed like a sardine?* Wasn't that one of the phrases that Ayishah had brought back from school? Syria was squashed like a sardine and Tripi no longer wanted to be squashed.

'Does she look like you?' asked Milo.

Tripi nodded. 'Yes, but more beautiful, and she has smaller feet.' He held up each foot in turn and laughed. Then he pulled out his photograph of Ayishah. The pale blue pinafore, the navy shirt, the orange scarf that looked like a tie – she loved that.

Milo took the photograph and peered closely. 'They show Syria on the news a lot.'

'Yes, people like to hear about war.'

'Maybe someone could spot her on the telly.'

Tripi had thought of this. But what could he do? Sit in front of the television all day and all night in the hope that, for a second, the camera might pick up the face of a twelve-year-old girl?

'Can I borrow the picture?'

'I don't know, Milo.'

'I'll get it back to you really quickly. I've got an idea for how we can look for Ayishah.'

This little boy, always coming up with ideas, like Ayishah. He nodded and handed over the photograph and then he looked at Milo and waited for the boy's eyes to settle on his.

'Milo? You will not speak too much of what I have told you.'

'The story about everyone dying in your town?'

'Yes. And the other things too, especially not to Nurse Thornhill.'

'Okay. We can trade, I've got a secret to tell you too.'

Milo crouched down, zipped open his school bag, pulled out a pack of photographs and held them out to Tripi.

'I've got pictures, but they're not nice ones like of your sister.'

Tripi took the photos and brought them over to the window. And then he dropped them.

'What is it?' Milo came over and picked them up.

'Milo, where did you get these?'

'That's what I was going to tell you, I found them in Gran's room.'

'You found photographs of naked women in Mrs Moon's room?'

'Yes, in her room at home, but they're not Gran's, they're Al's. The guy who's moved in – here.' He held out the photos again. 'This means he's bad, right?'

Tripi turned away. 'I can't look at these, Milo.'

'Why not?'

'Allah wouldn't like it.' Tripi tried to block out the image of the woman kneeling with her bosom pushed forward.

'Oh.'

'A lot of young men have photos of naked women – I do not think it is unusual, Milo.'

'No, they don't.' Milo flipped through the photographs. 'They have dirty magazines, like on the top shelf in Mr Gupta's shop. These are actual photos, which means that maybe he took them. He looks like the kind of guy who'd take dirty photos.'

Tripi noticed words written on the back of one of the photos. He reached for it, careful not to turn it over. A date, a time, a location and a name. He took another photo and it was the same, they were all labelled.

'Where *exactly* did you find these, Milo?'

'In Al's book. I found out that he smoked too and that he doesn't take his shoes off when he comes into the house. When I show these to Mum, she's going to have to kick him out, isn't she?'

Milo smiled. He had a gap in his bottom teeth, which made Tripi's chest tighten. He'd kept some of Ayishah's milk teeth, five baby stones rattling around in a matchbox at the bottom of his backpack.

'I don't think these photos are for . . . ' Tripi looked at Milo, nine years old. Did he know about these things? Tripi sighed. 'I don't think the man has these photos for his pleasure.'

'Well, why does he have them, then?' The boy's face fell into a frown.

'I don't know, Milo, it looks like he's doing some research. Is he a policeman?'

'A policeman? No, of course not.' Milo grabbed the photos out of Tripi's hands and shoved them back into his school bag. 'If he doesn't leave soon, I'm coming to stay with you,' he said. 'You've got plenty of room here.'

'You really want Mrs Moon to come home, don't you, Milo?'

Milo nodded.

'And you think she wants to come home too?'

'Of course she wants to come home – wouldn't you if you lived in that horrible place?'

Tripi thought about the food and the cold and the snappy snappy voice of Nurse Thornhill and how she held onto the old people's arms so tight that she left white marks on their skin. And how, in the Syria he grew up in, old people got to stay in their homes with their families.

Milo picked Hamlet up again and kissed each of his ears in turn. 'Hamlet misses Gran too, don't you?' Milo brought his watch up to his eyes. 'I want to see Gran before school,' he said. 'I'm going to bring her Hamlet.'

Tripi thought of what Nurse Thornhill's face would do if she found a pig in Mrs Moon's room.

Then Milo looked up at Tripi, his eyes so concentrated it hurt to look back at him.

'Will you help me, then? To get Gran back?'

Tripi thought about how much he needed to keep this job – the last thing he should do was to upset Nurse Thornhill. But then he looked again at the boy's determined eyes and thought of Ayishah.

'I will try, Milo,' he said. 'I will try.'

24

Milo

Milo came out of Mr Gupta's corner shop and stuffed the pile of photocopies into his school bag. He looked up at the fuzzy lights that hung along Slipton High Street and shifted his head to take in the shapes of the shooting stars and of big-bellied Santa on his sleigh. It was only the beginning of December and already the decorations looked droopy.

'Fifteen days till Christmas,' he whispered into Hamlet's white ear. 'Then we'll all be together again.'

So what if Tripi thought the photos weren't about Al being a dirty perv who liked looking at women's boobs? Milo would tell Al that he'd found the pictures and that he was going to show them to Mum. Maybe that would scare him into leaving.

And, in the meantime, he was going to find a way to get Gran out of Forget Me Not.

Get Al out and get Gran back: a two-pronged attack as

Mrs Harris had explained when they learnt about the Battle of Hastings. In 1066 William the Conqueror got his men to shoot arrows at the Normans so that they raised their shields and then the infantry came in and thrust their swords into the Normans' unprotected bodies. Milo wished the test had been on the stories he learnt about in history rather than on words and sums.

As he walked past the bus stop, Milo saw an advert that made him stop dead.

No One's Forgotten at Forget Me Not Homes, the words in a speech bubble coming out of Nurse Thornhill's mouth.

She smiled with her shiny white teeth and everyone else in the photo had shiny white teeth too like they'd had one of Mum's bleachings, and the lounge wasn't the real lounge: the one in the picture had big windows looking out onto a sunny garden with pink roses and perfect green grass. There were men and women in the photo, which wasn't the same at the real Forget Me Not either – apart from Petros, the guy who kept hanging around Gran. And on the photo, none of them had wrinkles and there was a fuzzy white haze around them, like they were in heaven. The old people smiled at each other and drank tea out of thin white cups and held plates with cucumber sandwiches and strawberry tarts and lots of other small cakes.

Milo supposed that was just what people did, made things look better in adverts than they looked in real life, like the houses Dad sold when he worked in Move-It on the High Street. Milo sometimes came along with Dad when he visited houses and no matter how scummy they were in real life, by the time Dad had taken out his camera and shot some pictures and passed them through his computer, they looked like the houses in Mum's magazines: light and shiny and colourful. *We'll make your home look like a palace*, he'd say to the owner as they left.

Milo looked away from the advert and headed towards the nursing home.

As he turned the corner a flash of yellow zoomed past the pinhole. He looked again. The cap, and under it, Petros. He took a battered leather wallet out of his pocket, emptied some coppers into the palm of his hand and counted them with his finger. Mum didn't have enough money but even she didn't count coppers.

Milo didn't think that the old people at Forget Me Not were allowed to wander around outside, not without special permission from Nurse Thornhill.

When he walked into Forget Me Not, Milo stopped at the nurse's station for a moment and waited for Nurse Thornhill to show up because of the rule that said you had to let some-one know you were here before you visited your relative. But then Hamlet began to wriggle under his coat and when Milo looked at his watch he saw that the big black hand was on twenty past. If he was late, that would give Mrs Harris some-thing else to see Mum about.

'Just stay still until we get to Gran's room,' whispered Milo, stroking the top of Hamlet's wrinkly snout. Milo's arms ached from carrying Hamlet who was growing much faster than the micro-pig charts said on the internet. Maybe he was a fast developer.

Out of the lounge came the smell of burnt toast and por-ridge and the telly was turned on so loud it made Milo's head hurt.

As winter sets in, the crisis in Syria worsens . . .

124

Syria, the place that Tripi and his sister came from.

Civil war, that's what Tripi had called it, a country turning against itself, like an argument in a family. Milo thought of Mum and Dad and Gran and how maybe that was a bit the same. That they were in a civil war and that was why people had to leave, like Tripi had to leave Syria and Dad had to leave England and Gran had to leave her room under the roof at home.

But Tripi was going to get Ayishah back, like Milo was going to get Gran back and maybe Ayishah would be here in time for Christmas, and they could both come home and have Christmas dinner with Mum and Gran and Hamlet.

The old ladies didn't seem to be eating their burnt toast or their porridge. Milo couldn't see whether their teeth were white like on the advert because they kept their wrinkly mouths shut tight, but he suspected they'd be yellow, like most old people's teeth. The good thing was that they were all looking at the telly. He dashed round and gave each of them a photocopy of Ayishah's picture and told them to look out for her and to let him know if they saw anything.

When he got to Gran's room he knocked, excited to see her face when she realised that Hamlet was with him.

Just as he opened the door, Nurse Heidi came out carrying a pile of sheets that smelt like Mrs Moseley's dresses.

Hamlet let out a small squeal.

'Shhh . . .'

Nurse Heidi turned round. 'What was that?'

'Nothing,' said Milo. 'What are you doing with Gran's sheets?'

'Oh, a little accident.'

Gran didn't have accidents, not when she was at home. She called for Milo and he came up and helped her to the loo.

The nurse dashed past.

Hamlet squealed, louder this time, and squirmed so hard that Milo dropped him.

'Milo, my friend!'

Milo spun round.

Petros the painter guy spread his legs, caught Hamlet, swung him up in the air and walked towards Milo.

'This pig yours?' Petros chuckled. 'The English and their pets.'

Milo took Hamlet and wrapped him under his coat and caught that scent again: plasticky lemons. Hamlet must have picked it up too because he twitched his nose and let out a series of small, soft grunts which he did when he didn't like the smell of something. Or someone.

'I wouldn't let Nurse Thornhill see your little friend.' He flicked one of Hamlet's ears. 'Come to see the beautiful Louisa?' asked Petros.

Milo scrunched up his brow. No one called Gran that. Lou, that was her name. *It's French for wolf*, she'd written on her pad when Milo had asked where her name came from. Though in French, the word had an extra 'p' at the end. It made Milo think of Red Riding Hood and how the wolf turned into a gran. Gran wrote that wolves got a bad press, that they were beautiful and intelligent and looked after each other and that they saw things other people didn't, like Milo with his special eyes.

And wolves love the moon, Gran had written. *So*

126

you see, I was meant for Great-Gramps. Gran had taken Great-Gramps's name even though they never got married.

And this guy had known Gran for what, five seconds?

Milo wrapped his arms tightly around Hamlet. He pushed past Petros, opened Gran's door, closed it quickly behind him so that Petros got the message not to follow and walked in.

25

Milo

When Milo walked into Gran's room, everything was cold and dark. Gran's bed was stripped and she sat asleep in her armchair by the window. He'd hoped that after he took away the dozy pills, she'd be back to her old self, but she looked tired again. Her head lolled forward.

He switched on the lights, opened the curtains and went over to give her a kiss. Her eyes opened for a moment and she reached out to touch his cheek.

'I know what you need, Gran, some sweet tea and short-bread. That will wake you up.'

He walked over to the tray he'd set up with the mini-kettle and Gran's tartan mug but the jar with the tea and box of shortbread had vanished.

He knew right away where they were. Confiscated by that nasty Nurse Thornhill. She wouldn't want Gran having anything nice to eat and drink. She probably took them away when Gran refused to eat those slimy dumplings and that stringy beef.

Milo looked at his watch. If he didn't get to school in the next few minutes, he'd miss registration, but he didn't care, this was more important.

'I'll go and get you some,' said Milo. 'The corner shop will still be open.' He went to Gran's raincoat that hung on the back of the door to look for her purse, but her pockets were empty.

'Where's your purse, Gran?'

Gran looked up at him, her eyes so confused he wanted to cry.

Milo felt a wave of anger pulling up through his tummy and into his throat. It was one thing to take away Gran's tea and her sugar bowl and her shortbread, it was another to take away her purse.

'Are you sure you didn't put it somewhere else, Gran?'

Gran shook her head.

'It's okay, Gran, I'll find it.' He gave her a kiss on the cheek, picked Hamlet up off the floor and went back out into the corridor.

The sounds of different TV channels drifted past him. He was surprised that Nurse Thornhill hadn't banned watching the telly too, though he guessed it was to keep the old people occupied and out of the way. Mr Todds who taught 5B and wasn't very good at getting his class to behave let them watch TV programmes in class all the time – it was the only thing that kept them quiet.

When he got to the nurses' station, Milo put Hamlet down on the counter and jabbed at the bell. He was going to ask Nurse Thornhill to explain why Gran was so sleepy all the time and whether it was because of those pills he found the other day and he wanted her to explain where Gran's tea things were and to do something about Gran's purse having been stolen. As director of Forget Me Not, it was Nurse Thornhill's job to do something about all those things.

When he took his finger off the bell, he noticed a drawer with big, block letters written on a piece of paper stuck to the front:

KEEP OUT

Milo went round and pulled at the drawer. It was locked but felt quite loose. Sometimes Mum watched Bear Grylls on TV. She said he was sexy and adventurous and went to exciting places and was the kind of man who wouldn't leave you in the lurch. Bear Grylls could get anything open, even a rusty old can of sardines. So Milo took out the mini penknife he kept on his key ring, a freebie from a cracker last Christmas, pulled out the mini-tweezers and pushed them into the lock and yanked open the drawer.

Mum said that Bear Grylls was resourceful; Milo hoped that she'd think he was resourceful for getting the drawer open.

It took Milo a moment to see what was inside. He blinked a few times, rubbed his eyes and leant in closer. The smell of old leather rose up from the drawer. And then he saw them, dozens of them, all piled up on top of each other: purses and wallets and card holders.

He rifled through them, snapping and popping and zipping them open. Apart from some old receipts and some passport photographs, every single one of them was empty.

Milo thought of those films where people went to jail and had all their belongings taken away from them and put in a plastic bag. He reckoned they got their money nicked too.

He looked around him quickly to check that Nurse Thornhill wasn't coming and then he took out the phone Dad had given him, put on the flash and took three pictures of the drawer. He knew exactly who he was going to show and this time Nurse Thornhill wouldn't have a leg to stand on.

'I want to see PC Stubbs.' Milo stood on tiptoe, leaning into the reception desk at Slipton Police Station.

Hamlet sat down at his feet. Milo didn't know what the rule was on police stations and pets so he hoped that no one would spot him.

'Shouldn't you be at school?' asked the receptionist, a woman with frizzy red hair.

Milo looked at the clock on the wall behind her. He'd missed most of the first lesson already. He'd go in after lunch and explain he had a last-minute eye appointment. Mrs Harris was used to Mum being disorganised.

'This is urgent,' he said.

'I'm sure.' The woman didn't look up, she just kept typing at her computer.

'It's my gran.'

She pushed her wheelie chair back to a filing cabinet, yanked open the metal door and rifled through the folders.

Milo thought of Nurse Thornhill's KEEP OUT drawer full of all the old people's empty purses and it made the blood surge to his ears.

'You have to listen to me. There's been a theft at Forget Me Not – we have to do something.'

The woman with the frizzy red hair turned round.

131

'A theft's not urgent.' She went back to her filing cabinet.

Milo leant further into the reception desk, his feet off the ground now.

'It *is* urgent. Nurse Thornhill's stealing all the old people's money and she makes them go to their rooms when it isn't even bedtime just because they complain about their food, which is horrible, and I'm sure you'd complain if you had to eat it, and she gives them pills to keep them quiet—'

The woman held up a skinny white hand in the same way the lollipop lady did outside Slipton Junior when she wanted a car to stop.

'Why don't you go home and speak to your mum. This isn't the place for a little boy.'

Milo sank back into his heels and stumbled backwards. Then he thought about what PC Stubbs had said: that they should all keep their eyes open to things going on in town and how he handed out cards and said that they could get in touch with him any time and he even said that Milo would be a good asset to the force. If he could find him, PC Stubbs wouldn't tell Milo to go home and speak to his mum. He'd listen and he'd rally a whole team of policemen, all of them in their blue and white chequerboard hats and their stab vests and they'd charge into Forget Me Not and arrest Nurse Thornhill.

Milo smiled at the lady with the frizzy red hair and stepped away from the reception desk.

'Thank you for your help,' he said.

He waited until she'd wheeled her chair back to the filing cabinet, grabbed Hamlet and darted down the corridor into the heart of the police station.

*

He didn't have the first clue where to look for PC Stubbs but he remembered what Gran had taught him about trusting the feeling in his tummy. Plus, he knew that if he listened carefully, he'd be able to make out PC Stubbs's low, clear voice, the one that made everyone in Class 5A shut up, even Stan.

Milo looked through the glass windows of five different doors before he got to the interview room where PC Stubbs was talking to a teenager slouched on a chair, his skinny body floating in his big grey hoodie and his loose-slung grey jeans.

'I thought I didn't hear you go out the front door!'

Milo felt a set of bony fingers crunch down on his shoulders. He spun round. The woman stood so close to him that all he could see through the pinhole was a frizzy ginger blur. And then it clicked: the receptionist.

'And what's that animal doing here?'

'He's my pet. I'm allowed to have him, I've got a licence.'

'You're not meant to be back here. I told you, you need to go home.'

Through the pinhole, Milo looked from the woman's red lips and back to the window of the interview room. This was his last chance.

'PC Stubbs!' he yelled.

Hamlet squirmed.

Frizzy ginger woman leapt back. Milo smiled inside. Maybe his voice was more like PC Stubbs's than he thought.

He heard the screech of PC Stubbs's chair and then the click of the door. His heart rate shot up.

It's okay, he kept telling himself. *He'll listen. He'll do something*.

PC Stubbs looked down at Milo, his brow all wrinkled up.

'You came to school,' Milo blurted out. 'You showed us the video and I got the answers right.'

Hamlet squealed like he was agreeing.

Frizzy ginger woman stepped forward. 'I'm so sorry, PC Stubbs, I'm afraid that this young man has got rather carried away. I sent him home but he snuck past reception and made his way here. I'll take him back now—'

She put her bony fingers on Milo's arms and he shook them away.

Milo took a deep breath. It was now or never. 'I came to find you because you said that we should come and speak to you if ever we saw something bad going on in Slipton and you said that I'd make a good policeman because I was good at spotting things and now I've spotted something, something really bad, and that's why I came and you have to come with me straight away to Forget Me Not nursing home, which is where my gran is staying, because there's this horrible nurse and she's stealing everyone's money and she's really mean and punishes the old people just because she feels like it and she probably spends all their money on herself and—'

PC Stubbs held up his hands like he had in class when they'd cheered for the video. Milo gulped to get his breath back and fell silent.

'Miranda, I think I can take it from here.' There it was again, that low, slow calm voice.

Miranda blushed and nodded. 'I was only trying to help,' she mumbled.

'And I'm grateful for that, thank you. I'll come and bring you a coffee when I'm done here with—'

'Milo – Milo Moon,' Milo chipped in, his chest relaxing. PC Stubbs was on his side. He was going to listen to him.

When Miranda had left, PC Stubbs turned to Milo and said:

'It's good to see you, Milo.' He leant in. 'And who's this?' He gave Hamlet a rub on the head.

'His name's Hamlet.'

Milo suddenly felt a bit foolish for having blurted everything out in one go without planning it out in his head first. He promised himself to be calmer now to make up for it. PC Stubbs was listening to him, that was all that mattered. And when he found out what Milo had uncovered he'd be really impressed and everyone else would be proud of him too like Gran and even Mum might think he'd done something right for once. And best of all, Mum would understand that it was time for Gran to come home again.

PC Stubbs cleared his throat. 'How long has your gran been at Forget Me Not, Milo?'

'A week and a bit . . . I don't know . . .'

Milo didn't understand why PC Stubbs was starting his questioning here. He had to steer him to the important bits.

'But that's not the point. It doesn't matter if she's been there for days or weeks or years. And it's not just her, it's all the old people – Nurse Thornhill's taken away everyone's money and—'

Milo gulped. He could feel himself getting carried away again.

'And she used to live with you, is that right?'

'Yes, but—'

PC Stubbs paused. 'You must miss her, Milo.'

Milo felt where this was going. His stomach tightened.

'This isn't about missing my gran.' His words came out in small stuttery bursts.

PC Stubbs paused and took a breath and made his voice go soft.

'Why don't you come and take a seat, Milo.' He pointed to couple of plastic seats across the corridor. 'And I could get you a drink from the machine.'

Milo shook his head.

PC Stubbs sighed and looped his fingers into his belt.

'You know, Milo, there are some things that don't make sense to us when we're growing up. We look at them head on and we think we understand what's going on, but there's a bigger picture.'

Milo clenched his fists; he felt his nails digging into the palms of his hands. This wasn't about seeing the bigger picture. This was about seeing what was right under your big fat nose and knowing it was wrong and doing something to put it right. That's what the police got paid to do.

'Nurse Thornhill's a pillar of the community. She gives a great deal to the old people of Forget Me Not.'

More like she steals a great deal.

'And you know what, Milo, I'm sure there's a very good explanation. She's probably put their money in a safe and is looking after it for them so that they don't lose it or so that someone doesn't walk off the street and take it from them. If you ask me, she's done the sensible thing.'

A pillar of the community? What was he going on about? Milo didn't want to listen any more. PC Stubbs was just as bad as all the other grown-ups. Coming here was pointless. Milo turned and walked down the corridor.

'We'll put your complaint on file, Milo,' PC Stubbs called after him.

Milo thought of that big grey metal filing cabinet that

Miranda rifled through. Hundreds of bits of paper that no one would ever bother to dig out.

'Come and see us any time. And keep those eyes and ears open.'

Milo's heavy footsteps on the thick linoleum floor swallowed PC Stubbs's voice. If there was one thing he'd worked out in the last hour it was that whatever he ended up being when he was older, it wasn't going to be a policeman.

26

Milo

Milo wasn't meant to run because he could trip over or miss things coming towards him, like that truck the night of the Christmas party, so he'd taught himself to walk really fast, faster than any of the kids at school. But this time he didn't care, he just wanted to get out of that stupid police station as fast as he could. His eyes heavy and tired and filled with grey fuzz, his heart knocking against his chest, he dashed out into the road.

A loud screech.

Milo dropped Hamlet, who darted across the road, squealing his head off.

A swerve somewhere close to Milo's body.

The crunch of metal.

Swearing.

And flowers, hundreds of yellow petals, falling from the sky over the tarmac.

'Bloody idiot. Why don't you look where you're going.'

Someone walking towards him. The thud of heavy boots. Milo stood frozen in the middle of the road.

'Milo?'

Milo looked up and rubbed his eyes.

'Christ, Milo, you nearly got yourself killed.' That Scottish accent.

'Hamlet – where's Hamlet?' Milo looked around frantically. His eyes wouldn't focus.

He felt the man moving away from him and then heard a squeal.

'Here.' The man placed Hamlet in Milo's arms.

Milo looked down into Hamlet's small, scared face. He had yellow petals on his head.

Milo shifted his head. A motorbike lay on the side of the road, a dent in its body.

'I . . . I'm sorry.'

Milo looked down through his pinhole at the man's hands: they were trembling, like Gran's. Then he looked up into his face. It was Al, the guy living upstairs.

'Are you okay, Milo?' Al asked.

Milo shook his head. He felt tears pricking the back of his eyes. 'They wouldn't listen to me.'

'I meant are you okay after nearly being run over.'

Milo kept going. 'They never listen to kids. They pretend they do, but when it comes down to it, when you try to tell them something important, grown-ups are all the same.'

'You're not making any sense, Milo. Come on, let's get you and Hamlet out of the road.'

Al took Milo by the elbow and guided him to the bench outside the police station and then went to get his bike and wheeled it over.

'I'm sorry about your bike,' Milo said, looking at the concave dent over the Harley bit of Harley Davidson.

'It'll live,' said Al, pulling a pack of cigarettes out of his leather jacket.

Milo noticed that Al's hands were still shaking. Al lit the cigarette, inhaled deeply and puffed the smoke up into the dark sky. With every puff, Al's face relaxed a bit more, and his hands too. Maybe cigarettes weren't as bad as all that, thought Milo.

'Why are there yellow petals everywhere?' Milo asked.

'I was taking roses to Gran.'

Milo felt a jolt. 'To my gran?'

'She's everyone's gran, Milo. Or she was back home.'

So it was true. Al was a relative of some kind. And he knew that Gran's favourite flowers were yellow roses.

'I'm her great-nephew,' said Al. 'One of the tribe from Inverary.' He dragged on his cigarette some more. 'Let me finish this and I'll take you home. Then you can explain to me what you were doing standing in the middle of the road outside a police station.'

Milo wasn't sure he wanted to tell anyone anything any more, not after what had just happened with PC Stubbs. And he wasn't sure he could trust Al, not yet. And he didn't want to go home, not if Mum was there. She'd give him a lecture about missing school. He had to talk to her when she was calm, get her in a good mood, so he could explain about Gran. Mum knew when things were unfair – if he could get her to believe what he'd seen, maybe she'd do something about it. He picked up his school bag and swung it over his shoulder.

'I've got to go to school,' he said.

'If you're sure you're okay.'

Milo nodded.

Al lifted the seat of his bike, pulled out a spare helmet and held it out. 'For you,' he said.

Milo widened his eyes. 'What?'

'I think you're safer on the bike than your feet, don't you?' Al laughed.

'But . . .'

'I'll drop you off, it's on my way.'

'You're still going to see Gran?'

'Of course. Though I'll have to apologise for coming empty handed.' He looked at the roses scattered over the street.

'Will you . . . ' Milo started and then hesitated. He took a breath. 'Will you let me know if you see anything . . . I mean, if you see anything that you don't think is quite right?'

Al shrugged. 'Sure thing, Milo.'

As Milo looked at Al's bike, he thought of his classmates at school and all those boys who could do things like play football and ride skateboards and play tag because their eyes were right. He'd be willing to bet that none of them had ever been on the back of a motorbike, not even Stan.

Milo nodded.

'Good.' Al strapped on Milo's helmet, lifted him by the armpits and settled him onto the back of the bike. Then he put on his own helmet and his gloves and sat in front of him. 'Grip me around the waist, Milo, and follow my movements.'

Milo passed his hands around Al's big leather jacket. It smelt like his skin and the attic room and like all the places he must have been to.

He still didn't like the thought of Al living in Gran's room and cluttering it up with his things and making it all smelly and smoking in it. And he knew that there was something wrong with those photographs he'd found, but for those few minutes, as they roared through Slipton, Hamlet squashed between them, tucked into Milo's school jumper, Milo forgot about everything: about Dad and Mum and Gran and Al and his photos and nasty Nurse Thornhill. He even forgot about his eyes. He just squeezed Hamlet in tight, closed his eyes, let the wind whip past him and imagined, for a second, that he was flying.

27

Tripi

Tripi stood in front of the television in the lounge at Forget Me Not and watched the snow fall on Syria. He and Ayishah had left in T-shirts and sandals; they were going to buy warm things when they got to England. She'd packed a blue cotton jumper for when the nights got cold, but the day they left Damascus the temperature climbed to forty degrees, so she kept the jumper in her backpack.

A man from an organisation called Save The Children stood in the television talking about one of the camps Tripi and Ayishah had seen as they neared the border. With a sad voice, the man asked for donations; the winter was cold, he said, the children hungry.

Every time Tripi looked at the news, he searched for Ayishah's face: the wispy curls around her forehead, how her cheeks went pink and chubby when she laughed.

Tripi looked from the screen to the old women sitting in the lounge. It was cold in here too and the porridge in front of them didn't look much better than the grey clumps of rice they served up to the children in the camp on the television. He watched Heidi, the young nurse, rub at an old potato stain on the front of Mrs Turner's dress. And then Nurse Heidi noticed that Mrs Turner had dribbled some porridge onto the front pocket of her dress.

'Silly thing,' said Nurse Heidi.

Mrs Turner smiled like it was a compliment.

'If you keep doing this, I'm the one who'll get it in the neck. Nurse Thornhill likes her clients to be clean.'

'Got 'em!' shouted Mrs Sharp from her armchair in the corner, tilting her iPad to one side.

'Be quiet, Mrs Sharp, you're disturbing everyone,' said Nurse Heidi.

Nurse Heidi did not look like a bad person, but she worked long hours so she was tired and that made her cross. And she had to please Nurse Thornhill to pass her diploma and pleasing Nurse Thornhill was hard work.

I'll never bring Ayishah to Forget Me Not, thought Tripi. He didn't want her to know that some bits of England were worse than Syria. Worse because there wasn't a war or a shortage of food and yet still they did not know how to be kind to each other.

Mrs Wong walked past Tripi clutching a piece of paper. A photocopy, a picture of Ayishah.

He'd told Milo to be discreet.

'What is that you have there, Mrs Wong?' Tripi asked, easing the piece of paper out of her hands.

'Milo told us to look for his friend.'

'His friend?'

Mrs Wong nodded. 'She is lost in that terrible country.'

144

So that is what people thought of his homeland now. A terrible country. And for some reason they believed that a twelve-year-old girl from Damascus was friends with a little boy in Slipton.

Tripi felt Nurse Thornhill come up behind him. 'You should be in the kitchen, Tahir, you're not paid to watch television.'

He handed the piece of paper back to Mrs Wong.

'Sorry,' he mumbled and gathered some breakfast bowls to look useful.

'I received your address,' she said.

Tripi's heart thumped.

'So, you live on the high street now, do you?'

Tripi balanced the bowls and watched Nurse Thornhill's thin eyebrows shoot up into points like paper hats stuck to her forehead.

He nodded. 'I'm staying with a friend.'

'A generous friend, it seems.'

'Yes.'

'Good morning, Nurse Thornhill.' Petros came into the lounge.

The hats on Nurse Thornhill's eyebrows softened and she smiled with her white teeth. 'Good morning, Petros.'

Petros went to inspect one of the legs on the coffee table.

Tripi did not understand why Petros got smiles from Nurse Thornhill or why she told Tripi to put more meat than potatoes on Petros's tray at dinner. Though he was glad that the old man got some food. He did not have supplies in his room like the old ladies who had biscuits and chocolates brought in by their families.

'Now chop, chop, Tahir, to work. There are people queuing up for your job.'

Not for the pay you give me, thought Tripi. Although she had insisted on his address, Nurse Thornhill had forgotten the other boxes on the form. He suspected that although she did not want a homeless man working in her kitchen, she was not too worried about him being an illegal immigrant without a National Insurance Number, not if it meant she could save some money.

'Heidi, come over here, I need you to help me get the front room in order,' said Nurse Thornhill. 'We've got a family visiting this afternoon.'

The young nurse nodded, got up and followed Nurse Thornhill with small, rapid steps. Tripi tried to catch her eye as she went past, but Heidi kept her head bowed.

He looked back at the television. *For Donations or more information, Call 020 70126400.* Maybe he could call the man in the television and ask him whether he had seen Ayishah.

'You shouldn't watch that stuff.' Petros went up to the television and flipped the channel to a cookery programme. 'It will only depress you.'

Watching nice food being made when all you got to eat were potatoes could be just as depressing for the old people, thought Tripi. And anyway, they had to keep the news on, they were looking for Milo's friend.

'Are you happy here, Mr Spiteri?' Tripi asked.

Petros shrugged. 'I try to be grateful.' He laughed but it was one of those laughs you release when you cannot think of anything else to say.

'Are you treated well? You and ... ' Tripi looked round the lounge. 'The other patients here?'

146

'Nurse Thornhill looks after me, yes. And the ladies? They are okay.' He took off his cap and twisted it between his fingers. 'It isn't for me to rock the boat. If I am not here, where will I go? Like you with your job, no?'

'Yes. I see,' said Tripi. But sometimes, when you saw things that did not feel right, it was your duty to *rock the boat*, wasn't it? That's what Ayishah would say.

28

Milo

When Al had roared away on his bike, Milo checked that no one was looking and turned out of the school gates. He wasn't in the mood for going to school any more. And anyway, he couldn't take Hamlet with him. Milo had always thought that Hamlet would enjoy going to lessons and learning new things. People think that pigs are stupid and dirty and do nothing but eat and roll around in the mud, but that's only because they haven't lived with a pig or read up on them. Pigs are the fourth most intelligent animal in the world and they learn things really quickly, like how to play computer games by moving the joystick with their snout and how to turn off light switches. If Hamlet went to school, maybe he'd get so clever he could sit those stupid tests in Milo's place.

Milo pulled his mobile out of his coat pocket. The contract was still in Dad's name and the phone hadn't cut out yet. Milo changed the setting to make his number *Unknown* and called the school secretary.

'Hello, Slipton Primary.'

Milo cleared his throat and put on his newsreader voice.

'Hello, this is Mr Moon, Milo Moon's father.'

'Good morning, Mr Moon, what can I help you with?'

Mrs Higgins didn't use that tone when she spoke to Milo, or to any of the other children at Slipton Primary.

'I'm afraid Milo won't be coming in today.'

Hamlet snuffled. 'Shhh!' said Milo.

'Mr Moon? Are you still there?'

'Yes. My son's got tonsillitis.'

'Oh dear, I am sorry, Mr Moon. Will he be well enough to come in tomorrow?'

'Probably, we will have to see how he feels.'

'Poor Milo.'

'Yes, poor Milo.'

'Well, call again tomorrow to give us an update on his progress. In the meantime, I'll have a word with Mrs Harris.'

'Thank you.'

He pressed END CALL and let out a laugh. Hamlet squeaked. Milo hadn't thought that his newsreader voice would work.

Now he had some time to think about how to get Gran out of Forget Me Not and away from that Petros guy and Nurse Thornhill who was giving her drugs to make her sleepy and stealing her money. But before that, there was something else he had to put right, something that might get Mum on his side so that she'd listen to him when he told her what he'd seen.

Mrs Hairy's house wasn't very different from the other houses in Slipton, but she'd done things to make it look posher like put a sparkly silver gate at the end of the path that led to her front door and built white columns by the door. Mum called it The Hairy Mansion.

Mrs Hairy worked as a head waitress in London, which is why she had to look her best. Mrs Hairy told Mum these cool stories about her guests, like this Zulu tribesman who came to dinner with nothing on but a leather pouch over his dangly bits and how he'd wanted to dance with her because she was black, like him.

Milo knew Mrs Hairy was in because she didn't go anywhere without her red Mercedes. Mum said she'd saved for it for ten years and that she loved it more than her husband.

'I've come to apologise.' Milo tried hard not to zoom in on the dark fuzz on Mrs Hairy's top lip.

Mrs Hairy took off her sunglasses and stared down at Milo.

'I'm Sandy Moon's son and it was my fault that Mum went off the other day. She was looking for me, she didn't mean to leave you waiting.'

'You're the boy with the pig?'

'What?'

'You came in the other day, with your pig?'

On his way here, Milo had stopped by the canal to pick up an old piece of rope from one of the houseboats. He'd used it to tie Hamlet up behind a flowerpot at Mrs Hairy's gate and hoped Hamlet wouldn't have one of his squealing fits.

'Yes, his name's Hamlet.' Milo gulped. 'And he didn't mean to come into the shed either.'

'Ah – "when sorrows come they come not single spies, but in battalions".'

'What?'

150

'Hamlet. I studied it at school. It means that bad things all happen at once.'

Well, that was true.

Up close, rather than from the door of the shed or through her car windscreen, Mrs Hairy looked quite young. Her neck was a bit wrinkly but the skin on her face was shiny, pulled up tight behind her ears.

'Could you come back, please?' Milo asked. 'So that Mum can finish ... doing ... so that she can give you some more treatments?'

Mrs Hairy laughed.

'She'll give you a discount.'

'Why don't you come inside, Milo?'

Milo wasn't sure about going into Mrs Hairy's house with its big gates and its funny columns, but he couldn't go home until after school was finished and that was hours away, so he might as well use up some time.

The hallway was built of sparkly pink stone; even without touching it you could feel how cold and smooth it must be. Plastic palm trees stood in pots leading up to the kitchen. At the end of the hall there was a swirly staircase that looked like it belonged in a castle rather than in a small house in Slipton. The kitchen was sparkly like the hall but smooth, black sparkly with glass walls all around.

Mrs Hairy poured Milo some orange juice, sat down on a high stool and crossed her legs. As Milo sat on the stool in front of her, he tried not to look at Mrs Hairy's legs because he remembered what Mum said about her being half-plucked and he worried that one of them would be really smooth and the other one would be really hairy and that Mrs Hairy would notice him staring and get offended.

151

'So, no school today, Milo?'

'I'm sick.'

'You are?' Mrs Hairy raised her plucked eyebrows. Milo wondered how bushy they'd get if she let them go wild like the hairs around her bikini line.

'I've got a bad throat.'

'Oh.'

Milo nodded and coughed and tried to make his voice sound croaky.

'Mum doesn't know I'm here. But I had to come and see you to explain . . .'

'Why your mother left me waiting for an hour?'

'Like I said, it was my fault.'

'I expected your mother to contact me herself.'

'She's embarrassed.'

'Embarrassed?'

'Because there's no money left in the bank and she has to pay the mortgage and you're her last client.'

There was a moment of silence which made Milo worry that he'd spoken too fast or said too much.

'I understand, Milo. Your mother told me about your gran going to Forget Me Not. My mother is there too, and it is an expensive place, no wonder your mother is struggling. But that still doesn't excuse—'

'Your mum's living there with Gran?' Milo mentally scanned through images of the old ladies. And then he got it: Mrs Moseley with her dark skin and the black hairs sprouting out of her chin, she must be Old Mrs Hairy.

'If it's so expensive, why doesn't your mum live with you, in your attic?'

'I'm afraid I'm not good enough for that.' Mrs Hairy's eyes went a bit watery.

'Why would you have to be good to have your mum living in the attic?'

'She's not really herself any more, not since my father died.'

'Gran's not herself any more either and when Gramps died she stopped speaking. But she isn't too hard to look after, we coped just fine when she was at home.' Milo thought of Gran sitting in the dark all sleepy without anyone looking after her properly and his throat tightened around his words. 'I'm sure if you tried—'

'My husband finds it difficult to have her here, there isn't really room for all three of us.'

Mum told Milo how Mrs Hairy was sad because she didn't have children and that that was why she spent so much time getting plucked and working in London, because it took her mind off things. So if Mrs Hairy lived in this house with Mr Hairy, there'd be plenty of room. Much more room than in Milo's house.

Mrs Hairy sniffed. 'It's the right place for her.'

Milo didn't know whether to say anything about it not being a nice place in case it made her more upset.

'Though goodness knows it's ruining me. I do nothing but write cheques to that place, all those special treatments she needs. "The extras", Nurse Thornhill calls them.'

Milo thought about the chandelier in Nurse Thornhill's flat and the furry purple walls and the bottle of champagne and the drawer full of empty wallets. He hoped that Mum wasn't paying for any extras.

'I haven't seen you there,' he said.

'I find it a bit hard, Milo. Visiting makes me sad.'

Milo understood what she meant. He'd thought going to see Gran every day would make him feel better, but the more time he spent with her, the further away she felt. Though he did think that it was sad that Mrs Hairy didn't go to see Mrs Moseley at all. Plus, if she went, maybe she'd see that the Hairy Mansion was much nicer than Forget Me Not and she'd realise they had plenty of space and that sending her away was a mistake like sending Gran away was a mistake.

'So will you come back to Mum's salon?'

'Like I said, Milo, your mother needs to rethink her approach to her customers . . . '

'But she didn't mean to leave the other day, it was my fault. Please—'

'I'll give it some thought, Milo.'

He was Insisting again and grown-ups didn't like that. But he had to show Mum that he cared about her business and that he understood they needed more money, especially if Gran was going to come back and live with them.

Mrs Hairy walked him back to the front door. Milo stepped out into the drive and then he turned round.

'Mrs H—' Milo coughed. 'Mrs . . . ?' What was her real name again?

'Yes, Milo?'

'I think maybe you should go and visit your mum. I think she'd like to see you.'

29

Sandy

Sandy sat at the kitchen counter eating a Hobnob and flipping through her salon diary. Every page blank, except for Gina's appointments, which Sandy now crossed out. She barely had enough left in the bank to cover the food bills, let alone the mortgage and the debts on the equipment for the salon. And Milo needed new school shoes and she wanted to do some nice things for him too, like take him to London Zoo and to the Planetarium, some quality time just the two of them, things to take his mind off Lou.

Sandy prised another Hobnob out of the packet and licked her fingertips.

And Andy, sending those bloody baby photos every few weeks. He said to pass them on to Milo but as soon as they came in, she buried the photos in Mr Overend's dustbin across the road. Andy didn't get to play happy families, not when he hadn't got the first clue what they were all going through.

Sandy loosened the cord of her tracksuit bottoms, poked a third Hobnob out of the packet and looked around the kitchen.

She'd banked on some damage, a few burnt tea towels, that sort of thing. But not this: the ash had got in everywhere, dirty marks on the walls, the top of the spice bottles sticky with soot, a grey film inside the mugs, dust at the back of her throat. Last night, the extractor fan above the stove screeched to a halt, clogged. And Milo's eyes, rimmed red, redder than usual. And the insurance company stalling, saying they needed to carry out some further investigations about the fire.

Sandy swallowed the last bit of Hobnob. She wasn't going to let them take away her house. It was their home, hers and Milo's.

She turned to the back page of her address book and found the number Andy had given her for his flat in Abu Dhabi.

She put in the international code, dialled the number and waited.

A few rings and the answerphone clicked in.

Bubbles of laughter.

Marhaba, The Tart's voice.

Hello, Andy's voice.

More laughter.

You have reached the home of Andy and Angela, they chanted together.

God, their names made them sound like children's TV presenters. And then she felt sick. *Sandy and Andy*, that was hardly any better. Worse, in fact. When they'd first got together, Andy had said, *You see, I'm part of you*, pointing to

156

how his name fitted into hers. Now the similarity of their names felt like a joke.

And Bella, our Habibti, the Tart sang out.

What the hell was a Habibti?

Our baby girl, said Andy.

Sandy had always wanted a girl, someone whose hair she could brush, a little sister for Milo. When they went for tests to find out why she wasn't getting pregnant, the doctor mumbled something about fallopian tubes and said that it was a miracle she'd had Milo, she should concentrate on him. And the worst part of it? She had to keep taking the pill to make sure she didn't fall pregnant.

Leave a—

Sandy took the phone away from her ear and was about to hang up when she heard a voice, not recorded this time.

'Hello?'

'Hi.'

'Is that you? Sandy?'

So he could still recognise her voice. 'Yes. It's me.'

'I'm sorry, the machine clicks in too soon.'

Or maybe you were busy, thought Sandy. *Fooling around with that Tart while the baby's sleeping, I bet that's a real turn-on.*

'How are you, Sandy?'

'Fine.' She dislodged a line of ash from under a fingernail.

'And Gran?'

Sandy swallowed. 'Oh, you know, same as always.'

'But you're coping?'

Coping? She could hear them now, talking about her as they sat on their sunny terrace drinking cocktails: *Poor Sandy, stuck in rainy Slipton, holding it all together . . .*

'I'm fine.'

'And Milo?'

'Uh-huh.'

'Doing well at school?'

'You know Milo.'

'We'd love to have him over sometime. Have you shown him the photos?'

'Abu Dhabi is too bright for him, he'd struggle.'

'Can't he wear his glasses?'

Sandy didn't answer. How long had it been since Milo had worn his glasses? And why hadn't she noticed?

'Was there a reason you called, Sandy?'

'What?'

'Only . . .'

'Only what?'

'Well, it's a bit of a busy time for us.'

Us. We. It made her feel sick. She bit the nail of her little finger down to the quick and a drop of blood bubbled up onto her skin. She smudged it and sucked her finger.

'I was just checking in. To see how you were doing. With, you know, the baby.' The words stuck in her throat.

'Wow, that's really nice of you, Sandy. Hear that, love?' he yelled out at The Tart. 'Sandy called to ask how we were, how the baby was.'

Sandy pulled the phone away from her ear.

'Angela's on top form, a natural mother. And she's looking great, her figure just pinged back into place, amazing. I don't know how she does it with all this delicious food around, I guess it's her fast metabolism.'

Sandy pulled at the raw bit of skin next to her thumb. Fast metabolism. Probably puked it all up as soon as his back was turned.

'How's the salon going?' he asked.

'Oh, Christmas rush, you know.'

'The agency's doing really well out here. Great properties in the Abu Dhabi area, very lucrative, come at just the right time too.'

Sandy pictured rows of white villas perched like storks in the clear, still water.

Andy babbled on. 'You know how it is, babies are such expensive little creatures.'

She recognised an old nervousness in his laugh.

'Yes, they are.' *And so are children. And old people.*

'About Christmas – and Milo's birthday,' Andy said.

Milo's birthday, something else she'd have to find money for.

'I thought it might be nice—'

The Habibti wailed in the background. Maybe she was turning into a demon. Sandy imagined her sharp teeth clamped to Angela's nipple.

'I'm sorry, darling – I mean, Sandy. I'm sorry, Sandy, I have to go – domestic duties.'

Since when had Andy cared about domestic duties?

'You know what, Sandy?' He sighed. 'I knew it would work out, you and me. That we'd build our lives up again.'

He made it sound like they'd been caught up in some kind of tsunami, a great natural disaster beyond their control, and that now they should pat themselves on the back for having clung to the life raft. Why couldn't he see that he was the one who'd landed a bomb in their lives? A big Tart-shaped bomb.

'You'd better go, Andy, sounds like you're needed.'

A beat of silence. 'You sure you don't need anything?' he asked.

'Yes. I'm sure.'

Sandy put down the phone. Then she grabbed the packet of Hobnobs, threw them against the wall, flung open the drawer and pulled out her bottle of diet pills.

30

Milo

Milo had a few hours to kill before the end of school so he went to the park. He sat on the swings, cradling Hamlet, and watched a mum pushing her little boy on a bike with stabilisers.

Getting a new bike, that's how it had all started. A proper, grown-up one with the saddle all the way down so that Milo could grow into it. Dad hid it in the garage behind a dustsheet and he and Mum kept saying that they were buying Milo socks for Christmas and a vest for his birthday and they nudged each other and winked when they thought Milo wasn't looking. But Milo had flipped to the picture in the catalogue so many times that he knew the shape of the bike by heart.

Sometimes having your birthday on Christmas day was the worst thing, because it felt like you get half of one and half of the other and nothing proper. Other years, it felt like getting double of everything, a better Christmas and a better birthday than if they'd been apart.

A year ago, Milo was sure that, with the new bike, this Christmas-Birthday would be doubly good.

The bike was expensive: Milo saw the numbers under the picture. But it was okay, because at the beginning of December Dad came home with a bottle of champagne and announced that he was now Top Dog at Move-It, which meant he got more money and a secretary and that he was in charge of loads of people and got to tell them what to do rather anyone telling him what to do. Milo heard him say to Mum: *It's okay, Sandy, we can afford to splash out this year.*

Mum was so excited about Dad getting the promotion that she said they should hold his Christmas work party at their house and if Milo helped, he was allowed to stay up for it.

On the day of the party, Mum cancelled her salon appointments so she could concentrate on making herself and the house beautiful and Dad came home early from work to move the furniture. Then he helped Mum and Milo make snacky sausages, which showed how happy Dad was because he never did anything in the kitchen. He wrapped the wrinkly brown sausages in bits of streaky bacon and called them Pigs in Blankets to annoy Milo because he knew that pigs were Milo's favourite animals in the whole world. Mum even let Milo try a bit of the mulled wine she was making and it tasted like hot Ribena, except without the water added, and with spicy things that made Milo's nose tickle and something else that caught the back of his throat and made his chest feel warm.

Milo whizzed around collecting people's coats and taking them up to his mum and dad's bedroom and got people drinks and handed around the sausages. He'd never seen so many people in his house. Mum put the slushy Christmas music on and everyone crammed in closer and closer and started swaying and someone dropped some mulled wine on the carpet, which Milo was sure would make Mum flip but she didn't, she just threw back her head and laughed and said she'd deal with it in the morning.

The only thing that made Milo sad about that night was that Gran wasn't at the party. She'd written on her pad that she'd rather stay upstairs and get an early night. Not that she'd be able to sleep with all the racket. It was from the night of the Christmas party that Gran started sleeping a lot: she'd fall asleep while she was having her lunch and during the Shipping Forecast, which was her favourite radio programme, and sometimes she even fell asleep while Milo was telling her a story or giving her a bath and washing her hair – and then he had to shake her awake because people had been known to drown in a bath, and when she woke up she stared at Milo, dazed, and said things like, *want to come in and join me for a swim? The sea ... it's so warm ...*

'Milo, go and get that stool from my salon,' Mum yelled above the music. 'We've run out of chairs.'

Mum had a special swively stool made out of white leather with shiny silver feet on wheels so that she could zoom around the shed and pick up products without having to get up.

Milo walked through the frosty grass, his head spinning from all the noise in the house. As he looked at the shed, it seemed to shrink in front of him. All the bits around the door were fuzzy. He rubbed his itchy eyes and re-focused. Now all he could see was the door with the padlock dangling off the metal clasp.

Mum never left the shed open. There was too much expensive equipment like the Microabrasion Machine (she'd tried it on Milo's nose and it had made it go pink and smooth and shiny) and the sunbed and the expensive creams with seaweed from the Red Sea in them. Plus the insurance wouldn't pay out if something was stolen and they found out that she hadn't locked it up properly.

As he got to the door, he heard a squeaky metal noise and a high-pitched giggle like someone had swallowed helium. He felt wobbly now, maybe it was the mulled wine. When Mum wasn't watching, he'd taken a few more sips from the ladle in the saucepan.

Milo flicked the switch by the door and stepped towards the bit of the room where Mum kept her stool. For a moment the brightness of the light hurt his eyes so much he wanted to switch it off again. But then he noticed that there was someone else in the shed. And then he realised there wasn't just someone, there were people. Two bodies tangled up on Mum's massage bed, their feet pushed into the donut ring you put your head in. A man with his trousers pulled down and his dangly bit all red and stiff and up and at an angle, and a woman with her skirt hitched up. And they were staring at him but Milo's eyes were so hot and scratchy that everything looked blurred and he couldn't make out who the people were.

'Milo? What are you doing here?' Dad's voice. And then Dad getting up and pulling his boxers up and the woman covering her boobs up with her arms. Milo saw the big bulge in Dad's pants and thought about what he'd said when Milo got a bulge, that it was your body getting ready for when you met a girl you really liked. Like Mum, he'd said.

Milo dropped the stool and heard it clatter to the floor as he ran out into the night.

He didn't go back into the house but ran round to the side gate and then through to the garage. He whipped the dust-sheet off his Christmas-Birthday bike, wheeled it out onto the drive, climbed on and set off full tilt into the road.

31

Lou

Lou lay in her bed at Forget Me Not drifting in and out of sleep. Somewhere deep in her mind, she heard a garage door whine open and the sound of pedalling on the drive. And that damned whistling, worse than the *jingle all the way* bleating from downstairs. Why couldn't he just pipe down and go to sleep like a normal old man. And then, as if he'd heard her thoughts, Mr Overend fell silent.

And after that a whine as loud as the foghorn across the sea at Inverary.

And a smash.

And the music snapping off mid *jingle* in the lounge.

Her voice came back in a rush, soaring up her body like it had been waiting for the moment for sixty-two years.

'Milo!' she cried from her room under the roof. 'Milo!'

But no one heard her. No one except Mr Overend who stood leaning out of his window, looking down at the road.

Milo had stayed in her room for days, handing her

fragments of what he'd seen: his father and the woman whose love he'd exchanged for Sandy's.

She stroked his hair and listened and cursed Andrew. The child worshipped his father, and look what he'd done.

Her eyes flickered open. Petros sitting on the chair by the bed, a gentle snore rolling off his breath. How could she explain to Milo these feelings she had for this old man who'd walked into her life?

Her head bobbed back down and she thought again of that night last Christmas, everything jumbled.

I saw him, Gran ... I saw Dad with someone else ...

Lou opened her eyes and looked around. Petros was gone, the room empty again.

Where was she?

A damp patch pressed into the soft skin inside her thighs. Behaving like a frightened child.

'Hello?'

An old woman stood in the doorway, her white hair down to her waist like a ghost.

'It's me, Mrs Zimmer.'

Lou had never heard her speak. She thought that Mrs Zimmer might have lost her words too.

'I heard you tossing and turning as I walked by.'

Mrs Zimmer came and lay beside Lou in the narrow bed.

'You don't mind, do you? I was sleepwalking and you woke me ... and I'm a little tired now.' She yawned and curled up and mumbled, 'I think I saw that girl, that little girl, though I can't be sure ... ' And then she fell asleep.

Lou looked around at the white walls and the white bedding and the window looking out onto the grey roofs of Slipton.

Forget Me Not, that's where I am.

The alarm clock on the bedside table clicked as it struck twelve. Lou must have drifted off mid-morning.

That same dream, of the night Milo found his father and his secretary in Sandy's shed. The night they realised Milo's eyes were broken.

She looked at Mrs Zimmer's face, her mouth open, a light snore pushing off each breath.

No, nothing had been right since that night.

32

Sandy

'You should have come in to talk to us about all this, Mrs Moon.' Mrs Harris sat in Sandy's kitchen, sipping a cup of tea.

She's old enough to be my mother, Sandy thought. *She's certainly talking to me like she's my mother, implying I can't look after my own son.*

First there'd been the phone call from Gina: Milo had shown up at her house, and then this woman stood on their doorstep demanding to be let in.

'I got a message that Milo's dad had called, which is when I twigged that something must be wrong.' Mrs Harris put down her mug. 'I gather he's moved abroad.'

I gather. Making a piece of gossip sound like it was something clever she'd worked out. Sandy had never liked teachers, interfering busybodies.

Mrs Harris cleared her throat. 'So this eye condition. Ret ... Retin ...'

'Retinitis Pigmentosa.'

'Right. It would have been helpful for us to work together to help Milo. We're doing all we can at school, but there needs to be some support from home.' Sandy slipped one of her bare feet out of her clogs and looked down at her chipped toenails.

'Mrs Moon?'

'Andy was going to do that. Liaise with the school.'

She was blaming Andy, but it was her fault, wasn't it? It wasn't like he was going to stay in touch with Slipton Primary all the way from Abu Dhabi.

Sandy remembered how she'd sat in that dark underground room with all those lamps and machines and eye charts as Dr Nolan explained why Milo had fallen off his bike. Why he'd been getting those headaches, why he'd jump whenever she came up behind him without warning.

You have to imagine looking at the world through a pinhole, Dr Nolan had said.

And he'd explained how that pinhole got even smaller at night and when it rained. And how, one day, the pinhole would close up altogether and Milo's world would go dark.

Cures? No. Dr Nolan shook his head. *But you can try Vitamin A, Omega 3, foods with antioxidants. There's some research to suggest those things might help.*

When had she last reminded Milo to take his pills? To eat those green leafy vegetables that were meant to make his eyes sharper?

Sandy wished she was the one with the bad eyes, she already knew what it felt like for the world to disappear.

Milo had sat on the chair, swinging his legs. He remembered every word the doctor said that day. *It's like an orange moon*, Milo explained to her in the car on the way home. He pointed at the picture of his retina that Dr Nolan gave him: the white shadows where the damage was, the network of nerves. *My eyes are like a lunar eclipse, Mum.* He'd been obsessed with seeing a bloody eclipse ever since.

And then Andy had bought Milo a picture of an orange moon to put on his bedroom wall. *You see, your eyes are special*, he'd said. As if that helped.

Sandy spotted a pile of mail on the counter: a note from the bank manager, a letter from the insurance company. She covered them up with a magazine. She'd move them to the shed later so that Milo wouldn't find them.

'It's been having an impact on his work, Mrs Moon.'

'Milo's fine.'

'I'm afraid he's not. He failed his recent maths and English exams – we put a breakdown in the post for you.'

A weight plummeted through Sandy. 'There must be a mistake. Milo's very clever, we had him tested.'

Mrs Harris examined a trail of ash on her fingertips and scrunched up her nose. There should be a *policy* against letting teachers turn up at people's houses without any warning, that's what Sandy thought.

'All I'm saying, Mrs Moon, is that maybe this condition, this problem he has with his peripheral vision, is getting in the way of his learning. If we can obtain some more information, we could help him—'

'He's got special lenses.' Sandy felt sick. Where were those damned glasses? 'Anyway, the doctor said it would be years before it became a real problem. If it had got that bad, Milo would have told me.'

Mrs Harris crossed her chubby knees. Sandy spotted some

dark hairs poking up through the teacher's flesh coloured tights.

'Children don't like to be different, Mrs Moon. They'll often go to great lengths to disguise a disability.' She paused. 'We have a special unit at school, staff trained to cope with pupils who have learning difficulties.'

Sandy felt the red rash prickling up her throat. She clawed at it, knowing she'd regret it later.

Mrs Harris continued. 'Maybe you should talk to him about how he's finding things at school.'

'Excuse me?'

'Sometimes it helps to sit down and—'

'I heard what you said, I'm just wondering where the hell you get off—'

'Your neck, Mrs Moon, you're bleeding.'

The front door clicked open and shut again. Milo came into the kitchen, his lips blue, his face as grey as the sky.

Mrs Harris stood up.

Sandy ran towards him. 'Milo . . .'

Milo stepped away from them both. He wrapped his arms around the padded shape that wriggled at the front of his duffel coat. That was Andy's contribution to this situation. While Sandy spent last Christmas dragging Milo from one eye specialist to the next, Andy stepped in with a poster and a bloody pig. Oh, and he got Milo a baby sister too.

'You seem to have recovered from your tonsillitis, Milo,' said Mrs Harris.

Sandy shot Mrs Harris a look. Weren't teachers trained in child psychology? Accusing Milo as soon as he came through the door wasn't going to help, was it?

'Can we talk, Mum? It's important.'

Sandy strained a smile. 'Of course, Milo. But why don't you come in here and join us for a second, tell Mrs Harris all those clever things you've been doing on your computer.'

'I can't talk to you when she's here.'

'Darling . . .'

'This is important, Mum. More important than anything I've ever told you.'

'Well, just give me a bit of time with Mrs Harris . . .'

Milo turned round and stomped upstairs. The bang of his bedroom door sent a shudder through the house.

Sandy spun round to face Mrs Harris, her eyes ablaze. 'He's too clever for your stupid tests, that's all. He doesn't need a special unit. You know where Milo should be? In an advanced class. Gifted and Talented – isn't that what you people call it? You'd think teachers were trained to recognise when a kid was bored. He finds it too easy – no wonder he can't be bothered to do any work.' Sandy caught her breath.

'We're just trying to help, Mrs Moon. It sounds like you've got a lot on your plate.'

'It sounds like you don't know how to mind your own business.' Sandy's skin burned. She opened the front door and held out Mrs Harris's coat.

33

Milo

The bogey car reversed out the drive. Milo watched one of Hamlet's droppings slide off the roof and down the back windscreen.

He held Hamlet up to the window so he could see.

'Serves her right for turning up to our house like that,' Milo whispered into Hamlet's black ear. He'd picked up the droppings in a poop-a-scoop bag when they were in the park. Hamlet's licence hadn't arrived yet, so Milo didn't want to leave any evidence.

He'd known that Mum would be too busy to listen. There was always something.

'You'll see Gran tomorrow,' he said as Hamlet burrowed his snout into Milo's arm. 'Tripi will take you. And you'll have to help us find out what's going on at Forget Me Not and then we'll get Gran out of there and we'll be together again.'

The loud voices from the telly started up again above

Milo's head, and that heavy metal music too. How could someone listen to the telly and music at the same time?

Milo looked up at the ceiling and thought about Al and how he'd let him and Hamlet ride on the back of his motorbike. Maybe he wasn't so bad after all, but then there were still the photos to explain. Before he could trust him he had to get to the bottom of those.

He put Hamlet down, took the photos out of his school bag and went upstairs.

Bang! Bang! Bang! He thumped on Gran's door.

No answer.

He tightened his fist and whacked harder. *Bang! Bang! Bang!*

The door flew open.

'Hi there.' Al smiled at Milo, which Milo hadn't expected after all his banging.

'I'm trying to do my homework, I can't concentrate.' Milo looked into the room at the big flashing television. Did Al watch anything apart from the news?

'Oh, I'm sorry, mate, I'll turn it down.' Al walked over, held a remote up to the telly and pressed until the voices went quiet and then he got another remote and did the same thing to his stereo.

'So you okay – after this morning, I mean?' Al asked.

'Kind of.'

Al's eyes flickered over Milo's hands. 'What's that you've got?'

Milo felt his fingers get hot and sticky around the photos. Was taking someone's stuff when he was in your home the same as stealing in the outside world?

Al kept smiling.

Milo made his eyes focus on Al's face. His dark hair and his big nose and his stubbly skin blurred in and out of focus. He drew up all the energy he had left and said, 'Mum wouldn't want this kind of stuff in her house.' He held out the photographs.

Al looked at Milo for a second and then laughed. Milo smelt smoke on his breath.

'Why don't you come in so we can have a chat?'

Milo put the photos down on the bedside table, but he missed the edge and they scattered over the floor. Bits of boob and puffy lips and bulging thighs swam in front of him. His face burned up, like Mum's rash.

Milo worried that one day, when he had a girlfriend and had to look at her naked, she'd come too close and he'd only see bits of her at a time and she'd get angry, because it's rude to stare at people's private parts.

'What do you think of them?' Al opened the window and lit a cigarette.

'They're ... They're ... ' Milo took a breath. 'You shouldn't have them. It's wrong.'

'I agree, Milo—' Al took a drag on his cigarette and let out the smoke through a corner of his mouth as he spoke, '—can I call you Milo?'

Milo nodded and then regretted it, he didn't want this guy calling him anything.

'Well, as you know, my name's Alasdair McCloud, but you can call me Clouds, like my mates do.'

Mates? Milo wasn't sure he wanted to be mates with someone who'd taken over his Gran's room and filled it with naked women and noise and smoke.

Al drew again on his cigarette, crouched down and picked up the photos.

'I was wondering where these had got to – can't do much without my evidence.' He blew hoops of smoke to the ceiling, which Milo thought was cool until he remembered he wasn't meant to like him smoking in Gran's room.

'Why have you written numbers on the back?'

'It's for the documentary.'

Milo's eyes went wide. 'I don't understand.'

Al sat down on the bed and patted the bare mattress.

Milo shook his head.

'Fair enough.' He laughed again. 'You know what a journalist is, Milo?'

Milo turned his head and looked at the television with the quiet voices. 'Of course I know what a journalist is.'

'Okay, so that's what I'm training to be.'

Milo didn't know where this was going or what it had to do with pictures of naked women.

'A special kind of journalist.'

'One who takes bad photos?' Milo felt proud of his comeback.

'Yes.' Al sucked on his cigarette. 'One who takes bad photos.'

'Mum wouldn't like it.'

'I dare say she wouldn't.'

Milo lifted his head. He was getting somewhere at last.

'You have to take bad photos if you want to catch bad people, Milo.'

'What bad people?'

'People who take advantage of girls like this. Who are involved in sex-trafficking.'

Milo didn't understand what sex had to do with traffic.

'Bad people who make them be naked?' he asked.

'Yes.' Al stacked up the photos and put them back in the book where Milo had found them with the orange writing that said *Hell's Angels*, a book Milo was sure Mum wouldn't like either. 'You know what an undercover reporter is?'

Milo nodded but he didn't, not really.

'It's someone who digs up the dirt, who goes to places and looks at things everyone else ignores, so that the people doing bad things get caught.'

'Isn't that what the police are meant to do?'

Al shrugged. 'Yeah, but they're sometimes a bit slow. We speed things up and we're willing to expose things in a way the cops aren't allowed to. We put the evidence on TV, on the internet.' Al looked up at Milo and smiled. 'You know what? I think you'd be quite good at it. Breaking in, snooping around—'

'I'm ... I ... I didn't—'

'It's all right, mate, I'm impressed. You thought I was the bad guy, so you came to find evidence – that's what I do.'

Milo came and sat on the end of the bed, leaving a good gap between him and Al. He thought about PC Stubbs and how he refused to do anything about Nurse Thornhill stealing all that money from the old people. Al was right, they were slow. In fact, as Milo saw it at the moment, they were pretty useless.

'So, how do you manage not to get caught? When you're getting your evidence?'

'That's the undercover bit. I pretend I'm one of them.'

'One of the bad guys?'

'Exactly.'

Milo's mind raced. Al was right, he'd be good at going undercover and finding stuff.

'Are you going to catch them? The people who made those girls get naked?'

'I hope so, Milo – we're getting close.' Al looked at Milo and blinked. Milo knew what was coming next – Al had given him the look everyone gave him when they realised there was something wrong. 'Can I ask you a question, Milo?'

Milo didn't feel like talking about it, but he nodded. Al had answered his questions, so it was only fair.

'You see things differently from other people, right?'

Milo felt it coming, the whole pitying him because of his eyes.

'It's just the way you look at things, like you can see more than we can. Deeper, I mean.'

Milo felt himself blushing. No one had ever made Retinitis Pigmentosa sound like a good thing, not unless you count Dr Nolan who went on about Milo's *unique condition*, and that didn't count because doctors were paid to find sick people interesting.

Milo shook his head. 'My eyes don't work.'

Al stubbed out his cigarette. 'Well, they worked well enough to catch me out.'

'I can't see the whole picture.'

Al laughed. 'Lots of people can't do that.'

Milo didn't understand. He curled his thumb and fore-finger together to make a small hole, nudged up the bed until he was wedged next to Al, and held his fingers up to Al's eyes. 'Look through here.'

Al leant into Milo's hand, squinting with his other eye.

'That's what I see. Kind of, only worse.'

'Wow, that must be amazing.'

Milo shrugged. 'Not really.'

'I mean, it makes you focus, doesn't it? I bet you see all kinds of things that other people miss.'

Milo had never thought of it like that.

'Yeah, but I miss the other stuff, outside of the hole.'

'The other stuff's overrated, mate. If everyone gets to see it, it's not very special. Now what you see, that's something.'

Milo thought about all the things he'd seen at Forget Me Not and how other people whose eyes were better than his didn't seem to notice it. Maybe Al was right, maybe seeing everything through the pinhole was some kind of super-power. Or maybe Al was just saying it to make Milo feel good so he'd forget about showing Mum the photos.

'So, once you see something that's wrong, you take photos?' asked Milo.

'Photos, film. Any evidence that will make what you say sound true.'

'And don't you get in trouble? If you get caught?'

'That's part of the job, Milo. Fear of getting caught gets the adrenalin pumping, it's what drives you.'

Milo got up and went to the door. He put his fingers on the door handle and hesitated. A part of him wanted to turn round and tell Al about Gran and everything he'd seen at Forget Me not and to get him to help him gather evidence to catch Nurse Thornhill, but he wasn't sure yet whether he liked him or whether he could trust him. Maybe he'd dismiss him just because he was a kid, like PC Stubbs had. No, he'd wait a bit longer and in the meantime, he'd find ways of gathering some evidence by himself.

Milo turned round. 'Did you get to see Gran?'

Al nodded. 'Strange place she's in, that's for sure.'

Milo felt a little skip in his heart. So he wasn't imagining it. Al saw it too. Maybe he would believe him if he told him all the things he saw.

'So, have I passed the test?' asked Al.

Al lay back on the mattress. He still didn't look right, taking up all this space in Gran's room.

'Maybe,' said Milo, and he couldn't help smiling a bit.

'Well, if we're going to be friends, you really should call me Clouds. It's what everyone calls me back home.'

'In Inverary?' That was where Gran came from.

Al nodded. 'Aye, in Inverary.'

Milo thought that 'friends' was maybe stretching it a bit, though he supposed that calling him Clouds couldn't do any harm. He nodded and said. 'Okay.'

Later that night, as Milo drifted off to sleep, he heard Clouds's biker boots clomping down the stairs and him talking to Mum by the front door. Even if what Clouds said made sense of the photos and why he watched the news all the time, none of that explained why he didn't have any pants or socks or other clothes in Gran's wardrobe or wash things in the bathroom. And why, most nights, Milo heard the roar of his motorbike pulling away and only heard it coming back first thing in the morning. He was right not to trust him yet.

34

Tripi

On Friday the fourteenth of December, Tripi plodded down the corridor with Hamlet snuggled under his chef's whites and Milo's mobile phone sticking out of his pocket.

Milo had come by the house before school, breathless with excitement about this man called Al who'd given him an idea about how to find out whether there was anything suspicious going on at Forget Me Not. He'd given Tripi the pig (for Mrs Moon) and the phone (to collect evidence). Tripi still wasn't sure about this, but helping the little boy couldn't hurt, could it?

He'd taken footage of the pills that Nurse Thornhill gave the patients – Milo said that was important – and although he had felt a knot in his stomach as he did so, he let Mrs Moseley show him the bruises that ran along her arm where

Nurse Thornhill had gripped her and pushed her under a cold shower.

Mrs Swift walked past him and smiled. It was amazing how these old people managed to stay happy in a place like this.

'You are looking very beautiful this morning, Mrs Swift,' he said.

'I could do yours too, you know.' Mrs Swift held up her red lipstick. 'I saw this show on the telly and they were saying that men wear make-up too now, they call them metrosexuals.'

'I will think about it,' said Tripi. 'Thank you.'

Mrs Swift went and knocked on Mrs Wong's door. 'Ready for your make-up?' she asked.

Every morning Mrs Wong let Mrs Swift give her what they called a make-over. And then Mrs Wong came to the kitchen to ask whether she could have some rice for lunch and he had to tell her that rice was not on the menu. Next Monday Nurse Thornhill was taking the day off, perhaps he would make Mrs Wong some rice then.

Heidi stood staring at the noticeboard. Tripi liked her soft smile, though she reminded him too much of a mouse, always scuttling after Nurse Thornhill.

'Looks like she got shortlisted.' Heidi adjusted the basket of washing under her arm and pointed at a poster.

The Greater London Nursing Home Awards. Underneath, a list of three shortlisted homes and home directors.

First on the list: *Forget Me Not Home, Slipton, Nurse Thornhill.*

Tripi shook his head. There was something wrong with this country, something more wrong than Syria.

'How did she get chosen?' he asked.

'Votes. I voted for her, so did most of the patients. Petros organised it.'

Heidi looked at the bulge under Tripi's coat and frowned. Tripi breathed in and held Hamlet tighter.

'You voted for Nurse Thornhill?'

She really was a little mouse. And Petros? Tripi wanted to like the old man, especially as Mrs Moon was so fond of him. But he was always, what was that phrase Ayishah had learnt at school? *Sucking up* to Nurse Thornhill.

'She said she'd give me a good write-up for my course.' Heidi looked at the poster again. 'She does work hard, you can give her that.'

She works hard at making people unhappy, thought Tripi. *There should be an award for that.* Then he had an idea. He slipped a hand into his pocket and switched on the red button of the phone, like Milo had taught him.

'So, Nurse Heidi,' he said, his voice loud and clear.

Heidi raised her eyebrows at Tripi's change in tone, though he did not worry too much about that: being foreign meant that people expected you to sound strange. 'Nurse Thornhill,' he pronounced the name really clearly, trying to lean his mouth towards his pocket. 'Nurse Thornhill told you to vote for her, did she?'

Heidi wrinkled her brow but nodded.

'Was that a yes?'

'Keep your voice down, Tripi.' Heidi looked up and down the corridor. 'Yes,' she whispered.

He hoped the phone had picked her up, it would be good evidence for Milo. Hamlet shuffled. A teacup pig, wasn't that what Milo had said? More like teapot pig.

184

'What's that?' She nudged her chin at the bulge under Tripi's chef whites.

At that moment, Nurse Thornhill's tall, white figure appeared at the end of the corridor.

Heidi went pale. 'I swear there are CCTV cameras in this place.'

That was a good line for the recording, thought Tripi.

Hamlet let out a squeal.

Tripi looked at Heidi's washing basket. It stank of sleep and urine. Nurse Thornhill sacked one of the cleaners for spending too much time talking to the old ladies so Heidi was having to do all the work the cleaner did plus her own nursing duties. Tripi lifted one of the dirty sheets, placed Hamlet into the basket, placed the sheet back on top and leant in towards Heidi. 'Bring him to Mrs Moon and tell her to hide him.'

Heidi's eyes nearly popped out of her head. 'What? No. I'll get in trouble. Tripi!' She kept looking from the basket to Nurse Thornhill who was now walking towards them.

'Okay, I'll do it,' said Tripi, grabbing the basket.

'Having a mother's meeting?' asked Nurse Thornhill, looking from Tripi to Heidi.

Tripi didn't know what *a mother's meeting* was, but he quickly stepped in with: 'I thought I would help Nurse Heidi.' He lifted the basket a little, praying that Hamlet would stay quiet. 'To collect the washing. My shift doesn't start for another thirty minutes.'

Heidi nodded a bit too hard.

Nurse Thornhill narrowed her eyes, but then she caught sight of something behind Tripi and her white teeth pushed through her lips.

'Ah, the poster's arrived.'

'Yes, I put it up,' said Nurse Heidi.

The three of them stared at the poster with Nurse Thornhill's name written in thick black letters.

'The Award Inspectors are coming on Tuesday. We have the weekend to make the place look spick and span.'

Tripi knew what *spick and span* was: it meant bringing in roses and cream cakes and smoked salmon sandwiches like when they had visitors.

A pillowcase slipped off the pile of washing in Tripi's arms and floated to the floor. Hamlet's curly black tail poked out. Tripi leant over, picked up the pillowcase and whipped it back into the basket, and as he did so, he felt the phone slide out of his pocket onto the floor. Before he had the chance to do anything, Nurse Thornhill leant over and picked it up.

'This yours, Tahir?' She turned the white phone over between her long fingers. 'Looks rather expensive.'

One minute he was being accused of being a terrorist, the next of being a thief.

Tripi nodded. 'It was a gift from a friend.'

He felt like a five-year-old.

'Ah, the generous friend with the house?'

Tripi nodded, balanced the basket under one arm and took the phone.

'You left it on, Tahir,' said Nurse Thornhill, tapping her fingernail on the red light at the top of the screen. 'You should be careful with that.'

'Thank you.' Tripi's heart banged so hard he thought his chest was going to explode.

Heidi had shrunk back behind Nurse Thornhill.

'Excuse me?' A voice came down the corridor.

Tripi looked up and saw a woman in a tight pink suit coming towards them down the corridor. When she got closer, he noticed that she had skin browner than his and black hairs on her top lip. *Women with moustaches*, Ayishah had giggled and pointed them out and said that if she ever got a moustache, she would pluck the hairs out so hard that they would never dare to grow back.

'Ah, Mrs Downe.' Nurse Thornhill exposed her teeth again. 'Thank you for coming in. Let's go to my office and we'll have a talk.'

Heidi scrabbled after them. *Definitely like a mouse*, thought Tripi. He'd thought English women would be stronger and more courageous than this. He would have to take lots more film for Al to edit, a little bit of footage on each of the old ladies at Forget Me Not.

'I'm so glad you've decided to come in at last,' Tripi heard Nurse Thornhill say as she walked next to the woman. 'Your mother's doing exceptionally well.'

35

Lou

Early on Saturday morning Milo lay on the carpet of Gran's room in Forget Me Not, his head in her wardrobe.

'I think he likes it here, better than the garage, that's for sure. Mum hasn't even noticed he's gone. I bet she thinks I'm hiding him in my room.'

Lou's eyes burned. She'd got up three times in the night. Once to clean up Hamlet's mess (the potatoes she fed him for dinner must have disagreed as much with his insides as they did with hers), once when he squealed (she found him choking on one of her shoelaces) and finally when, with all the strength she could muster, she carried him over to her bed. She struggled with her left leg, pulling it behind her like a petulant child. Her whole body was being petulant, ignoring the messages from her brain, deciding to do its own thing.

Lou had set her alarm to get Hamlet back into the wardrobe before Nurse Thornhill did her rounds.

Though Milo was right about one thing: Hamlet kept her warm, his plump body pressed against hers through the early hours of the morning.

'We've got a lodger, Gran, his name's Al. Well, it's Clouds, that's what he likes to be called, but his proper name is Al. He's your great-nephew. He came to see you the other day.'

She looked out through the window and across the rooftops of Slipton. Alasdair. Even as a boy he was a rebel, going against his mother's orders and swimming with Lou in the cold sea of Inverary.

'At first I wanted him to leave because he smokes and he's messy and he sneaks out of the house in the middle of the night and I don't know where he goes and it's your room, not his – but apart from that, I think he might be okay. He told me about how he's an undercover reporter and it gave me an idea. I'm going to make a documentary on Forget Me Not. Maybe, once you come home, Clouds can stay with Tripi, because Tripi's got a house now. Tripi's helping me with the documentary. He's got the mobile Dad gave me and he's recording everything.' Milo got up off the floor, smiling. 'You'll see, Gran, we'll get you out of here.'

Lou felt Milo's excitement flap in her chest.

Milo came over and stood next to her. She watched him shift his head before resting his gaze on her left arm.

'Is it getting worse, Gran?' Milo took her hand in his soft fingers.

Lou shook her head. Feeling a strand of hair come loose against her chin, she slipped her hand from under Milo's and reached up to her face. She felt the fluttering of her fingers against her skin. She couldn't find it, the strand of hair. She fumbled clumsily by her ear.

189

'Here, let me do it.' Milo leant forward and in one quick movement, tucked the strand behind her ear. 'You see, Gran, you need me around. That horrible nurse isn't any help, is she? And I'm going to work out what she's done with all your money. I bet she's stolen it. And Gran, I need you back home too. Mum's lost all her customers and she's stressing about my schoolwork and bills keep coming in and she tries to hide them in the shed but I can tell they're bills from the envelopes when they come through the door.'

Dear Sandy, she never did understand how to save. Lou wished that she'd let her help. She had a few savings, enough to get her through this bad patch.

'I wish Mum would get up and do something about it, but she doesn't, she just sits there, eating Hobnobs and staring at the telly. She was better when you were at home.' Milo took a breath. 'We were all better.'

Lou thought about her small room at the top of the stairs. Had she liked it there? Those hours spent on her own looking out onto the roofs of Slipton?

Milo shifted his head to where the bagpipes stood propped up against the wall. 'Can we have a lesson? I want to learn Great-Gramps's song.'

Gran looked down at her trembling hand and her thin arms. Had Milo forgotten what had happened last time? When the air in her lungs ran out before the first note? She'd have to ask Alasdair to teach him.

A *rat-a-tat-tat* on the door like someone beating out a tune.

'Louisa! Oh, and Milo. Hello, Milo.'

Lou felt something sink inside Milo. He turned away and went back to the wardrobe.

Petros walked into the room with his creaky knees, an arm behind his back.

'I have a surprise,' he announced.

Lou felt the slump of Milo's shoulders and the pressure of his eyelids as he screwed them shut, hugging Hamlet closer.

She wished he'd give Petros a chance.

'For an English rose.' Petros took off his yellow cap and held out a single pink rose, tipped red, like it was blushing.

'She's Scottish,' Milo mumbled.

Petros gave a small bow. 'I beg your pardon. A Scottish rose.'

Lou took the rose and breathed in the scent of the petals. Not an artificial floral scent, just cool and fresh and alive. So few things smelt alive these days.

'Aren't you married?' Milo mumbled, staring at the ring on Petros's left hand.

Petros cupped his hand to his ear: 'What was that?'

'Shouldn't you be giving flowers to your wife?'

'Ah. Well, that is a little difficult, Milo, her grave is far away, in Greece.'

Milo's ears flared red and he went back to stroking Hamlet.

Petros found a glass, filled it with water, trimmed the stem and placed the rose on the windowsill. Then he walked over to Milo and peered into the wardrobe. 'In Greece,' he said, 'pigs are for salami.' He rocked back on his heels, patted his stomach and laughed.

What a silly man, thought Lou. *A lovely, silly man.*

Milo got up. 'I think I'll go now, Gran.'

Lou stretched out her good hand and tried to get a

message to him. *Please stay*, she whispered into his mind, but Milo had tuned out.

The shaking in Lou's left hand got worse.

Milo turned to face Petros, his eyes focused. 'By the way, you don't know anything about pigs. They're clean and they're clever – much cleverer than you – and Gran loves Hamlet, so if you're trying to impress her, talking about salami isn't going to work.' Then he walked over to the windowsill and stared at the pink rose. 'And Gran prefers yellow roses. Whole bunches of them.' He came over, brushed Lou's cheek with a kiss and walked to the door.

Petros stood at the wardrobe, grinning at Hamlet. Lou looked to see whether Petros had his hearing aid in. Luckily she couldn't spot the plastic curling into his ear. Perhaps he'd forgotten to put it in this morning. And perhaps he hadn't picked up on too much of what Milo said.

Lou heard Hamlet snuffling around her shoes. She knew that sound, the same one he'd made in the night: he was trying to find Milo. Clever, that was true, and clean – most of the time. And they needed love, that made them special too.

When Andrew had come back with Hamlet last June, a piglet no bigger than the palm of her hand, she'd written a note for him, tried to explain that the piglet was too young, that he needed his mother. And then she watched Milo feed Hamlet milk through a pipette he brought back from school, and she understood that the little pig had a better mother in this small boy than he'd ever have had in his pen.

Hamlet's perfect, Gran, Andrew had said. *Good peripheral vision, bad focus – they'll make the perfect team.* Lou had advised him to keep that particular insight to himself. He'd upset Sandy enough.

'I'll give you an update tomorrow,' said Milo as he stood at the door. 'How the plan's going – only ten days to go.'

Ten days until Christmas, until Milo's birthday. Lou gripped her trembling hand and squeezed it hard. She wished it were a few days closer.

36

Milo

As Milo walked out of Gran's room, he heard a crash from the next door.

He stepped closer.

Mrs Moseley's door stood ajar, just wide enough for Milo to look through. There didn't seem to be anyone in the bedroom area but there was lots more noise: another crash and the sound of water gushing and a gasp and then a loud, deep voice he recognised straight off: *We can't afford to be washing you day and night. Cleaning your bed sheets. Cleaning your clothes. Cleaning you.* The next thing Milo saw was Nurse Thornhill pulling Mrs Moseley into the bedroom.

Milo made his eyes zoom in. She didn't have her cane so she was wobbling a bit, her nightdress was sopping wet, her lips blue and chattering and her grey hair stood up in clumps. Her face looked lost like Gran's when she forgot where she was.

Nurse Thornhill ripped off Mrs Moseley's nightdress and threw it at Nurse Heidi.

Now Mrs Moseley stood naked in the middle of the room. Greyish-black hairs sprouted from under her armpits and a thin tangle, the same colour, sat on her private bits.

Milo's eyes felt like they were on fire.

The young nurse came over to the door, saw Milo and slammed it shut.

A tap on his shoulder.

'Milo? You are still here?'

Milo turned round. Petros.

'Did you see that?' asked Milo.

'See what?'

'Just now, what happened in there?' Milo nudged his head towards the door. 'What they did to Mrs Moseley?'

Petros put his arm around Milo's shoulders. 'Things are not always, how do you say it in English? How they look.'

'How they seem,' corrected Milo.

'Yes, things are not always how they seem.'

Milo thought about what Al had said. 'They are how they seem, you're just not looking properly.'

'Milo, please . . .'

'And you can leave Gran alone. She loves someone else, someone much nicer than you.'

Milo had to go and speak to Al, to tell him everything and to enlist his help in exposing Nurse Thornhill. He heard Mum's voice in his head: *Don't run, Milo.* But he shook it off, pushed into his legs and ran out of Forget Me Not as fast as he could.

37

Milo

When Milo got home he went straight to the kitchen, put four slices of toast in the toaster and switched on the kettle with melted handle from the fire. He got out two mugs, poured milk into the bottom of each one, put in two teaspoons of sugar and a teabag, filled them up, squeezed the teabag hard, dumped the teabags in the sink and then buttered the toast and topped it with Fluff. Balancing the plates and mugs on the small tray he used to use to bring things up to Gran, he clomped all the way up to the top of the house.

He'd noticed that Clouds liked to sleep in so he was worried he might get angry at being woken up, but this was urgent, and at least he'd made him breakfast.

Milo knocked on Gran's door.

No answer. His motorbike was outside, Clouds was definitely in. Milo knocked again.

A groan. A clomping across the room. And then Clouds opened the door.

Through the pinhole Milo saw that Clouds was wearing nothing but his boxer shorts. His dark hair stuck out in tufts from the top of his head and he had a big hairy chest and hairy legs and there were hairs sprouting on his toes too.

'Christ, Milo, where's the fire?'

'The fire?'

'It's not even ten o'clock.'

Milo held out the tray. 'I thought you might be hungry.' Milo never saw Clouds eat and even if he wasn't hungry, he'd have space for Fluff on toast and sweet milky tea.

Clouds gave Milo a tired, wonky smile. 'I suppose that now I'm awake, I could eat something.' He took the tray.

Milo followed Clouds into Gran's room, sat down on the edge of his bed and waited for him to have slurped some of the tea and munched through some of the toast.

'This is good,' said Clouds, licking a bit of sweet white Fluff from the corner of his mouth.

And that's when Milo told him. He started from the beginning, from when he'd first noticed that the nursing home was cold all the time and how Nurse Thornhill's flat was nice and warm and that she drank champagne while the old people had to eat slimy dumplings and about how she'd punish the old people for complaining about the food and how he'd spotted the dozy pills amongst Gran's things and then found out that her purse was missing and gone to speak to PC Stubbs, who hadn't listened, not properly, and how he hadn't been able to tell Mum either, and then today, what he'd seen happening to Mrs Moseley.

'So run this by me again, Milo. You think Nurse Thornhill is stealing the old people's money?' Clouds took another sip of tea. 'And that she's . . . ' He shook his head. 'That she's mistreating the people at Forget Me Not?'

'She's treating them really badly. And she must be stealing their money. Why else would she have all their empty purses stashed away in her private drawer?'

Clouds went over to open the window and took out another cigarette. Milo noticed that he had tidied up since he'd last been in here: his clothes were folded on Gran's chair and there weren't saucers full of cigarette butts lining the windowsill.

'Maybe PC Stubbs is right,' Clouds said.

'What?' Milo felt that hot, angry flush rising up into his cheeks again. Up to now he'd thought Clouds was on his side.

'It's important to look at things from every angle, Milo. Maybe she's keeping their money safe.'

Milo shook his head. 'She wouldn't do anything nice like that. And that doesn't excuse all the other bad stuff she's been doing.'

'Okay. And so what did PC Stubbs say before you left?'

'That he'd put it on file.'

Clouds laughed. 'Yeah, I know that line well.'

Milo dropped his shoulders. 'We have to stop her.' Milo gulped. 'Otherwise she's going to get away with it.'

Clouds nodded and smiled. 'You don't miss a thing, do you, Milo?'

When Clouds said that, Milo felt a warm glow in his chest, but then he remembered that he'd felt the same glow when PC Stubbs complimented him on working out what was going on in the crime scene video, and look how that had turned out.

Clouds stubbed out his cigarette on the outside bit of the window ledge and dropped it in the bin.

'Sounds like you've got a case, Milo.'

Milo's heart skipped a beat. 'I do?' He felt a surge of confidence. 'Well, I thought about what you said, Clouds, about the police being rubbish—'

'Well, that's not quite true, Milo. It's just that they have to stick to lots of rules and procedures which slow everything down. And they have other things to be dealing with too, like speed cameras and road accidents and people getting drunk and having a punch-up on a Saturday night – so sometimes they get distracted from the important stuff. That's why they need a helping hand.'

'Okay, so maybe they do try to get things right. But the point is that right now they're not helping us with what's going on at Forget Me Not.' He caught sight of the photographs of the women lying on Clouds's bedside table. 'Just like they're not helping those women who are being treated badly, which is why you're doing your own investigation. I thought that maybe we could do the same thing for the old people at Forget Me Not. I've already started gathering evidence with this really cool guy called Tripi, who I know you'll like, but we don't really know what we're doing.' Milo took a breath. He knew that how Clouds responded to the next bit of what he said would determine whether or not he could trust him. 'You could teach us. You could help us catch her.'

'One thing at a time, Milo. First of all, I'm not going to catch anyone – you are. Undercover reporters don't walk on each other's turf. And second, before you leap in and try to get Nurse Thornhill thrown into jail, you need to see if your theory matches up with the truth. You need to do some proper investigating.'

Milo looked at Clouds and any anger he'd felt at him being here and making Gran's room smelly and cluttered lifted. Besides Tripi, this was the first time since he could remember that someone had actually listened to him and believed him and wanted to help.

Just as Milo was thinking that, Mr Overend started whistling across the road. For a second, it felt like the old days when Milo came up here to speak to Gran.

'Now, *he*'d make a good undercover reporter,' Clouds said, leaning out of the window and giving Mr Overend a wave.

'He would?'

Clouds nodded. 'Think about everything he must see looking out onto the street day after day. I bet nothing much gets past him.'

'So will you teach me?' Milo asked. 'I mean, to be a proper undercover reporter, like you?'

Clouds smiled. 'Sure thing, Milo. Sure thing.'

38

Sandy

Sandy stood in front of the Co-op, staring at the job application form. The Christmas lights swayed above her. Andy had managed to spoil that as well: her favourite time of year, the time she associated with the joy they shared ten years ago when Milo came to them. Like the doctor said, a miracle.

As the doors swished open and shut, Sandy looked in at the women wearing green nylon fleeces and black polyester shirts. She wasn't sure she could bear it, that beep-beep-beeping all day long.

She took a breath and walked on. When she got to the corner of the high street, Sandy noticed that lights were on in the pink house. The front garden had been cleared of rubbish, the hedges trimmed back. The kitchen window was steamed up and a sweet, warm smell drifted out into the cold December air. And someone was singing a jumpy, energetic tune that sounded oddly familiar.

Perhaps Big Mike was back at last from Thailand with

Lalana, the wife he couldn't stop speaking about whenever he came to the salon to have his shoulders waxed. He'd waited and waited for her visa to come through and then, one day, he had enough: he resigned from his job, packed his bags and booked a one-way ticket to Thailand.

The front door clicked open.

'It is me, Tripi. We met the other day.'

Tripi?

The young man lurched down the front steps. Sandy had never seen anyone with such, big, clumsy feet. When he reached her he looked her up and down and smiled.

'I saw my green waterproof through the kitchen window, it suits you.'

'I'm not sure.' Sandy looked down at the green nylon that stretched over her bust and pinched at her waist. This man with the brown eyes and the thick eyelashes must be twice her height and half her weight.

'The colour,' said Tripi, 'like pistachios. It goes with your eyes.'

'Oh.' Sandy hadn't given a thought to her eyes in a long time. In some lights, the blue did look green, didn't it? Like Milo's.

'The other day when we met, I did not catch your name.'

'I'm Sandy,' she said, holding out a rain-wet hand.

Tripi laughed and held up his palms. 'Sorry, sticky fingers. I have been baking.'

A man who baked? Sandy looked up at the house. 'So you live here?'

Tripi kicked at one of the front steps with his big feet. 'For the time being.'

'Your baking smells good.'

His face lit up. 'Yes, come in, come in, you must try some.'

Sandy looked around her. 'Okay,' she said. 'Just for a moment.'

It was strange. All of Mike's things were still in his house: his pictures of Thailand, his golf equipment, a pile of mail stacked on the table in the hall.

'You're a friend of Mike's?' Sandy pointed at a photo of Mike with his pasty white arm draped around Lalana.

'We are like friends,' said Tripi, going over to the kitchen counter and taking a spatula out of the utensils pot. He eased the spatula under a sheet of sticky golden squares and prised one of them loose.

'Well, you're doing a good job looking after his house.' Sandy glanced through the door that led into the lounge. She'd never seen the place so tidy. 'It's been empty for close to a year now, I was worried that squatters might move in.'

Tripi dropped the spatula onto the floor.

'I am sorry,' he said. 'I am clumsy.'

'Me too.' Sandy smiled.

He lifted one of the golden squares from the baking tray and held it up to Sandy's mouth.

'What is it?' Sandy moved her head back a bit and felt herself blushing.

'Baklava, our national sweet.' He beamed. 'I have used my first pay cheque to buy the ingredients. Pistachios are expensive in your country.' He whistled through his teeth. 'What do they say? "A rip off".'

Sandy smelt honey and sugar and butter and warm pastry and looked at the scattering of crushed pistachio nuts on the top; they made her think of green jewels. She opened her lips and let Tripi place the parcel on her tongue. She closed her eyes, allowing the pastry to melt and the flavours to swim around in her mouth.

'You like it?'

She nodded and wiped a pistachio crumb off her lip. 'Everything should taste like this.'

'So you agree?' Tripi smiled. 'Not like your potatoes.'

'Our potatoes?'

'All you eat here are potatoes.'

Sandy laughed. 'Maybe you're right.'

Tripi arranged some more of the pastries on a plate, poured black coffee into glass tumblers and put everything on a tray. He didn't look clumsy at all, not when he was doing this.

'Come.' He held the tray above his head like a waiter. 'You can dry off from the rain.'

Sandy hung the green waterproof on the back of a kitchen chair and regretted having worn her tracksuit bottoms out of the house. She noticed a smear of chocolate Hobnob on her sweatshirt.

'Come through!' called Tripi.

She sucked in her stomach and followed him into the lounge.

Sandy stared out into the garden and then she noticed a pink mat propped up against the back door.

'Is that yours?' She went over and picked up the yoga mat.

'It was lent to me.'

'Lent to you?' She grabbed the mat, rolled it out onto the carpet and pointed at the initials in the corner. 'SM. *Sandy Moon*. That's me! What are you doing with my yoga mat?'

Tripi's eyes darted around. 'I ... I ... Like I said. It was given to me, a gift.'

'Given to you?'

'A little boy, Milo. He said I could have it, for my prayers.'

'Your prayers?'

'To Allah, my God. I am a Muslim. It was so that I did not have to pray on the sleeping bag.'

'The sleeping bag?' Sandy's head spun. Her yoga mat? Milo?

39

Milo

As he walked down the high street, Milo's eyes kept burning. Maybe they'd turn to ash like the kitchen back home. He blinked, wanting that picture of Mrs Moseley to go away.

Fairy lights and jingle bells and tinsel.

Why did everyone look so cheery? Couldn't they see what was happening?

He caught a glimpse of the advert in the bus stop, Nurse Thornhill smiling with her white teeth. He didn't care if she'd had ten fiancés and they'd all been blown to bits, no one was allowed to treat people like she did. Bad things happened to people all the time and they didn't take it out on everyone else.

Now that he was a proper undercover reporter, he had to rally the troops, get people on board who'd support his cause. His first stop: The Hairy Mansion. As soon as Mrs Hairy found out what was happening to her mum, she'd put an end to it.

Only he didn't have to walk that far.

When he got to the traffic lights outside Tony Greedy & Sons, he spotted Mrs Hairy zooming down the road in her red Mercedes.

'Stop!' He yelled, doing star jumps on the pavement to get her attention.

A bunch of carol singers walked out in front of him.

Away in a manger, no crib for his bed . . .

Who cares about Jesus's stupid bed? With God on the case, Jesus was going to get one anyway, wasn't he? What about Mrs Moseley and Gran and all the other old ladies at Forget Me Not?

The carol singers crossed the road. Mrs Hairy slowed down to let them pass.

'Excuse me.' Milo pushed through them.

The stars in the bright sky looked down where He lay . . .

'I need to get past.' He elbowed someone in the ribs, but he didn't care. He had to stop Mrs Hairy and tell her about Mrs Moseley.

'Ow! Watch where you're going.'

He found himself face to face with Jill, a woman who, before Dad left and everyone went off Mum, acted like Mum's best friend and came to use the sunbed in the shed for free.

Milo ignored her and pushed on forward.

Mrs Hairy pulled away from the zebra crossing.

Milo lurched in front of her.

Her eyes bulged and she swerved to the right, crashing the flat nose of her shiny Mercedes into a bollard outside The Cup Half Full. Milo looked at the white brushstroke scraped along the front of the car and the number plate which swung down and clunked against the tarmac.

Mrs Hairy leapt out of her Mercedes.

'What the hell are you doing?'

Milo had underestimated how close he'd got to the car and that Mrs Hairy had already picked up some speed.

'You trying to get yourself killed?'

'It's your mum. We have to get her out of Forget Me Not.'

Mrs Hairy's ears went bright pink.

'I've had just about enough of you.' She leant over and looked at the white scratch along the front of her car. 'I'll be sending a bill to your mother.'

A bill? Mum couldn't afford to pay the bills she had, let alone a new one for hundreds of pounds. But that wasn't important, not compared to what Milo had to tell Mrs Hairy.

'You have to listen to me.'

Clouds had said to go slowly, to be discreet, and Milo had planned to do that but somehow, bumping into Mrs Hairy like this in the middle of Slipton high street, everything had spun out of control.

The carol singers, who'd stopped singing when Milo nearly got run over, gathered around the car and started up again. Opportunists, that's what Dad called people who tried to get money out of you the minute you had your defences down.

Bless all the dear children in Thy tender care . . .

'Just shut up, will you!' yelled Mrs Hairy.

Milo nodded in agreement.

The carol singers went quiet, except an old man at the back who hadn't heard. *And take us to Heaven to live with Thee there*, he croaked. Someone must have poked him because he stopped. They looked at each other and shuffled their feet and walked off down the pavement.

Milo followed Mrs Hairy as she got back into the driver's seat.

'I saw your mum – they were being horrible. You need to come and rescue her.'

Mrs Hairy continued to ignore Milo. She strapped herself in and lowered the window.

Then she let out a heavy sigh. 'I know you miss your gran, but you can't go around making these wild accusations.' She leant forward and her face softened a bit. 'Your grandma needs professional help now. Keeping her at home wasn't good for any of you. It's for the best, Milo.'

Mrs Hairy hadn't got a clue. The only person who knew how to look after Gran was Milo and the only thing that would be *for the best* would be for Gran to come home.

'Please come with me, I'll show you, it won't take long.'

'I'm late.' She started the engine.

What could be so important that she didn't have time to check that her mum was okay?

'I'm sure whoever it is can wait.'

Mrs Hairy let out a snort as though it was the stupidest thing she'd ever heard. 'There are some people you can't keep waiting, Milo.'

Mrs Hairy closed the car window and started the engine.

Milo banged on the glass. 'Your mum's more important than a stupid celebrity getting their tea.' He banged again. 'They'll find someone to cover for you, you have to come with me—'

But Mrs Hairy didn't hear Milo. She'd already pulled away from the bollard. Her number plate fell off the front of her car with a clunk.

40

Milo

At the end of the garden, Milo pushed through a gap in the fence.

'Tripi!' he called out.

He took long strides across the grass and walked straight into the lounge.

And then he noticed that there were two people standing in the lounge, staring at him. Through the pinhole he noticed a set of chipped pink nails.

'Mum?'

'You are his mother?' Tripi looked from Milo to Mum and then sat down on the sofa and let out a long, slow breath.

What was Mum doing here and how did she know Tripi?

'Of course I'm his mother. What on earth are you doing here, Milo?'

Milo's felt his eyes go dark. He was tired of looking out onto the world and finding things he didn't like. Sometimes he wished his eyes would hurry up and go blind altogether.

'Tripi's my friend, you shouldn't be here,' he said.

'Your friend? What are you talking about?'

Tripi stood up. 'Your mother is my friend too, Milo.'

'I am?' Sandy stared at Tripi.

'You are both my friends.'

The ringtone from Milo's phone sounded. Sandy looked to Milo but when she worked out the noise wasn't coming from him, she turned back to Tripi.

'Why does Tripi have your phone?' she asked.

Tripi held up Milo's phone. 'It is your father, he has been calling you.'

'Dad?' Milo leapt forward and grabbed the phone.

As he waited for an answer, he noticed Mum's shoulders sink. Whenever he asked why Dad never called, she said it was because he was busy looking after the baby. He noticed the rash inching up her throat. This morning, he'd watched her spreading calamine lotion over it until her throat ended up looking like a body part for a Madame Tussauds statue.

'He's hung up,' said Milo, staring down at the phone. He swiped his fingers over the screen. 'And the number's blocked.'

'He will call again,' said Tripi. 'He wants to talk to you.'

'You spoke to Dad?'

'Only briefly. I explained I was your friend and looking after your phone, but I don't think he understood.'

'Of course he didn't bloody understand. My son's friend? How old are you? You shouldn't be picking up young boys and taking them into your home. You could be arrested for that.' The red rash spread into her cheeks.

'Mum, Tripi's not like that. Tripi's—'

'It is okay, Milo.' Tripi stood up and cleared his throat. 'I am twenty-four and I work at Forget Me Not and I know Mrs Moon – Old Mrs Moon, not you. Milo came to me. But if you do not want us to be friends, I understand. In my country it is the same: the mother always decides.'

'No, she doesn't. She doesn't get to decide.' Milo rubbed his eyes; they felt raw and bloodshot. Red dots swam in front of him. 'She made Dad go away and now she doesn't even have a job and no one's paying the bills, and I keep trying to tell her things about that horrible place where she put Gran, but she won't listen. She never has time to listen. So she doesn't get to decide *anything*.'

Mum stepped backwards.

Tripi stood staring at Milo.

'I ... I think I'll go.' Mum turned and walked back through the kitchen.

'Stay and have some more baklava and some coffee,' Tripi called after her. 'We can talk, the three of us.'

But Mum didn't listen. She walked through the front door and a moment later she stepped out onto the pavement into the rain, the green waterproof sitting inside on the back of a kitchen chair.

41

Tripi

As the Lovely Sandy disappeared through the front door, Milo walked out through the back door. Tripi had upset both his new English friends, though he didn't quite understand why.

'Milo,' he called after him. 'Please stay.'

When Milo reached the gap in the fence he stopped but did not turn round.

'Do not be angry, Milo.'

Tripi came and stood behind him. He wanted to touch his shoulder but then he thought about what the Lovely Sandy had said: about Tripi being too old to have a friend like Milo and how it had made Tripi feel sick in his stomach, like the smell of the potatoes at Forget Me Not.

He had not once thought about their ages, that he was twenty-four and that Milo was nine and that their friendship could be seen as strange. *You're barking up the wrong tree,* that's what he wanted to say to Milo's mother. But sometimes people did not like his phrases and she was already angry with him.

'You went behind my back,' said Milo, twisting a laurel leaf between his fingers until the green flesh was crumpled and bruised.

'I do not understand.'

'You're just like Mrs Harris, you went and told my mum.' Milo threw the leaf onto the grass. 'I can't trust anyone.'

Tripi heard a wobble in Milo's voice and, although it was in English, it was the same wobble he used to hear in Ayishah's voice when she was upset about something.

'Please, Milo, I did not know she was your mother.'

Milo turned round. He fixed his eyes on Tripi, his little mouth set hard. 'So you're saying it's a coincidence, that you were sitting having coffee with Mum in the house I found for you?'

Tripi shrugged. 'Allah works in mysterious ways.'

'Well, I don't like the sound of Allah.'

Ayishah had once said that, too. When their parents explained that they had to leave, that Tripi would look after her until they were together again, they told her to trust Allah that all would be well. And she turned round and said: *If Allah's so great, you wouldn't have to leave at all.*

Sometimes Tripi struggled with his faith, but Allah was the one good thing he had left to hang onto.

'I saw your mother standing in the rain looking at the house, and we got talking and I asked her to come in.' Tripi thought that telling Milo he had met her at Forget Me Not the other night would confuse things.

'You didn't know that she was my mum?' Milo's eyes and his mouth softened. 'You really didn't?'

214

'I really did not know, Milo.' Then a big smile spread across Tripi's face. 'Though if you had told me that you had such a beautiful mother . . .' He allowed himself to ruffle Milo's hair.

Milo scratched his head.

'Come on, let us go in and you can taste some of my baklava. Your mother liked them, maybe you can bring some home to her.'

They walked back down through the garden and into the house.

'I have some good evidence, it will make you happy.'

'Recorded on the phone?'

Tripi nodded.

'I saw something today, Tripi, with Mrs Moseley and it was horrible. And I talked to Clouds and he's going to teach us to be proper undercover reporters. Once we're finished with her, Nurse Thornhill will be running away from Forget Me Not as fast as her legs will carry her.'

'Nurse Thornhill has been shortlisted for The Greater London Nursing Home Awards and the inspectors are coming on Tuesday to help them with their decision.'

Milo turned round and his face burst into life. 'There are inspectors coming on Tuesday? To Forget Me Not?'

Tripi nodded.

'That's perfect.' He bounced on his feet. 'We can show them what it's really like, we can tell them about Nurse Thornhill and how horrible she is and get the patients to talk about how they are treated and she'll be exposed and they'll take her away. We have to start planning now.'

'Planning?'

'What you're going to do to make sure that they find out about her.'

215

'Me?'

'I have to go to school, Tripi. I got into loads of trouble for not showing up the other day. I'll help you with all the preparations but you have to be in charge on the day.'

Tripi sat down on the couch and sipped at his coffee that had now gone cold.

'These inspectors, Milo, are they like the police?'

'Kind of.'

Tripi stared at his big feet and shook his head. 'Then I cannot help you.'

'They're not the real police. But they have the power to do things, like we have inspectors who come into school and if our teachers aren't teaching us properly they can report to the Head and the school gets a warning and if it's really bad it might even get closed down.'

Tripi still didn't like the sound of having to deal with these inspectors.

'I am in a delicate situation, Milo, I need to keep my job. If you want me to take photos and make recordings, I will do that, but that is all. The police cannot find out about me ... ' He had hoped not to have to tell Milo, he didn't want his new friend to think of him as a criminal.

'Find out about what, Tripi? You're worried they'll think you're a terrorist, because of your backpacks?'

An illegal immigrant was bad enough, but a terrorist? And, if Nurse Thornhill got her way, a mobile phone thief too.

'I could explain that you're a nice Muslim, that you pray for good things, for your sister and for Gran and for me, and that you're not interested in blowing up the Americans.'

Tripi suddenly felt very tired. Part of him wished that he

216

had never met this Milo and the Lovely Sandy and Old Mrs Moon, and that he still lived in the park with his sleeping bag. Things were simpler then.

'Milo, I must tell you a secret and you must promise me to keep it to yourself.'

'Okay. Except if you are a terrorist, I'll have to tell someone, otherwise I could go to jail for withholding information.'

'I'm not a terrorist, Milo, I'm a refugee. I think I am allowed to be here because my country is at war, but I have not filled out the papers yet. I do not even have a work visa.'

'But you work at Forget Me Not and you look after the old people and you're a really good cook and you're nice. Once they see what you're like, they'll let you stay.'

'I'm afraid it is not so easy, Milo. If the police find out that I have not been following the rules, they might lock me up or send me back to Syria.'

'The police in Slipton won't do that. If you explain what happened, they'll understand. Anyway, I don't think they'd even notice, they're too busy filling out forms for their filing cabinets.'

'I don't think the police in Slipton will have much of a choice. It is the big police in London, the police who decide who gets to stay in the UK and who has to leave.'

Milo came and sat on the sofa and took Tripi's hand in the way that he took Mrs Moon's hand at Forget Me Not.

'Well, we'll just have to make sure they don't find out, then, won't we?'

Tripi looked at Milo's hopeful face and knew he couldn't say no.

'Okay, Milo, you win. But we must be careful.'

He thought about Ayishah and about how he hoped that maybe someone out there was helping her, like he was trying to help Milo. He believed in these things, that there were threads that connected all the good people in the world and that it was the good people's job to make those threads stronger.

'So did my Dad really call?'

'Yes. Is that not usual?'

'He hasn't called since he left. Mum said he was busy and that we should give him some time.'

Tripi remembered what Milo had told him about his father being in Abu Dhabi, not so far from Syria. It began to make sense now.

'So your mother and father are no longer together?'

Milo shook his head. 'It was my fault.'

'I do not think that can be—'

Milo interrupted. 'I found Dad with someone else, and then I fell off my bike so everyone found about it and when my eyes got bad, Dad's Tart got pregnant and then he left. If it weren't for me, Dad would still be here.'

Tripi found it difficult to follow, maybe it was the English.

'Did he leave a number?' asked Milo.

Tripi thought about the Lovely Sandy and how she had not been happy when he mentioned the phone call from Mr Moon. He shook his head.

Milo rubbed his eyes again and sniffed. Although Tripi did not like the idea of there being a Mr Moon, even if he was far away, he could see that Milo missed his father and that was something he understood.

'Your father wanted to discuss Christmas.'

'He did?' Milo's voice lifted.

'Yes. "I need to talk to Milo about Christmas." That's what he said.'

Milo flung his arms around Tripi and squeezed him so hard that Tripi had to loosen the grip of the little boy's fingers so that he could breathe.

'It's all going to be okay,' said Milo, picking up a piece of baklava. 'This is going to be the best Christmas-Birthday ever.'

42

Lou

Lou's eyes fell on the advent calendar propped up on the windowsill. A present from Milo. *To help you remember the dates, Gran*, he'd said. *It's the same as mine. So you can open it here and I can open it at home and it'll be like we're together.*

So he had noticed that too, how the days were slipping out of her mind.

Lou reached out. Her fingers fumbled at the cardboard window, trembling. Numb or shaking and nothing in between. The small battles fought inside her body.

But not to have the strength to open a child's advent calendar?

She reached out again and the calendar fell – a clatter of plastic and cardboard against the thin carpet.

Lou had been able to haul in nets twice her weight, to keep the fishing boat steady in the wind that swept off the Inverary coast.

And now?

She shook her hand, willing it to work. Her fingers trembled harder. *Mocking me, are you?* Both hands now, like a comedy duo; the jazz hands of an old woman.

She hadn't been able to concentrate on a thing since Milo left yesterday. His eyes so wide and sad. How could she tell him that the fondness she had for Petros was a world apart from the love she had for him, her little Milo, her brave soldier? Petros brightened her days, warmed up her cold room. He made her laugh. If Milo gave him a chance, he would like him too.

Lou looked down at the seventeenth of December.

Below her on the street, the front door slammed.

Milo? Is that you?

She willed her legs to go stiff, the blood so slow to move these days, and pushed herself up and leant out of the window.

The white shadow had turned dark. A long black coat, a black hat pulled down low over her grey hair, a bunch of lilies in her black-gloved hands.

'Mrs Moon?' A knock on the door. 'Mrs Moon?'

Nurse Heidi stood at the door and then came over and stared out of the window.

'I'll be holding the fort today. Nurse Thornhill's taken the day off, she's escaping to London.'

Lou reached for her pad.

Where is she going? She nudged her head towards the window.

Nurse Heidi hesitated. 'She's off to Harrods. She lost someone there – the 1983 bombings, I believe. There's a photograph in her flat.'

Lou nodded. She remembered reading that in the papers –

news from London always made it to Inverary: thirty years ago today. She closed her eyes. Was it the article she was seeing now? Or was she confusing things again?

Six people killed . . . she remembered that.

'I think it was her fiancé,' Nurse Heidi said.

Yes, six people killed. And a young nurse on her lunch break coming to meet her fiancé the journalist, Philip May, twenty-four. She'd remembered the story because it had reminded her of David, how she too had lost the man she loved who'd been promised to her for life.

Nurse Heidi leant further towards the window. 'Looks a bit like a crow, doesn't she? All that black?' She laughed and took Lou's elbow. 'Anyway, enough of this gloom and doom. We're going to have a nice day.' She steered Lou towards the wardrobe. 'Let's find you something colourful to wear, something to put a smile on Mr Spiteri's face.'

43

Milo

After school on Monday, Milo went straight to Forget Me Not. At lunchtime, he'd called Tripi from the payphone outside the canteen to ask when Nurse Thornhill was due back from her trip to London, but no one seemed to know, not even Nurse Heidi, so they couldn't risk waiting a minute. She could sweep back in at any moment and before that, Milo had to make sure everything was ready for the big day.

It was already dark as Milo skipped down the high street. Looking up through the pinhole at the pale moon, nearly full now, he felt a buzz of excitement in his tummy. He was like William the Conqueror gathering his troops before battle. Clouds had taught Milo that he had to organise a briefing meeting: *everyone has to know what their role is*. He said that it was *essential to the successful execution of a plan*. And Milo was determined that his plan would be successful. By this time tomorrow the inspectors would be marching Nurse Thornhill out of Forget Me Not, never to return.

'You're sure this is the best place to meet?' Milo asked Tripi as he looked around the cold, dark storeroom behind the kitchen.

Tripi nodded. 'She never comes in here. The van delivers the goods to the kitchen door and I load up the shelves.'

Milo scanned the rows of dusty steel cans. Tinned lamb and tinned beef and tinned mushy peas and tinned carrots. No wonder all the food on the old people's plates looked the same. The labels were black and white with an **ECONOMY** logo printed on the top next to a pound sign. They didn't have any colour or any pictures of the food inside like the cheap ones Mum bought from the supermarket.

Milo noticed that Tripi was blushing and staring at his big feet.

'I try my best to make them nice food, but what can I do? The only fresh thing in this kitchen are the potatoes.' His gaze flicked over the big hessian bags of white potatoes. Even they had the **ECONOMY** logo stamped onto them.

Milo took one of Tripi's big hands and squeezed it tight. 'Don't worry, Tripi. At home Mum only makes microwave meals, which isn't much better than eating out of tins. And anyway, once we've got rid of Nurse Thornhill, we'll get you a proper job in a nice restaurant and one day, when you're a famous chef and you have your own kitchen, you can order in all the fresh food you want and famous people will come and eat the yummy things from your menu.'

Tripi looked up from his feet and gave Milo a sad smile. 'You speak like my sister, Ayishah.'

'Well then, Ayishah must be right. Now, let's gather every-one for the meeting.'

They divided up the old people between them. Tripi went

to get Mrs Turner, Mrs Wong and Mrs Swift and Milo collected the others.

'Hello, Milo!' Nurse Heidi waved from the end of the corridor.

Milo stopped still, his arm clamped under Mrs Moseley's. He turned round slowly.

Nurse Heidi came up to Milo. 'Your gran's on good form today, she'll be pleased to see you.'

'I'll see her later,' said Milo.

'Where are you taking Mrs Moseley?'

Milo had debated with Clouds about whether or not to involve Nurse Heidi but they decided it was too risky. She was being trained to be a nurse by Nurse Thornhill so maybe she was more on her side that she let on. They couldn't risk her telling Nurse Thornhill about the plan and spoiling everything.

'I'm taking Mrs Moseley to the lounge,' said Milo. 'She's going to help me with a school project on the Caribbean.'

Mrs Moseley held up her tape player. 'Yes, the music of Jamaica.'

'Don't forget to say hi to your gran.' Nurse Heidi smiled and walked on.

Milo and Mrs Moseley waited until she'd disappeared round a bend in the corridor and then took off towards the kitchens.

One by one Milo and Tripi sat the old ladies on the plastic crates in the storeroom.

'It's like a bunker!' exclaimed Mrs Swift, looking around at concrete walls and the concrete floor and the tiny dusty window right at the top.

Milo had learnt about bunkers at school, they were the

places people went during the war to keep out of the way of the bombs.

He got out the list he'd made with Clouds.

'So, Mrs Turner, when the inspectors come and shake your hand, you're going to show them your pockets.'

Mrs Turner stood up as if she was in class and held open one of her pockets. 'I've got it all ready now.'

As Milo looked down into the grey mushy peas and bits of potato, his tummy churned. 'Brilliant, thank you, Mrs Turner. Just make sure you wear that same dress tomorrow.' He hoped that Nurse Thornhill wouldn't make her change it.

'Mrs Wong, you're going to talk about the menu, how there's never any rice, even though it's your favourite food.'

Mrs Wong nodded.

Milo thought that maybe the inspectors wouldn't mind much about the rice so he'd planned another job for her too. 'And make sure Mrs Foxton comes out of her room and talks about her conservatory and how Nurse Thornhill never listens to her.' Milo reckoned that if you were a nurse, you were meant to listen to old people, even if they didn't make sense. The inspectors should know that Nurse Thornhill never had time for the old ladies.

'Savages!' Mrs Foxton exclaimed. 'Breaking my windows. Stealing things.' She shook her fist.

Mrs Swift raised her hand. She reminded Milo a bit of Nadja at school: always wanting to get things right. 'And I'll tell the inspectors how Nurse Thornhill stole my make-up bag while I was doing Mrs Zimmer's eyeshadow. She yanked it right out of my hand.' Mrs Swift rubbed her fingers along her wrist. 'And she still hasn't given it back.'

As well as listening to the old people, it was Nurse Thornhill's job to help them be happy and doing other people's make-up was what made Mrs Swift happy. Plus, she shouldn't be allowed to confiscate personal belongings from her patients, not when they hadn't done anything wrong. Milo had briefed Tripi to show the inspectors the **KEEP OUT** drawer. He didn't want to bring it up in front of the old ladies in case it upset them.

'And I'll tell them how she stole my iPad,' chipped in Mrs Sharp. 'She said she was sick of hearing the Angry Birds theme tune, even though I turn the sound really low not to upset her.' That was mean too, because the iPad was a present from Mrs Sharp's godson and playing Angry Birds made Mrs Sharp happy like it made Mrs Swift happy to do people's make-up.

Mrs Zimmer sat on her crate, swaying in and out of sleep. She'd be too sleepy to talk to the inspectors, but Tripi would explain how Nurse Thornhill didn't always wake Mrs Zimmer up for meals and that Mrs Zimmer got really cold sitting in the lounge all day without the heating on. Milo also suspected that Nurse Thornhill gave Mrs Zimmer too many of those green and white dozy pills.

Milo scanned down his list. On their own, these things weren't that bad, but once Mrs Moseley came out with the wet patch on the back of her dress and the bruises on her arms, they'd have to see that something was wrong.

'Mrs Moseley, you're ready too?' asked Milo.

Mrs Moseley nodded. Her cheeks shone.

'You'll tell them about the cold baths?'

A picture of Mrs Moseley standing in the middle of her room, shivering, flickered in front of Milo's pinhole. He stood up straight and took a breath.

'We have to show the inspectors what it's really like here, and how Nurse Thornhill treats you all. But it's really important that you don't let on, not before they get here.'

The old ladies looked at Milo and nodded.

'Where's Lou?' Tripi asked. 'And Petros?'

Milo stared up at the bare, dusty light bulb swinging from the ceiling. He'd hoped that no one would notice they weren't here.

Tripi and the old ladies looked at Milo and waited for an answer.

'They're busy,' Milo said. And it was true. Gran was busy smelling that stupid rose of his and Petros was busy sucking up to Gran. They were so wrapped up in each other that they probably didn't get half of what was going on at Forget Me Not.

Mrs Moseley broke the silence. 'Tomorrow, we'll have a party!' She turned up the volume on her tape recorder. Bob Marley's voice boomed out. It was so sunny and bouncy that even sleepy Mrs Zimmer seemed to sway to a different rhythm.

Let's get together and feel all right.

Milo felt his heart lifting. Everyone was on board: his plan was going to be a success.

Then Tripi stumbled to the stockroom door.

'What is it?' Milo asked.

Tripi put his index finger to his mouth. Milo went over and turned down the volume on Mrs Moseley's tape recorder.

Footsteps; quick, squeaky footsteps.

'It's Nurse Thornhill!' exclaimed Mrs Wong. 'She's coming!'

Mrs Swift gasped.

The door flew open.

Nurse Heidi's small figure stood in the doorframe.

Milo didn't know whether or not to be relieved. At least it wasn't Nurse Thornhill but if Nurse Heidi told on them, it might just as well have been.

'I was wondering where you'd all got to,' said Nurse Heidi. She closed the door behind her and came to sit next to Mrs Swift on one of the crates of tinned tomatoes. 'So, are you going to fill me in on the plan?'

For a moment, everyone was silent. Milo looked at Tripi to check his reaction. His mouth was half smiling and half worried, as though he wanted to believe that Nurse Heidi being here was a good thing but didn't quite trust himself.

'We're going to catch the witch,' said Mrs Moseley. 'We're going to show those inspectors what that nasty white witch is really like.'

Milo and Tripi and all the old ladies looked at Nurse Heidi, waiting for her to respond.

Nurse Heidi brushed down the skirt of her uniform, looked up at them and said: 'So, what's my job then?'

44

Milo

Milo snapped the chocolate out of the plastic casing. A picture of Mary and Joseph knocking on the door of the Inn, Mary's belly as big as The Tart's before she left for Abu Dhabi with Dad.

Tuesday eighteenth of December: eight days until Christmas.

He packed his bag for school and skipped downstairs, whistling Great-Gramps's bagpipe song.

'You seem happy,' said Mum, scooping yellow powder out of her SlimFast tin.

Milo nodded and sat down at the kitchen counter. He watched Mum pouring skimmed milk into a cocktail shaker.

'Can I have one of those?'

'It's not for kids.'

'It looks like a milkshake.'

'Well, it is, sort of. It's milkshake medicine.'

During one of their rows, Dad had told Mum that his Tart was a size zero. *She has this amazing metabolism*, he said, like it was a talent. Mum had run out of the room, crying. Milo thought that size zero sounded pretty pointless, like saying size nothing, which didn't make sense because no one was size nothing otherwise they'd be invisible. Anyway, since then, Mum had been on a diet, taking pills that made her jittery and drinking shakes, but she kept eating Hobnobs too, so the diet wasn't working. Mum couldn't fit into any of her old clothes and when she sat down on the kitchen stool, her thighs bulged over the edge.

'Here, you can have some Fluff on your toast.' Mum thumped down the jar on the counter.

Before, when Dad was still at home and Gran was living upstairs and Milo's eyes hadn't gone wrong, Fluff had only been allowed for special occasions because it was bad for his teeth.

'So you're going to wear your special glasses today? To help you read the board?'

They'd been through all this yesterday.

'And you're going to tell Mrs Harris if you're struggling?'

Milo took a gulp of orange juice. 'Yes.'

Mum's eyes went narrow. 'You okay, Milo?'

'Fine.'

'You just seem . . . I don't know.' Mum shook the cocktail shaker and then poured the yellow frothy liquid into a glass.

A bit of Milo wanted to tell Mum about the plan and how today was the big day, how they were going to catch Nurse Thornhill. But he was worried she might go in and ruin everything. Anyway, she was still acting weird about him being friends with Tripi.

Mum took a sip of her shake, pulled her mouth back over her teeth like she'd sucked on a bit of lemon.

'I'd better go,' said Milo, jumping down off the stool.

'Wait a minute.' Mum came over and held Milo's chin up and looked straight into his eyes. 'Now, don't let them put you in their special unit. I've called the Head and he's made me a promise, but that teacher of yours . . .'

She'd said that yesterday too.

Milo nodded. 'Don't worry, it'll be fine, Mum.'

Mum gave Milo a kiss on the forehead and said 'I love you' against his skin.

'Love you too, Mum.'

When the time was right, he was going to tell her about being an undercover reporter at Forget Me Not, but first, he wanted to put everything in place. When he stood back he saw that her eyes were all shiny. Maybe living with Mum wasn't so bad after all.

All day Milo tried to hold down the excited feeling that had been growing in his tummy ever since Tripi mentioned the inspectors. They'd made the perfect plan. Everyone knew what they had to do. By the end of today, Nurse Thornhill would be out of Forget Me Not.

At school, Milo wore his glasses, like Mum said, and let Mrs Harris know when he was having trouble with a sum or with a word or when his eyes were so tired that he couldn't take in any more writing. But every spare minute he got, Milo's brain whizzed around with pictures of what must be happening at Forget Me Not.

Of Nurse Thornhill being handcuffed and dragged out through the front door and of everyone cheering and saying

Well done Tripi, which Milo wouldn't mind, even though the plan had been his and Clouds's idea. And he imagined the police showing up with their flashing blue lights and how they'd be so impressed with what Tripi had done that they'd help him find Ayishah.

It might take a day or two to get in touch with the old people's families but soon they'd all be picked up, like Mrs Moseley who'd go and live with Mrs Hairy in the Hairy Mansion and the horrible white nursing home would be shut down and Gran would come home.

Milo felt a bit bad that Clouds wouldn't have a room any more, especially as he'd been teaching Milo all about what it takes to be an undercover reporter, but he could stay in Milo's room until he found a new home. And anyway, he was always out at night so he must have another place to go to.

At three thirty, as soon as the school bell sounded, Milo speed-walked straight to Forget Me Not.

Nurse Thornhill stood at the top of the steps leading to the front door of Forget Me not, her white teeth gleaming.

Milo crouched by the railing, watching and listening.

'It's been a pleasure,' said a man with a grey suit and fuzzy grey hair.

'If only everyone took so much pride in their work, this country would be a better place,' added a tubby bald guy with a clipboard.

'You're in with a strong chance,' said a third man with a faded black suit and gelled hair.

'More than a chance,' fuzzy grey-haired guy said.

'We probably shouldn't tell you this, but you're the horse

everyone's backing,' said the bald guy. 'No one's as good as you, Ruth.' And then he winked at her.

Nurse Thornhill held her fingers to her chest and said, 'Oh, goodness . . . really . . . I am flattered.' She was back in her starched white uniform and she wore lipstick and eye shadow and blusher and when she touched the black-suit guy's arm, her cheeks went pink.

'We're very grateful,' black-suit guy said.

'No, I'm the one who has to thank you. It was so good of you to come and visit our little family.' Nurse Thornhill's voice was fake-soft, like Mr Whippy ice cream that melted on your tongue before you had the chance to taste it.

'It would be great if you got a little film ready to show the home at its best. Patient interviews, that kind of thing,' said the gelled-hair guy. 'If you win, the film will be broadcast at the ceremony.'

'I'll try to find someone to do that.'

'We'll see you on Friday night, then,' said the bald guy. 'Make sure you have your acceptance speech polished.' Another wink.

Milo sat back, his head ached. Everything was happening backwards: they were meant to be handcuffing Nurse Thornhill and taking her away. And where was the police car? And the cheering? And where was Tripi?

Nurse Thornhill went back inside and Milo watched the three men drive away.

As he walked into the front hall of Forget Me Not, Milo smelt roses and air freshener. Heat blasted so hard out of the radiators that he had to take off his duffel coat. He went straight to the kitchens.

Milo dumped his school bag on the kitchen floor and heard a crunch. His glasses. He'd been so quick to leave the last lesson, that he hadn't put them back in their case.

'What happened, Tripi?'

Tripi wiped his hands on his white apron and shook his head. 'I am sorry, Milo.'

'What do you mean, you're sorry?'

'The plan did not work.'

'How . . . I mean . . . why . . . ?'

'Early this morning, when my shift started, Nurse Thornhill came in and talked to the patients, all of them together, in the lounge. She promised them nice things if she won the prize. She said she would use the prize money to make their rooms beautiful and to get them nice food. And she said they would be proud to be at the best nursing home in Greater London.'

'And they believed her?'

'I think they were scared, Milo. If the plan didn't work, they were the ones who would be in trouble.'

'But the plan would've worked, it was *foolproof*.' Milo felt his voice coming out higher and higher like a squeaky violin.

'The old people get scared more than you or me, Milo. They worry that they won't have anywhere to go.'

'What about the evidence? Didn't you show them that?'

Tripi shook his head. 'I am sorry, Milo, but I have to keep my job. When all the old people decided that they were going to say nice things about Nurse Thornhill and Forget Me Not and when Heidi told the inspectors that Nurse Thornhill was the best person she had ever worked with and when all those nurses turned up from the other Forget Me Not homes to make the place look beautiful and acted like they were here all the time to look after the old people, I got worried. If it is only you saying something against all the other people, you get in trouble. That is what I learnt from Syria.'

Milo watched Tripi's face come in and out of focus until he was just a blur. Milo rubbed his eyes. What was he saying? That the inspectors didn't suspect a thing?

'What about Mrs Moseley?'

Milo had gone through the story with her over and over: all the things he'd seen that day when he walked past her room, and the other things he hadn't seen that happened in the bathroom. Everything apart from the naked bit, which he thought would make Mrs Moseley feel embarrassed.

'Nurse Thornhill locked her in.'

'Where?'

'In her room. She told the inspectors that Mrs Moseley was sleeping because she needed her rest.'

Milo turned round and walked to the swing doors.

'Milo . . . ' Tripi called after him.

'I thought I could trust you,' said Milo. 'I thought you'd understand.'

45

Tripi

'Milo! Your bag!' Tripi pushed through the swing doors, holding Milo's school bag, but Milo had already disappeared.

'Ah, Tahir.' Nurse Thornhill walked towards him from the other end of the corridor. 'Just the person.'

Petros walked a few steps behind her holding a video camera.

'Our chef has worked in some of the world's best hotels.' Nurse Thornhill turned and showed her stretched smile to the camera. 'Tahir is part of the Forget Me Not family.'

Her voice sounded like one of the political broadcasts in Syria. Both sides did the same: called the people of Syria *brothers and sisters*, told them that they were *part of the Syrian family*. As long as they obeyed, of course.

'Here we are, the kitchen. Food is so important to our clients.' She pushed past Tripi.

Petros followed.

'Hygienic. Purpose built. As you can see, we've had a feast

today.' Nurse Thornhill swept her arm across the work counters, which were littered with the leftovers of cakes and canapés. First thing this morning she had made Tripi go and collect them from The Cup Half Full on the high street.

'Tahir, why don't you tell us about your speciality? What you love cooking most.'

Tripi stood in front of the camera, blinking. Potatoes. That's all he could think of: pale, sweaty potatoes.

'Tahir?' Nurse Thornhill said through her clenched smile. 'The camera's waiting.' Then she turned to Petros. 'You said we could edit, didn't you?'

Petros nodded.

'So Tahir, tell us about your favourite dish.'

'*Mezze.*'

'No, no. Petros, turn it off. Tahir, we need you to say English things. Victoria sponge cake, shepherd's pie, lemon meringue.' She waved her hand at the camera. 'It's for the awards ceremony.' She sighed and turned to Petros. 'I'll leave you to it, Mr Spiteri, I've got work to do. Make sure you show me the video when you're done.'

Petros nodded and Nurse Thornhill swept out of the kitchen, just as she had swept in that morning just before the inspectors arrived.

We'd hate them to find out about your little immigration problem, wouldn't we, Tahir? She had smiled while she said it, her teeth glowing under the kitchen strip lights. *To lose your job after only a couple of weeks? To be sent home with all those bombs going off?*

On Monday, when she came back from London with red eyes looking pale and tired as though she had been to a funeral, Tripi had felt sorry for her. But it was like she put

238

that person away along with the black coat and the black gloves.

He should have been courageous. *Taken the bull by the horns* and spoken to those inspectors, regardless of Nurse Thornhill's threats. Milo was right, he had let him down, he had let everyone down. Ayishah would be ashamed of him.

'Isn't that Milo's bag?' asked Petros, looking at Tripi's hands.

Tripi went back to the sink to finish his washing up. He did not want to talk to Petros. Not telling the inspectors the truth was one thing, but making a propaganda film for Nurse Thornhill?

'Tripi? Don't you want to talk to the camera?'

Tripi plunged his hands into the hot water and shook his head. He scrubbed at a pan.

'I thought we were friends, Tripi? Both foreigners cast away on this strange island.'

Tripi turned round, his face red from scrubbing.

'You don't see the truth of what is happening?' asked Tripi. 'You want to help Nurse Thornhill?'

Petros took his hands off the camera and let it dangle against his chest. 'It is not so simple.'

In Tripi's experience, when people said that, it usually meant that things were very simple – only that they didn't like the simplicity. Like when Tripi begged the soldiers from the Free Syrian Army to help him find Ayishah, showing them the photograph. Like when he'd gone to the government and told them over and over that Ayishah was too young to be walking around on her own, that she'd be scared with all those bombs going off and that they had to help him find her.

But the soldiers had not bothered to look at the photo and the government officials had thrown Tripi out of the building.

Both sides had said the same thing: they had more important things to worry about, they did not have time to search for a little girl.

'Even Milo sees it, Petros.'

'Milo is upset that Louisa is not at home and that she and I are friends.'

Tripi looked for a sign from the old man: did he not understand that there was more at stake than a little boy wanting his gran?

'You are not brave, Petros.'

Petros took off his yellow cap and rubbed his bald patch. 'Maybe I am not brave. Or maybe I do not have a choice.' He twisted his cap between his hands.

No wonder it was so frayed, thought Tripi, all that twisting. It is what people did when they were scared, like when Ayishah poked her thumbs through the cotton sleeves of her school jumper when there were gunshots in the streets of Damascus or when Milo pulled at the straps on his school bag as he talked about Old Mrs Moon or when Lovely Sandy twisted the hem on the waterproof he had lent her when she was not sure whether to come into the house.

'Petros, are you afraid?'

Petros pulled his shoulders back and puffed out his chest. 'Afraid? Why would a Greek man be afraid?' And then he slumped his shoulders. 'It is like I said, Tripi, I do not have a choice.'

'There is always a choice, Petros. Always.'

'It is easy for you to say, my friend – you are young, you do

240

not depend on anyone. But one day you will know how this feels.'

Tripi thought that he would like to be old enough to feel what Petros felt. Many of the people from his homeland would never reach his age. Some children would never finish school.

Looking past Petros's blank face, Tripi noticed a label on Milo's bag. His name: *Milo Moon*, and his address: *7 Crescent Way*.

'I've got to go,' he said, wiping his hands on a dishcloth.

On his way out of Forget Me Not, Tripi saw Nurse Thornhill talking to Nurse Heidi and hid behind the corner to watch and listen.

'I warned you.' Nurse Thornhill stood over Heidi, her hands on her hips.

Heidi sniffed, her eyes red and swollen. 'I'm sorry.'

Had he found out that Nurse Heidi had been involved in their discussions on Monday?

'You let me down today,' said Nurse Thornhill.

'I didn't mean to.' Tears dropped out of her eyes and onto her cheeks like her eyes were raining.

'If you've cost me the award ...' Nurse Thornhill sucked in her breath.

'I'll explain to the inspectors that it was my fault.' Nurse Heidi wiped her nose on her sleeve.

'Forgetting to wash your hands after you've handled a client – such a basic, basic thing, Heidi. Did you see how they made a note of it?'

'Maybe if you tell them that I'm a trainee, that I'm meant to get things wrong.'

'You're *my* trainee,' Nurse Thornhill said, her voice loud now. 'And that means you don't get anything wrong.'

Tripi changed direction and headed for the back door.

'Tahir?' Nurse Thornhill's voice. 'Tahir? Where are you going?'

But Tripi didn't turn back.

46

Milo

'You've got to think bigger, Milo.' Clouds turned down the news and sat on his bed. He had his naked women pictures all lined up on the carpet with post-its stuck over their nipples and fuzzy pubic bits.

'How can I think bigger? It's all ruined now. She's going to win the prize and everyone will think she's wonderful and that Forget Me Not is this amazing place and Gran will have to stay there for ever. Not that she wants to come home, so I don't know why I'm even bothering.'

'Gran likes to make up her own mind about things, I'm sure you know that already, Milo.'

Milo looked up at Clouds. 'But she belongs here.'

Clouds held Milo's gaze for a moment. 'You're not only doing this for your gran though, are you, Milo? You're doing it because there's a story that needs to be told.'

Milo shrugged. 'But no one's going to listen.'

'Not if you give up they're not.'

Milo lowered his head.

'You still want to be an undercover reporter, right? Someone who shows the world the truth?'

'I suppose so.'

'Then you have to persevere. Especially when the best opportunity for getting your story out has just been dropped into your lap.'

Milo looked up again. 'What do you mean?'

Clouds nudged his head at the television.

A presenter stood in front of a map of Syria. He pointed to a line of dots that started in Damascus, Tripi's home, and snaked across to a town on the Syrian border and then across the border to Turkey. A film started playing of children ducking under the barbed fence separating the two countries. Milo shifted his head in time with the newsfeed along the bottom of the screen: *thousands of refugees have fled along this route.*

He wondered whether Ayishah was there and then he felt bad for having shouted at Tripi.

'You mentioned that Nurse Thornhill was going to make a film of the home, for when she collects her prize?'

Milo nodded. On his way out of Forget Me Not, he'd seen Petros walking behind Nurse Thornhill, carrying a camera. He'd made Milo think of a little sausage dog, wagging his tail. If only Gran could see what an idiot he was.

'And you've got some evidence, from that friend of yours, Tripi? Things he's recorded on your phone?'

Milo nodded.

'Well, there you go. You've got your way in.'

'What way in?'

'You swap the films.'

47

Sandy

A thump on the door. Sandy tried to block it out; if she didn't answer, maybe they'd go away and leave her alone.

She looked at the television, a couple kissing by Niagara Falls. *The most romantic destination on earth*, said the presenter.

Another thump.

The kitchen walls shook; brittle bones, like an old person. Perhaps one of these days, when a Boeing 747 rumbled overhead, the house would crack and fall down with her inside it. She pictured it lying like a flat pack in the middle of Crescent Way. A gap in the road like a missing tooth.

They couldn't expect you to pay a mortgage on a collapsed house, could they? And anyway, no one would find her under all that rubble.

Sandy pressed mute on the TV and walked to the door.

'Who is it?'

'It's me.'

She knew the voice. And then, as she looked through the peephole she recognised the dark hair, the brown eyes, the thick eyelashes.

How had he found out where she lived?

'You shouldn't be here,' she called through the door. 'I'll call the police.'

She heard him shuffle closer.

'I am sorry to disturb you, Young Mrs Moon, but I need to talk to you about Old Mrs Moon.'

Young? At twenty-seven, Sandy felt ancient. She opened the door.

Tripi came in and handed Sandy Milo's schoolbag. He pointed to the address label. 'I am not, what do you call it here? A stalker.'

The way he smiled, like he was holding out a gift, made Sandy smile back despite herself.

'I work in the kitchen,' he said. 'At Forget Me Not, that is how Milo and I met.'

Sandy looked at his chef's whites. Clean. Ironed. Spotless. Nicer than her green polyester fleece and the nylon skirt that dug into her waist. She'd gone and done it. Signed up for a job at the Co-op. They were so desperate for staff that they'd made her fill in a form right then and there, sent her to the Ladies to put on her new uniform and put her straight onto the tills.

'Milo came to see me and he forgot his bag.'

Half an hour ago, Milo had trudged upstairs, not saying a word. After this morning, she thought they'd turned a corner, but it looked like she'd done something wrong again. For a nine-year-old he sure was behaving like a teenager.

Tripi glanced round the kitchen. 'You have a nice house.'

246

Sandy looked at the black stains on the linoleum, melted curtains, the dark smears against the fridge – and couldn't help but laugh. 'It used to be.'

'Milo told me about the fire. He said Old Mrs Moon had a moment of forgetting.'

'The insurance company doesn't quite see it that way. Looks like we're going to be stuck with a burnt kitchen.'

'Oh.' Tripi furrowed his brow. Then the television screen caught his attention. 'You like holidays?'

Sandy looked at the presenter standing in her skimpy bikini on a long, white beach. *Honeymoon Hideaways.* That was the name of the programme.

'Yes. I like holidays,' she said.

Tripi brushed his palm over one of the stools at the counter and sat down. 'What are these?' He picked up a tub of pills. 'Vitamins?' He read the label out: '"Burn Fat Fast".'

Sandy took the tub out of his hands and shoved it in the cutlery drawer.

'You want to burn fat?'

'Doesn't every woman?'

Tripi shook his head. 'In Syria, if a person is thin, she is considered either poor or sick.' He looked directly at her. 'You are just right.' He drew a curvy figure in the air with his hands and then blushed. 'Food is there to make you happy. One day, I will make you a banquet.'

Sandy felt dizzy. She hadn't eaten anything since the SlimFast shake this morning and her toner belt pinched at the folds of her stomach.

'Thank you for the bag, I'll make sure it gets back to Milo.' She moved towards the kitchen door. 'I'm afraid I have rather a lot of work to do.'

A soak in the bath, that's what she needed. Eight hours at the till next to the chill cabinets; she still couldn't feel her fingers.

'Milo is not happy,' said Tripi.

Sandy's dropped her shoulders. 'No.'

'I let him down.'

Sandy smiled. 'Well, that makes two of us.'

'What did you do?'

'Everything. Everything that a mum can possibly do wrong, I did it.'

'I do not believe that.'

'Oh, you should. Just ask him.'

'I was meant to help Milo catch Nurse Thornhill.'

Sandy wondered whether Tripi was struggling to find the right word in English. 'Catch her?'

'He wants Forget Me Not Home to close down.'

'He what?' Sandy swayed on her feet. The diet pills were kicking in.

Upstairs, she heard Milo's footsteps on the landing. She'd recognise the sound of his walk in a crowd of a thousand people. His deliberate steps as he avoided tripping over objects outside his line of vision.

'Milo is a sensitive boy, he sees things. He sees things in here.' Tripi pointed to his heart. 'He is not happy with how they treat the old people at the home and I am not happy either. The inspectors came and I did not tell them, but I am going to help him now. Milo was right and I was wrong.'

None of this was making any sense.

'We need to help him, Mrs Moon.'

'He's right, Mum.'

Milo stood at the bottom of the stairs.

248

'Milo, if this is another one of your crazy ideas for getting Gran back home . . .'

'It's not.' Milo came into the kitchen. 'I mean, it is, a bit. Gran should be with us, I can look after her better than any stupid nursing home, but it's more than that. The place is horrible. You haven't seen what it's really like, Mum. When we dropped Gran off Nurse Thornhill put on a show, like she always does for visitors.'

Sandy looked from Milo to Tripi. Her pulse raced from the caffeine in the pills. *To be taken as part of a calorie controlled diet . . .* 110 calories so far today, how was that for controlled?

'Are you okay, Mum? You look a bit . . .'

White dots swam in front of her eyes. She should have gone to see Lou, but it was all too much.

'Mum?'

Milo's voice faded.

The burned linoleum shifted under her feet.

The house wasn't falling; it was rising, coming up from the foundations like a tide. And Sandy hadn't learnt to swim.

'Mrs Moon . . .' These were the last words she heard, far away. And then falling and a soft landing, softer than her body expected. And then nothing.

'Mrs Moon?'

'Mum?'

Someone was shaking her arm.

'Sandy?'

Sandy looked up and blinked.

That Scottish accent. Al.

'Here, have this.' Tripi handed her a tumbler. 'Tea with honey.'

'I don't understand—'

'Low blood sugar, Mum, take it.'

She sat up and sipped the warm, sweet liquid.

'In Syria, honey is like medicine,' said Tripi.

'You had us worried there, Sandy – didn't she, mate?' Al slapped Milo on the back.

'You need to eat, Mum – proper stuff, not just shakes and pills.'

So she hadn't even been able to keep those from him.

'I will make you some real food,' said Tripi.

'Sounds good,' said Al. 'Some of the best food I ever had was in the Middle East.'

The red rash crept up Sandy's throat. 'I . . . I'm fine, thank you.' She pulled down the black polyester skirt that had crept up her thighs and then realised that her fleece and her shirt had lifted up over her belly to reveal the black toner belt. She tugged them both down, got onto her feet and took a breath. 'I'm fine now.'

'Steady there,' said Al, taking her arm as she swayed.

She took her arm out from under Al's and walked to the kitchen. 'I'm really fine, why don't you all go back to whatever it is . . .'

'If you're okay now, can I walk back with Tripi?' asked Milo. 'We've got to discuss our plan.'

Fragments came back to her. Tripi on her doorstep, a problem about the nursing home. She was too tired to work it out. She looked out of the window and saw that it was already dark. 'I'm not sure, Milo. You're not so good in the dark.'

'I'll be fine, Mum.'

'Well, at least wear your glasses.'

For months she'd let him go out without them. Simply forgotten. Wasn't that unnatural, for a mother to forget the needs of her child?

Nocturnal vision is a real problem for Milo. It's a surprise he's coped so well, Dr Nolan had said, handing her the clear lenses Milo had to swap for the sunglasses as soon as it got dark. And then everything had blown up with Andy and Angela and the great announcement that the bloody Habibti would be joining them soon.

'I forgot them at school. I'll be okay though, Mum, I'm good without them.'

'I'd better get back to my lair, work to do.' Al gave Milo a wink and headed up the stairs.

Sandy saw Tripi look at Al with a sad, dazed expression. He didn't think that she ... and Al? Surely not?

'Mum? Can I go, then?'

'I'll come with you,' she said. 'The fresh air will do me good.' She swung back her head and finished the tea, waiting for the last bits of sticky honey to trickle down her throat.

48

Lou

'I'm glad you were on your best behaviour for the inspectors,' said Nurse Thornhill, pinching at a bit of Lou's arm as she yanked the sheets around her body. 'We can't afford to have any problems, not before the awards ceremony.' She stood up and looked towards the door. 'What was that noise?'

Lou held her breath.

'No wandering around the corridors after bedtime. How many times do I have to tell that woman.' She stormed to the door, poked out her head and yelled: 'Mrs Zimmer, I've told you before, no loitering after bedtime.' She turned back to Lou. 'If I catch her . . . '

Nurse Thornhill clicked the light off, leaving Lou in the dark, and squeaked away down the corridor.

Lou waited a few beats. And then she heard his footsteps, followed by his breath.

'Louisa?' Petros whispered her name into the dark room. 'The coast is clear, she is in her flat.'

Lou knew when a man was afraid and when he was lonely. No money, no family, the same clothes day in day out.

He plodded to the window, took the pink rose from the vase, threw it out of the window, revealed a new one from behind his back, yellow this time, like Milo had taught him. He placed the rose between his dentures and walked to the bed. Then he spat it out and yowled. '*Na pari i eychi!* Damn it!'

Hamlet, who'd been asleep under the covers, woke up, got onto all fours, scrabbled his way out from under the sheets and squealed.

'A thorn,' said Petros, touching his bottom lip.

Silly man. Kind, silly man. Lou patted the bed beside her. How long since a man had sat on her bed, had lain at her side, his body cupped into hers?

She wasn't ready, that was all. It takes time to let go, not so much of the memories, there weren't many of those, but of the dreams of what could have been.

'You are letting little salami sleep in your bed again?'

Lou nodded. Once he stopped calling Hamlet salami, Milo would grow to love him. Young enough to be a good grand-father, well enough to live at home in her small room under the roof. Petros shouldn't be here.

Petros took off his shoes – the only patient who didn't wear slippers – and squeezed in next to Lou.

'Well, I suppose I should be glad not to have found Mrs Zimmer.'

In the last few days, Mrs Zimmer had taken to sleeping in Lou's bed. She liked to come and see Lou and then as soon as she arrived she got tired and lay down for a nap.

Petros rubbed Hamlet behind his white ear. 'You spoil him, Loiusa.'

And I spoil you, she thought. A man she barely knew who reminded her she was still alive.

Petros moved Hamlet down to the bottom of the mattress and propped up some pillows next to Lou, which gave Hamlet just enough time to plod back up to the top of the bed. Hamlet pressed his snout against Petros's hand and settled his fat body down between them.

Lou leant over and touched the drop of blood on Petros's lip. *Dear, silly man*. Forgetting that a rose had thorns.

She switched off the bedside light and lay back, staring up at the ceiling. It was a good thing that she was so slight or the three of them would never fit in this narrow bed: an old woman, a fat pig and a Greek painter with a generous belly.

'I will have to find a way to win Milo's heart.' Petros rested his hand on Hamlet's head.

Lou stroked Petros's hand. Could she ever have imagined that, at ninety-two, she would have to choose between her grandson and a lover?

All these impulses surging through her body like the beam from the Inverary lighthouse as it swept over the sea – the way she kissed his cheek the other day, and now, this longing for more. She leant over and took his face in her hands, her fingers still and strong, and pressed his lips to hers.

Their mouths were clumsy at first. And then she pulled away for a second and looked at his face, at the blood on his lip, at his closed eyes and she leant in again and got lost in him. As his mouth pressed against hers, his hand brushing her breast, parts of her body stirred that she thought had abandoned her long ago.

'I love the smell of your skin,' he said. 'Like fruit . . .'

Apricots. The perfume Milo had given her last Christmas.

'Hmm . . . warm and sweet.' Petros held his cheek against hers.

Lou knew she had to act fast, before she lost her nerve. She leant over to her bedside table, grabbed her paper and pencil, wrote the words in the dark, and handed the pad to Petros.

'What is this? A secret note from my Louisa?' Petros held the pad close to his face and squinted in the dim room.

And then a silence so long Lou thought that her heart had stopped.

Petros lifted Hamlet off the bed, held him to his chest, kissed his head and then looked at Lou with the softest, kindest eyes she had ever seen.

'You want to marry me, Louisa?'

She nodded.

'Then you are mad. There is nothing I can give you.'

She wrote on the pad again: *You give me everything.*

Petros's eyes shone in the dark room. 'Are you sure, Louisa?' His voice trembled.

She nodded again.

He closed his eyes like he was saying a prayer and then he opened them and looked right at her: 'Yes, Louisa. I will marry you. Though I think we should ask Milo's permission first, don't you?'

Hamlet grunted softly; the corners of his mouth turned up.

It had been a long day, the inspectors in and out of the room, Petros running after Nurse Thornhill with that camera. Had she heard right? Had he said yes? Or was her mind slipping again?

Lou's fingers began to tremble.

Stupid hands. Stupid body. How could she marry him? An old woman like her?

'Are you all right, Louisa?'

Lou reached her hand to Petros's face.

She nodded. For a second, her fingers went still and then Milo's face appeared in front of her, those eyes of his, wide and focused and sad.

49

Milo

'So we're going to make this video and swap it with the one Petros is making and then, when she goes up and gets her prize, they'll show it, and everyone will see what Forget Me Not is really like and that it's all Nurse Thornhill's fault. And Clouds and me were thinking that it would be really cool if all the old people came along too, maybe you could drive them, Mum, in a minibus, and then we'd burst into the ceremony, like a surprise, so that when everything goes tits up—'

'Milo!'

'That's what Clouds said.'

Milo skipped ahead of Mum and Tripi on the dark pavement. He didn't care about the grainy blur in front of his eyes because what he could see was much better: a stage full of the old ladies from Forget Me Not, smiling and cheering as Nurse Thornhill was carried away by the police. Everything was falling into place.

'Well, you don't need to copy everything he says,' said Mum. 'Clouds is cool.'

Tripi hunched his shoulders and sank his hands deeper into his pockets. 'Anyway, when Nurse Thornhill gets kaboomed, we'll all burst in and the local newspapers can take photos of all the old people and I'll take a film on my phone and send it to Clouds who'll put it on the internet, along with our film that he'll have released already.'

At last Mum was listening; with her on board, they could really do this.

'I still don't understand why we can't just call Slipton Council or whoever it is that oversees nursing homes around here. Go through the proper channels. If what you say is true, all it will take is a few complaints . . .'

'No, it won't, Mum. You should have seen Nurse Thornhill with the inspectors, she had them eating out of her hand. They think she's like this superhero nurse. And Clouds said the local authorities wouldn't want any negative publicity so they'll hush it up. This way, we get maximum exposure. And Clouds said that it will trigger a wider discussion, which is the point of being an undercover reporter – you find one example of a bad thing and you prove it and then they have to look into all the other things too. There are probably horrible nursing homes all over the UK, Mum. Clouds said—'

'Slow down, Milo.'

Tripi scratched his head and asked: 'Can we trust him, this Clouds?'

'Of course,' said Milo.

'There was a time when Milo didn't like Al, isn't that right, Milo?'

'That was before, Mum.'

They reached the high street with its droopy Christmas lights.

'Do you like him, Young Mrs Moon?' asked Tripi.

'Please, call me Sandy, like I said when I came to your house.'

This was a good sign, thought Milo. If Mum liked Tripi, that would help them work together.

'Sandy, like on *Honeymoon Hideaways*, like the sand in Syria.'

Mum smiled. Milo didn't know what Tripi was going on about.

'Sandy,' he said again, like he was learning it. 'My question is: do you like this Al, or Clouds as Milo calls him?'

'Milo's pretty good at reading people,' said Mum.

Although Milo was pleased by what Mum said, he didn't think that Mum liking Clouds was the point. Why did grown-ups have to muddle things? They were a team now, Milo and Mum and Tripi and Clouds and the old ladies. Even Nurse Heidi was backing them. And once they realised what was happening, even Gran and Petros would join in.

Together, they'd close down Forget Me Not for ever.

They got to the end of the high street and stood outside Tripi's house.

'Did you leave all the lights on?' asked Milo.

'Looks like Big Mike's back.' Sandy pointed at the grey Ford Mondeo parked in the drive.

Tripi took in a sharp breath.

'He'll be pleased with how well you've looked after the place,' said Sandy.

Milo glanced at Tripi. So that's the story he'd given Mum.

Tripi cleared his throat. 'Eh . . . yes. I do hope so. I hope he will be happy in his home.'

Milo saw that, despite the cold, small drops of sweat had sprouted up on Tripi's forehead.

'I wonder whether he's brought Lalana with him,' said Sandy. 'He's been trying to get her a visa for over a year now. I've only seen her in pictures, but she's—'

'I had better go inside,' said Tripi. 'I must talk to MailOrder—to Mr Mike. If you will excuse me.'

Milo wanted to tell Tripi it was okay. That if they told Mum that he didn't have a home any more, she'd let him stay with them. 'Mum, the thing is—'

Tripi shook his head and his eyes pleaded so hard it made Milo think of Hamlet when he was hungry.

'Well, give Mike my best. Tell him if his wife needs some beauty treatments . . .'

'I must go.' Tripi's voice sounded tired.

In the distance, Milo heard police sirens.

'We'll talk tomorrow.' Milo said the words really slowly so that Tripi would know that they'd talk about Mike coming back and finding Tripi a new home just as much as they'd talk about the Forget Me Not plan.

A police car swerved round the road. Milo recognised PC Stubbs sitting in the front.

'I wonder what the police are doing in this neck of the woods,' Mum said.

Milo's eyes darted from Mum to Tripi to the pink house to the police car. He had to get Mum out of here or she'd find out that Tripi was squatting in Big Mike's house.

'Tripi, are you okay?' Mum asked. 'You've gone very pale.'

Tripi was staring at the police car.

'I think I have forgotten something in the kitchen at the nursing home,' he said. 'Please excuse me.'

Milo wished he could tell him that it was going to be okay, that he hadn't done anything wrong, or nothing that they couldn't explain anyway, but he'd made a promise to keep Tripi's secret.

'See you tomorrow!' Milo called after Tripi.

Through the pinhole, Milo watched his friend running away into the dark December night.

50

Lou

'What on earth!' Nurse Thornhill strode across the room and tore open the curtains.

Lou's eyes strained against the morning light.

Hamlet chewed on the piece of paper from her pad. *Marry Me.* Lou covered him with the blanket.

'I knew that you two couldn't be trusted.'

Lou turned her head. Petros snored on the pillow beside her, fully dressed, the sheet taut over his belly.

'Mr Spiteri, wake up!'

Did she need to shout?

'Mr Spiteri!'

Petros's arm twitched. He rolled over and kept snoring.

Lou tucked the blanket tighter over Hamlet's body and prayed he wouldn't move or squeal and that Petros wouldn't wake up suddenly and disturb him.

'This is not a holiday camp.'

Lou tried to lift her legs over the side of the bed but they wouldn't move.

'Mrs Moon, I am waiting for an explanation.'

Lou gave up on her legs and looked up at Nurse Thornhill. She couldn't help but laugh inside: a ninety-two-year-old woman caught in bed with an old man and a pig.

Nurse Thornhill sucked her teeth. 'Oh, of course, I forgot – her ladyship doesn't speak.'

She walked round the bed and ripped the blanket off Petros's body.

Petros tugged it back in his sleep.

Nurse Thornhill tugged harder.

Hamlet spat out Lou's marriage proposal, bounced onto his feet and ran around the bed squealing.

'What in heaven's name!' Nurse Thornhill leant over the bed and stared at Hamlet.

Petros rubbed his eyes.

'Heidi!' Nurse Thornhill shouted through the open door.

A few moments later, Nurse Heidi ran in.

'What is it? Is something wrong with Mrs Moon?'

Lou smiled at the young girl.

'Yes, something is wrong with Mrs Moon. And with Mr Spiteri. And with this animal they've let into the room.'

'An animal?' Nurse Heidi's eyes fell on the bed. 'Oh, the piglet.'

'"Oh, the piglet"? You knew about this?' asked Nurse Thornhill. 'Something else you wanted the inspectors to see?'

'No, I just—' Nurse Heidi looked from Hamlet to Lou to Petros.

As Lou watched Petros sit up, she had to hold herself

back from reaching out and passing her hand through the grey strands of hair sticking up at odd angles around his head.

Petros rubbed Hamlet's head. 'I told Nurse Heidi that Mrs Moon's grandson had a pig. We showed her a picture, that is why she recognises him.'

Hamlet grunted.

'Take him out. Now.' Nurse Thornhill clasped her forehead. 'If the inspectors had seen this . . . goodness knows . . .'

'Is everything all right?' Mrs Moseley stood at the door in her nightdress. She pressed PLAY on her tape recorder and held it to her ear. 'Makes him feel close,' she said. 'Dear Roland.' Her brown cheeks shone.

'Turn that thing down and go back to your room, Mrs Moseley,' said Nurse Thornhill.

Lou heard Mrs Moseley scuttle away – in the opposite direction to her room.

'I thought I could trust you, Mr Spiteri.' Nurse Thornhill paused. 'We have an understanding. Come to my office, please.'

Nurse Heidi lifted Hamlet off the bed. 'He's heavier than he looks, isn't he?' She carried him to the door. Lou stretched out her hand towards Hamlet.

'Don't worry, Mrs Moon, I'll make sure he's okay.' Nurse Heidi smiled.

'Stop being sentimental, Heidi. Pigs are dirty farm animals, just get rid of it.'

Petros was on his feet now. He walked to the door, his knees creakier than ever from his long sleep on a narrow bed. 'Please, Nurse Thornhill, the pig belongs to Milo, he is Milo's special pig. He is very clever and he is clean, cleaner than we are. You cannot take him away, Milo will never forgive me, or Louisa.'

'This is ridiculous. Nurse Heidi, go!'

At that moment, Hamlet wriggled out of Heidi's arms, dropped on the floor snout first and squealed. The four of them watched him dash down the corridor, ears back, corkscrew tail lifted to the ceiling.

'After him, Heidi.'

'Ooh, a pig!' Mrs Swift called out from the corridor.

Maybe she'll do his make-up, thought Lou.

Nurse Heidi dashed out of the room.

Nurse Thornhill's face went grey as a tombstone.

Petros pushed past her and made his way down the corridor after Heidi and Hamlet.

'Mr Spiteri, come back here!' said Nurse Thornhill.

Petros turned round and walked back to Lou's room.

'Remember our arrangement, Mr Spiteri?'

His broad shoulders sank.

Lou didn't like all this talk of arrangements and special understandings. Her head ached. So tired. Slipping . . . slipping again . . . What was she doing here? And where was Milo? Why wasn't he here yet?

'You haven't forgotten, have you, Mr Spiteri?' Nurse Thornhill asked Petros. 'That you owe a special debt to Forget Me Not? To me?'

Petros nodded.

And then it came back to Lou. Petros's lips in the night, her proposal.

She propped herself up in bed and cleared her throat.

Petros and Nurse Thornhill turned to look at her.

Lou coughed again and asked: 'What debt?'

The room fell silent.

Had she really spoken? Had the words actually come out?

'Did you say something, Mrs Moon?'

'Louisa . . . ?' Petros reached out for her.

Lou sat up straighter, rested her fingers on her throat and tried again.

'What debt?' Her voice like a stranger's.

Nurse Thornhill brushed down her uniform. 'So you've found your voice again, Mrs Moon? Well, I'm afraid this is none of your business.'

Words pushed up Lou's throat, aching to get out.

Lou had thought that maybe her voice would never come back, like an engine left to go cold, but here it was, waiting in her mouth, ready to carry her words.

Sixty-three years of silence, banished in a moment.

She gripped her throat and spoke again. 'T-there is every reason for m-me to get involved. P-Petros and I are getting m-married.'

'Gran?'

Milo stood at the door, his eyes wide and bloodshot like that night a year ago when he'd found his father in the shed; the night his eyes let him down and he fell off his bike into the path of an oncoming truck.

If the driver hadn't looked up, seen Milo intrigued by the whistling and reached for the brake, . . .

If he hadn't swerved onto the pavement at just the right time.

51

Milo

Milo had met the old ladies standing in the corridor in their nightdresses. Mrs Moseley had whispered in his ear: *They've gone and done it now ... naughty children ...* And then they'd followed him to Gran's room.

Mrs Moseley led the way, propping up Mrs Zimmer who'd just woken up, followed by Mrs Sharp Mrs Swift Mrs Foxton Mrs Turner Mrs Wong.

When they heard Gran speak, they started clapping.

Mrs Moseley turned up the volume on her tape player and Bob Marley's dreadlocky voice filled the room.

'I'll do your make-up for the wedding,' said Mrs Swift.

'My Roland can come and play with his band,' said Mrs Moseley.

Milo left them behind and walked to the wardrobe. He stared at Gran's empty shoes.

'Where's Hamlet?'

He didn't care about anything any more. What was the

point in trying to get Gran back home when all she wanted was to marry that stupid Greek guy and stay in this crummy nursing home? He was even angry at Clouds for having made him believe he could be an undercover reporter and actually make things better. It was all hopeless. From now on, he was going to let the grown-ups sort out their own mess.

He'd take Hamlet home, close his bedroom door and not let anyone in. And he'd refuse to go to school or to do anything any adult told him to do ever again.

Kneeling down, Milo looked under the bed. He made his eyes zoom in and out and shifted his head an inch at a time so he didn't miss a bit. The duskiness made it difficult to see but he knew that if Hamlet was under there, he'd hear his pink snuffling.

'Milo . . .' Gran's fingers fluttered on his back. She'd pulled herself out of bed. 'Hamlet wouldn't fit under there, not any more.' Her voice sounded rough and croaky like she'd been smoking one of Mrs Harris's cigarettes.

He didn't want Gran to talk, he wanted things back to how they were before: Gran with her pad and her pen and her funny pictures. He wanted to be the one who looked after her.

Milo pulled away from Gran's hand and stood up.

'Where is he, then?'

Mum came into the room. She'd been taking Milo to school this morning, the first time in ages. They set off early so they could stop by Forget Me Not. She wanted to come in and check whether everything Tripi and Milo had said was true.

And so Mum had heard everything too. Gran speaking

268

for the first time – and Gran saying she was going to marry Petros.

Everyone had heard it.

'If what you're referring to is that filthy pig . . . ' Nurse Thornhill stood in the doorway.

Petros stepped forward. 'He is with Nurse Heidi. She is giving him a wash.' He rubbed under his armpits and grinned.

Nurse Thornhill looked at Petros and shook her head.

'He doesn't need to be washed,' said Milo.

'Well, Heidi thought he'd like a bath, a bit of special treatment.'

Why was Petros getting involved? And what did he know about Hamlet? Only a few days ago, he'd implied all Hamlet was good for was salami.

Nurse Heidi ran in, her cheeks flushed. 'Excuse me,' she said, pushing through Mrs Moseley Mrs Zimmer Mrs Sharp Mrs Swift Mrs Foxton Mrs Turner Mrs Wong. 'I can't find him.'

Milo saw Petros put his finger to his lips but Nurse Heidi didn't notice.

'I ran after him down the corridors and round the lounge and then out towards reception – and then he disappeared.'

'Yes, I saw him disappear,' said Mrs Swift. 'Fast as an arrow, that pig.'

'What do you mean, he disappeared?' asked Nurse Thornhill.

'Why were you running after Hamlet?' asked Milo.

'Well, Nurse Thornhill asked me to take him away—'

The room went quiet.

'So, you weren't giving him a bath, then?' asked Milo.

Gran sat down in her armchair and rubbed her brow. Petros came and stood beside her and touched her shoulder.

'A bath?' Nurse Heidi looked from Nurse Thornhill to Milo.

Milo pushed past Nurse Thornhill and Mum and all the old ladies and walked straight down the corridor and out through the front door.

Although it was Tuesday morning, the high street buzzed with Christmas shoppers. They were all laughing at him: the mums buying last minute presents; the sellers on the market stalls shouting out two for one offers on crackers and cards; toddlers in Santa Claus hats with chocolate smeared round their mouths.

And then it got worse.

Milo walked past the front window of Bill the Butcher's. Pieces of paper tacked to the window. *Closing Down Sale. Everything Must Go.* And then a hand-drawn poster with a big lump in the middle: *A Ham for Christmas!* Milo looked down at the pink shiny bits of meat in the window display. Rashers of bacon and fat, pale sausages and big lumps of gammon.

He hated Christmas.

Milo focused his eyes down the street. Where would Hamlet have gone? Would he have managed the steps outside the front of Forget Me Not? Would someone in the street have picked him up and taken home? Mum said that teacup pigs were expensive and that Dad shouldn't have wasted so much money on a pet. Maybe someone had stolen him and was going to try and sell him.

Milo stopped at the RSPCA shop. In the window was a

picture of a Labrador puppy, so thin his bones poked out of his chest, sore patches on his back, his eyes two shining black pools.

'I'm afraid I haven't seen him,' said Mrs RSPCA. Milo had never found out the name of the woman who sat behind the till. 'But I'll keep an eye out. Why don't you make some posters and put them around Slipton? I could put one in the window for you.'

Mrs RSPCA was the only one who understood how important Hamlet was. And she was right – if he didn't turn up in the next hour, Milo would make some posters. He'd think of a reward. He still had the bike Dad gave him last Christmas sitting in the garage going rusty, it wasn't like he was ever going to be able to ride it again, so he could sell that. He could photocopy the posters at Mr Gupta's, like he'd done with Ayishah's picture. *Ayishah*. For the first time Milo realised how sad Tripi must be. Last summer, he had looked for Ayishah for weeks and she was somewhere dangerous, much more dangerous than Slipton was for Hamlet.

He screwed shut his eyes. *Hamlet? Where are you?*

When Milo talked to Hamlet in his head he could tell Hamlet understood because he stopped snuffling and the shape of his eyes changed. Gran talked to him too. But they'd never tried it when Hamlet wasn't in the same room.

Wherever you are, Hamlet, stay away from Bill the Butcher's. And if someone tries to grab you, run away.

Milo didn't know where to go next. Without Hamlet or Gran, home wasn't home any more.

He walked past the pink house and saw Big Mike standing at the kitchen window smiling out onto the street. He must have found a way to get Lalana to come home with him.

And then Milo thought of Tripi and how he'd lost his home too.

That's what he'd do, find Tripi, the one person he could still trust.

Milo turned off the high street and walked along the canal. He crawled under the bench to see whether Tripi's things were there, but then he realised that they'd probably still be in Big Mike's house. Maybe they'd even been taken away for inspection by the police. So that meant Tripi must have spent the night without a sleeping bag and without his things. And what about Ayishah's red backpack? Tripi would flip if he didn't have that.

When he couldn't find him at the canal, Milo went to the park where he'd first seen Tripi doing his prayers on the grass. But he wasn't there either.

Then he had an idea.

He went to one of the old payphones on the high street. It smelt of beer and wee and stale smoke. After slotting in 50p, he dialled his own mobile number. Tripi had answered it when Dad called, maybe he'd answer it again.

Milo counted each ring tone. If Tripi didn't pick up within the next two rings, the messaging service would kick in.

'Hello?'

Tripi sounded miles away.

'Tripi, it's me, Milo. Where are you?'

In the background, Milo heard traffic whooshing past. Horns beeping. The clatter of a lorry.

'I've been looking for you everywhere,' said Milo.

'I'm sorry I took your phone.'

'What? I don't care about the phone.'

'I didn't know where to leave it.'

'Where you are? I have to speak to you.'

A pause.

'I'm going to London.'

'What do you mean, you're going to London?'

'I'm hitch-hiking.'

Hitch-hiking was one of the most dangerous ways to get to places, that's what Mrs Harris said. It was like inviting a stranger to bundle you into his car and kidnap you.

'What are you doing to do in London?'

'When MailOrderBrideMan came back and I didn't have a place to stay any more, a light bulb went on.'

'What do you mean, a light bulb?'

Milo heard another lorry rattle past. He hoped that Tripi wasn't standing too close to the motorway.

'I've been wishing that Ayishah will come here and find me, but that's not going to happen, is it, Milo? She's twelve years old. How would she get to England on her own? I've got to go back to Syria to find her. If I go to London I can earn money faster for the plane ticket.'

Looking up into the sky Milo saw a plane, its nose angled up at the clouds as it made its ascent.

All the bits of his life were slipping away. He couldn't keep hold of anything good, could he? Not Dad, not Gran, not Hamlet and now Tripi was leaving too.

'But what if you don't find her? What if you starve or get sick? What if you're blown up?' Milo thought about the pictures he'd seen on Clouds's telly last night. A mother carrying a boy Milo's age, a bullet wound in his chest.

273

'That doesn't matter, Milo, all I know is that I shouldn't be here, I should be with Ayishah.'

'Please, Tripi, please come back so we can talk.' Milo's brain whirred. He had to think of a good reason to change Tripi's mind. 'Clouds said he could help. He saw Ayishah on the news.' He gulped down the lie.

'Ayishah?' Tripi's voice went quiet. 'He saw Ayishah?'

Milo took a deep breath. 'He watches the news all the time. I showed him the copy of Ayishah's photo.' Milo screwed shut his eyes and opened them again. The numbers on the keypad blurred. 'If you come back, we'll help you find her.'

Milo had kept secrets before, like about sneaking Hamlet up to Gran's room when Mum thought he was still in the garage, like about failing his maths and English exams. But this was the first time he'd said a big, out-loud lie.

'Okay,' said Tripi. 'Okay. But if we do not find her, I am leaving, I am going back to Syria.'

'We'll find her. I promise.'

52

Sandy

'M-Milo? Where's Milo?' Lou called out.

Sandy woke up with a start and looked across the room. Lou speaking and craning her neck, the left side of her face sunk lower than the right, her arm collapsed under her as she tried to prop herself up. She'd had a few strokes in the past, and the scars they'd left on her body and on her face came to the surface when she was tired or anxious.

Milo was right, she'd gone downhill since she was here, one more item to add to the list of Sandy's failures.

Sandy stood up from the armchair by the window.

'Lou, you need to rest.'

'Where's M-Milo . . . ?'

'It's okay, Lou.'

'W-who are you?' Lou's face creased.

'It's me, Sandy.'

'Who's Sandy?'

Good question. Sandy took a breath. 'I'm Milo's mum.'

'Angela?'

Sandy felt a stab at Lou confusing her for Andy's Tart. Before they left for Abu Dhabi, Andy had arranged a meeting between Angela and Lou at The Cup Half Full; Sandy had hoped that she'd been slotted into the lost property department of Lou's brain.

'No, it's me, Sandy.'

'Where's Milo?'

'Al found him wandering the high street and took him home.'

Lou smiled weakly and closed her eyes. 'I.' She took a breath. 'I thought y-you'd like Alasdair.' Her voice was small and slurred and she jolted over her words, but it was coming back, that old muscle gaining strength with every word. 'L-lovely little Alasdair, swimming with me in the sea, never afraid of the cold. He reminds me of Milo.'

After he moved south, Andy had lost touch with his relatives in Scotland. His parents came down twice, once for the wedding and once when Milo was born, but then the journey got too much for them and Andy never quite found the time to drive up. Anyway, it was Lou who'd brought him up, his parents too busy working, living their own lives in Glasgow. They'd never wanted children, his mother had let slip once. *I don't owe them anything*, Andy had said whenever Sandy suggested a visit.

Lou turned her head to the clock on the wall. 'H-how long have I been asleep?'

Sandy looked out of the window at the darkening sky, at the Christmas lights blinking over the high street. 'You've been asleep for most of the day.'

Her face clouded over again. 'W-where am I?'

One moment Lou was here, her brain in the present, and then, all of a sudden, it slipped.

'You gave us a fright, Lou. When Milo left, your heart went into overdrive – I had to persuade Nurse Thornhill to get the doctor in, he'll be coming back later.'

Tripi and Milo had been right about Nurse Thornhill. She'd come close to suggesting that Lou had over-exerted herself on purpose like an attention-seeking child. What made someone like her become a nurse?

'Where's H-Hamlet?' asked Lou. Her eyes welled up. 'Where's little Hamlet?' She puckered her lips and made some small sounds as though calling a cat. 'Hamlet?' she called.

'God knows where Hamlet is, Lou. He hasn't been seen since this morning, looks like he couldn't get out of here fast enough. I don't blame him.'

'It's not so bad. The roof's started leaking and I need to fix the front steps, they're rotting away – the sea can be vicious, you know. Petros could help me, don't you think? Such a practical man. No, it's not so bad.'

'You're here, Lou, at Forget Me Not. And it *is* so bad, Lou. Milo told me what he saw. If I'd have known ... ' Sandy scratched at a raw bit of skin on her throat. The rash used to come and go, but now it looked like it was here to stay. 'To rely on a child to notice that something's wrong.'

'Milo ... always ... always sees things.'

Sandy came over to sit on the bed next to Lou. 'I'm sorry.' She looked around the room. 'I'm sorry about all this.'

Lou lifted her hand and placed it over Sandy's fingers. Her face settled into the present.

'I shouldn't have let you come here.'

277

'The fire . . .' Lou started. 'You had to . . . the kitchen.' Her cheeks flushed pink. How much did she remember of that day?

Using words on one side and paper and pen on the other, they'd discussed it. That it was time for Lou to move out. That Milo could no longer carry the burden of looking after her. But Sandy hadn't expected Lou to take it into her own hands, to set fire to the kitchen to give her a reason to move out. They could have made a plan, something safer.

Lou stroked the edge of Sandy's green fleece. 'You're wearing a uniform?'

'I was meant to be at the Co-op today, my second day at the tills. I imagine they'll sack me for not turning up.'

'The Co-op?'

Sandy nodded. 'It's just for now, until I get back on my feet.' She laughed. 'I can hear the beeping from that stupid scanner in my sleep. I keep thinking it's the alarm clock.'

'I have some m-money . . .' She reached a clumsy hand into her pocket as though looking for loose change. 'Enough m-money . . .'

Sandy took hold of Lou's hand and stilled it.

'I have to learn to stand on my own two feet, isn't that what you always told me, Lou? I've spent ten years taking money from Andy, I'm not going to spend the next ten taking money from his Gran. I'll find another job.'

Sandy didn't have many principles, not ones she stuck to, anyway, but taking Lou's money? She'd never do that. After decades of being battered by the Atlantic, Lou hadn't been able to give her cottage away, let alone sell it. In the end, they'd demolished it to make room for some beach huts, the cost of the land barely covering Andy's loft conversion.

Sandy had resented it at first, wondered why Lou couldn't be looked after by her own children, but then she'd seen it, how much the old lady loved Milo, how when they were introduced it was more like a reunion than a first meeting. And family didn't fall into neat lines, she understood that now.

Anyway, whatever Lou had left wouldn't add up to more than a few pennies, some pocket money for Milo. No, Sandy wouldn't touch it.

'Andrew?' asked Lou. 'He has m-money ... ' She shook her head. 'He was always saving as a boy, saving pennies in the jam jar, pennies for sweets ... '

Sandy looked at the bare bulb hanging from the ceiling. With the fees they were charging, you'd have thought Forget Me Not could afford lampshades. She should have told Andy that Lou wasn't living at home any more, maybe he'd have checked the place out.

'He's got a new baby to think of and anyway, it's down to me now. I'm going to focus on the things that matter, like making sure Milo's happy and that you're looked after. When you're strong enough we'll get you out of here, Lou, move you to a nice place.' She looked back at Lou's small hand covering her fingers. 'Oh, and it turns out I might have a wedding to organise?'

Lou's eyes brightened and then suddenly dimmed again. 'Milo?' she began.

'Milo will come round. Isn't that one of life's lessons? That we have to share the people we love?'

'It w-wasn't your fault, Sandy.' Lou stroked her hand. 'Andrew ... he leaves ... h-he's always leaving ... '

Sandy pressed her thumb into the corner of one eye, then the other, and tilted her head up to reverse the flow of tears.

'So, do you think you'll convince Petros to give up that cap of his?'

Lou let out a bubble of laughter. 'I-I'll try.' Then she patted her head, her hair matted from sleep, from not being washed.

Back home, Milo had bathed Gran, washed and blow-dried her hair. Sandy had let him do too much.

'He's very fond of you,' Sandy said. 'Tripi had to drag him back to his room.'

'Tripi?' Lou's face lit up.

'Yes, Tripi. He turned up late for his shift, but he's here.'

'B-but h-he left. He said g-goodbye.'

Sandy felt the rash heat up along her throat. Tripi had planned to leave?

Nurse Thornhill had threatened to sack him, but Tripi had taken it, standing there listening to her, no sign of anger or irritation on his face. Sandy had wanted to step in and defend him, to tell Nurse Thornhill that she had no right to talk to him like that. That Tripi was her . . . her what? Her friend? The man who'd been kind to her son? The first man since Andy had left who'd made her feel like maybe, under all those flabby rolls of flesh, she was still a woman?

Nurse Thornhill must have lost someone, been left, maybe like Sandy, and then turned bitter. Sandy refused to let that happen to her: she'd get over Andy. She'd fall in love again.

She blinked away the thought. 'Tripi's gathering evidence, as instructed by Milo. I imagine you've heard about this film they're making?'

Lou nodded and her eyes went far away. 'Alasdair's always c-clicking away on his camera. Click, click, click. D-dropped it in the sea once, cried for days.'

'Milo will fill you in tomorrow. I can't believe I'm letting a nine-year-old take on a nursing home.' Sandy laughed. 'But then again, perhaps it takes a nine-year-old to have the courage . . .' Sandy stood up. 'I'd better get home. Make sure he's okay.'

'Petros?' Her eyes suddenly wild.

'What is it, Lou?'

'A d-debt? A debt? What did she mean? Tell him not to worry, tell him that I'll take care of it, that w-when we're . . . when we're . . .'

'When you're married, Lou?'

Lou nodded and Sandy noticed that pink glow pushing up into Lou's cheeks again.

'Take him home . . . with you and M-Milo. Take P-Petros home.'

'If that's what you want, Lou.' Sandy picked up her bag and her coat and walked to the door.

'Sandy?' Lou's hands trembled, the left side of her face joining the rhythm until her whole body shook. 'It's such a long time to wait for him.' She looked out of the window. 'I'm not . . . I'm not sure I'll make it. I mean, until Christmas.'

53

Tripi

On his break, Tripi went down the corridor to visit Old Mrs Moon and to check that she was okay. *She got upset when Milo left,* Nurse Heidi had told him. *We thought that maybe she had a fit, she's had a few in the past, but the doctor said she's just over-tired. She'll be okay.* Nurse Heidi smiled. *She's enjoying having her voice back.*

At first, Tripi didn't understand the word. He thought that, in this country, *fit* meant beautiful, like Lovely Sandy with her big smile and her soft skin. But Nurse Heidi said it like it was a noun, *A Fit,* that it was when the body fought against the mind.

Thinking of what the word meant made Tripi remember that all his things, including Ayishah's backpack and her pocket dictionary, were still in MailOrderBrideMan's house. He had nothing left but her school photograph, tucked into the back pocket of his trousers.

Maybe, when he went to Milo's house later tonight, they

could find a way to get it all back. Milo had called the mobile again and said that Tripi could stay at his house, that his mum had agreed. This made Tripi feel better, that Lovely Sandy wanted Tripi in her home even with that Al man living upstairs.

As he walked past Room 7, Tripi heard zipping and thumping and Petros saying things in his Greek language that sounded similar to the Syrian words that people used when they were angry.

'Petros?' He opened the door and looked in.

The bed was stripped, bags piled up in a corner, Petros's paintings of Greece taken off the walls and propped up by the bin.

Petros stood on a chair, pulling a suitcase off the wardrobe. It landed on the carpet with a thud.

'What is going on, Petros?'

The old man breathed heavily, his hair stuck up around his bald patch like bits of straw, his yellow cap on the floor.

'I'm leaving,' said Petros.

'Why?'

'Nurse Thornhill needs my room.'

'But it is your room, Petros, you are a resident here.'

Petros shook his head.

'I don't understand.' Tripi went over and helped Petros off the chair.

'My daughter stopped paying.'

'Stopped paying for what?'

'For my place here. She said it was too expensive, she has gone back to live in Greece.'

'But didn't you come to England because of your daughter?'

Petros stared down at his cap. 'She thought it would be nice for her children to have me close by. It turned out they weren't so interested in spending time with an old man.'

'And Nurse Thornhill let you stay? Without paying?'

Petros nodded. 'Although to my grandchildren I am ancient, next to the ladies here, I am young. And I am a man, good for the Forget Me Not profile.'

Tripi thought about how Petros followed Nurse Thornhill around with his camera the other day. How he never seemed to notice when she did unkind things or made decisions that were not in the best interests of the old people. But Nurse Thornhill must have more of a reason than this for letting Petros stay.

'What else, Petros?'

Petros sat down on the chair, put on his cap and bowed his head. 'I tell her things.'

'What things?'

'Information about the patients.' He slumped his shoulders. 'And other people.'

'Like me?'

Petros nodded.

'And Nurse Heidi?'

'Everyone.' And then he lifted his cap a bit and smiled. 'Well, not everyone. Not me and Louisa, that was meant to be a secret.'

Tripi closed the door. 'Nurse Thornhill makes you spy on us?' he whispered.

It started to make sense. How Nurse Thornhill always turned up at just the right time. How she knew everything that was going on. Tripi thought about what Nurse Heidi said the other day. Petros was Nurse Thornhill's CCTV.

'It is like I said yesterday in the kitchen, I do not have a choice. If I did not do what she said, I knew I would be homeless.'

Like I was, thought Tripi. He could understand that a man would do a great deal to keep a roof over his head.

'But your daughter?'

'She has not phoned in months.' He looked up. 'I did not look after her mother as I should have, in those days when she was sick. I couldn't, Tripi. I couldn't sit with her and watch her die.'

'But your daughter must understand ... if you need her help.'

'I am a proud man, Tripi, I am not going to beg.'

Tripi looked around the bare room. 'But where will you go?'

'It does not matter.'

'Of course it matters. For a start, Old Mrs Moon loves you.'

Petros gave Tripi a crooked smile. 'You think? Well, maybe a little.'

'I think maybe a lot.' Tripi had heard a muddled message from Milo about a marriage proposal. He liked the idea of two old people getting together; it gave him hope that one day he would find someone too.

'She will not want to know me any more, not when she finds out what I have done.'

'Old Mrs Moon is very understanding, Petros. She has lived for a long time, longer than you. She knows that it is not easy.' All that listening without saying a word. 'She will not judge you, Petros.'

Petros shook his head heavily. 'Please, you cannot tell her. She trusted me.'

A knock on the door.

'Petros? Are you in there?'

Petros and Tripi looked at each other.

'Petros? It's Sandy, Milo's mum.'

Tripi jumped up just in time to see the Lovely Sandy walking into the room.

'Tripi?' When she said his name, it was like a small bird flying out of her mouth.

He looked from Sandy to Petros to his bags and boxes and the bare walls and knew what he had to do. An old man could not sleep on a park bench or by a canal.

'Petros must stay with you,' he said to Sandy.

'But—' Sandy started.

'I do not mind, I have another place to go. Petros must come to Crescent Way.'

'I don't understand,' said Sandy.

'Petros has been kicked out by Nurse Thornhill, he is homeless.'

'Why? What have you done, Petros?'

Petros's eyes clouded over.

Tripi stepped in. 'Because of the marriage proposal.'

'That's ridiculous.'

'She said it is policy.' Tripi had heard that word so often on Nurse Thornhill's lips that he was certain Sandy would believe him. He tried to imitate Nurse Thornhill's deep voice. 'The policy is: "No couples at Forget Me Not". Only single people. So you see, Sandy, he must come home with you.'

'She really doesn't like people being happy, does she?'

Tripi looked at the Lovely Sandy and thought of how, in a different life, he would have liked to make her happy.

Petros took off his cap and twisted it between his hands. 'I am fine, thank you. I don't need a place to stay.'

'Do not listen to him, he must go. I willingly sacrifice my place.'

'Your place?'

'He must stay instead of me in your house in Crescent Way.'

'And what about Lou? Milo's gran? I can't leave her here alone,' said Sandy. 'She needs you, Petros.'

'I will look after her – until we have made the film and caught Nurse Thornhill, then everything will be fine. Then ...' His voice trailed off. *Then I will find Ayishah.*

Last night, Tripi had stayed on his old bench by the canal.

For hours he could not find sleep, the cold too sharp on a body that had got used to the warmth of a house. But he told himself that this was his life now. Not in a nice home marrying a nice English girl and having a job as a chef. As long as he had not found Ayishah, he did not deserve any of those things. When at last he fell asleep, he dreamt of that hot day in July when they left, the bombs falling on Damascus.

'From the Four Seasons to Buckingham Palace: we are stylish tourists,' Ayishah said.

She laid out the papers: their new identities, a copy of the letter from their fictional uncle in England and the job recommendation from the chef.

Tripi felt his heart swell under his ribcage. For Ayishah, this was a big adventure. Unlike him, she wasn't worried that they were leaving in a hurry, two weeks earlier than planned, nor was she scared by the three days of bombardments that they'd just lived through or anxious when the driver they'd paid to take them across the border announced that this was their last chance to get out, that he would not be coming back to Damascus.

'What will be, will be,' she said, smiling at having slipped in an English saying.

Gunshots through the night, the city lit up like a firework display. He looked at her shining eyes.

'And this means we will get to England faster,' Ayishah said. 'That is a good thing.'

The Toyota would take them to the Turkish border. And then onwards, through Europe: Greece, Italy, France. If all went well, they would reach England by the end of September.

They sat together in the back of the open pick-up and held hands, Ayishah because she was excited, Tripi because he did not want to let go of his little sister, not with all these guns and strangers. Her small palm fitted perfectly into his. He remembered how, as a baby, she'd loved to clamp her fingers around his, how she cried when she was pulled away from him, her big brother.

'We are squashed like sardines,' she whispered and then leant in closer. 'With smelly sardines.' She giggled and held her nose.

One of these smelly strangers stood up in the back of the pick-up and yelled at the driver. 'Hey, why are we going to Aleppo? The plan was to go straight to the border.'

'We have more people to collect,' the driver called back

Anything for a few Syrian pounds, thought Tripi. For some, business was more lucrative in times of war than in times of peace.

Another man pulled a mobile from his ear and yelled.

'Things are not good in Aleppo. I have a friend there, he says not to enter the city.'

'Just following orders,' said the driver.

'I've never seen Aleppo,' said Ayishah, her eyes wide at all these new things. 'And it's good, isn't it? To be helping more people?'

Tripi nodded and kissed her forehead. Ayishah had a way of chasing away his selfish thoughts. Picking up more people felt like an unnecessary delay, an extra danger, but as ever, his little sister pricked his conscience. Perhaps there were more people like them, brothers and sisters, parents and children, who needed to leave the city, to start a new life.

The Toyota coughed its way into the streets of the second largest city in Syria, and then screeched to a halt. A rush of air, the car tilting to one side under its heavy cargo, a flat tyre.

'Everyone off,' said the driver. 'Everyone off.'

Gunshots bounced off the buildings. The two men who had shouted at the driver were right: they should not be here.

For the first time, Ayishah's eyes darkened.

'It's okay, Ayishah,' Tripi said. 'We won't be stopping for long.'

Three hours of waiting and still the driver had not returned with a spare tyre. Tripi and Ayishah played the game where they wrote long English words on each other's arms and the other had to guess what they were. They'd used up just about every word they knew and Ayishah, tired from all the excitement, was beginning to get sleepy. He drew her close and felt her weight lean into him.

Darkness fell on the city. Troops poured into the streets.

Some shot at the sides of the Toyota, just for the pleasure of it.

Murmurings rippled between the passengers. Ayishah looked up and rubbed her eyes. They listened to people's ideas for what to do next:

Shall we leave on foot?

Yes, we must get out of Aleppo before we get blown to pieces.

No, we should wait for the driver, we have paid so much.

How far is it to the border?

Are the roads safe?

Some left. Others sat on the road and waited for the driver.

Tripi wished he could turn back time to those days when he worked long hours in the kitchen, when Ayishah came back from school, full of English words and stories.

'What do you want to do, Ayishah?' Tripi asked.

He watched his little sister open her mouth, always more decisive than him, and then, out of nowhere, a cloud of noise and dust tore up between them.

Tripi got up off the pavement, his head pounding, shards of glass lodged in the palms of his hands. His head thumped so hard and the smoke was so thick and acrid that he found it hard to keep his eyes open. He hardly knew where he was. A burnt-out car. The Toyota too had caught fire.

'Ayishah?' He called. 'Ayishah?'

He staggered up and down the road. A few of the passengers from the Toyota had been injured and thrown to the ground like Tripi; others had left already. How long had it been since the explosion?

On the side of the road, a sheet covered a small body: a flower of blood seeped into the white cotton.

'Ayishah?'

He lurched forward and then saw that a mother was sitting by the body, crying.

'Halim ... My Halim ... ' she said, over and over.

'Ayishah!' he called out, his voice raw.

Dark now, the street silent. The fighting had moved on. And no Ayishah.

When Tripi woke up by the canal, he knew he had to go back and find her, that he should never have left Syria. So he took to the road, hoping for a free ride to London. He would find a job, pay for a flight home. Or if that did not work, he would hand himself in to the police.

But then Milo had called and persuaded him to come back. He had said that Al had seen Ayishah on the news and that, after the awards ceremony, they would find her together.

'Tripi? Tripi?' Sandy touched Tripi's arm. 'Did you hear me? I said okay, Petros can come with me. If you help him with his things, I'll bring the car round to the front door.'

Tripi gave Sandy a small bow. 'You have a very fit heart.' Sometimes he liked making up phrases of his own. He wanted to let her know that she was kind to take Petros in.

She smiled at him, but she frowned at the same time so he was not sure that he had said the right thing.

54

Milo

Milo had been sitting in the garden for what felt like hours, waiting for Big Mike and Lalana to get out of the way. Clouds was being his lookout on the pavement at the front of the house. Milo had had to persuade Clouds to come with him. *It's undercover work*, he'd said, which made Clouds happy, though Clouds said they had to be quick. Mum had asked him to babysit Milo until she got back from Forget Me Not and he wasn't sure that breaking into someone's house was the kind of babysitting she had in mind.

After dropping a note through Mrs Hairy's letterbox (an apology for stepping in front of her Mercedes and an invitation to the awards ceremony – when she saw the film they'd made, she'd have to believe him), Milo and Clouds sellotaped posters of Hamlet along the high street, Clouds had printed them off his computer and made them look like WANTED signs to catch people's attention. Then they went to Big Mike's house.

Milo watched Big Mike kiss Lalana with his fat lips.

He watched Big Mike pull off Lalana's jumper and squeeze her small titties with his plump, white fingers.

After that, Milo watched Mike lift Lalana off the ground – she was tiny compared to Big Mike, as small as Milo, nearly.

And then he watched Big Mike swing her round and round like on Strictly Come Dancing, except not as well.

At last, with his face frozen numb and his eyes fuzzy from staring, Milo watched Big Mike carry Lalana upstairs to the bedroom. He knew what would happen next: Big Mike would get on top of Lalana and they'd rub their bodies against each other and make grunting noises, like Hamlet when he needed a poo. Milo was a bit worried about Lalana getting squashed under Big Mike, but he didn't allow himself to think of that for long. He had to concentrate on getting in and out of the house without Big Mike noticing.

Now that Tripi was coming to live at home, Milo wanted him to have all his things, like the photo of the Queen that Ayishah liked and his pocket dictionary and Mum's yoga mat that he needed for praying.

Milo planned to set everything up in his room as a surprise for when Tripi came home after his shift. It was his way of saying thank you to Tripi for coming back from London to help him catch Nurse Thornhill.

He eased his hand through the broken glass, turned the handle and walked into the lounge.

Big Mike's house was a mess, not like when Tripi lived there. Swimming trunks and bottles of sun lotion and straw hats and towels lay scattered around the lounge. Cereal and crumbs and puddles of milk sat on the kitchen counter. In the hall Big Mike's suitcases lay snapped open, spilling out more clothes. And then, thrown in a pile under the stairs, Tripi's things. Milo breathed a sigh of relief that they hadn't been taken by the police.

Maybe, once Big Mike saw how nicely his house had been kept, he'd decided not to press charges. Anyway, he was probably too busy squeezing Lalana's titties to worry about anything else. Milo thought it would be nice to have something that made you so happy that you forgot about all the things that weren't right in your life.

Milo put Ayishah's backpack on his shoulders and Tripi's backpack on his front, slotted Mum's yoga mat under one arm and Tripi's sleeping bag under the other and headed for the front door.

'Who the hell are you?'

Milo jumped and shifted his head around the hallway. It took him a second to locate where the voice was coming from.

Heavy footsteps came down the stairs.

'What are you doing in my house?' Big Mike stood at the bottom of the stairs in his boxer shorts. His shirt hung open over his hairy belly, his face red and sweaty.

Milo yanked at the front door.

'Hey! Don't I know you? You're the kid—'

Please, please don't recognise me, thought Milo. He'd only just got Mum on board with The Plan; he couldn't afford to get in any more trouble.

Milo flung open the front door and felt a heavy hand pull on Ayishah's backpack.

If he wanted to get away, Milo knew there was only one option.

He eased his small shoulders from under the straps, dropped the sleeping bag and Mum's yoga mat, pushed through the front door and clattered down the front steps onto the High Street.

Clouds and Milo speed-walked all the way home.

'You did the right thing,' said Clouds. 'You couldn't risk him catching hold of you.'

Milo shook his head. 'I failed the mission. I didn't get Tripi's things and now I bet we'll never get them back.'

'You did the best you could, Milo. Tripi will be grateful for that.'

Milo wasn't sure.

When they turned into Crescent Way, Milo heard Mr Overend whistling and saw him lean out of his window and stare at Milo's house like on the day Clouds moved in.

Milo had an idea. He went to stand on the pavement under Mr Overend's window.

'Where are you going?' asked Clouds.

'You know what you said, about Mr Overend making a good undercover reporter? Well, let's see how good he really is.'

Milo tilted his head and looked up through the pinhole.

'Mr Overend?'

Mr Overend stopped whistling.

'Have you seen my pig, Hamlet?'

Mr Overend didn't say anything, he just stood there looking out at Milo's bedroom window.

'Well, seeing as you look out onto the street so much, could you keep an eye out for him? He might try to find his way home.'

Mr Overend gave Milo a wink and started whistling again.

What a loon.

Milo and Clouds came through the front door and stood in the hallway to catch their breath. And then Milo smelt something funny, a smell that definitely shouldn't be in his home.

He looked around. Brown cases and boxes cluttered the hallway, and paintings. It was the paintings that made Milo recognise the smell: the smell that had hung around Gran ever since she'd moved into Forget Me Not. Plasticky lemons.

'Milo? Is that you?'

Mum was home. Milo prepared himself for a lecture.

She came out of the kitchen, kissed his forehead and didn't say anything about Milo being out when he shouldn't have been.

'Sorry, Sandy – we went for a quick tour of Slipton to see if we could find Hamlet,' said Clouds.

'Thanks, Al,' said Sandy.

As Clouds made his way back up to his room, Milo saw Petros sitting at the kitchen counter drinking tea out of Milo's favourite mug, the one with the flying pigs that went with the side plate.

Petros held the mug out to Milo like he was saying cheers.

'What's he doing here?' asked Milo.

Mum gave Milo a *don't-be-rude* glare. 'Petros is staying with us for a while.'

'Where's Tripi?'

'Tripi?'

'I left a message on your phone.'

'Oh. I'm afraid I haven't had time—'

Milo put down his bag. He picked up Mum's phone, jabbed in the code for the message service, waited for the electronic voice to stop speaking and held out the receiver. His recorded voice rang out into the kitchen.

'I'm sorry I didn't get the message, Milo.'

Milo looked at the raw patch on Mum's neck; drops of blood sat on her pink skin.

'Darling, we don't have room for Tripi, not with Petros staying.'

'What's wrong with Petros's room at Forget Me Not?'

From what Milo had seen, Petros's room was bigger and nicer than any of the old ladies' rooms.

'It's complicated, Milo. He doesn't have anywhere else to go now.'

Tripi didn't have anywhere to go. And *Tripi* was a friend. And *Tripi* hadn't tried to steal Gran away.

'You have a very nice room, Milo,' said Petros. He placed his wrinkly lips over one of the flying pigs on the rim of Milo's mug and slurped his tea. Gran hated bad table manners.

'You've put him in *my* room?'

Mum chewed the nail on her little finger and didn't answer.

Milo stormed upstairs and flung open his bedroom door.

He shifted his head around his room and noticed something lying on his bed: that stupid painting from Forget Me Not with the small sailing boat lost in those big waves.

Clouds hadn't yet made it all the way up to his room, so he came back down the stairs and stood at Milo's door.

'Come on, Milo, don't worry about all this stuff. Let's start work on that film.'

Milo shook his head. He took the painting off his bed and stared at the little boat, then he put the painting under one arm, grabbed his duvet and his pillow, pushed past Clouds, stomped down the stairs, walked through the kitchen, dumped the painting at Petros's feet and went out through the back door into the garden.

As long as Petros was in Milo's home, Milo would stay in the shed. It wasn't like it was being used for anything else.

55

Milo

Whenever Milo came in here, it was so quiet that it felt like someone was pushing cotton wool into his ears. Dad had insulated the shed to block out the engine noises from the planes. *We can't have your mum's clients getting disturbed*, he'd said, taking Mum by the waist and giving her a kiss. Milo used to turn away when Mum and Dad did that yucky lovey stuff, but now he missed it.

Milo dumped his duvet and his pillow on the floor and switched on the desk lamp. He grabbed his duvet and his pillow and curled up by the door.

He let his mind scan through the last twelve months. He couldn't think of a single good thing that had happened since last Christmas. Except getting Hamlet, and even he was missing now.

Milo screwed shut his eyes. He played Great-Gramps's bagpipe song in his head until he fell asleep.

*

As Milo sunk deeper into sleep, his mind wandered into dreams. He was still dreaming at midnight, when he got up off the floor and opened the door to the shed. He stretched and yawned and then tilted his head to the dark sky: only a tiny chunk to go before a full moon.

The house stood dark and quiet.

Milo floated out of his body, walked across the wet grass and out through the side gate onto Crescent Way.

As he stood in the middle of the empty street he noticed that Mr Overend hadn't moved from his window: he stood there in his PJs whistling like when Milo had come home.

When he spotted Milo standing under the street lamp, he stopped whistling and disappeared from the window. The next moment he was standing at his front door with wellies and a coat over his PJs.

'I've been waiting for you,' said Mr Overend. 'Are you ready?'

Milo was surprised that he could talk. Apart from the whistling, he'd thought Mr Overend was mute, like Gran. Or like Gran before she decided to get her voice back and announce she was getting married.

'Ready to go?' Mr Overend asked.

Milo nodded.

Together, they walked down Crescent Way and through Slipton's windy streets to the canal. When they reached the line of houseboats, Mr Overend pointed to the bench. A dark bundle lay wrapped in a sleeping bag.

'Go closer,' said Mr Overend.

Milo went and stood above the bundle and looked down at Tripi's face. His dark hair fell over his eyes and his lips curled up at the sides. His head rested on Ayishah's red bag. How had he got his things back?

'You see?' said Mr Overend.

Milo nodded.

'Come on, we don't have long.'

Milo followed Mr Overend down the high street until they reached Forget Me Not. Mr Overend pointed up to Gran's window. The curtains were open and the light from the moon lit up Gran's figure as she sat in her armchair. Her face looked peaceful.

Next to her, in a little vase, stood a yellow rose. Petros must have taken Milo's advice. Its golden petals leant into the dark night like a shooting star.

'You see?' said Mr Overend.

Milo nodded slowly, though this time he didn't really want to see.

'Nearly time to go home.' Mr Overend took Milo's hand and guided him past the high street to the park. As they stood peering through the gates, Milo heard a rustling in the long grass by the lake.

'Look,' said Mr Overend.

Milo shifted his head. And then he saw Hamlet, bigger than he remembered, snuffling at the earth.

His black ear and his white ear stood stiff and tall, his small black eyes shone, reflecting the nearly-full moon and, for a second, Milo was sure Hamlet was looking right at him.

Milo turned to Mr Overend to say thank you, but Mr Overend had vanished and when he looked back through the park gates, Hamlet had disappeared too.

*

Milo woke with a start, shivering. Through the pinhole, he looked up at the window to the shed: the glass was webbed with ice.

A gentle crunch on the grass outside. And then a bang at the base of the chipboard door followed by a yelp and a *stupid, stupid door.* And then someone walking away.

He stood up and opened the door just a crack. Cold air swept in. The smell of wet grass, the night sharp with frost. The moon shone like a big white coin, nearly full now. Clouds's light was on in the attic and blue flashes flickered through the lounge window. And then Milo saw something move across the lawn: Mum, hopping away towards the back door.

Milo's gaze flicked down to the patch of frozen grass in front of the shed where he spotted a plate heaped with buttery toast, white Fluff smeared thickly, right to the edges.

He felt a flutter in his chest, just by his heart, and then Gran's voice:

Give her a chance, Milo. Just a little chance.

'Mum!' he called out, his voice small in the night.

She stopped hopping towards the house, stood still and then turned round.

For a moment they looked at each other across the garden, neither of them knowing what to say.

Milo picked up the plate and held it up. 'Do you want some?' he called out to her.

Mum nodded and walked slowly back towards the shed.

When she got close, he noticed a pearl of blood sitting on her little toe.

'You stubbed it again,' Milo said.

Mum nodded.

'Does it hurt?'

Mum's eyes welled up and she bit her lip. 'A little.'

When the beauty business was running properly, she'd stub her toe on the shed door all the time. She wore open-toed mules to show off the nail-varnish she sold to her customers: a new colour every week. Sometimes, she'd let Milo paint it on for her. But the bottom of the shed door hung forward further than you thought it did when you looked at it face on, and there was a gap where it was meant to join the frame. So when she went to put the key in the padlock, she'd forget and her little toe would get caught. Dad had promised to fix it, but that was before The Tart came along.

Just because she'd brought him Fluff on toast and just because she'd stubbed her toe, didn't mean that Milo was going to forgive Mum. But she looked cold and her eyes were sad and there was more toast than he could manage on his own, so he opened the door a little wider and let her in.

They sat on the floor, their backs against the shed wall, and for a few minutes the only sound was them munching toast.

'Couldn't you sleep?' Milo asked, thinking of the blue flashes in the lounge.

Mum shook her head. She pressed down on her little toe to stem the blood. 'I think there's a splinter in there, that's why it won't stop bleeding.'

Milo stood up, went over to Mum's eyebrow kit and took out the tweezers, the ones with the little battery-operated light attached so you could catch the tiniest of tiny hairs. Then he sat down beside her and took her little toe in his hands. He focused his eyes, switched on the tweezers and bent over. There, nestled just under the nail, was a small brown splinter.

'It's going to hurt a bit, Mum,' Milo said.

Mum laughed as though Milo had said something funny.

He poised the tweezers over her skin and then pinched at the tiny brown thread.

Mum let out a small gasp.

'Got it!' Milo said, holding up the tweezers and the splinter to show her.

'I think you should take over the salon,' Mum said, looking around the shed. 'You'd make a great eyebrow plucker.' She sighed. 'In fact, I think you'd do a better job of running this whole damned business than I ever did.'

'I want to be an undercover reporter, Mum, like Clouds.'

'You do?'

Milo nodded. It was the first time he'd said it out loud, like it was a real plan, beyond helping the old people in the nursing home, like it was something he wanted to do for the rest of his life. For a second, he panicked and wished he hadn't. He knew what Mum was thinking – that it wasn't a proper job, that it was too dangerous, that it got you in trouble with the police, that it didn't make enough money and that he'd struggle with his eyes.

'Well, I'll have to train someone else to wax Mrs Hairy, then,' she said and they both laughed and the air between them felt lighter.

'Do you miss Dad?' Milo asked.

Mum went to get a wad of cotton wool from a glass jar on the shelf and wrapped it around her little toe. Without turning round she said:

'Every day.'

'I miss him too.'

'I know, Milo.' Her voice wavered. 'I know.'

'Are you angry with him? About Angela and that he left?'

Mum turned round and came back to sit beside Milo.

'For a while, I was angry. But now I suppose I'm just sad.'

'Because you wish he'd come back?'

Mum shook her head. 'No. I know that won't happen – he's got a new life and a new baby – and he's happy, Milo. Happier than he ever was. The reason I'm sad is because I wish I'd handled things differently. Mainly for you.'

Milo didn't think Mum had ever considered his feelings in any of this. It was all about her and Dad and how she somehow didn't know how to operate without him around. It was as if when he left he'd taken some of the screws that held her together and now all she could do was walk around all wonky and falling apart.

Mum paused for a moment and then she wrapped one of her big, pudgy arms around him and pulled him into her chest. Milo felt the softness of Mum's skin and the warmth of Mum's body pressing into his and for once he didn't mind the sticky perfume that clung to her nightie – he liked it even, because it smelt like something he knew. He couldn't remember the last time that Mum had given him a hug.

Milo suddenly felt tired, more tired than he'd felt in weeks and weeks. His body softened against Mum's.

'Why did you make Gran go away?'

He felt Mum take in a sharp breath and then she held it for a second, as though she was scared to let it go.

'She needed proper care, Milo, more than either of us could give her. It wasn't fair, she was becoming too much of a burden on you.'

A lump rose in Milo's throat. 'But she wasn't a burden. I loved having Gran here, I loved looking after her.' His voice swelled and grew thick. 'Everything was better when she was here.'

Mum stroked the back of Milo's head. 'I know, darling. I know.'

Milo pulled away from Mum and looked her in the eye. 'And it didn't work, did it? We went and stuck her in that horrible, horrible place where she didn't get proper care after all. She would have been better off at home.'

Mum's tired eyes filled up and the tip of her nose went pink. She closed her eyelids and two fat tears plopped down onto her cheeks. She sniffed.

'I got so much wrong, Milo. But we're going to make it okay, I promise.' She swept her index finger under each set of eyelashes to get rid of the tears. 'And because of you, we're going to improve the lives of more than just Gran – we're going to make it better for all those old people at Forget Me Not.'

'You think it's going to work?'

Mum smiled. 'Of course it's going to work.'

Milo waited a beat and then he asked:

'And you'll help me find Hamlet? We'll put out adverts and everything?'

She laughed lightly and kissed his head. 'Yes, we'll find Hamlet. From now on, everything's going to be okay, I promise.'

56

Lou

Milo's face when he heard her voice. He saw her love for Petros as a betrayal of the grandfather he'd never met. Another betrayal, like that of his father when he took his love away from Sandy.

Lou shook her head. Milo was right. A sentimental old fool, that's what she was; falling in love again at ninety-two, clutching at her last chance of a wedding she'd been waiting for her whole life.

Most nights Lou slept in her bra and pants and tights. Without Milo's help there was too much elastic, too many fiddly hooks to cope with on her own. She walked to the wardrobe, dragging her left leg behind her. The leg had joined the protest of her left arm and the left side of her face.

She picked out the dress she'd kept for special occasions. Red poppies on white cotton, the dress Milo made her wear on her birthday. Strange how, as you got older, your clothes seemed to grow until they swam around you, their vast folds of fabric swallowing you up.

Lou wanted to make an effort for Milo – Tripi had told her about the awards ceremony and how much it meant to Milo. She had to be well for that.

With one hand she eased the dress over her head, and then it got stuck. She pushed harder, the collar ripped, her right arm gave way.

Milo, I need your help, she whispered.

He'd always known when she needed him, would come tearing up the stairs to her small room under the roof to help her out of bed, to fill up her glass of water, to tie up her hair.

Milo . . .

'Need a hand?' Mrs Moseley stood at the door, propped up on her cane. Her dress was clean today, no stains.

'No, no, no.' Nurse Thornhill swept past Mrs Moseley and strode into the room. 'It's too cold for that.' She whipped off Lou's dress and shoved it back into the wardrobe. 'Like a child.' She shook her head. 'Haven't you looked out of the window? There's ice on the pavements.' Nurse Thornhill pulled a jumper and a woollen skirt out of the wardrobe.

'You could turn the heating up.' Lou's words came out slurred. For years she'd wondered how her voice would sound if it came back one day. Would it sound new and unused, out of sync with her old body? Would she still have her Scottish accent?

Nurse Thornhill stared at Lou. 'Maybe you should go back to being quiet.' She turned away and called for Nurse Heidi through the door.

Nurse Heidi's footsteps in the corridor. And then her face at the door.

'Morning, Mrs Moon,' she said, her voice as light as a bird's.

'Heidi, I need you to take Mrs Moseley back to her room, please.'

Nurse Heidi slipped her arm under Mrs Moseley's elbow and guided her as she shuffled down the corridor.

'Now get dressed, chop, chop.' Nurse Thornhill turned to Lou.

She slammed the door behind her and left Lou standing in her bra and knickers and tights.

Milo ... I'm slipping ...

Lou looked at the window, stars of ice on the inside of the glass panes, the cold creeping in.

I'm slipping away.

57

Milo

'Time to wake up, Milo, or you'll be late for school.'

Mum poked her head round the shed door. She smiled, walked in and kissed the top of his head.

'Here's your uniform – no time for a shower this morning, I'm afraid.'

She placed a clean shirt and clean underwear and clean socks along with his tie and his trousers and his jumper on the massage table.

Milo couldn't remember the last time she'd laid out his clothes for him.

'I've made some breakfast, but you might have to grab and run. Can't have Mrs Harris complaining again.' She gave him a wink.

He noticed that she had a new dress on and she was wearing make-up and she'd even painted her nails. He felt his whole body lighten. Things were going to be okay after all.

When she'd gone back to the house, he stretched and looked around the shed. And that's when he saw some papers that didn't look like Mum's beauty leaflets or her holiday brochures or even the bills she tried to hide so he wouldn't worry about their money problems.

He scanned the heading: *Slipton Star Home Insurance*
Dear Mrs Moon . . . the letter started.

The words twisted in front of Milo's tired, fuzzy eyes. But there was one part he found easy to read: a section in bold, right at the bottom.

Our insurance inspectors have concluded that the fire which occurred on Saturday 1st of December does not come under your accidental home insurance policy. There is evidence that the fire was started deliberately. You will therefore not be receiving an insurance payment from Slipton Star Insurance.

Mum had said that the insurance would pay out for a new kitchen, that it was guaranteed.

Milo rubbed his eyes and focused on the next few lines:

Furthermore, due to clear evidence of interference, Slipton Star Insurance will be undertaking an independent fraud investigation.

Fraud. That meant cheating and lying and trying to get something for nothing. But the fire was an accident. All the insurance inspectors had to do was go and visit Gran and they'd see that she forgot things like that the tap was still running and that the lid wasn't on the kettle so it boiled dry and that Great-Gramps was dead.

Gran wouldn't set fire to the kitchen on purpose. Milo swallowed hard. Would she?

The morning of the fire came back to him. How he hadn't heard the clatter of the pan, which meant that she was going to make her tea on the hob instead of the kettle, how, for the first time ever, it had taken him ages to realise there was a problem and that she needed him and that by the time he got down to her, the kitchen was already on fire.

He felt an ache in his chest and the ache got worse when he looked at his clothes all neatly folded up on the massage table. The Christmas Party, that's when everything started to go wrong.

That's when they found out about Dad's Tart.

That's when Milo nearly got run over and they had to go and see Dr Nolan who told him that his eyes didn't work any more.

That's when Mum stopped sleeping and started watching holiday programmes day and night and eating too many Hobnobs and getting rashes and losing all her customers.

That's when Gran started shaking and forgetting things and talking about Inverary.

And that's what led to the fire and Gran getting kicked out and going to that horrible nursing home with evil Nurse Thornhill and lechy Petros.

He'd wanted to believe Mum last night: that she was sorry, that she cared about him, that things were going to be okay. But she was probably lying again, just as she'd lied about the fire and Gran and the insurance.

He pulled on his uniform and ran out across the lawn and

ducked round the back of the house so that Mum wouldn't see him. The last thing he felt like doing was eating her stupid breakfast.

'You're late, Milo,' Mrs Harris said as Milo crashed into a desk at the front of the class.

'I don't care,' he mumbled under his breath.

Beside him, Nadja gasped.

Milo slumped into his seat.

'What did you say, Milo?'

Through the pinhole Milo stared at Mrs Harris's twisted yellow tooth.

'He said he didn't care,' announced Stan.

Milo shut his eyes. Could this day get any worse?

'Sorry,' he blurted out. But he wasn't sorry. He wasn't sorry about anything any more.

'Well, seeing as you're in such a good mood today, Milo, why don't you start us off.'

Mrs Harris sat in her chair behind her desk, got out her mark book and waited.

'Start doing what?'

Nadja stared at him, her eyes wide. Laughter rolled in from the class behind him.

'If you'd turned up on time, Milo, you'd know, wouldn't you?'

He hated that, how teachers got bees in their bonnets when you did something to upset them and then found ways to punish you over and over.

'Your special pet, Milo?'

All at once Milo's body flooded with panic. He felt like he was being filled up with concrete like one of those craters in the middle of Slipton High Street, and now he couldn't breathe and couldn't move and couldn't get out of the way.

The Speaking and Listening presentation. The one that was meant to make up for his bad marks in English and Maths. He'd forgotten all about it.

'Come on, Milo, get your notes out, we don't have all day.'

Milo cleared his throat. 'Could I have a word with you in private, Mrs Harris?' he asked.

He wanted to explain to her that he hadn't had time. With everything happening at home and at Forget Me Not, he'd got behind on his schoolwork. If she gave him until tomorrow, he could prepare tonight. Even she had to understand.

'I don't think that will be necessary, Milo. Just say what you've got to say out here.'

She was still punishing him for having been rude when he came in. He wished he could take the words back and start again.

'I need a bit longer to prepare,' he said.

'I'm afraid that's not an option.'

'Or maybe I could . . . I could write an essay on the computer instead. I could make it twice as long as the talk. I'll try really hard. It's just that I haven't had the time . . .'

Mrs Harris put her elbows on her desk and pressed her hands together like she was going to pray. Then she looked right at him and spoke really slowly.

'It's time you took responsibility for your learning, Milo. I can't always be making exceptions – that wouldn't be fair, now, would it?'

'Good point,' chipped in Stan.

'Be quiet, Stanley,' barked Mrs Harris, which made Milo feel one millimetre better about the mess he was in.

'I'm sure you've got lots to say about your pet – just see this as an opportunity to learn some improvisation skills.'

Nadja tilted her head to one side and looked at him with such sad eyes he thought she might cry. She was probably thinking about how worried she'd be if she had to give a talk without having prepared it.

Milo got up onto his feet and went to stand in front of the board.

He coughed and tried to focus his eyes, but all he could see through the pinhole was the blur of his classmates, and even then, only a small, select blur. He imagined all the ones he didn't see smirking and pulling faces at him.

'The thing is . . . ' Milo started. 'The thing is that I don't have a pet any more.' A picture of Hamlet flashed in front of his eyes: he was sitting in his cage in the garage, his black ear and his white ear standing on end, his curly tail twitching, squealing as the smoke and the flames came in from the kitchen. If what the insurance letter said was true, if Gran started the fire on purpose, Hamlet could have died. If Milo hadn't found the fire blanket and held it in front of him and got to Hamlet on time, he could have burnt to a crisp. And all because she wanted to go to some stupid nursing home. And who was looking after Hamlet now? Who'd make sure he didn't get trapped in a fire or run over or chopped up and put into sausages?

Milo closed his eyes and gulped. He didn't want to cry, not here.

'What is it, Stan?' Mrs Harris's voice came in from the side.

Milo shifted his head. Stan had his hand up.

'Are we allowed to ask questions?'

'Not yet. Let Milo finish.'

'I was just wondering how he managed to lose a pig.'

Milo clenched his fists. 'You don't understand. Hamlet . . . he . . . he . . . ' Milo stuttered. 'He ran away from Forget Me Not.'

'You took your pig to a nursing home?' Stan let out a big belly laugh. Others joined in.

'Be quiet, Stan. Remember that you're being marked for your listening. Let Milo go on.'

But Milo couldn't go on. The words stayed trapped in his throat, right under that big lump that had come up when he thought of Hamlet darting around the streets of Slipton all on his own.

He hung his head and dropped his shoulders and stared down at his feet.

'Milo?' Mrs Harris's voice had softened a bit. 'Milo?' She stood up.

Milo walked slowly back to his desk and slumped down into his chair. He'd thought this day couldn't get any worse, but it just had – worse than he'd ever thought possible.

58

Tripi

Tripi watched Nurse Thornhill rub her lips together in the reflective surface of the oven door. She had gone a shade brighter today. Her hair looked whiter too, pulled back so tight he saw the pink of her skull. And she had swapped her white clogs for sharp, beige heels.

He thought back to Monday and how she'd worn those black clothes that drained the colour out of her face. She must be keeping secrets, he thought, like the rest of us. *People do bad things when they are unhappy*, that was what Tripi's father taught him. He understood that unhappiness could be dangerous, he had seen it on the streets of Damascus and in Aleppo on that hot day in July when Ayishah disappeared behind the rubble. He had thought that sadness would creep under his skin and change him for ever too.

Nurse Thornhill's starched uniform crackled as she walked. He hoped that she wouldn't check the storeroom, which is where he'd been sleeping for the last few nights. Sandy had tried to persuade him to come and stay in the house, that she would make up a bed on the couch, but he thought he should stay here, near the old people.

Tripi carried the heavy pan of potatoes to the sink and emptied it into the colander. He felt her eyes watching him and his hands slipped. A pale potato rolled across the tiles. He wiped the steam off his brow, picked up the potato and took it over to the bin.

'Back into the colander,' she said.

'But it is dirty.' At The Four Seasons, the Head Chef had explained how tourists had delicate stomachs. *Everything must be clean*, he said. *So our customers don't get sick.*

'We can't afford to be wasteful, Tahir,' said Nurse Thornhill.

Tripi angled the camera phone in his pocket to make sure it caught those red lips. He already had a picture of the stock-room with all the cheap tinned food and of the locks on the outside of the old people's doors; now he wanted to get Nurse Thornhill on film.

'I'll only be a few hours, Nurse Heidi's in charge. Don't forget, not too much meat, we've got plenty of potatoes.'

Tripi wondered what Nurse Thornhill would be eating at the dinner to which she'd been invited. He pictured her pushing fat forkfuls of steak through her red lips, gravy running down her chin.

Nurse Thornhill straightened up and pushed out her small bosom.

'They might come in here tomorrow to take some pictures.' She swept around the kitchen and wrinkled her nose. 'What's that sweet smell?' Nurse Thornhill was twitching her nose like the rats that sniffed at the rubbish bins by the canal.

Tripi had got up early to make baklava. They were going to have a party after the awards ceremony, a double party to celebrate Nurse Thornhill's departure and the engagement of Old Mrs Moon and Petros. The Lovely Sandy had brought over the brown sugar and honey and filo pastry and pistachios. Was it possible that the ingredients could make Tripi long for home and for Sandy at the same time?

I wish I could take you to my restaurant in Damascus, he had told her. *I would make you a thousand dishes from my homeland.*

She had blushed and sucked in her stomach. *I'll need to go on a diet first.*

He had shaken his head. *No diet, no diet.* He did not want there to be any less of her.

She released her stomach.

Sandy explained that she and Milo had made up, that they were friends now and that everything was going to be better.

She smiled her Lovely Sandy smile. *He's ready to fight the powers of evil. Been through a lot, the little man, most of it my fault. But from now on, I'm going to be there for him.*

And that made Tripi feel sad, because he could see how much Sandy wanted to be a good mother. And it also made him sad because it made him think of Ayishah and how much she had been through and that maybe if he had looked after her better, they would not have been separated.

He should never have given up looking for her. Two months, hundreds of kilometres, every refugee camp on the

Turkish border, clutching the photograph that no one wanted to look at. They had seen too many pictures of missing children.

And then the thought had come to him: perhaps his clever, resourceful little sister, who could charm her way into anyone's heart, had travelled through Europe on her own. She had her papers and she knew her destination: Buckingham Palace, London.

Every day of October, Tripi stood outside The Queen's gates, scanning the faces of little girls with dark curly hair, looking for Ayishah's brown eyes.

Soon his money ran out. Policemen stopped him in the street and asked to see his papers. And then the job advertisement at Forget Me Not, a small town called Slipton, a place where he could hide from the authorities.

But now there was hope, wasn't there? Milo had said that this man, Al, had seen Ayishah on his television screen, that he was investigating. And then, like a sign from Allah, he had found his things: his sleeping bag and Ayishah's red rucksack sitting by the bins outside MailOrderBrideMan's house.

Miracles happen every day, Tripi.

Knowing that part of Ayishah was close to him again had allowed him to sleep well, despite the cold.

'Tripi? I asked you about the smell?'

'Perhaps it is the cleaning product. I have been scrubbing the surfaces, like you said.' He held up the bottle and read the label: 'Lavender and pine.'

'I'd better go.' She rubbed her lips together and brushed her hands down the smooth plane of her uniform.

Tripi took a breath. 'Perhaps with the award money,

you could buy some nice food for the clients, as a celebration?'

'The money is for more pressing things than food, Tahir.'

Like filling your purse, he thought. Nurse Thornhill would have done well out of the war in Syria, Tripi was sure of that – she would have charged the casualties for every bandage, for every bullet hole she stitched up.

Tripi knew that, for Milo's plan to succeed, Nurse Thornhill had to win the prize: she had to go up on stage and collect the trophy and give her speech so that they could show the film. But oh, how he wanted her to – what was that phrase Mrs Moon had written on her pad the other day? *Eat humble pie.* He would like to see Nurse Thornhill eating so much humble pie that it made her vomit.

When she got to the door, Nurse Thornhill turned round.

'Oh, and Tahir? After tonight we'll need to reconsider your contract. With a raised profile I have to make sure our paperwork is in order.'

As soon as she left the room, Tripi switched off Milo's phone.

Her threats could not hurt him any more.

Half an hour later, Tripi heard a knock on the swing doors and then a hushed voice.

'Hey, Tripi, got the phone?'

Al's eyes darted around the kitchen. Tripi still didn't like the thought of him living in Sandy's house.

He handed Al the phone.

'Excellent, mate, I'll get that loaded up.'

An undercover reporter, that's what Milo called Al. Milo had told Tripi that when he was older, he wanted to do that

321

job, but Tripi had seen too many undercover things in his life. He wanted to live in a world where everything was out in the open, where no one spied on their friends or made up stories.

'Sandy'll swing round with the bus in about an hour to collect you all.'

Tripi didn't like Lovely Sandy's name being in Al's mouth. He cleared his throat. 'Do you have any news?'

'What's that, mate?' Al was already scanning through the video footage. 'This is cool stuff.'

'I was wondering whether you had any news about my sister?'

'You have a sister?' Al looked up from the phone.

Tripi felt a hollow thud in his chest.

'Ayishah ... Milo said you had seen her on the news. That you could help me find where she was.'

Al scratched his head. 'I don't think so.' He kept looking at the phone; his eyebrows shot up whenever he saw something he liked. 'Where's your sister, then?'

Tripi's throat felt small and tight. He could barely push the words through his lips. 'In Syria.'

Al looked up. 'Oh, right, the girl on the photocopy.'

'So you have seen her, then?'

'Seen her?'

Tripi saw Ayishah's face a second before the explosion. What would her answer have been? That they should leave Aleppo and go on foot to the Turkish camp, or stay and wait for the driver? If he had heard her words, perhaps he would have found her.

Al put the phone in the pocket of his leather jacket. 'It's a needle in a haystack, mate, there are millions of them.'

'She is twelve years old. She is alone.'

Al shifted from one foot to the other. 'Christ. Well, I'll take another look at the photocopy, see what I can do.'

Tripi closed his eyes and pictured her face, smiling at him across the rubble. *I'll find you, Ayishah*, he promised. *I'll find you soon.*

59

Sandy

Sandy watched the last blue and white pill swirl down the toilet bowl and felt the muscles in her chest relax. She wanted Milo to be proud of her. From now on, she was going to do everything right, even the little things. They were going to build a new life together. No more pills or dieting or thinking about Andy or worrying about money.

She slipped on the dress she'd bought from the RSPCA shop that afternoon. The dress had a halter neck and it had spun as she'd turned to look at herself in the changing room mirror. And it was orange, Milo's favourite colour – a soft, peachy orange like that special moon on the poster in his room. As she'd floated around the shop in her new dress, she'd noticed Milo's torch in there and the woman had explained how he'd come in to exchange it for a travel kettle for his gran. Sandy had sobbed onto the orange dress and bought the torch back and promised herself that as soon as she'd saved a bit, she'd buy him a proper torch, one of those metal ones that sat heavy in your palm and shot out beams of light for miles and miles.

She flushed the loo one last time to make sure the pills were gone for good and then went down to the kitchen and pulled out the television plug. No more holiday programmes. No more wishing her life away.

She stood in the hall and wound a cream coloured scarf around her neck. Perhaps, when all this was over, her rash would disappear.

'You look beautiful.' Petros stood at the bottom of the stairs in a white shirt and a yellow polyester tie that Andy had left behind. Nothing frayed, except for the cap that pressed down on his ears.

'And you are handsome,' said Sandy. 'Lou will be proud to have you on her arm.'

Petros took off his hat, held it to his chest, and bowed. 'I am going for a little walk, to get some air.'

She nodded. 'Make sure you're back by six.'

Then the phone rang and Petros disappeared through the front door.

'Hello?'

A clicking on the other end.

'Milo? Is that you?'

A baby's cry.

'It's me.'

Sandy's hand flew up to her throat. 'Andy?'

'*Just take her,*' she heard Andy say, his mouth pulled away from the receiver.

The baby's cry dimmed. Perhaps Habibti had turned into a demon after all.

'How are you, Sandy?'

325

She wanted to laugh. How am I? Was he serious?

'I'm busy, Andy, I don't have time to talk now.' She scratched at the raw skin under her scarf.

'I'm coming home.'

For a moment, the world froze. The clock on the microwave stopped blinking, the hum from the refrigerator rattled to a halt, the drip from the tap stood suspended in mid-air.

'What?'

'Things aren't working out here.'

Sandy gripped the back of one of the high stools at the kitchen counter.

'Sandy? Are you still there?'

How long had she waited for these words? To hear Andy say that he'd made a mistake, that he was coming back to her, that he was a stupid fool who'd taken her for granted? That he missed her and he missed Milo and wanted them to be a family again. And she'd be cross a while and give him a hard time and then she'd give in and laugh and say that she was sorry too, that she'd try harder and she'd tell him she loved him and that of course he could come home. That she and Milo were waiting for him.

'Angela is struggling with the language.' He paused. 'And the culture. It's all too much for her.'

'What?'

'She misses her friends.'

The world started spinning again. The drop from the tap splashed into the sink. The microwave blinked.

'And we want to raise Arabella in England.'

Sandy sat down on the stool and laughed. Andy, Angela and Arabella.

'What's funny?'

'Nothing.'

'We'll be selling the house, Sandy. We need the money.'

The red rash, creeping up again. Blood under her finger-nails. 'You haven't paid a thing since you left.'

'I paid the mortgage on the house you're living in for ten years.'

It's slipping. That's how Lou described what her mind did on days when she felt she was losing her grip on the world.

The front door clicked open and shut again.

Milo came into the kitchen and put down his school bag.

'So why are you so busy?' Andy asked.

'Oh, we're just closing down Lou's nursing home.' She glanced over at Milo and gave him a wink.

And then she realised what she'd said.

'What the hell are you talking about, Sandy? Why's Gran in a nursing home?'

Shit.

Milo looked up, his hearing so sharp that he'd have got all of that.

'Sandy?'

'Oh, for Christ's sake, Andy, what did you expect? Waltzing off to the other side of the world on a mid-life crisis. We couldn't cope with her any more.'

'Milo knew how to—'

'Milo's a fucking child.'

Milo stood in the middle of the kitchen and stared at her. Sandy stretched out her hand towards him. 'Darling . . .'

He stepped back.

'She's my grandmother, I get to decide where she goes,' Andy roared down the phone.

'You're not here and you're not paying the bills, and Milo's too young to look after her. She's ill, Andy. Her mind's slipping.'

Milo picked up his school bag.

'Andy, I've got to go.'

'We need to talk about this. And about me coming back.'

'I couldn't give a fuck about you coming back. Just piss off, Andy.' She slammed down the phone.

Milo was already at the back door.

'Milo, come back.'

He walked straight to the shed.

Sandy ran after him. 'Milo!'

This wasn't how it was meant to happen. She'd made a plan:

She'd be waiting for him when he got back from school. He'd see her in her new orange dress with her make-up, her hair twisted up in a bun to show off her long neck, just as he liked it. And she'd tell him all about how the preparations had been going.

That Al was at his girlfriend's putting the finishing touches on the film.

That Sandy had got permission from Mrs Harris to borrow the school minibus.

That everyone was ready to head to London.

That they'd organised a party for afterwards.

And she'd tell him that she liked Tripi, that she was glad he was in their life.

Above all, she'd squeeze him tight and tell him how exciting it was, that her little Milo was going to save the day.

Milo closed the door of the shed.

Sandy stood outside, the wet grass seeping through her

tights. She knelt down and held her hand to the shed door. 'Milo, please listen. You weren't meant to hear that.'

'You lied,' he said, his voice small and wobbly. 'I trusted you when you came and spoke to me last night, but you're always lying.'

'I try to protect you, my darling.'

'You lied about telling Dad that Gran's in the nursing home, you lied about Gran and the fire—'

'The fire?'

'I saw the letter on your desk. It makes sense, what you said about her knowing it was right to leave. She wanted to go. She did it on purpose.'

Sandy took in a sharp breath and held it for a second.

'Gran knew it was time to go, Milo.'

'What do you mean?'

'It's like I said last night. She didn't want to be a burden on us any more. On you, Milo.'

Milo didn't answer.

'Please let me in now, please. We can talk, like we did last night. I can explain.'

'So she set fire to the kitchen to make you get rid of her?'

There was a long pause. 'It was Gran's way of showing us that she needed more help than either of us could give her. It was her choice, Milo.'

And Sandy had messed that up too.

'And you keep moving people in without asking me,' said Milo.

'I had to, Milo. I'm sorry.' Sandy couldn't think of anything to say to make things better.

'And Gran – you didn't tell me she was ill. I mean really ill.'

'But Milo, you must have seen.'

'If you'd let her stay with us, she'd have been okay, I would have looked after her.'

Sandy paused. She couldn't tell Milo that he was only a little boy, that with the best will in the world he couldn't look after Lou.

'Please come out, Milo.' She wanted more than anything to hold him, to make him feel that everything was going to be okay, that they'd work it out, the two of them. 'Please, Milo. This is what you wanted – for everyone to see Forget Me Not for what it really is. I'm going help Nurse Heidi get the ladies ready, I'll come back to collect you in an hour. I've put out your clothes upstairs – your favourite orange sweatshirt. It matches my dress . . .'

'I'm not coming.'

'But Milo—'

'There's no point any more.'

She heard a thud against the door and pictured Milo's legs hitched up into his chest, his eyes pressed down onto his knee caps.

Sandy took a breath. 'Please come out.'

But there was no answer.

60

Lou

She heard his footsteps coming down the corridor, the weight of him walking across the room, the creak of his knees as he bent down in front of her.

'I wanted to see you again,' he said. 'To make sure my Louisa was okay.' He reached up and stroked the side of her fallen face. 'And to give you this.'

He held out a rolled-up piece of card.

Lou did not have the strength to unroll it, or to speak, so he opened it for her.

She looked at the lines of pencil that made up her face, her hair, an urgency in their strokes as though he wanted to get it done before she sailed away like his wife.

'I will paint you,' he promised. 'But this is for now.'

She reached out her hand and touched his arm. A new white shirt, no frays at the cuff.

Levering her thumb under her third finger she eased off her engagement ring and dropped it into Petros's hand.

'Marry me,' she whispered. 'Marry me now.'

He took the ring and kissed it and slid it onto her other hand.

'The left hand is for David, the right one for me.'

Petros got up off his knees. 'I must go and find someone before the awards ceremony. I will see you there, Louisa.'

Lou nodded and watched Petros walk back across the room, heard his steps down the corridor, through the front door, and watched the top of his head shining under the street lamps as he headed to the park.

61

Tripi

An hour later Tripi stood outside the shed with Sandy.

'Milo, it is Tripi. We have to leave now, we have the film, it is very good and it is all your work. You must be proud and come with us.'

Silence.

'And Al has gone to his office so he can release it on the internet when the award is announced.'

More silence.

Tripi forced himself not to blame Milo for lying about Al having found Ayishah. He was trying to save Old Mrs Moon and to help the old people at Forget Me Not. Tripi only wished that he had not been so quick to believe him because it made him feel foolish. *It is easy to pull the wool over your eyes, Tripi*, Ayishah had said.

He should have learnt by now that good news did not come so easily.

'Everything is ready, Milo, you will be pleased.'

Still nothing.

Sandy placed her hand on Tripi's arm. 'It's no good.'

Strands of blond hair had come loose at her neck, curled by the damp night. Standing there in her orange dress, she reminded him of the sunsets in Syria. A wave of homesickness swept over him.

Tripi pulled away from her. After tonight, he would go straight back to London. He had no right to form attachments he could not keep.

The light in Sandy's eyes flickered off.

Tripi held out his hands. 'If Milo wants to stay here, there is nothing we can do, but we must find Petros or Old Mrs Moon will be upset.'

After the excitement of recovering her voice, Old Mrs Moon had remained silent all afternoon. Twice, he had found her asleep in her armchair in the lounge. He was not sure that she was up to this awards ceremony.

'You don't think I know that?' Lovely Sandy's voice broke.

He had upset her, he had been unkind to draw away from her touch.

'I am sorry, Sandy.'

She stepped away from him and tears spilled out of her eyes. 'He went for a walk,' she gulped. 'I reminded him to be back by six. And then Andy ... ' She choked on her words. 'And then Milo ... '

Tripi had never seen a grown woman cry like this, big, fat tears. Her whole body heaved, streams of mascara ran down her cheeks. She had got dressed up, she had wanted to make Milo happy and now she was crying and it was his fault.

He stepped forward and folded her into his arms. Her muscles relaxed and her body sank into his chest.

334

'It is okay,' he said, smoothing down the back of her head. He placed his fingers at the nape of her neck and stroked the loose strands of hair. 'It will all be okay.'

She lifted her head to him, her eyes swollen, the tip of her nose red from the cold, and then she reached up and kissed him.

He closed his eyes and felt her lips and, for a moment, the world fell away.

When he opened his eyes, he saw a smile coming through the streaks of her tears.

Tripi rocked backwards, his heart swelling.

He looked at his watch. 'Okay, let us get going. We might find Petros on our way out of town.'

They walked across the grass to the house, Tripi holding Sandy steady as her heels sank into the soft grass.

Before they went back into the kitchen, he looked over his shoulder at the shed: Milo's face peered out of the small window.

Every seat in the bus was taken, the air full of old ladies' perfume, rose and lavender and soap. With Mrs Swift as an apprentice, Sandy had done their hair and their make-up.

Mrs Zimmer had stayed awake long enough to get onto the bus.

Nurse Heidi had rescued Mrs Sharp's iPad from Nurse Thornhill's confiscation box so now she could play Angry Birds all the way to London.

They were excited that they might be on the news, especially Mrs Turner who said she would show the cameras all the food she had stored in her pockets and Mrs Foxton who thought that maybe she could ask The British Public whether they'd seen anyone throw that brick into her conservatory.

As for Mrs Wong, she knew for sure that there'd be Chinese restaurants in London and that meant rice.

Above the bus an old man stood whistling at his window and for some reason, Mrs Moseley recognised the tune and joined in. She had not stopped smiling since she left Forget Me Not.

Sandy switched on the ignition, her small plump body lost behind the steering wheel.

'You are sure you are happy to drive?' asked Tripi.

She looked at Tripi as Ayishah had whenever he had said something stupid. Sandy pressed on the accelerator and the bus lurched down the road.

62

Milo

Milo stepped out of the shed. The whole house was dark now, even Gran's room. He looked up and zoomed in on the full moon and felt like he had to say sorry to it: he'd wished it into existence and now here it was, ready for the big night, and he'd given up. But he couldn't go to the awards ceremony, could he? Not after all the lies. Even Gran had lied. She hadn't told him that she started the fire on purpose. She hadn't said she didn't want him looking after her any more.

And then Tripi kissing Mum, right there in their back garden.

He'd trusted Tripi – he was meant to be Milo's friend, not Mum's. But now Milo realised that Tripi probably only came back from London for her: because he wanted to grab her titties, like Big Mike with Lalana and Dad with his Tart and Petros with Gran. When he was older Milo wasn't ever going to kiss anyone or have a girlfriend or get married.

After what happened at school, Milo should have known that the day would end badly.

And then when he got home he heard Mum talking on the phone to Dad and all the lies she'd been storing up and that made his day even worse.

Maybe he could run away and live like Tripi with nothing but a sleeping bag and a backpack. He could work in a kitchen doing the washing up to earn money for tea and Fluff on toast.

Or maybe his eyes would suddenly get worse, quicker than anyone expected and he wouldn't be able to see anything any more, not even the tiniest pinhole, and then the world would be black and he could pretend it wasn't there.

Milo heard footsteps on the pavement outside the house and then saw someone walking towards him across the grass. A man wearing a yellow cap, a big black and white lump in his arms.

'Milo?'

Milo stepped back towards the shed.

'Milo, look what I found.' Petros came and stood in front of him and held out Hamlet. 'He is very heavy. Here, take him.' He dropped Hamlet into Milo's arms and Milo nearly fell over backwards from the weight of him.

Hamlet snuffled and grunted and rubbed his wet snout against Milo's chin. Milo held him in tight against his chest and buried his face into his fur and sighed into it. 'I thought you'd gone,' he said over and over. 'But you came back. You came back.' He breathed in the scent of Hamlet's skin: he smelt of earth and leaves and of the night sky; he even, Milo thought, smelt of the bright sharp moon looking down on them. 'You came back,' he said again, his voice all choked up.

'He has been looking for you. I found him in the park, he told me you liked the park and that you would come and find him there.'

Milo didn't believe Petros: Hamlet wouldn't speak to him, not in a million years.

'So, are you ready to go?'

'They left without us,' said Milo.

'I know.' Petros held up Milo's phone. 'Al gave me this before he went to his office. He called me to ask where I was and I said I was busy and not to say anything to Lou or Sandy or Tripi.'

'You went out looking for Hamlet?'

Petros nodded.

'You said that pigs were only good for salami.'

Petros laughed from his belly. 'Well, maybe I was wrong, or maybe some pigs are different, like your Hamlet, though he has got so fat that he would make very good salami . . .'

Milo didn't like Petros's jokes, though he had a point: Hamlet was getting fat, much fatter than the pictures of fully-grown teacup pigs on the internet. Milo had asked Dad for Hamlet's birth certificate, like it said you should do on the website, so that you can be confident that the teacup pig has come from a good litter, but Dad had laughed and said it wasn't necessary.

Petros gave Hamlet a little rub behind his black ear. 'So, are you coming, Milo?'

'We can't go – I told you, they've left.'

'Ah, but I have a much better means of transportation than a bus, Milo.'

Milo didn't like that Petros just assumed he was coming

when he hadn't even made up his mind about whether he wanted to go or not.

'Come with me. You can bring Hamlet if you like.'

Petros walked across the grass to the gate.

'Are you still marrying Gran?' Milo called after him.

Petros stopped and turned round. 'With your permission, Milo, that would make me very happy, yes.'

Milo looked at Hamlet and then up at the moon and then back at Petros and he thought how Petros wasn't nearly as handsome as Great-Gramps in his army uniform. But Petros made Gran happy, didn't he? And Gran wouldn't let just anyone make her happy, especially as she still loved Great-Gramps. Plus, she must have asked Great-Gramps about it.

'How are we getting to London, then?' asked Milo.

Milo hadn't felt so car-sick in all his life. Lurching forwards and backwards, getting pressed up against the door when the car veered around sharp bends, the clunk of speed bumps, the starting and stopping and the rattling of the old engine and the smell of petrol and exhaust fumes.

'How old's this car anyway?' asked Milo.

He'd walked past the rusty Volvo a thousand times but he'd never thought Mr Overend could drive it.

'Probably as old as me!' Mr Overend laughed and swerved down a side road.

The dream he'd had last night. Mr Overend helping him find Hamlet. Mr Overend coming to the rescue. It had been pointing to this moment.

With his slippers on, Mr Overend didn't have a proper grip of the pedals and so he kept missing the brake and pressing the accelerator instead.

Milo made sure the seatbelt was still secure over Hamlet and then gripped the door handle.

Dad used to complain about old people driving. He said that once someone got over seventy the government should make them re-sit their driving test every few years. At the time it had made Milo laugh, thinking about all those old people whizzing around in driving school cars with the big L plates on the back, but maybe Dad had a point.

As they stopped at the traffic lights, people glanced into the car: they stared at Mr Overend in his PJs and at Milo holding Hamlet in the passenger seat and at Petros with his yellow cap in the back seat.

What if a policeman walked by and arrested them for looking weird and threw them into a mental home? Milo had seen this film where that happened and the more the people who got locked up tried to persuade the doctors and the nurses and the police that they were sane, the crazier they sounded and the more people thought they really were mad and in the end they went properly crazy from staying in the mental home with all the other crazy people and they had to stay there for ever and have their brains zapped by electrodes.

'We're here!' Mr Overend pulled up behind the Slipton Primary minibus parked in the disabled bay outside The Prince Albert Hotel.

It turned out Mr Overend used to be a London cabbie and knew the roads better than an A-Z. He told Milo and Petros how London cabbies were the cleverest people in the world and that it had been proven that they had bigger brains than normal people because they had to remember everything in 3D, except that had changed now because of satnav so the cabbies were as thick as everyone else. And some of the roads and roundabouts and road signs had changed since Mr Overend last drove around London too.

Milo climbed out of the car with Hamlet and Petros, and Mr Overend said he would drive the car back to Crescent Way and that he looked forward to hearing all about what happened to Nurse Thornhill. Before he left he handed Milo an envelope of photographs.

'They are of your baby sister,' he said. 'I found them in my dustbin.'

'Photos of my sister?'

Mr Overend nodded. 'She looks like you, Milo.'

Milo tucked the photos into his pocket. He would look at them later and work out why they'd ended up in Mr Overend's dustbin.

63

Milo

The old women from Forget Me Not filled the lobby of The Prince Albert Hotel. They looked almost normal in their frilly dresses with their make-up and their hair done in tight buns or curls, though most of them still wore their slippers, like Mr Overend. And Mrs Moseley still smelt of wee but she looked happier than she did at Forget Me Not. She stood at the window waving at Mr Overend with her cane as he did a three-point turn in the middle of the main road. Cars whooshed past and honked and people poked their heads out of their windows and yelled at him: *Get out of the road, Grandad!* But Mr Overend just grinned and so did Mrs Moseley. Maybe Gran and Petros and Mr Overend and Mrs Moseley could have a double wedding.

So this was the plan: as soon as the guy on stage announced

the prize and the techie people switched on the film, Gran, Mrs Moseley, Mrs Zimmer, Mrs Swift, Mrs Sharp, Mrs Foxton, Mrs Wong and Petros would burst through the back doors and point to Nurse Thornhill and they'd all shout something that Milo hadn't worked out yet, because he'd planned to think of it before he decided to stay in the shed and since then he'd forgotten.

It took a while for them to notice Milo, but then Hamlet squealed and everyone turned round and Hamlet did his business on the floor of the lobby and the hotel staff went mental, but it didn't matter because Gran came over and gave Milo a hug. Even though she walked really slowly and her face looked lopsided, as he stood there wrapped up in her arms smelling her apricot skin, Milo felt that maybe everything might be okay after all.

'Quick, Milo, they're about to make the announcement.' Petros came over and stretched out his arms for Hamlet. 'I'll look after your little pig.'

Milo clung onto Hamlet.

'We're friends now, aren't we, Hamlet?' said Petros, rubbing behind Hamlet's white ear. Hamlet wriggled and didn't look convinced but Milo handed him over all the same.

Mum poked her head round the door of the conference room and waved at Milo to come over.

Gran squeezed Milo's hand. 'Go,' she said. 'Be brave.'

Milo liked the sound of Gran's voice. And he liked that soon she'd be back home and he'd get to hear it more and more. They wouldn't have to write everything down any more, they could have proper conversations.

*

344

Milo didn't know where to look. So many people all crammed together, rows and rows of chairs, a platform full of grown-ups in suits and robes.

The swirly red bits on the carpet made Milo feel dizzy and the ceiling felt too low and there weren't any windows.

He tugged at the collar of his orange sweatshirt.

Tripi came over and rubbed Milo's shoulders. 'I am glad you came, my friend.'

Milo nodded, though he couldn't look him in the eye, not with that picture still in his head of Tripi standing in the back garden kissing Mum.

He turned to Tripi. 'Did you give the sound people the new film?'

'Of course. We are a team now, Milo, I would never let you down. Nurse Thornhill is in for a surprise.'

'Shhh!' said a woman with fuzzy purple-grey hair sitting at the back.

Milo looked at Mum in her orange dress and thought about how pretty she looked and about the hug they'd had last night in the shed, and all the bad thoughts melted away. He went up to her and put his arms around her waist. 'You look beautiful, Mum,' he said.

'Had to look the part for your special day, Milo,' she said and bent her head over his and squeezed him tight.

Mum, Tripi and Milo took their seats.

'And now, the moment you've all been waiting for,' said a guy with a black gown and loads of gold medals round his neck. 'Drum roll, please,' he said, except there wasn't a drum roll, just people fidgeting in their seats and coughing and sniffing and waiting.

The pictures of three nurses came up on the screen behind him: Nurse Thornhill in the middle with her wrinkles ironed out, though with the same stuck-on smile.

'In third place . . . ' The medallion guy opened a gold envelope like at the Oscars and read out the name: 'Miss Theresa Bone from Bird's Eye View Home for the Elderly.'

Milo thought Bird's Eye was a type of fish finger.

There were gasps and claps and a woman shuffled out of the front row. She smiled but you could tell it was pretend smiling because her lips were too tight. Milo thought it must be hard to come third when you'd hoped to come first and to have everyone stare at you while you went up and got an award you didn't really want.

'We're getting closer now,' said medallion guy. 'In second place . . . .' He yanked at the envelope. 'Daphne's been using superglue on these things,' he said and laughed. Daphne must be his secretary. Maybe medallion man had slept with her like Dad slept with his Tart. 'In second place . . . Nurse Thornhill from Forget Me Not, Slipton.'

Milo looked at Mum and then at Tripi. Their faces froze. And then he looked back to the front of the room and saw Nurse Thornhill getting up and her stuck-on smile was worse than ever, and her face went as red as the swirls on the carpet and he nearly felt sorry for her before he realised that their plan had been blown out of the water.

You're the horse everyone's backing, that's what the bald inspector guy had said on Tuesday. *No one's as good as you, Ruth*. He even winked at her.

Milo had to do something.

'Tripi, go to the sound and lighting deck and tell them to play the film.'

'But they won't listen to me ...'

'Yes, they will. Just tell them how horrible she is and if they refuse, say you'll give them some money.'

'Milo ...' started Mum.

'It's okay, Mum, once they've seen the film they'll forget about the money.' Tripi knocked into people's knees, stumbled out into the gangway and disappeared through the back doors.

'Mum, get everyone ready in the lobby.'

'Milo ... are you sure?'

'You wanted me to do this, right? That's what you said back home, outside the shed?'

Mum put the nail of her small finger in her mouth and then nodded and followed Tripi through the back doors.

Milo took a deep breath and stepped forward.

A yellow fuzz pulsed in front of his eyes from the contrast between the darkness over the audience and the spotlights at the front. Milo closed his eyes and opened them again and tried to focus.

Gran said *Be brave*, and Milo knew what that meant. Brave like Great-Gramps when he fought in Korea and won the Battle of Pakchon, even though his regiment was really small and didn't have enough weapons. Even though it meant he had to die as part of the winning.

Medallion guy's voice boomed on. 'Nurse Thornhill's work at Forget Me Not has been exemplary. She came a very close second and should be hugely proud of her achievements.'

The bald inspector guy sat on the front row, smiling. Milo reckoned he'd told all three nurses the same thing – about them being the horses that everyone was backing.

Milo climbed onto the platform and as he walked past the row of important people, he tripped over a microphone cable and grabbed the leg of a woman who wore the same black gown and medallions as the guy doing the talking. She gasped and pulled away and Milo fell down. Behind him, Milo heard mutterings from the audience and the medallion guy stopped talking and as Milo got back onto his feet and shifted his head, he caught sight of Nurse Thornhill, her red face bang in the middle of the pinhole.

'Young man, you shouldn't be up here,' said someone who didn't look important because he wasn't wearing a suit or a gown with chains, but jeans and a faded black T-shirt.

Milo regained his balance and walked towards the microphone. He hoped that Mrs Harris would get to see this on the local news and that she'd have her mark book with her because one thing was for sure, he wasn't doing this again in front of the class.

'Could I borrow your microphone, please?' Milo asked the medallion guy. 'I have something I'd like to say about Nurse Thornhill and Forget Me Not Homes.'

'Um ...' Medallion guy turned round to look at the other grown-ups sitting on the stage but none of them said anything.

'It's really important.'

Medallion guy stared at him and then someone called out from the back of the auditorium.

'Milo! Milo! Listen to Milo!'

Mrs Hairy stood in her high heels next to Mrs Moseley, who started clapping and calling Milo's name too.

And then Tripi joined in from the sound and lighting desk, and someone else too, and he sounded foreign, like

Tripi, but a curlier kind of foreign and Milo realised that it was Petros and that he was lifting Hamlet in the air and Hamlet was squealing like mad, as if he wanted to join in.

All the old ladies from Forget Me Not streamed in through the Emergency Exit door and when they heard Mrs Hairy and Mrs Moseley and Petros, they joined in with the clapping and chanting. And then random people from the audience shouted Milo's name too, and all of a sudden the whole room was yelling and there were flashes from the photographers in the front row and Milo noticed the TV cameras too and how they were zooming in close to his face.

Nurse Thornhill yanked medallion guy by his gown.

'Get him off the stage,' she said through her tight, stuck-on smile.

But medallion guy didn't listen to her. Instead, he handed Milo the microphone and sat back down in his chair.

A *shhhhhhh* swept over the audience and people stopped calling Milo's name and the flashes stopped too and then silence.

Milo stood on the big stage and took a breath. It wasn't nearly as scary as he thought it would be because when he looked into the spotlights everything went blurry, the whole audience and everyone on stage so he could pretend he was up there alone, just talking to himself or to Gran.

'I've got a pet pig called Hamlet.'

A few people laughed.

'Dad gave him to me as a present, to cheer me up when I found out that I had Retinitis Pigmentosa – which means that my eyes don't work properly and that one day I'll be blind.'

There were some gasps.

'And also because he wanted to say sorry for having sex

with his Tart rather than with Mum and because his Tart was pregnant and they were moving to Abu Dhabi and I wouldn't get to see him for a long time.' He paused.

Several people in the audience started talking now. Mrs Harris said it was rude if people talked during someone's speech so Milo waited for them to stop before he continued, which is what Mrs Harris did when she wanted the class's attention.

'Just let the kid talk!' yelled a man from the back.

Milo leant into the microphone. 'Hamlet's the best pet you could have. He's not hard to train like a dog and he doesn't scratch you like cats. And he listens to what you've got to say, even when everyone else is too busy.' He swallowed. 'Plus, he's really warm, so you don't ever need a hot water bottle.'

Milo squinted to see whether he could spot Hamlet because he thought he'd quite like that hundreds of people were hearing about him.

'But some of the time, when Hamlet lived with us, he wasn't very happy.' Milo felt bad about saying the next bit in front of all these people, but it was part of his speech, so he couldn't leave it out. 'He wasn't very happy because Mum made him stay in the garage. And the garage gets really cold, especially in winter, and there isn't much light and it smells of petrol fumes. Plus we don't have much money so we can't buy him the luxury food from the pet store, only economy food, which you can tell he doesn't like very much but eats anyway when he realises he's not getting anything else.'

Milo stopped to catch his breath. He was worried that he was doing what Mrs Harris called *going off the topic* and *losing your audience*, so he decided to get to the point he wanted to make.

'The point is that I didn't notice he was unhappy, not at first. But then, when I let him into the house and watched him snuggle up under the heater or on my duvet and when I gave him leftovers from my tea, his snout went all pink and wet, which the internet says means he's healthy, and he smiled and I know you probably think that pigs can't smile, but they can, because I've seen him do it. And he never smiles when he's in the garage, he only ever smiles when he's in the house, with me.' Milo took a breath. 'So what I'm saying is that Forget Me Not is like the garage and that Nurse Thornhill keeps it like that because it's cheaper, even though it makes the old people sad and cold and hungry and then, when the inspectors come, she pretends that it's really nice and they believe her because they don't bother to look properly.' He knew Mrs Harris would say that he'd taken too long to get to his point, but he'd get marks for structure – especially for putting the punchline at the end so that everyone would remember the important bit. 'And I've seen her flat and it's really posh, so I think she must take all the money from the old people and use it for herself.'

Nurse Thornhill stumbled backwards and her eyes darted around like how Gran described the fish that got caught in her fishing net in Inverary.

The flashes started again and this time the TV cameras pointed at her, not at Milo.

'And now we'd like to show you an undercover film we've made so that you can see for yourself what it's like, because that's proper evidence and not just me giving my opinion.' He stood up straighter and tried to make eye contact with his audience even though all he could see was one face at a time and even then it was blurry because his eyes were tired.

'When you've seen the film and thought about what I've said, I hope you'll understand why we think that Nurse Thornhill shouldn't be given any prize at all and that she should be locked up and that all the old people from Forget Me Not should be allowed to go back to their families.'

He did the thumbs up sign to Tripi but the sound and lighting guy was already on the case. The screen behind Milo flickered to life.

The first shot was of Mrs Moseley, her lovely cheeks glowing and shiny and like chestnuts, clutching her tape recorder and dancing. For a moment Milo was worried that they were showing the wrong tape, the one of Forget Me Not like it looked on the posters. But then she turned round and the camera zoomed in on the back of her dress. On video the stain looked worse than ever, layers of yellowy-brown like she'd wet herself over and over and no one had ever bothered to clean her properly. Milo heard the audience gasp.

Then came a shot of the dark corridor where all the old people's rooms were. The camera panned over the locks on the outside of the doors. You could hear Mrs Foxton's voice behind her door calling for Nurse Thornhill. *We need to call the police, we need to report the break-in ... my conservatory ...* And in the shadows, a white figure, tall and skinny, gave the door a thump. She hissed, *Be quiet!* and walked on.

A cut to the lounge, to a row of plates heaped up with potatoes and gloopy stew and on each plate only a few tiny bits of grey-looking beef. A close-up of Mrs Turner's toothless smile and then the lens zoomed into her pocket, which she held open for the camera: mushy peas covered in gravy all squished into the fabric of her dress.

Milo looked through the pinhole at the audience. Their eyes were fixed on the screen. Some of them held their hands to their mouths. There wasn't a rustle or a cough, just the whirring of the projector and the sounds from the old ladies on the film.

Get up! Get up! Nurse Thornhill's voice boomed onto the screen. The camera wobbled. Mrs Wong, who always went on about being an Olympic gymnast, doing one of her exercises, holding out a hand because she'd got stuck in a squat. A few members of the audience laughed, because it was funny, despite Nurse Thornhill's shouting, but they soon fell quiet when they saw how she grabbed Mrs Wong by the armpits and heaved her up, not even giving her the time to find her balance. Nurse Thornhill pulled so hard on Mrs Wong's arms that Milo was worried that they might pop out of their sockets.

At the back of the room, Milo saw someone in a black leather jacket push through the swing doors. Clouds. He'd come! Milo wanted to tell him what a good job he'd done of editing Tripi's film, how without him they'd never have been able to show everything that was going on at Forget Me Not.

The room gasped again and Milo flicked his eyes back onto the screen.

Another trip down the corridor. A zoom over the radiator dials, set at zero. Frost on the inside of the windows. The posh visitors' lounge locked up and dark. Mrs Sharp standing in the corridor with her iPad, shouting *Got 'em!* and then the white shadow sweeping past again, grabbing the iPad and then a second later, a picture of the KEEP OUT drawer with all the empty purses and the iPad shoved in too. On the

353

handle of the drawer Milo spotted Nurse Heidi's delicate fingers. She must have helped Tripi with the film.

A few more shots of the old ladies. Mrs Zimmer asleep in her armchair in the lounge, a pile of green and white dozy pills in a paper cup beside her. Nurse Thornhill yanking a lipstick out of Mrs Swift's hands. Mrs Moseley standing in the middle of her room with wet hair, shivering, saying, *I don't want a bath . . . I don't want a bath . . .* and then a cut away to Gran's room.

Milo looked over to Mum. She was standing up, her hand gripping her throat. This time he felt glad that Tripi was there, standing beside her, holding her shoulders. Mum scratched at her throat; Milo knew that she felt what was coming next, just like he did. He thought of those times when he'd tried to see Gran and Forget Me Not was all locked up and when he'd found Gran in her room with bruises on her wrists.

The screen flickered.

Gran sitting in her armchair by the window, a tray of food on her lap. She hadn't touched her plate. A moment later, Nurse Thornhill's voice filled the screen. *Come on, Nurse Heidi, if her ladyship isn't going to eat, we're going to have to give her a helping hand.* The camera phone must have been on Nurse Heidi because it didn't look like there was anyone else in the room and the only people on screen were Gran and Nurse Thornhill. Gran shook her head. *No arguing!* shouted Nurse Thornhill. Milo couldn't breathe. He wished he'd never left Gran alone, not for a second. Gran scrabbled around, looking for her pad, but Nurse Thornhill grabbed it and threw it across the room. Then she went and stood over Gran. She pushed a fork into Gran's fingers, gripped her tiny wrist, levered some food onto the fork and yanked it up to Gran's mouth. Gran kept her mouth closed. *You're going to eat!* Nurse Thornhill yelled.

The audience gasped. Milo's heart beat so fast he thought his chest was going to explode. So that's where Gran had got all her bruises from. Nurse Thornhill grabbed Gran's wrist and tried again. This time she flicked the food at Gran's mouth, but Gran kept her mouth closed. The food dribbled down her chin and onto the front of her dress. And then the screen went black.

Milo swayed on his feet, feeling the silence press in on him. Then, as the audience kept quiet, he worried that maybe he'd said something wrong in his speech, or hadn't explained properly, or maybe he'd gone off the topic so that no one understood what he was talking about. Or maybe they didn't get the film and why they'd made it.

But then he felt someone standing up behind him and when he looked round he saw it was the lady with the gown and the medallions whose leg he'd grabbed when he tripped over the cable. She was clapping.

'Got 'em, the buggers!' shouted Mrs Sharp from the back of the room. And people laughed, because they remembered her voice from the film. And then everyone else on stage joined in with the medallion woman's clapping and soon the whole room was on its feet, cheering and clapping and stomping and it was so loud Milo kind of wished it would stop because his head hurt, but he was kind of glad too because when people were brave, they got clapped and Gran had wanted him to be brave. Maybe Great-Gramps would be proud of him too.

But then, as Milo narrowed his eyes and made the pinhole come into focus, he noticed someone walking in the opposite direction to everyone else. Someone who wasn't clapping or looking at him: Nurse Thornhill, striding towards the Emergency Exit.

'Look!' Milo shouted. 'She's getting away!'

A hundred heads turned and followed the line of Milo's outstretched arm.

Mrs Moseley hobbled over from where she was standing with Mrs Hairy, then she stepped past Mum, Mrs Zimmer, Mrs Turner, Mrs Swift, Mrs Sharp, Mrs Foxton, Mrs Wong, Petros and Gran and held her cane across the Emergency Exit. Nurse Thornhill tried to push through but someone from the audience grabbed her from behind and after that she got swallowed up by the crowd and Milo couldn't see her any more. But he didn't mind because he knew that they wouldn't let her go.

64

Tripi

The old people clambered out of the minibus, buzzing. Petros chanted a Greek song from his hometown in Patitiri and Mrs Moseley led the old ladies in her version of one of the Bob Marley songs she liked called 'I Shot the Sheriff', which Tripi guessed must be her way of celebrating getting rid of Nurse Thornton.

Nurse Heidi stood at the front door, her cheeks glowing.

'You did it!' She stretched out her arms to the old people.

'You're in charge now,' cried Petros.

The officials had asked whether there were nurses back at the home who could look after the old people and they had explained that Nurse Heidi was waiting for them and that she was more than capable of holding the fort until morning. *The fort*: Tripi liked that, the idea of a home as somewhere strong and safe. Tomorrow someone would come over from Slipton Town Council to decide what should happen to Forget Me Not and its residents.

Mrs Hairy parked her red Mercedes outside the front of Forget Me Not and stepped out of her car carrying a huge cake box with golden swirly letters on the top.

'Sandy told me about the party,' she said, smiling. 'And there's always spare cake hanging around the kitchens where I work.'

Tripi watched Mrs Moseley hobble towards her daughter with her cane. They had the same straight nose, flared at the nostrils. *You can't hide family*, thought Tripi.

As they walked up the steps to the front door, Lovely Sandy hugged Milo to her, ruffling his hair and kissing his cheeks over and over.

And between their feet, fatter than ever, grunting and snuffling, Hamlet ran around in circles.

Tripi wanted to join in the singing, or sing his own song from Syria, perhaps even the national anthem 'Ḥumāt ad-Diyār', Guardians of the Homeland ... *The flutter of our hopes and the beats of our hearts* ... his favourite lines. But instead, he just stood and watched and listened. Before he left, he wanted to take all this in. He looked up at the sky and watched a plane fly into the clouds.

He helped the old ladies down from the minibus. They took his hand and stepped lightly onto the pavement. Carried on this wave of release, knowing that Nurse Thornhill was never coming back, it was as though they had forgotten they were old.

He felt a little proud that perhaps he had helped to make this possible. And sad too: he would miss his new friends. But tonight he was still here and there was baklava in the kitchen and a cake and an engagement party. Petros said that he wanted to get married before Christmas so that he could see in the New Year with Lou. He had looked up a place called Gretna Green that he had found on the internet. They could take the bus there and get married straight away. Tripi had smiled, listening to Petros speaking with the excitement of a young man.

'Tripi?' Mrs Zimmer placed a piece of paper into Tripi's hand. One of Milo's photocopies of Ayishah. 'She has kind eyes,' said Mrs Zimmer.

Tripi nodded, *kind and mischievous*. 'I love this photo,' Tripi said, smoothing over the crinkles.

'No, not on the photo.'

Mrs Zimmer was always either falling asleep, asleep or waking up. Her thoughts were never very clear. 'What do you mean, Mrs Zimmer?'

'On the television.'

Tripi's heart sped up. 'You saw her on the television?'

Mrs Zimmer rubbed her eyes. 'I . . . I . . . I don't know. Milo told us to look, so I have been watching the news. Everyone thinks I sleep all the time but I usually have my eyes a little open.'

'You saw her on the news?' Tripi wanted to lift the old lady off her feet and spin her around. 'When?'

'This morning. But I'm not sure it was her, Tripi, my eyes aren't that good any more and the picture flashed by so fast. She was in the background, I think. Maybe it wasn't her . . . I just thought you could look into it, that it wouldn't hurt.' Mrs Zimmer took the photocopy out of Tripi's hands and turned it over. 'I made a note of the time when I saw the little girl on the screen.'

Tripi read Mrs Zimmer's wobbly words written in pencil: *Tripi's sister? BBC1. 8:03am.*

His blood crashed in his ears. He could look on the internet and find a clip of the news programme. He could see for himself if it was Ayishah, if she was alive. Five months and not a single lead, and now this – a note scribbled by a tired old lady.

'How did you know that the photo Milo gave you was of my sister?'

Mrs Zimmer smiled. 'We are not so foolish, Tripi. A friend of Milo's, in Syria?'

No, not foolish at all.

'The little girl you saw, did she look okay?'

Mrs Zimmer hesitated. 'A bit skinny. I don't think they have enough potatoes in Syria.'

'And the programme – did it say where the film was from, which camp?'

'I didn't catch that. Maybe you can look it up on a computer.' She folded up the photocopy and gave it to Tripi. Then she squeezed his hand. 'I don't want to get your hopes up, I wasn't sure whether to tell you ... I might be wrong ...'

But Tripi wasn't listening. His mind raced. Al. Al would know how to find the bit of footage.

Tripi looked up at the dark sky, at the stars of Slipton. *Yes, Ayishah, you were right, miracles do happen.*

He watched Mrs Zimmer walking back into Forget Me Not, yawning. He had to believe that what she saw was a message from Allah, it would give him the courage to go back.

This time I won't stop looking until I find you, Ayishah.

Tripi glanced one last time around the bus. And noticed a small dark figure in the back seat.

'Old Mrs Moon?' He walked down the aisle.

She opened her eyes. 'I am a little tired,' she said, her voice hardly there at all.

'Let us get you inside, for your party.'

'I told Petros to go ahead. I would like to sleep for a little while.'

'To sleep? Here?'

Old Mrs Moon nodded. 'Here, yes.' She closed her eyes. 'Come back for me later, Tripi.'

Tripi did not like to leave Old Mrs Moon on her own in the dark bus, but if there was one thing that the old ladies should be allowed to do now that Nurse Thornhill had left, it was to decide what they wanted and not be forced into things.

'Please,' she said. 'Please go and enjoy the party.'

Tripi leant forward, kissed Old Mrs Moon's cheek and whispered, 'Sleep well.'

65

Milo

Milo walked back from Gran's room with her bagpipes squashed under his left arm and the vase with Petros's yellow rose clutched in his right hand.

Great-Gramps's bagpipe song played over and over in his head like a victory march.

We did it, Great-Gramps, we did it.

And then Milo looked at the yellow rose, and for some reason he felt like he'd seen it before. Petros had listened to him about yellow roses being Gran's favourites. And he'd found Hamlet. Maybe he wasn't so bad after all.

Petros is okay, Great-Gramps, Milo said. *Not as good as you, but the way I see it, he'll keep Gran happy until you're back together again.*

He stood for a moment at the door of the lounge and shifted his head to take in every bit of the room. Only a few hours ago, it would have been cold and quiet, the news buzzing in the corner, the air filled with the smell of wee

362

and plasticky lemons and cold potatoes. But now it was alive.

Mrs Sharp was teaching Mrs Wong how to play Angry Birds. She'd worked out that having an opponent would be more fun than playing on her own.

Mrs Moseley twirled her cane like she was a lead in a West End musical, her tape player switched to max. He'd heard the tape so many times he recognised the song right off, 'Could You Be Loved', one of Mrs Moseley's favourites.

Mrs Foxton, Mrs Turner and Mrs Swift jiggled along with her as though the middle of the lounge were a dance floor.

Even Mrs Zimmer tapped her foot to the beat as she sat in her armchair, her eyes closed. Poor Mrs Zimmer, she hadn't got much sleep today.

Mrs Hairy stood at the dining table, arranging the cake she'd brought in.

By the window, Petros climbed onto a stool, held steady by Nurse Heidi, and fastened balloons to the curtain rail. Milo would give him the rose to present to Gran before he gave his engagement speech. Petros had practised it with Milo on the way back from London and it had sounded kind of cheesy (*I love you more than all the raindrops in England*, that sort of thing), but Milo thought Gran would like it.

Milo shifted his head again. Tripi arranged one of the small steel bins on the coffee table, dragged a massive hessian sack across to the other side of the room, put his hand in the bag, took out a potato and handed it to Mum. She laughed and blushed like it was a precious gift rather than a wrinkly brown potato, and then she lobbed it across the room. The potato landed with a clatter into the steel bin. Hole in one. The dancing old ladies turned round and clapped. Mum jumped in the air and threw her arms around Tripi.

Milo shifted his head again. The telly was still on, switched to mute, pictures of that place called Syria blinking out into the room. Ruined buildings, white flashes over a dark city.

Clouds had gone to collect his girlfriend, he was going to bring her to the party.

And Gran? Shouldn't she be here by now? Tripi said she was tired and wanted to stay in the bus and that he'd go back for her in a bit. She sometimes did that at home too, sat in her room in the dark, looking out over Slipton.

Milo did another inch-by-inch scan of the lounge. She definitely wasn't here.

Still carrying the bagpipes and the rose, Milo went out through the front door and stood at the top of the steps. Through the pinhole, he saw a car pulling up at the traffic lights at the end of the road. The car was a deeper richer red than Mrs Hairy's Mercedes, and it was posher too, so posh it didn't even have a number plate.

Milo went down the steps and walked up to the Slipton Primary minibus parked up on the kerb. For a second he looked up at the full moon.

'Thank you, Moon,' Milo whispered. One day he'd see an eclipse but for now a full moon was as good as he could hope for.

It was cold in the minibus, as cold as Forget Me Not when Nurse Thornhill was in charge. The air smelt of hairspray and Petros's plasticky lemon aftershave and old people's breathing. But most of all, it smelt of Gran's apricot perfume. The orange streetlights turned the inside of the bus into a grainy darkness.

He walked down the central aisle, moving his head from side to side as he checked the seats. Then he heard a snuffle.

He sped up and got to the row of seats at the back.

In a corner, the shadow of a street lamp over her small body, sat Gran, sleeping. Hamlet lay warm and fidgety on her lap. Gran really was shrinking; her feet didn't even touch the floor.

When he saw Milo, Hamlet's head shot up and their eyes locked.

Milo put down the bagpipes and the rose and sat next to Gran. He took her hand and stroked it like he always did when he wanted to wake her without giving her a start.

'Gran,' he whispered. 'Gran.'

But she didn't move.

Milo looked out of the minibus windows and through the pinhole he saw the lounge, lit up yellow, Petros's balloons bobbing up and down against the curtain rails.

'My brave Milo.'

Milo shifted his head back to Gran. Her eyes fluttered open, the fingers on her left hand trembled and she smiled. And then she closed her eyes again.

'Gran . . . ' Milo squeezed her hand. 'Gran, you're awake.'

But her eyes stayed closed and her small body sunk deeper into the seat and then the tremor in her hand went still.

Outside, a motorbike roared up the road and came to a rattling halt by the side of the bus. Milo tore out of the minibus.

Clouds stood on the pavement, removing his helmet. Behind him, a girl dressed in leather trousers with the same leather jacket as Clouds climbed off the Harley.

'Hey, Milo, what you doing out here?' asked Clouds.

Milo couldn't answer, the words stuck in his throat.

'This is my girlfriend, Kasia.'

Kasia stepped forward. 'I gather you're quite the hero.' She took off a leather glove and held out her hand to Milo.

So that's where Clouds had been disappearing off to every night, why he never kept his pants or his toothbrush in Gran's room.

Clouds grabbed Kasia by the waist and looked up the lounge window. 'So, the party's in full swing, eh?'

Milo couldn't breathe.

'You okay, mate? You look a bit shell-shocked.'

'It's Gran.'

'Didn't catch that?'

Milo cleared his throat. 'Gran's in the bus, she's not breathing.'

Clouds's face darkened. He let go of Kasia and leapt onto the bus.

'In the back,' Milo called out, following him.

Milo picked Hamlet off Gran's lap and hugged him close. Clouds sat next to Gran, lifted her small wrist and felt her pulse. Then he bent forward and held his ear to her mouth. In the dim light of the bus, Milo saw thick watery drops gather in the corners of his eyes. 'I'm here, Aunty Lou,' he said, over and over. 'I'm here.'

66

Sandy

Sandy watched Al carry Lou down the corridor, followed by Milo, Nurse Heidi and a woman who turned out to be Al's girlfriend. Petros stayed in the lounge, staring out through the swing doors.

'I have to go and talk to Petros,' said Sandy.

Tripi gently pulled Sandy's little finger from her mouth. 'It will be okay, I am here with you.'

Sandy squeezed Tripi's hand, took a breath and turned back to the lounge. They walked over to Petros who sat in one of the big armchairs staring at the yellow rose that Milo had just given him. Hamlet lay slumped at his feet eating a piece of Gina's cake.

'Petros?' Sandy asked.

Petros twisted the yellow rose between his fingers.

'We need to tell you something,' said Tripi, kneeling down in front of the old man.

Petros still didn't look up. He knew already, didn't he?

Above Mrs Moseley's music and the old ladies' chattering, Sandy heard a sound that didn't belong in a nursing home.

'Did you hear that?' Sandy asked Tripi.

There it was again, a cry.

Sandy ran to the door of the lounge.

Coming towards her down the corridor was Andy and a few steps behind him Angela holding the crying Habibti in her arms.

For months after he left her, bits of Andy floated like small ghosts on the air. The smell of the duvet as she pulled it out of the washing hamper. The sight of his broad, pink shoulders steaming from the shower. She'd look in the mirror and see his face, the spot that would blaze up on his temple when he was overworked. The feel of his thinning hair between her fingers as she snipped at it every month. She'd found a few strands on the kitchen tiles when she'd swept up after the fire.

And now? Tanned, his blue eyes lighter, blond hairs on his arms, a different cut to his jeans, a better fit.

She didn't know him any more.

Andy marched up to her. 'What the hell's going on?'

His duty free shoes shone. Abu Dhabi, the new world.

'We got this message on our phone from a guy called Tripi and then we heard Milo's voice on the radio as we drove here from the airport.'

Sandy heard the doors of the lounge swish shut and then she felt Tripi moving in behind her.

Andy looked around. 'So this is the place where you dumped Gran?'

The Habibti kept yelling. Why didn't Angela take her out and wait in the car?

368

'And what are you staring at?' Andy looked at Tripi.

'This is Tripi. He's my ... ' Sandy took a breath and looked at Tripi's kind face. 'He's my partner. We're together.'

'You're going out with him?'

She knew what Andy was thinking. She was going out with a younger man to get back at him. But she didn't care what he thought any more. She grabbed Tripi's hand. 'Yes, I'm going out with him. He's been here for Milo.'

Tripi gulped, his Adam's apple bobbed up and down his throat.

Andy threaded his fingers through his hair. *Still thinning,* thought Sandy, that hadn't changed. Tripi had a good hairline: strong, reliable.

'So where's Gran, then?'

Petros took off his cap, stepped forward and held out a hand. His old blue eyes misted over.

There was a pause. The music from Mrs Moseley's tape player dimmed behind the closed doors of the lounge; overhead, a faulty neon light flickered.

A small voice came from behind Sandy.

'She's gone, Dad.'

Milo stood in the corridor, his eyes wide.

67

Milo

At 3 a.m. Milo curled up on the bare mattress in Gran's room under the roof. Hamlet nestled into the crook between Milo's knees and his stomach; he'd thrown up Mrs Hairy's cake in the back of the car on the way home and then had fallen asleep.

Milo leant over and whispered into Hamlet's black ear. 'Do you know that Gran's gone?' He stroked the tuft of fur on his head. 'Did you know she was leaving, like you know when there's going to be a thunderstorm?' Hamlet twitched his nose in his sleep but his eyes stayed shut.

Springs from the mattress pushed up against Milo's thigh. Why hadn't Gran told him how uncomfortable it was? He could have bought her one of those soft memory foam ones from the ads on the telly.

I'm sorry, Gran, he thought, digging his nose into the mattress, breathing in the smell of Al's cigarettes and behind it, the scent of apricots. *I should have looked after you better.*

A knock on the door.

'Milo?' Dad's voice.

Milo didn't answer.

In those hours after the party, when Nurse Heidi called the doctor, when the men from the ambulance carried Gran out of the bus, when Clouds went home with his girlfriend and Mum agreed to let Dad, The Tart and baby Arabella come home with them – through all of that, Dad had kept trying to strike up conversations with Milo, had reached out to stroke the back of Milo's head, had asked him how he was doing. But every time Milo pulled away.

'Can I come in?'

Dad pushed open the door and came to sit on the end of the bed, his face puffy and blotchy. He held Arabella in his arms.

'I wanted you two to meet properly,' he said, holding her towards Milo.

Arabella squirmed and screwed up her face and pushed a bubble of spit through her small pink lips.

Milo turned away to face the wall.

'I'm sorry, Milo.'

Milo didn't answer. Hamlet got up onto his legs and walked over to Dad and Arabella. He let out a squeak.

'Looks like Arabella's got a fan,' said Dad, a smile in his voice.

What gave Dad the right to come in here and act like he wasn't to blame for all of this? To make out like everything was okay? Anyway, Hamlet didn't like Arabella, he was just curious because she was pink and wrinkly and smaller than him.

'Milo, did you hear what I said?' Dad cleared his throat. 'About being sorry?'

Milo sat up and looked right into Dad's face. 'Sorry for what, Dad?'

Dad's face flushed red. Milo wished Dad would get Mum's rash so he could feel what it was like to have his skin catch fire.

'I'm ... I'm sorry about ...'

'About leaving Mum? About not sending us any money? About not caring what happened to Gran? Or about not getting in touch, not until a few weeks ago when you spoke to Tripi, and even then you didn't call back, did you?'

'Mum didn't pass on the cards – and the photos?'

Milo thought of the pictures Mr Overend had given him and then he understood why they'd ended up in the bin.

When Dad had left, Milo had thought it was Mum's fault. That she could have tried harder to keep him at home. Because Dad was the nice one, wasn't he? He was the one who understood Milo and how much he loved Hamlet and how he didn't want people to treat him differently because of his eyes and how he preferred spending time with Gran than with people his own age. He'd thought that Mum must have been the one to blame. But now Milo understood that the people who loved you were the ones who stuck around.

'You chose to leave, Dad.'

'It's more complicated than that, Milo.'

Milo turned back round to face the wall.

'We're staying here for a few days, until after the funeral.'

Milo didn't get it, why Mum had made up her bed for Dad and The Tart to sleep in, why she'd helped The Tart make up a cot for Arabella in a corner of the room, why she'd said she'd sleep on the sofa. She was letting them walk all over her. Couldn't they go to a hotel and leave Milo and Mum and Hamlet alone?

'When you feel like talking, Milo, I'll be waiting.'

'What about after the funeral?' Milo mumbled at the wall. 'Will you go back to Abu Dhabi? Will you leave us again?'

Dad leant forward and put his hand on Milo's shoulder; it felt like a stranger was touching him. He wiggled his shoulder away. Arabella snuffled, like Hamlet did sometimes, and he felt a bit sorry for her, getting caught up in all this.

'We're moving back to Slipton. We'll find a house, Milo, with a room for you and space for Hamlet to run around in the garden.'

Dad was coming back? For good?

'I know I've messed up and I know it will take a long time for you to forgive me, but I promise that I'll make it up to you.'

Milo closed his eyes and listened to the water rushing through the pipes from Mum's en-suite bathroom. Was The Tart washing her face in Mum's sink? He listened to Hamlet's heavy breathing as he fell asleep again. Milo longed for Mr Overend's whistling or for a plane to fly overhead and drown all this stuff with Dad.

Milo screwed up his eyes tighter. *Gran, I wish you were here.* And then a tune started up, really quiet at first, jolting along like a horse galloping closer and closer.

Great-Gramps's bagpipe song, except there were two people playing now, a duet.

Milo opened his eyes and stared at the wall. 'Have you said sorry to Mum?'

He heard Dad shifting Arabella from one arm to another.

'We haven't had the chance to chat yet, Milo. But I will, yes – of course I will.'

The sound of the bagpipe duet got louder in Milo's head.

'Well, when you have, then we can talk.'

68

Sandy

In the basement of Tony Greedy and Sons Funeral Home, Sandy stroked Lou's skin. Cold as marble but still that softness. She smoothed down her eyebrows and pencilled in a little colour to trace their shape. Sandy had never seen them raised, as though life had run out of ways to surprise Lou Moon.

She'd asked permission to do Lou's make-up. She didn't want a stranger painting her face.

Andy knocked on the open door.

'Working your magic, Sandy?'

She looked up. 'You're here?'

'Arabella's fallen asleep at last.' He cleared his throat. 'Thank you for lending us your room.'

Sandy had made up a bed for herself on the sofa. After Andy left, she spent many nights down there, the television flickering into the early hours, her gaze fixed on the shed.

Andy came over and put a hand on her arm.

How long had it been since he'd touched her? She stepped forward and buried her face in his chest. That familiar smell, and another one, too, of his new little girl.

Andy stroked the back of her head and she knew she should pull back, but she wanted to stay here, just for a moment.

'I'm sorry, Andy. I'm sorry that I didn't speak to you about Lou.'

'I should have been here.'

Yes you should, you selfish bastard – wasn't that what Sandy was meant to say? And yet, as they had all walked home last night, as Milo had slipped his fingers into her hand and told her for the first time since she could remember that he loved her, something broke loose, an untethering, and the anger she had for Andy melted.

She stepped back and smoothed down her hair.

'It'll be good for Milo to have you home.'

He shook his head. 'He hates me, Sandy.'

Even a day ago, those words would have pleased her, a small victory. But they didn't, not now.

'He's been through a lot, surely you understand that? But he'll come back to you. He loves you.'

Andy went over and took Lou's hand. Sandy came and stood beside him.

'Andy, I need you to look after Milo.'

'Of course ...'

'I mean, really look after him. Make sure his eyes are okay, that he works hard at school, that he's happy. He needs to make friends, children his own age.'

'We'll do it together, Sandy. The fact that I've got Arabella now, and Angela, that doesn't change anything.'

A new woman and a new child in his life and nothing was different? The old naïve Andy was back.

Andy blushed. 'I mean it doesn't need to affect how we care for Milo.'

Sandy shook her head.

The thought had only just come to her but already she was certain it was the right thing.

She looked over at Lou, lying there like she was asleep. Where was she now? And what was she thinking as she looked down on them all?

My true love came first, said Lou before she fell asleep the morning she proposed to Petros. *And now I have a second love. Perhaps for you, Sandy, it will be the reverse.*

'I need you to take the lead for a while,' said Sandy. 'There's something I have to do, something important.'

69

Tripi

'You will give this to your mother after the funeral?' Tripi took the envelope out of Ayishah's backpack and handed it to Milo. A letter, to explain why he had to leave.

'So you're really going back to Syria, then?'

'Not Syria, not right away. But I must leave Slipton. I will go to London. And to other cities too. There are people in England who will help me find her – and other lost children. I will fight for it, like you fought to save the old people at Forget Me Not.'

'I'm sorry about lying.' Milo squeezed Hamlet closer into his chest and buried his nose in his fur.

'Well, you did not really lie, Milo. Al has helped me, he has given me ideas, names of organisations that will listen to me and help me to look for Ayishah.'

Whether the little girl Mrs Zimmer saw was Ayishah or not, Tripi knew he would find her: either in the camp they had shown on the BBC News, one of the 28,000 refugees in

Ceylanpinar, and if not there, then somewhere else. Ayishah was alive, he could feel it.

Milo looked up. 'And when you find her, you'll come back?'

'Of course. I will find a way to get Ayishah back to England. You will be good friends, I am sure of it – and she will love Hamlet.' Tripi rubbed the top of Hamlet's head.

'And you're really not going to tell Mum?'

Tripi looked over at Sandy who stood by the open casket smoothing down Old Mrs Moon's hair. She held a bottle of perfume in her hand and sprayed it behind Lou's ears and on the front of her dress. The smell of apricots drifted across the room.

'I do not want to spoil this day,' said Tripi. But he knew that it was more than that. If he told the Lovely Sandy, she would try to persuade him to stay and he was worried that he would lose the courage to leave.

Milo tucked the letter into the pocket of his trousers and walked back to the front of the chapel. He gave his father Hamlet to hold and then leant over and stroked baby Arabella's head. The Tart that Sandy had talked about so often looked at Milo with kind eyes. She did not seem so bad in the end, not as beautiful as Lovely Sandy, of course, too skinny.

Tripi stood at the back and watched everyone take their seats.

Petros came and sat on the other side of Milo, a yellow rose in his buttonhole as if this were his wedding day.

Kasia, Al's girlfriend, sat on her own. What a fool he had been to think that Al was a rival in his love for the Lovely Sandy. Al, a relative from Scotland who Sandy had never met. And he had a girlfriend from Poland, a woman who, like Tripi, was far away from her homeland but had found her place in England, like he would too, one day.

Mrs Moseley hobbled past with her daughter, a woman Milo called Mrs Hairy. For once Mrs Moseley did not have a stain on the back of her dress. She had moved out of Forget Me Not and was living in The Hairy Mansion.

Nurse Heidi helped the other old ladies to their seats. Because Heidi hadn't finished her training, they'd put someone new in charge, but Tripi was certain that one day Heidi would run a home of her own and that she would make sure it was warm and that the old people were happy and that potatoes would never be on the menu.

And then Al came through the doors in his kilt with Old Mrs Moon's bagpipes and began to play. Milo put Hamlet down on the chair, walked to the end of the row and went to hold Sandy's hand. He whispered in her ear.

Hamlet stood up on his chair and grunted and everyone shuffled to their feet.

Tripi felt a sting at the back of his eyes. He must not let himself get sentimental, he must think of Ayishah.

He turned to go.

'Tripi?'

He tripped on a rucked-up bit of carpet.

'Where are you going?' Sandy had slipped round the side of the room. Milo stood beside her, still holding her hand.

Everyone sat down except Andy who went to the microphone in front of Old Mrs Moon's casket.

Tripi looked at Sandy and took a breath. 'You did a beautiful job on Old Mrs Moon, you are an artist.'

Sandy laughed. 'She would have hated it. I don't think she

wore make-up a single day of her life.' Sandy sniffed. 'Always had such beautiful skin; apricot skin, like Milo.'

Milo blushed, but Tripi could tell the little boy was pleased that he had a bit of Old Mrs Moon in him.

'I think you should give Mum your hankie,' said Milo.

Tripi pulled a handkerchief out of his pocket and handed it to Sandy.

'I suppose I did it for me – the make-up, I mean.' Sandy wiped her nose and dabbed at her cheeks. Then she looked at Tripi through her blurry eyes. 'Milo says you're leaving. He gave me this.' She held up the letter.

Tripi hesitated, thought of a thousand excuses he could give her to make it easier for him to leave. But that was not fair.

'I wanted you to find out later, Sandy.' He glanced at Milo but Milo gave him the same cheeky grin Ayishah had when she knew she was winning an argument. 'But yes, I am leaving.'

'To find your sister?'

'Yes.' *The needle in a haystack*, he thought. Ayishah would like that phrase.

Sandy put her hand on his arm. She had painted her nails a pale pink, only the little one on her left hand was chipped.

'Mum's got something to tell you, Tripi,' Milo said.

Sandy took a breath and said: 'Take me with you.' She looked him in the eye. 'I'll help you find Ayishah. We'll travel around the country together, we'll bang on doors and campaign until they find her and bring her here.' Her face was alive. 'I want to do something important. I want to do this, Tripi.'

Andy finished his speech at the microphone and sat down.

The sound of an electronic organ started up, people got onto their feet again, opened their service sheets and started singing.

Abide with me; fast falls the eventide . . .

How beautiful, thought Tripi. *Abide with me*. That must be an English saying too.

'We've talked about it and we think Mum should go with you. They'll take you more seriously if you have someone English with you.'

Sandy stepped closer to Tripi. 'Milo and I had the same idea. It seems we're not so different after all, eh, Milo?'

Milo smiled. 'Well, not in this, Mum.'

'But who will look after Milo when we are away?' asked Tripi.

'I'll be okay,' said Milo, which made a couple of tears plop out of Sandy's eyes. 'I've got Dad to look after me – it's his turn, right, Mum? I haven't forgiven Dad yet because I think he needs to earn it, but I don't mind living with him. And I'll go and visit Petros and the old ladies at Forget Me Not and Al said he'll come back after he's celebrated Christmas in Scotland. And there's always Hamlet, he'll make sure I'm okay.'

'But, Sandy . . . ' Tripi couldn't take in her words. There were too many obstacles, surely?

'We'll only be away for a few days at a time, a week at the most. We'll come back often. I've spoken to Andy, he's promised me that he'll take good care of Milo – and Milo will hold him to it, won't you?'

Milo nodded. 'And you won't be long, not with Mum's help. And once you've found Ayishah, you'll come straight back and we'll all live together.'

382

Sandy travelling alongside him? Helping him so that he did not have to do this alone? Was it possible?

'I've got to go,' said Milo, looking over at the empty place next to his father at the front of the chapel.

Sandy and Tripi watched him walk down the aisle.

'You are sure Milo will be okay?'

Sandy nodded. 'Milo will be more than okay.' She handed Tripi back his handkerchief. 'So, are you going to let me come with you or not?'

Tripi put the handkerchief in his pocket and looked back at the congregation, still on their feet.

Through cloud and sunshine, Lord, abide with me . . .

He did not believe what people said about Allah being so different from this Christian God.

Tripi watched Milo pick Hamlet up off his seat and stand next to his father. And then Milo turned round and shifted his head and Tripi wasn't sure whether Milo could see him and Sandy, but the small boy's eyes widened and he smiled. And then turned back round.

'Ready?' Sandy slipped her fingers into Tripi's.

He took her hand to his mouth and kissed her knuckles and whispered, 'Ready.'

70

Milo

'Can I hold her for a while?' Milo asked Dad, looking into Arabella's small, scrunched-up face.

Dad nodded, lifted Arabella out of her cot and placed her in Milo's arms.

'I want to introduce her to Gran.'

Dad shot Angela a look.

'It's okay, Andy.' Angela turned to Milo. 'Go ahead, we'll wait for you outside.'

As everyone filtered out of the chapel, Milo carried Arabella to Gran's open coffin.

'Gran doesn't like make-up,' Milo whispered into Arabella's ear. He looked down at Gran's red lips. 'But I think Mum was trying to be nice.'

The lipstick was already fading, though, the edges around her mouth blurred. He wondered how long it would take for every bit of Gran to fade away.

'Gran, this is Arabella.' Milo held Arabella out so they

could see each other. 'Look, Arabella, it's Gran.' Arabella blinked. She opened her small eyes for a second and then closed them again. 'I think she's tired, Gran, she's had a long day.'

He nestled Arabella into his arm and then looked again at Gran.

'I hope you like where you are now, Gran,' Milo whispered. He hoped that she felt less confused than she did when she was here, never sure of whether it was then or now or later. Everyone kept saying she was in heaven but Milo wanted her to be somewhere more concrete – a place she loved, like in Inverary on her fishing boat or swimming in the sea. And he hoped that Gramps would be there too.

'Do you promise you'll keep watching us, like you always did?' Milo asked. 'Gran sees everything, Arabella.' He caught a bit of dribble on Arabella's chin. 'Now that you're family, she'll look out for you too.'

He was sure of this, that wherever Gran was, she'd be looking out for them all, seeing the world as he did, flutters of light through the pinhole.

'Gran will see everything, Arabella, everything.'

She'll see The Hairy Mansion where Mrs Moseley has switched on Mrs Hairy's stereo: together they'll be dancing in the marble hallway between the plastic palm trees.

She'll see Forget Me Not, where Nurse Heidi will serve up a Christmas dinner with the new Director, Nurse Barnett, but everyone calls her Pam because it's a friendly place. The old people's plates will be filled with all the trimmings – everything except roast potatoes. The bag of King Edwards will have mysteriously disappeared from the pantry.

She'll see Petros hammering a nail into the wall of the

lounge, the painting of the fishing boat resting at his feet. And she'll see a new old lady, Susie, eighty-four, moving into Lou's room where the yellow rose still blooms. There's a draught coming through the window – Petros will have to see to that.

'I promise to visit Petros every day,' Milo whispered, his eyes still closed. 'And Arabella will come too, won't you?'

After that, Gran will see the Harley leaning in close to the road as Clouds turns onto the A819 leading to Inverary. He'll spend Christmas with his family, he wants to introduce them to Kasia. Kasia will sit on the back clutching Al's waist, breathing in the sea air that reminds her of Poland. Perhaps Al will bring her to Inverary in the summer, too, and they'll leave their clothes on the beach and they'll swim in the dark sea, like Gran and Gramps used to do all those years ago.

She'll see Mum's head resting on Tripi's shoulder. They're asleep, rocked by the motion of the train that's taking them to a human rights campaigner who lives on the south coast. Maybe, from where Gran is, she'll be able to reach out and touch them. And she'll keep watching them to make sure they're safe, that Tripi doesn't get sent away, and she'll help them find Ayishah and then she'll watch them bring her home. Maybe they'll get married, like Big Mike and Lalana, so that Tripi and Ayishah can stay in England for ever. Gran will be at the wedding too, Mum's bridesmaid, holding a bunch of yellow roses.

And in a few days, after the candles and the cake and the unwrapping of a quilted bed for Hamlet, Gran will watch Milo take Hamlet in his arms and walk up to her old room under the roof. On the wall next to Gran's bed, next to the newspaper cutting of Gramps in his uniform, Milo will have tacked up the photographs Mr Overend gave him of baby Arabella. For a while Milo will sit next to the crib, watching the rise and fall of his baby sister's chest. Hamlet will snuffle and grunt and nudge the crib with his nose. It turns out Dad was right, Hamlet does like the little girl.

Gran will watch Angela come in, and she'll watch Milo help her carry Arabella to the small basin in Gran's bathroom, take Gran's flannel and smooth it across his baby sister's new skin.

You're her brother, Gran whispers behind Milo's eyelids. *You'll keep her safe and one day, when the world goes dark, she'll be your eyes.*

When Arabella is washed and dressed, Gran will watch all five of them, Milo, Arabella, Angela, Dad and Hamlet, walk to Forget Me Not where they'll have Christmas pudding with the old ladies and Petros. Mrs Zimmer has taken a shine to Hamlet: she lets him sleep on her lap while she dozes off in front of the news.

I think we're missing someone, Gran whispers.

Of course, Milo smiles.

After the thrill of his drive to London, Mr Overend will get bored of staring out of his window, so Gran will watch him open his wardrobe, put on his old suit, his black lace-up shoes, get into his Volvo and drive out of Slipton.

'Where will he go, Gran?'

No one's sure, Milo. But if you close your eyes and listen really hard, you'll always be able to hear his whistling. I can hear him now . . . .

'Milo, are you coming?' Dad's voice floats down through the chapel.

Milo keeps his eyes screwed shut. 'Just a minute, Dad.' He squeezes Arabella against his chest.

As he looks through Gran's eyes one last time, Milo sees the night sky at the end of the dark tunnel, a bright, white coin of light.

Bye, Gran, he says.

And then the hole begins to close, the moon shrinks to a dot, to the shiny head of a pin and then nothing.